CALIFORNIA
SCREAMING

Doug Guinan

SIMON & SCHUSTER

SIMON & SCHUSTER
Rockefeller Center
1230 Avenue of the Americas
New York, NY 10020

SIMON & SCHUSTER and colophon are registered trademarks
of Simon & Schuster Inc.

Designed by Lovedog Studio
Manufactured in the United States of America

1   3   5   7   9   10   0   6   4   2

Library of Congress Cataloging-in-Publication Data
Guinan, Doug.
California screaming / Doug Guinan.
p.   cm.
I. Title.
PS3557.U368C3   1998
813' .54—dc21   98-5494 CIP
ISBN 0-684-84936-4

ACKNOWLEDGMENTS

If you want a fun and easy life, arrange to have Jed Mattes as your agent.

If you want to look smart, get Chuck Adams to be your editor.

If you want good advice early on, call Richard Alleman.

For all your other human needs, call either my father, or Peter, Jim, Laurie, Greg, or Jeff, like I do.

Unless of course you want the impossible—for that you'll have to call the fixer, Michael Chianese.

FOR KEE AND PHILIPPE

CALIFORNIA SCREAMING

"Collect call from Kevin Malloy. Do you accept the charges?"

"Collect?"

"Accept the charges, Ma!"

"But your father . . . Kevin, where are you?"

"Will you accept the charges, ma'am?"

"MA!"

"All right already! Yes, operator. I accept the charges. Kevin, what are you doing? Why are you calling collect? Your father will be furious."

"I'm at Kennedy airport."

"What?"

"I'm getting on a plane."

"What kind of trouble are you in? Are you with Anthony?"

"No."

"Kevin! What is this?"

"This is the final boarding call for American Airlines flight twenty-seven, nonstop service to Los Angeles. All ticketed passengers should proceed immediately to gate five-B. Once again, this is the final boarding call."

"Kevin, are you trying to break your mother's heart? Or just kill me? Tell me, one or the other, just so I'll know."

"Okay, Ma, pay attention. Anthony and I were more than friends. Do you get it?"

"What are you saying, Kevin?"

"I'm gay."

"You're not gay."

"Ma, listen. Hot Tip found out."

"Oh my God. Wash your mouth out!"

"So I got to get out of New York right away. I'm going to California."

"Don't talk that way, Kevin! You're not gay. My hairdresser, John, he's gay. Trust me, I know gay."

"I gotta go, Ma."

"Kevin, I made baked ziti tonight and I want you to come home now! I promise I won't tell your father any of this!"

"I have to hang up, Ma. I'll call you. Don't worry."

"Kevin!"

PART ONE

"MERRY CHRISTMAS"

CHAPTER 1

Kevin.

Well, the central fact about Kevin was that he was extremely good look-ing. He wasn't pleasant looking, he wasn't handsome, he wasn't merely *a head-turner*. No, Kevin, thank God, had something much rarer. Ten seconds alone in an elevator with Kevin and you'd suddenly have the irrefutable proof that life is unfair. Ride up two floors with him and you'd feel as-saulted. Ride up three floors and you could cancel that self-esteem work-shop. *So what if you lose your deposit?* It was useless. His looks were that profound. They inspired people—to just *give up*.

Now Leon was just good looking enough for Kevin to be friends with him. Kevin might go to an afternoon movie with Leon, but he would not take him to certain parties in the hills. Leon accepted this arrangement readily because the entire foundation of their friendship was a deep and abiding respect for the Hollywood gay pecking order. Perhaps they recog-nized this quality in each other when they met in the lobby of that outfit on Fairfax called "Roommate World." Nevertheless, for a time, they made a good team. Had they lived in another part of America, they could have eas-ily been mistaken for a pair of frat brothers.

But, here in LA, in an area sometimes mistakenly called "Beverly Hills adjacent" by the real-estate mavens, anyone who cared to look could see what they were: Kevin and Leon were a couple of users who hoped that one day, they could forget each other. Their arrangement, touching and heartwarming as an episode of *The Waltons*, was *totally* familiar to anyone living west of Doheny.

• • •

Kevin was twenty-eight and Leon thirty-two, but they both affected the clothes of trip-hop teenagers. This is not to say that they each didn't have a Donna Karan suit hanging in their closets, but most of the time their clothes boldly stated:

"Although it is neither a source of solace nor enchantment, I have read Pop Monitor Profiles *and now understand exactly the career trajectory of Matthew McConaughey."*

At a glance, anyone brave enough could see that they were on the private mailing list for the biannual presale sale at Maxfield's, that they had accepted drinks bought for them at Muse by too many entertainment lawyers, that they knew where Sofia Coppola lived, and that at any moment they could be invited to do lines with a writer of sitcoms out in Marina del Rey.

In their John Bartlett stovepipe hip-huggers for men (made of acetate, rayon, and other fossil fuels), they were everywhere and nowhere at once; poster boys of America's Golden State, shining emblems of the Great Washed.

No one with half a mind would ever, in a million years, entrust them with a Nielson box.

The apartment they shared was in the walled city of West Hollywood, on a street called Westmount. Situated behind the Athletic Connection, a pricey health club where gay doctors, lawyers, and assorted industry types fought valiant battles with the laws of aging, it was a dingy affair featuring gray wall-to-wall carpeting. Those carpets may, at one time, have contributed to a look optimistically termed "high-tech," but no longer. Clearly, no one in the building had the energy or the wherewithal to alert the landlord to the fact that brown was the new black.

Razor-sharp aluminum venetian blinds hid a view of a dusty carport filled with Hondas and Saturns. Scattered about Kevin and Leon's dank living room were hundreds of CDs, but not a single chair or couch. They wanted furniture, of course, but neither of them had any credit left. And they were simply *not* the kind of guys who would drive out to the IKEA in Burbank and pick up something for six ninety-nine, no matter how many gay ads the store ran. Skimping, at this stage of the game, was just not an option.

Each had a bathroom to himself, and their rusty medicine cabinets were crammed with expensive products: shampoos from Lazartigue and Furterer, defrissants from Phyto, cuticle closers from Phillip Kingsley. Unopened soaps from The Body Shop, wrapped in recycled paper and tied with softened twigs, competed for space on the floor under the sink with cunning eye pencils from MAC. Bags of cotton balls sat on the toilet tank, as did numerous toners, astringents, and moisturizers. A cramped hallway linen closet contained still more: volumizers, texturizers, body boosters, hydroglazes, sunless tanning creams, unguents, palliatives, tinctures, exfoliants . . . and hundreds of Elizabeth Arden ceramide capsules. Like many youngish people in LA, they could not imagine buying a house, but a forty-dollar bottle of hair conditioner did not seem unreasonable. It seemed, in fact, absolutely right.

Only the most anonymous of tricks had ever set foot in the apartment, but none of them were ever received beyond the living room. Kevin or Leon, after lighting a candle from Diptyque, would tangle with them briefly on the living-room floor. Perfunctory caresses produced quick, pungent orgasms that were wiped away with a mid-priced paper towel. (None of it ever spilled onto the carpet.)

It was, of course, easier this way, what with intimacy being *just so five minutes ago*. Besides, according to the latest wisdom (dispensed by a celebrity who had not only just trekked through Tibet, but who had also managed the far trickier feat of making the leap from TV to movies), the distinctly *Western* act of ejaculation was thoroughly overrated. Its only real benefit, said celebrity stated at an airport press conference, was to prevent the prostate, twenty years down the road, from enlarging cancerously.

After only a few months under the hot Los Angeles sun, both Kevin and Leon thought this kind of logic made perfect sense.

Lately, Kevin's career as a fashion photographer had come to a standstill. Leon still yearned, one day, to realize his boyhood dream of becoming a set designer on a soap. When they first arrived in Los Angeles, there was a flurry of activity and a few paying jobs, but that was almost five years ago.

The problem was, they were fresh faced, but they were no longer *fresh faces*.

So, like so many others, they fell into the respected local habit of giving their lives over to the care of their physiques. Tuesdays, for example, were completely devoted to their triceps. Wednesdays *meant* chest and calves. Thursdays? Quads and glutes. Recently they had become very enthusiastic about a new exercise that worked the base of their necks. Abs, the key to the whole look, were, of course, tended to every day. And so on and so on, day after day, until Saturday night, when the whole package was showcased at a spooky club called Prod. Kevin and Leon's bodies, as dictated by a small and ruthless cabal of Milanese fashion designers, defined the end-of-century ideal of male perfection.

After an arduous night at a hastily thrown together underwear party, Kevin and Leon woke up late this Christmas morning to dry mouths, throbbing headaches, and a booming voice on their answering machine.

"Leon? Sweetheart? It's your mother. Your father and I wanted to wish you a merry Christmas!"

There was a muffled transferring noise.

"Hello, son," said his father. "Merry Christmas!" The phone was passed back to Mom. Leon imagined his father's plaid shirt, his unshaven jowls. The boys, lying on the floor in single-stripe Adidas sweatpants, listened closely but did not pick up.

"Give us a call when you can, dear. This is long distance so I don't want to stay on too long." A pause. "We love you." Another pause. "Oh, your brother is driving up with the kids. Your father shoveled the driveway this morning. We got seven inches last night! Bye, honey . . . Bye . . ."

Leon pushed the erase button and the LCD indicator went back to zero.

"Forgive me if I let the obvious pun pass," drawled Kevin, "but could you perhaps explain why your mother feels the need to shout into the phone?"

"Because it's long distance, you jerk!" Leon was not, at least this early in the day, in the mood for what his mother would call "smarmy remarks."

"Don't get testy," said Kevin. "I understand. And I adore your parents. I have to adore any white people that would put the name Leon on a birth certificate. They obviously felt pretty confident in you from the start."

"Like a boy named Sue," replied Leon, not for the first time in his life.

After that, no one else called.

They spent the morning watching an *AbFab* marathon on Comedy Central. Then they pulled out their Ab Rollers and did fifteen hundred sit-ups. After that they drank their MetRx. Around two o'clock they became quasi-interested in real food, but no nearby grocery stores were open.

"I'm anxious," said Kevin, on his feet now in the living room, peering through the venetian blinds. "I'm hungry and I'm anxious. I feel a need to be in the company of models. I think I'll go up to Chin Chin on Sunset and see if they're open. Chinese people don't celebrate Christmas, do they, the heathens?"

"I don't think so. Do you want company?" asked Leon.

"No. I'll bring you back a Chinese chicken salad. I think today we can treat ourselves to the fat."

Kevin went into his room, where the sight of his unmade bed depressed him. He stripped off his sweatpants, removed his underwear, and then put the sweatpants back on. He then opened the mirrored door of his closet. Inside was a vast assortment of ironed T-shirts on hangers, in all sizes, arranged by hue. He selected a white Hanes, medium, which was one of several that he'd had specially cropped by a Mexican seamstress in her basement apartment on Harper. It left a sliver of ab muscle exposed.

He had a fleeting urge to put on some kind of jewelry, but, as yet, had never given in to it.

It was a cold but bright afternoon, and there was a disconcerting absence of glare and smog. Kevin, climbing into his silver Miata, tried to imagine what LA must have been like in its heyday, when Mack Sennett bathing beauties on their day off took the Santa Monica Boulevard trolley all the way down to the ocean. When Marion Davies used to sit around the Hearst beach house demanding baked potatoes smothered in caviar. When Peg Entwhistle leapt to her death from the top the Hollywood sign. LA must have been sort of okay back then. Maybe even sort of fabulous.

There were was an amazing lack of traffic and Kevin slipped over the streets like a drop of mercury. It would have been a great day to shoot some test shots. In this clear light, he could have put a girl in the middle of Sunset Boulevard and created something really stark and apocalyptic. His portfolio, overly influenced by Madonna's Steven Meisel period, certainly needed fresh material. Oh, well. Maybe next year, he thought. *If I'm still stuck here.*

Chin Chin, along with every other shop on this stretch of Sunset, was closed. He decided to pull a U-turn in the parking lot behind Sunset Plaza and take in a view of downtown, a place he'd never been. Because everyone was at home with their families on this one day of the year, there were no auto emissions blocking his view. He could actually make out a battleship gray Asiana Airlines 747 lifting off out of LAX. A breeze came up and

Kevin felt the strangely unpleasant sensation of semi-clean air on his face. Moving quickly, he opened his glove compartment. Under a pile of cassettes, he found a sample pack of Japanese cigarettes from a job he assisted on a few months back, and some matches from the Boom Boom Room.

He lit up.

As Kevin sat in that empty parking lot, smoking idly, thinking, as always, about New York, a white stretch limo pulled up alongside his tiny car and slowed to a stop. Kevin snapped out of his reverie, ready to bolt. A white limo was hardly a strange sight, but what was it doing here, today? After a few moments, a black window smoothly descended and a very tan hand, holding a bubbling glass of champagne, reached out.

A face leaned forward.

"Merry Christmas."

It was Brad Sherwood.

When their eyes met, Kevin instantly remembered what they once called him in a fat September issue of *Vanity Fair.* "Brad Sherwood: The Mogul's Mogul."

There is nothing Brad Sherwood abhors more, exclaimed the writer of the glowing puff piece, *than an unscheduled minute. From early morning to late at night, he is always looking ahead, planning, arranging, pushing deals through—Making Entertainment Happen! Behind him, like gulls trailing after an ocean liner seeking scraps, assistants, secretaries, trainers, dietitians, and lawyers dip and flutter in his wake, desperate for a glance, a nod, a millisecond of life-altering recognition. Whether plucking newcomers from the maw of obscurity or turning down dinners in his honor from Washington socialites, Brad Sherwood is always in demand.*

Magnet Entertainment, the empire he founded, was a ragtag collection of companies that had been casually cobbled together over the years until some point in the eighties, when they began spontaneously replicating and self-perpetuating on their own. The record group is still the jewel in the crown, but there is also "filmed entertainment," a publishing subdivision, three southern television stations and a newly formed CD-ROM wing. A twenty-four-hour cable-news linkup has recently been acquired. The books-on-tape department alone employs twenty-five people. Theme restaurants, theme parks, and a Flatiron-district Magnet Superstore (the entire building done in trademark green and purple) are all in the works.

Make no mistake—the man has an aura! On a slow day, he fields about a hundred calls. Would-be players all get on the phone with rehearsed speeches, offering projects, knowing that only Brad Sherwood *can cleanse the stench of failure that permeates their lives. If Brad says, "I'll get back to you," they immediately call their real-estate agents and upgrade. But if he says, "That's something I don't want on my plate right now," they eye outdated mood inhibitors that have accumulated in their medicine cabinets over the years with new interest . . ."*

"Happy Kwanzaa," replied Kevin evenly, his eyes slits.

Brad handed the champagne to Kevin and a certain sort of timeless gay deal was set in motion. It was all in the eye contact, the currency of the realm. Brad stared with intensity and Kevin raised his chin, agreeing to the challenge. Neither blinked.

Kevin toasted the famous mogul and then took a small sip. Like all the best champagnes, it slid down like fresh ginger ale.

There was an earsplitting subsonic trill and before Kevin could even identify the origin of the sound, Brad had a phone clamped to his ear and was speaking rapidly. "Jane, only you could find me! Merry Christmas! Of course I RSVP'd; I'm so looking forward to it . . . But I signed it myself . . . Well, if it makes you feel any better, heads will roll. A Christmas Day firing, if it makes you happy. My best to Ted." He clicked off his phone and turned back to Kevin.

"My parents live up there," said Brad, with a jerk of his thumb. "They wanted to be close to the old neighborhood, God knows why. It isn't safe any more. I put them in a condo, but now they complain they can't walk down the hill. *Where are we going to go? Tower Records?* They're hard to please. They wanted pecan Danish on Christmas morning so who's going to drive all the way out from Malibu to get it for them?"

To Kevin's amazement and delight, Brad Sherwood seemed nervous. Knowing when to press an advantage, he decided to get out of his car and treat Brad to a view better than the one that lay before them. As he came around to the open window to shake hands, even the limo driver, a man in his fifties who had seen it all, reddened with embarrassment.

Kevin's substantial cock, draped in those shiny, threadbare sweatpants, had a mighty swing to it.

"I see." Kevin transferred the cigarette from his right hand to his left and then proffered his right hand for a shake.

"Hi. I'm Brad Sherwood."

Kevin knew perfectly well who sat before him. Brad was not merely a much-photographed Hollywood supermogul. He was also a shadowy superstar of the ne plus ultra international gay A-list circuit!

Kevin, a star in a much tinier galaxy, bravely held his gaze. "Of course you are," he said.

The phone rang again. "Get that, Jeremy," said Brad. The driver picked up the line from an extension in the front seat.

"Sounds like you're a real mama's boy," said Kevin. Not the most inspired line, but he was stalling, figuring the odds, calculating the options. *How to play this. How to play this.* Think! Cool? Sassy? How much do I know? Friendly? Good manners? Nah. *No way.* If there was anything he'd learned after five years in LA, it was that good manners *never* played. *Never* do the right thing. Do the *rude* thing.

He really had only two options: pulsate or smolder. And when in doubt, smolder.

But what about the cigarette? Was it a turn-off? What about dropping it on the ground? But hadn't he read somewhere that Brad Sherwood was a major contributor to Greenpeace? Kevin decided littering, under the circumstances, would not be attractive. Then he struck upon a better idea. He turned around and bent over into his car, in the process exposing, almost, but not quite, the velvety crack of his rock-hard ass.

Damn. His insurance and registration were in the ashtray. Should he take them out? Then they'd be in his hand and he'd have to find a place to put them. There were no pockets on his sweatpants. Finally he just slammed the cigarette in among the papers and closed the miniature door. So what if they caught fire? The insurance had expired long ago.

"Great car," commented Brad. "I haven't been in a convertible in years. Seems like after the riots, everyone I know got rid of theirs."

"No wonder they're such a bargain," said Kevin.

"It doesn't bother you? Being so close to the ground?"

Kevin did not appreciate the tone of Brad's remark. It had the bitchy cadence of a well-practiced dig. It was so depressingly familiar, too. More than once Kevin had been up for jobs and an imperious art director would make it clear that the work was his in exchange for a little action. So far, Kevin had never quite gone the whole hog. Oh, he had taken off his shirt for them, or swam naked in their pools, but it was all just amateurish teasing.

This, however, was a whole new game.

"Has it really been so long for you, Brad?" asked Kevin, batting his eyelashes. "I mean, since you've been in a convertible. There's no traffic today, how about a spin? The danger, I think, would be minimal. Even gang members celebrate Christmas in some form, don't they?"

"That almost sounds like a dare."

"Maybe it is."

Brad spied a slithering passel of industry wannabes approaching from a distance of at least twenty cars. He had learned over the years how to avoid them before they could introduce themselves or worse, press a handwritten song upon him. *("Get this to Babyface!")* They had a straggly presence, and Brad always knew when they were about to pounce. "Okay," said Brad, rising out of the limo. "I'll take you up on that offer. But I want a ride home. I live in Malibu. Jeremy, follow us, will you? I'm going to get a ride with my friend."

Brad's driver nodded, his face a professional blank. He was certainly irritated, though. All of Brad's household staff had the day off and he knew from past experience that he would now be asked to guard the beach house while the boss fooled around. He decided to call his wife and tell her and the kids to go ahead and open their presents. There was little chance he would make it back to Redondo before midnight.

Brad grabbed his phone, his address book, and the bottle of champagne and lowered himself into the Miata. His back twinged and he stifled a groan. Now, logically, in an ordered world, Brad was too old for this kind of adventuring. But then he reminded himself that this was certainly a lot more pleasant than crushing heads in a boardroom in New York, his original plan for Christmas Day. Besides, it had been quite some time since he had picked a trick up off the street, and he had to admit it felt good.

Kevin decided to give Brad a real ride. Even if they got stopped for speeding, it was unlikely a cop would give anyone with *Brad Sherwood* a ticket on Christmas morning—not if they ever wanted to moonlight as security on a location set ever again. Kevin noticed Brad staring at his hand on the stick shift. He seemed mesmerized. Good. Sassy seemed to be working. Feeling charitable, Kevin decided to treat Brad to his smile.

Brad felt soaked. When he tried to smile back, the spontaneity just wasn't there. Smiles, real ones, had always been a struggle. They came easily only when he was being photographed or being introduced to Japanese investors.

"Just take Sunset all the way to PCH," said Brad. "It's such a pretty ride." The wind tugged at Brad's new plugs, but they seemed to be holding. He touched them briefly, resisting the urge to seek out a mirror on the visor. Instead he took a swig off the bottle of Cristal. Brad, as he had all his life, wanted to feel young, unburdened, and Californian.

"How about a sip of that good champagne?" asked Kevin.

"No way. The curves in Beverly Hills by UCLA are too scary even if you're sober. You can have some when we get to the house. If you get drunk, I can have Jeremy drive you home and another member of my staff will drive your car back tomorrow."

Kevin ignored the hint that was implicit in Brad's remark. It was too early for these sorts of complex negotiations, a breach of good taste. He wasn't going to get drunk off of one sip of champagne, for Christ's sake. And Kevin still had not decided whether he would actually let Brad Sherwood touch him. Oh well, no matter. What an adventure it was to be taking off for Malibu, especially after such a foul morning. Thoughts of Chinese chicken salads and that phone call from Leon's goofy parents had long since evaporated.

Kevin accelerated and glanced in the rearview mirror. Jeremy was keeping up, but the limo kept swerving over the center divider line. Kevin sadistically pushed down on the gas pedal. *If I'm a whore, so are you, Jeremy.* Really. As if it were something to be ashamed of.

"I gave my cook the day off but I think we can manage on our own," said Brad. "Or I can call the Bel Air Hotel and have them send over a Christmas dinner. I think they'll do that. Should I call them?" Brad reached for the comforting presence of his phone.

"You sure are quick with the assumptions, Brad. How do you know I don't have a family waiting for me at home? I only offered to take you on a quick ride and here I am on my way out to Malibu."

"Just a sixth sense," said Brad. "But you're right. I'm sorry."

"Relax. I'm a little crabby today. No, I don't have a family waiting for me at home. Just a roommate. Who is waiting for me to bring back some food. Whom I have completely forgotten about."

"Roommate. Now there's a word with a lot of hidden meaning."

"Yeah," conceded Kevin. "I agree. It's an all-purpose, innocent kind of word. But in my case it only means roommate. He's not my lover, if that's what you're wondering."

"Now look who's making assumptions," said Brad. "Speaking of words, isn't 'lover' a bit unusual nowadays? I thought the official word going around was 'partner.'"

"I think partner is what people say after the sex has died. Personally, I liked what Joe Orton called it. 'Friend.' *Can I bring my 'friend'? I'd like you to meet my 'friend.'* It sort of implies that one has only the one. It really carries the most weight. Andy Warhol used to say 'friend,' too, I think. That whole repressed fifties crowd was so great. They ran everything, yet still had time to run down to the Anvil and see who was in the sling that day."

"I knew Andy," said Brad, surprised at the reference to the famous New York sex club. He had been dragged down there a few times himself, usually in evening clothes. Brad was momentarily reminded of those long-ago seventies nights, when he hung with the wrap-dress-wearing, disco-bag-carrying international jet set. Talk about innocence. The thought of going to one of those West Side bars, a tacky lark back then, now filled his heart with dread.

"Andy hated to say anything too specific," said Brad. "If someone was gay, he said they had a 'problem.'" Aware that he was name dropping, he changed the subject. "Are you from New York?"

"Isn't everyone?" responded Kevin.

"Why did you leave?"

Why did you leave? The second-most-asked question in LA, after where do you work out. But it was a fair question. Why did anyone come out here, to this vast hardscrabble landscape of imported palm trees, Taco Bells, and ex–New Yorkers? Because they screwed up back east, usually. That's not what they said, of course. They said, I want to start over; I want to take a shot at my dreams; I want to get a degree in psychology. But New York would always be alive in their hearts. They would ache for it, even as they sat on their flagstone patios drinking iced tea by their pools, in January.

That's not why Kevin had come, though. Quite simply, he had come out here to wait for an old hard-on back east named Hot Tip Capozi to kick. Or get sent up.

"Well, I grew up in Westchester County," Kevin told Brad, "moved to Manhattan, and then one day, on my way to Citibank, I stepped into this huge pile of black slush just as I was leaving my apartment. My right foot was wet the whole day. That night, I thought, enough. It's over. LA of course was the only option."

For good measure, and to establish his "I know things" credentials, Kevin smiled and added confidentially, *"South Beach had already happened."*

"Oh, yes," said Brad. "The quintessential moment of clarity, New York style. I grew up here, so I worship New York, but I cleared out right after Ford said 'Drop Dead' to the city. Sometimes I still kid him about it when I bump into him on the golf course in Palm Springs. Anyway, I'm an only child, so my parents were thrilled to have me come back."

Kevin downshifted for a red light at the south gate into Bel Air. Maybe it was the mood created by the dense foliage hanging low over the center of the road, but a wisp of honesty escaped. "I think about going back every day."

"But, hey!" exclaimed Brad, "Who needs real seasons, right?"

"Right," replied Kevin. "Stay out here, be young forever. Isn't that the point?"

"Exactly," said Brad.

"You know," mused Kevin, "you and I, if we didn't have this 'problem' of ours, would no doubt have a few kids by now. We'd be unwrapping presents and planning our next excursion to Wal-Mart. Of course, we'd probably have to shovel the driveway first. *Yeccch."*

Brad had always liked New Yorkers, although he often didn't get their jokes. They spoke too fast and could really be negative. Still, he enjoyed Kevin's company. The kid had an *edge*—the kind the demographically desirable, post-ironic youth market opened their wallets for. (Brad would never forget the lessons of a twenty-four-year-old vice president of programming: "Edge is fine," she snarled in a meeting, "but you better make sure it's tempered with a *self-conscious, knowing phoniness!"*)

They rounded a final downward curve, flew past the Krishna Temple and suddenly the Pacific Ocean heaved and glittered before them. Kevin, barely slowing, made a screeching right on red and headed north. Jeremy, a few cars back, got stuck at the light.

There was a wet chill in the air and Kevin looked forward to getting to Brad's house. He'd seen it featured in a Hollywood issue of *Architectural Digest,* but what he really wanted was to get out of the wind. The skin on his face was feeling chapped, and Kevin, always conscious of how aging the elements could be to a face, was more than ready to *be there.* But they had crossed into Malibu now, so it would look silly if he pulled over to put the top up.

He was surprised at how comfortable he already felt with Brad. Looking over at him, he wondered idly what the sex would be like. Brad was altogether not bad looking. Movie-star short, which was a plus; short guys in LA held all the cards, and tall was blatantly loserish. And he had that new-world-order face: in Mexico, he'd be taken for Mexican; in France, for French; in Bali, for Balinese. How modern of Brad to have one before anyone else, how youth giving. And there was probably a decent body underneath that Gap T, those wrinkled Calvin chinos. As for the eternal question of body hair, Kevin, weighing it, thought Brad could go either way. A few gray hairs around the nipples maybe, but nothing he couldn't handle. (Unless, of course, the nipples had that over-chewed look—now *that* was a *real* problem these days.) As for the micro-graft lawn reseeding happening at the top of the scalp, well, Brad, to his credit, seemed very much on top of the situation. So many lost heart halfway through.

All right then! Based on the preliminary figures, it looked like the package might get a green light!

When they reached the gates of the Malibu Colony, they were waved through by a smiley, ruddy-cheeked chap dressed as Santa.

"The next house up on the left," instructed Brad.

Kevin spotted a colossal, hangar-like structure wedged between an authentic Massachusetts saltbox and a postmodern Gwathmey-esque children's playhouse. The back of the house was deceptively nondescript: white garage door, an austere rock garden (one rock) and a vaguely Japanese entryway. Perched jauntily on the edge of the roof, like a beret, sat a tiny satellite dish. Every house on the street featured one.

Brad, holding the bottle, opened the little car door and braced himself for his exit. He made a mental note never to ride in a Miata again; it was like riding in a go-cart. At the door, he hunched a shoulder to block Kevin's view and punched in a security code. The mechanism emitted a satisfying and expensive-sounding click.

"Well, here we are. Come on down to the kitchen." Brad entered a few more numbers on another pad inside. "Jeremy should be here in a few minutes."

"Relax, Brad. I only steal ashtrays from hotels."

"What? Oh, I didn't mean to . . . Oh, you . . ."

In the brightly lit white foyer, a pin spot showcased a small Georgia O'Keefe lilac. Kevin remembered it from *AD*, but before he had a chance to admire it, Brad led him around a corner and down a short flight of stairs. Brad's immaculate tennis shoes squeaked on the polished blond wood.

A cavernous living room, done entirely in shades of white, opened up before them. Beyond, a vast panorama of gray sea, full of living things, loomed vividly close through an inch-thick glass picture window. Great expanses of dense clouds were magnified through rectangular skylights. Set-like and forbidding, the room had a supremely hushed quality. Huge white couches, white throw rugs on white marble, and white lamps on white end tables seemed not at all inviting. An extremely flattering four-paneled Warhol of Brad dominated the southern wall.

Passing a Rothko, a Pollock, and a Hockney along the way, Brad crossed the room, motion-sensor lighting glowing on warmly with every step. He led Kevin to another small staircase. This one was circular, and at the bottom, there was another door. It, too, had a key-code pad. Brad punched a few more numbers.

They entered another living room, this one considerably more livable. It was furnished in nubby beige tones that struck a strong southwestern note. Sliding doors led out onto a deck. Gusts of cold ocean air rattled the windows every few seconds, making the entire structure shudder. Piles of scripts, documents, and huge parcels of mail bound in thick rubber bands obliterated the surface of the coffee table. A life-size promotional cutout of Tom Cruise stood in a corner, watching everything.

"The room upstairs is hermetically sealed," said Brad. "It protects the art from the salt air. I usually come in from the garage. Follow me. The kitchen's down here."

Brad guided Kevin toward another flight of stairs.

"Have you ever had a feng shui expert in here?" asked Kevin. "I think all these short staircases have some meaning."

"Yes, I have," said Brad. "Not a good sign, I'm afraid. I was told to bury a silver flute under the garage."

"Did you?"

"Of course. I flew the guy in all the way from Hong Kong! But the steps keep my parents out, mostly. They've never really liked this place. They can't take the damp. But it's one of the first houses I ever had built from scratch, so I'm a little nostalgic about it all."

The kitchen was on sand level, where was also a casual spare dining room. Brad went to a huge subzero refrigerator and pulled out a tin of goose-liver pâté and another bottle of Cristal. He then selected two champagne flutes from a cabinet that had been built to order around six authentically weathered colonial windowpanes.

"If we're lucky, somewhere around here are some Triscuits," said Brad. "They're my secret vice."

Brad found them in a pantry and then showed Kevin the way to the deck. Outside was a grouping of plush oversized couches. Brad unlocked the sliding glass door, set the pâté and Triscuits on a blue kidney-bean-shaped table, and went over to a gas heat lamp and switched it on. The little area warmed quickly and Kevin suddenly understood just how much rickety beach shack atmosphere $6 million could buy in today's market.

Brad popped the cork and it went sailing out onto the beach.

"You better go get that later," warned Kevin. "Bruce and Demi's dog might choke on it."

"You're right," said Brad, completely seriously. "I don't want to get sued. They're very good friends of mine."

Brad poured the champagne rather inexpertly. Foam streamed over the sides and Brad, entirely unused to pouring anything, became a bit unglued. Finally, when the glasses were reasonably full, they toasted each other. Neither could, for the moment, hold the other's gaze, so they stared out at the sea. An elderly man in a purple jogging suit played with his dog at the water's edge. Kevin wondered if it was Johnny Carson. Of course it was!

A knock on the sliding glass door startled them. Behind them, on the other side of the spotless glass, stood Jeremy.

"Excuse me, Mr. Sherwood. I just wanted to let you know I was here."

"Thank you, Jeremy. Why don't you go watch TV in Rosa's room. I may need you later."

"Sure, Mr. Sherwood, I'll be there if you need me." Jeremy threw Kevin another of his pointed, sissyish glances. Kevin put his feet up and batted his thick eyelashes back at him in a most queenly fashion. Jeremy retreated in a huff.

Brad polished off his champagne and then refilled each glass. With at least one member of his staff in attendance, he felt free to enjoy this hot number. "What a great day," he said, awkwardly aware of an impending conversational lapse.

Kevin said nothing, so Brad invoked the ancient words, the words he had relied on a thousand times before. They were the only words that ever came to him at times like this. But no other words were ever necessary.

"Would you like to have a Jacuzzi?"

"Sure," said Kevin. *Uh-oh,* he thought, *show time.* "Where is it?"

"Follow me, take your glass." Brad got up and led Kevin around to the side of the house. Along the northern wall was a heated lap pool. Steam rose off its surface as a large inflatable Daffy Duck bobbed gently at one end. Behind the pool was a tidy little open-air cabana with a navy blue awning. Next to that was the Jacuzzi and a curved shower stall with four heads. A glass-brick wall shielded the area from the house next door. Recessed far enough back from the beach to block the view from any joggers, the setup was perfect for private poolside hijinks at any hour of the day.

"There's towels, swimsuits, and robes, I think, in there," said Brad, directing the scene with an open palm. "Anything you need. Excuse me. I just need to make a quick call to my parents. I'll be back in a minute."

"Fine," replied Kevin. "This is great." His throat had gone dry, so he took another gulp of champagne and then headed purposefully toward the cabana. Inside, he found a small sauna and some standard-issue metal gym lockers, a fetishistic bit of design overkill. He opened one and found a mangled tube of Bain de Soleil, SPF 2. In another he discovered a tiny pile of neatly folded Raymond Dragon bathing suits. He selected a black-and-gold one with a wide elastic waistband and held it to his nose. The nylon gave off a slightly mildewy odor of chlorine. The fabric caught on his chin stubble.

Brad, by this time, had entered the house. He headed straight through the kitchen and into the adjacent laundry room. Once there, he opened a large closet that hung over the washing machines. He took down a few bottles of Dash and Snuggle and put them on the lid of the dryer, then shoved aside a false plywood panel. Behind it was a series of controls for three video cameras. One was trained on the cabana interior, another had a view into the sauna, and the third was built into the lap pool for lurid underwater shots. He turned them all on with a flip of a toggle switch. (Well, it *was* an older model—but sturdy and faithful; still, Brad reminded himself to upgrade.) Satisfied that the cameras were running properly, he went back outside.

The sun was just beginning to set and soon it would be bitterly cold. Since the cabana was an open-air unit, Brad thought he'd give Kevin a few more moments of privacy. He picked the Cristal up off the patio table and savored the view. Before he raised the bottle, he whispered, "Happy birthday, Christ," and then took a deep swig.

Kevin took off his T-shirt and shivered. It was getting late and he was starting to think he should call Leon and at least let him know where he was. But of course he wouldn't. How often did one get to spend Christmas Day with Brad Sherwood? Kevin loosened the knot in his sweatpants and they dropped to the concrete floor. He was about to put on one of the swimsuits, but then decided the thing to do was remain naked, just to show Brad what the "season of giving" was all about. He unfolded an old *Apollo 13* promotional beach towel, looped it over his forearm, and strode out into the ferocious wind.

Brad was waiting with the bottle. "You must be freezing," he said evenly.

"How can you tell?" said Kevin, meeting his gaze.

Brad chuckled and tried not to stare. But that, of course, was impossible.

Kevin's body was sleek and magnificent, and there was a hint of tan line left over from last summer. His thighs were rounded, but deep cuts delineated each muscle group. His aureoles were perfect brown silver dollars.

But what was most striking about Kevin, before one even had a chance to dwell on the sleek perfection of his features, was his hair. Incredibly shiny, it hung down in an enviable style that cannot be duplicated, despite today's excellent and highly researched straighteners. Every filament was a triumph of nature. Kevin's hair didn't just move, it *cascaded*. Thick, black, and featuring a widow's peak, it had been, all his life, as good as money in the bank. Kevin allowed the wind to whip it around a bit, knowing as he stood there perfectly still, that Brad, like all the rest, was dying a thousand deaths inside.

"Are you coming in?" asked Kevin.

"Maybe."

Brad was not yet drunk enough to consider taking his clothes off in front of this fantastic-looking youth. Perhaps after the sun went down. He went over to a control switch and activated the whirlpool jets.

"Suit yourself," said Kevin. He stepped forward and tested the rumbling water with a foot. It was very warm, almost unpleasantly so. Nevertheless, he put his glass down and inched himself into the swirling cauldron. When the leaping water gurgled around his balls, soaking the fine hairs of his inner thighs, Kevin stopped and stretched, holding his wrists up against the sky like the youthful and resourceful model he once was.

"Too hot," said Kevin, folding his arms. His upper body broke out in goose pimples and his nipples hardened into fine pencil erasers. Off in the distance, lights went on all over an oil tanker. A gust of wind sent Daffy Duck into a furious spasm of bobbing.

Brad, a little drunker now, summoned up his courage and touched the back of Kevin's neck.

Kevin, his green eyes limpid and vulnerable, turned.

In front of them, the sky was a crashing medley of purple and orange.

"This is where we kiss," whispered Kevin. Eyes lowered deferentially, like a geisha, he put his arms around Brad's narrow shoulders.

Brad had not kissed anyone, other than hustlers, in years. And unless it was part of a pre-negotiated fantasy theme, kissing, while commonly included in the rental price, was rarely considered an integral part of the act. Still, he went with the program. When an erection flowered, Brad felt a deep sense of mastery and power. Something he hadn't felt in ages.

Kevin, sensing Brad's willingness to go the distance, parted Brad's lips with his tongue.

CHAPTER 2

On the long, winding drive home from Malibu the next morning, all of Kevin's innate New York driving skills were put to the test. Christmas, apparently, had taken a lot out of everybody, and as a result the entire population of Greater Los Angeles seemed to have made a group decision—to get back in their cars.

Obviously, it was the only place they could produce, phone, think, and eat in peace. Every driver Kevin passed seemed greatly relieved and deliriously happy as the talk-radio stations reassured them repeatedly that home-equity lines of credit could easily be obtained by calling an 800 number, that BreathAsure would save them from further embarrassment with their bosses, that Ford Rangers could still be leased for no money down. And while it might seem to the uninitiated that many of the drivers were talking to themselves, they were clearly just *rehearsing their lines.*

Kevin heard the CD player blasting the Barbra Streisand Christmas album as he approached his apartment door. He paused and tried to think of a few excuses to give Leon for not calling, but none came to him. Finally, he just pushed the door open.

He found Leon lying on the floor with their neighbor Shane. They were flipping through back issues of *Vogue Hommes.* Everything was back to normal here, too, thought Kevin. No one was doing anything.

"Oh, God," drawled Leon. "He must have been really something if you stayed overnight." Leon pointedly did not look up from his magazine.

"Hi, Kevin!" said Shane.

Shane was a flight attendant, and saying "Hi!" in a chirpy, upbeat tone was one of his talents. He was from a suburb outside of Chicago, had lived in West Hollywood for about a year, and, as per city-ordinance mandate, had gone blond minutes after his arrival.

Shane Dunne vacuumed his apartment every day and had a bumper sticker on his car that proclaimed, SOME DAY MY SHIP WILL COME IN— *BUT WITH MY LUCK I'LL BE AT THE AIRPORT!* Like most of the guys in the building, he lusted after Kevin but tried not to be too obvious. When he moved in next door, he nervously brought over a baked chocolate-and-Rice Krispies confection, just to be neighbor-like. Kevin and Leon, of course, immediately threw it out.

Kevin went over to the blinds, yanked them open and then slid back the window, even though he knew it would have no effect on the air quality in the apartment. The ocean breezes only reached as far as Beverly Hills.

"Shane came over with Christmas presents for us, Kevin," Leon stated. "Wasn't that sweet?"

"Yours is right here," said Shane. He handed Kevin a carefully wrapped box. A plastic sprig of holly was Scotch-taped to the top.

"This is gorgeous," commented Kevin, barely glancing at it, "but is there any coffee? I won't be able to give it my full attention until I have some coffee." He put the gift down on the floor.

"I'll make it," exclaimed Shane, delighted to be of service.

"That would be lovely." Kevin mugged, rolled his eyes at Leon, and then headed toward his bedroom. Leon leapt up and followed.

"So, where did you end up?" hissed Leon. "I hope it was huge and I want all the details because I'm furious. I hung around here last night until eleven, starving. I almost ordered a pizza! There was nothing in the house but Chromatrim gum!"

"Well," said Kevin, pulling his chlorine-encrusted T-shirt off in front of the mirror, "events took a turn. I would have called but I was sort of occupied."

He felt a bit guilty. He could have apologized, but instead absentmindedly pulled down his pants, giving Leon a rare treat. It was simpler this way. The sight of Kevin, gloriously nude, except for white socks and sneakers, put a stopper on Leon's questions. Kevin then lazily searched in his closet for a towel; the good one, from the Ramada. If Shane hadn't been so consumed with the task of making the coffee, he could have stolen a peek, too. It would have been the fulfillment of his fondest dream.

Kevin yanked his shoes off. "Well, I suppose I can fill you in on some of the less gruesome particulars. But get rid of Shane. I have to take a shower. I'm covered with large chunks of debris."

In the kitchen, Shane had shoved aside a pile of bills and then placed three coffee cups on the wobbly pine table. He was now busy folding squares of paper towels into artful little sailor hats.

"Oh God, my mother used to do that," said Leon.

"Well, I couldn't find any serviettes."

"You're quite the fussbudget, aren't you, Shane. You'll make some man very happy one day."

Shane beamed. "I know. I belong in an apron, barefoot and pregnant. Too bad the queens around here can't appreciate my homemaking skills."

"Oh, someone will come along. Are you dating?"

"Yes, constantly," replied Shane. "I meet tons of guys, but not the marrying kind, I'm afraid."

"Well, you're looking in all the wrong places."

"That's not true! I always work in first class on my flights. There are always a lot of gay businessmen going to New York and Boston. And then I go two-stepping in Long Beach on Monday nights. I never go out in West Hollywood, and in the summer I go to Will Rogers Beach. What am I doing wrong? I tan really well."

"I have no idea. It sounds as if you're doing everything right."

"If I don't sleep with a guy on the first date, they don't call. If I sleep with a guy on the first night, they don't call."

"What's your type, Shane?" Leon gave Shane the once over. Shane was about five-nine, with a cuddly little body, and sweet, close-set eyes. His ass was his best selling point, plump yet firm. The bleach job, however, was a disaster. Pulled through a cap and left in way too long. Roots for days.

"Oh, you know. Good looking, with a good job, a nice car, a nice apartment. I'm not asking for anything special! Just someone nice."

"Well, do they have to be white?" asked Leon.

"No. Black, Latin, Iranian . . . I don't care anymore. But no gym queens."

"Well, hon," said Leon, now bored with the subject, "I'm afraid you're really in the wrong town. Cute as you are, you're just not bartering your gay currency effectively. Listen, just find a daddy in Silver Lake and start buying Kleenex boxes that coordinate with your bath mats. You'll be much happier. Someone about to turn forty would be thrilled to have you lounging about. Keep your chin up! And by the way, if you want to date Iranians, you better start calling them Persians."

Kevin came in, his hair still wet. He wore ripped Levi's and a bright-yellow golf sweater, no shirt. Shane lunged for the coffee pot. Kevin picked through the unopened bills.

"Cream and sugar, Kevin?" whispered Shane.

"Just black dear," said Kevin, not looking up. Shane poured all around and then boldly sat down.

"Do you want your present now, Kevin?" asked Shane.

"Oh, that would be great."

The bills remained unopened.

Shane jumped up from the table and retrieved the box. "I didn't know what you wanted but when I saw it I just thought of you," explained Shane, as he shyly offered the gift to Kevin. "I mean, it just made me think of you."

Kevin tore away the ribbon and the plaid wrapping paper and let them drop to the floor. He recognized the box from a high-priced tchotchke emporium at the Beverly Center. Inside, he found a sort of green frog piggy bank, with a slit at the top and a cork plug underneath. It came with a small rectangular Lucite pedestal.

"Wow, Shane. This is really . . . great."

"Do you like it? They also had other animals but this one was the nicest. You can return it if you want—I still have the receipt."

"No, I wouldn't dream of it. It's totally fabulous. What did Shane get for you, Leon?"

"I got a very beautiful book about healing your inner child."

"I think all gay people need to heal their inner child," said Shane.

"You're absolutely correct," said Kevin. "Heal the little bastard before he starts getting notions. Leon, haven't you healed your inner child yet?"

Leon shook his head.

"Really? You're a disgrace."

"I haven't healed him yet, but I'm going to. Maybe this afternoon."

"Good. I think that would be wise."

"Don't you have a flight today or something, Shane?" asked Leon.

"No, not for a few days. I go to Denver and then on to Chicago. I'm going to see my family on my layover."

"Well, then we better break up this little fete. Kevin and I have a thing to go to today. Remember, Kevin?"

"Yeah, we better get moving. We'll see you later, Shane. Thanks for the presents."

"Oh, okay. I'll be home all day doing wash, but I may have to go to my Readyteller later. Knock on my door if you want."

"Whatever," said Kevin.

Shane went compliantly out the door and Kevin shut the adjacent window—it was the kind of building where everybody could hear everything.

"That was easy," said Leon. "He's putty in your hands."

"Really?" responded Kevin. "Can he get us free flights or something?"

"I don't know. You might have to sleep with him."

"Oh, I have bigger fish to fry. After last night."

"So, where were you?" said Leon.

"I was in Malibu. Shaking my money maker at the home of Brad Sherwood."

"Oh my God!" yelped Leon. "You're kidding."

"Yeah, pretty weird, huh? He cruised me up in the parking lot behind Sunset Plaza. First he plied me with champagne, and then later he got down to work on Wee Willie Winkie."

"Holy cow," said Leon.

"I should never drink. Pawing led to groping, which led to an underwater Jacuzzi blow job. I had a stream of water shooting up my ass for half an hour. I don't remember him once coming up for air."

"Oh, my God, I can't believe I'm hearing this," said Leon. "*Magnet Entertainment* Brad Sherwood?"

"Wait, it gets better. But is there any more coffee? And are there any cigarettes in the house?"

"Yeah, hang on, here's some." Leon grabbed a carton of Merits out of a kitchen cabinet and then refilled their coffee cups. An encounter with a celebrity was always a valid reason to smoke.

"Now, wait a minute," said Leon. "I have to hear everything. How did you wind up in the Jacuzzi? Did he have a big one?"

"Mmmhhh, let me think. It was . . . reasonable. Who can remember? I was bombed. The only image I can conjure right now . . . is that of an L-shaped studio apartment."

"A what?"

"You know, an L-shaped studio apartment. It's a Manhattan real-estate term that describes a kind of cookie-cutter . . ."

"Kevin! Don't hold back on me! This is the most incredible news I've ever heard. Ohmygod! Brad Sherwood!"

"Oh, relax. I'm sure I wasn't the first to be drawn into the boiling waters of his hot tub." Kevin lit a cigarette and continued. "I suppose he thought it was an expert seduction. He kept leading me down staircases until we were on the beach. At that point, the sun was starting to set, which was, as you can imagine, very mood-enhancing. But I had made up my mind long before he did. I just played the helpless maiden. Once he got rid of his creepy chauffeur it was a fait accompli."

"Chauffeur?"

"Yes, his chauffeur. I think the butler had the day off."

"So what was the house like?"

"Oh, Leon, you can't imagine the hideousness! Clean lines and sofa art. Really gay and cold, like Lucille LeSeur overdosing on her new Pepsi money. Windows where windows *ought to be,* if you know what I mean. California classy. Fabulous lap pool, though. Steely Dan piped in through underwater speakers."

Leon stared at Kevin with new awe. Now, Leon had had his share of rich tricks, but he'd never quite entered the inner sanctum. It was not a question of looks. Leon was handsome and would always do well. But he just didn't have a secret in his eye, or a twinkle. His features were regular, but they were too symmetrical and open. His skin was clear, but it didn't glow. His dark-brown hair was straight, but it didn't shimmer. His jaw was firm, but there was a bit too much space happening between the lower lip and the chin.

He was regular gorgeous, not Hollywood gorgeous, and that was his unpardonable sin.

The phone rang. Leon answered immediately, breaking, in his excitement, the cardinal rule of the house: to screen.

"Hello. May I speak to Kevin, please."

Leon's eyes widened.

"Hold on, I'll see if he's here."

"Brad Sherwood!" mouthed Leon, silently. "Brad Sherwood!"

Kevin waving the cigarette around, whispered, "No, No!"

"Uh, sorry, he's not here," said Leon, with more aplomb than Jane Hathaway. "May I take a message?"

"Yes. This is Brad, uh, a friend of his. Listen, I left something in his car that I need. An address book. Do you know when he'll be back?"

"Uh, no," said Leon, grabbing a pencil and writing "address book" on the back of one of four Visa bills. He shoved it in Kevin's direction.

"Well," continued Brad, "I'd like to get it back this afternoon. Actually, I have someone heading in the direction of West Hollywood right now to pick it up. If Kevin's not there, he'll wait. What is your address?"

"Uh, my address?" said Leon.

"Yes."

Leon paused a beat too long.

"Who is this?" said Brad.

"This is Leon, his roommate. Kevin's not here so I can't help you."

"Leon," said Brad patiently, "I'm sorry, I'm not making myself clear. This is Brad Sherwood. I think I left something in Kevin's car. It's nothing, really; just a little address book with phone numbers in it. My driver is on his way over to pick it up. If Kevin isn't there, he'll wait. Do you understand?"

"Uh, sure, Mr. Sherwood."

"Good. Now what is the address?"

"Seven forty-four Westmount, number five."

Kevin leaped up and waved his hands wildly, two inches from Leon's face.

"Thanks." Brad hung up without saying goodbye, which Leon thought was really rude.

Kevin started yelling but Leon cut him off.

"Where are your keys?" he asked Kevin. "You've got Brad Sherwood's address book in your car. His driver is on his way over here right now to pick it up."

Kevin ran into his bedroom. His car keys were on his dresser. He grabbed them and ran barefoot out the front door.

There was a ticket on the window of the Miata. Damn. Street cleaning between ten and twelve. No wonder he had no trouble finding a spot. He jammed the key in and ripped open the passenger door. The thin, black-alligator address book was on the floor. Kevin's heart pounded and a passing jogger startled him. The guy cruised him and then veered off and smashed his shoulder into a telephone pole.

Kevin ignored him and ran back into the apartment. "I got it," he said, panting. He locked the door, drew the blinds, and then he and Leon slammed themselves back down at the kitchen table.

"Jesus," marveled Leon. "Brad Sherwood's address book. Open it up."

Kevin stared at Leon and then opened to the first page: "A."

The first entry was for someone named Fentress Atkinson. A list of phone numbers followed: New York, home and office; London, home and office; Bedford, home; Hobe Sound, home. Kevin turned the page.

"Anita Baker, Detroit, home," gasped Leon. "Oh my God, I love her. It's her private phone number!"

"She's on his label, dummy," said Kevin, imparting to Leon the knowledge that everyone got off the news, off the radio, from the paper—the kind of knowledge you couldn't avoid these days, even if you wanted to. Somewhere along the line, entertainment news *had become the news.*

He turned another page.

"Connie Chung, Joan Collins, Tom Cruise," read Leon. "Wow, keep going."

"D. Marvin Davis, crossed out. Dominican Republic (Consul General), Neil Diamond, Barry Diller, Matt Dillon, Dr. Dre . . . *Bobby* De Niro . . ."

"Wait!" shouted Leon. "Go to M."

Kevin quickly flipped to the M section.

And there it was, plain as day. *Madonna.* LA, New York, Miami. Numbers had been crossed out and rewritten so many times she had an entire page to herself.

"Oh, my gosh," said Leon.

"Get a pencil," said Kevin.

Leon's jaw dropped.

"I'll read them off and you write."

Leon hesitated but then leapt up and grabbed a pen and a few sheets of paper.

"Okay, ready," said Leon, his hand trembling. "Start with Madonna."

Kevin read off the numbers.

"Who's next?" said Leon.

"How 'bout . . . Liz Taylor?"

"Cool."

"There's a lot of rock people in here . . . Elton John, Axl Rose, Sting . . . John Tesh?"

"Who?" said Leon.

"Don't write him down."

For the next half hour Kevin and Leon copied numbers diligently, without pausing. Neither questioned why. It was, if you had any dignity, the right thing to do.

After they got through all the big celebrity names, they started adding some of the others.

"Mike Brazier," said Kevin.

"Who's that?"

"Big agent. Wife, two kids, charities, boyfriend."

"Got it. Next?"

On and on they went, page after page. Leon's wrist began to ache. So many names. Most had either a New York or LA street address, plus a few phone numbers. Some of the people in the book had numerous homes: Aspen, Santa Fe, Southampton, Miami, Puerta Vallarta, Greenwich. A few Londons and Tokyos. There were Washington, D.C. numbers, too, including one that had "WH" next to it in parentheses. Cellular numbers, car phones, offices, private home lines, fax numbers, all carefully written in pencil. The sheer volume was amazing. As they perused and copied the numbers, Kevin slowly began to comprehend that these people were Brad Sherwood's personal friends. These were the people he called just to chat.

An hour passed before they were almost finished. Kevin felt awed by all the pages they had filled. These were the names of the people who ran the world. Imagine knowing them? Imagine having such a large life?

Maybe it was time to pour on some fresh charm. This was the stuff of salvation. Kevin knew Brad now, sort of intimately. Did he want to participate in this world? It was a titillating thought. Something to do, a goof, before he escaped and put all this LA nonsense behind him. It might be nice to be treated well in Hollywood for a change, instead of as just another sleazy boy-toy.

A knock at the door broke the spell they were under. Kevin swept up the papers and gave them to Leon.

"I'll go," whispered Kevin. "You get lost."

Even through the distorted lens of the peephole, Kevin could see that Jeremy, Brad's driver, had a peeved expression on his face. He really doesn't enjoy his work, thought Kevin.

"Jeremy. What a pleasant surprise."

"I'm in a hurry," he said. "Do you have Mr. Sherwood's address book?"

"Yes, of course," replied Kevin. "Would you like to sit down and have a drink while I fetch it? The drive from Malibu must have been exhausting. How about a Kir Royale?"

"Just hand it over."

"My, my, wasn't Santa good to you this year?" Kevin nonchalantly swiped the address book off the kitchen table.

"I haven't had Christmas yet. Mr. Sherwood wanted me to remain in the house as long as you were hanging around. Thanks to you, my kids are still waiting for their presents."

"Well, I'm sure you're well compensated. What is family anyway, Jeremy, when you're so close to the glamour of Hollywood? They're LA kids, they'll understand. Brad is more important, wouldn't you say?"

Jeremy snatched the address book from Kevin and turned on his heel. Kevin noisily locked the door behind him.

"Guess who I just hung up on?" yelled Leon.

"*What?* Oh, God."

Kevin ran into Leon's bedroom. It was the smaller of the two, tidier than his, and full of secondhand Victorian furniture, artfully restored. The walls were painted a soothing heliotrope. Jagged thunderbolts and fanciful gray clouds stenciled on the ceiling obscured a dreary series of ancient water stains.

Leon was on his bed, dialing a number on an old rotary phone. The numbers they had copied were spread out all over.

"I just hung up on Goldie Hawn," gasped Leon. "It was definitely her voice!"

"Are you crazy? They can trace calls instantly now. What if she has star sixty-nine? Or call return? Or caller ID?"

"Oh, relax. I didn't ask her when she's going to remake *Private Benjamin*. I just hung up," said Leon.

Kevin scooped up the phone numbers. "Come on. Let's go to the gym. You're losing all perspective, darling."

CHAPTER 3

"Oh, darling, I had the most fabulous trick last night."

Brad was on the phone with his old friend Rob. Glints of sun bouncing off the Pacific warmed the shine of his antique biblical-limestone kitchen floors.

Around him, maids were swarming. FedEx had come and gone, as had Gelson's, his landscape architect, and his trainer, who had left him sore. Jeremy had dropped off his address book and the pool guy was on his way—as soon as he fished a dead seagull out of a drain two doors down. To Brad, it all looked like his life was in running order and the illusion was good.

"On Christmas Day?" asked Rob, from his mansion in Beverly Hills.

"Yeah, can you believe it? I met him in West Hollywood, coming back from Midge and Sy's. He was hanging around the parking lot behind Sunset Plaza and he drove me home. In a Miata."

"No!"

"Yes!"

"How lurid!"

"Well, I had Jeremy follow," continued Brad. "Then we started drinking and somehow, one thing led to another and we wound up in the Jacuzzi."

"I thought you were going to New York."

"I was, but I wormed out of it. I wasn't up to facing the Magnet board. Besides, I need to think some things through. Have you decided, by the way? Are you coming to Maui with me?"

"Yes," answered Rob. "The tour is going really well. In fact, we've extended the run another week—my skaters are on the train to . . . Belgium?

Liechtenstein? Oh, who knows. Anyway, yes, I'm coming. I could use a few days on a beach."

"Good. Call the Royal Waleia, just to make sure. I think they're still holding your suite. And the spa cuisine will do us both a world of good. Did I tell you they're having a no-alcohol New Year's Eve party? There's also a charity five-K run and a Polynesian-themed midnight aerobics class."

"Well, I don't know if I'm up for all that," said Rob. "I just want to get some sun and lose five pounds."

Rob Erikson had a finger in a lot of pies, but his ice-dancing troupe, surprisingly, was one of his steadiest earners. He had been a figure skater himself many years back and had rescued this old show from bankruptcy, catching, in the process, a cyclical wave of ice-dancing popularity. The show, called *Fantasies on Ice,* was currently touring Europe. Rob was quite proud of it, especially since he had once asked Brad to invest in it. Brad declined, so Rob impulsively had sold off his Montana acreage to close the deal. It proved to be a smart move. He had only bought the land as part of some cowboy fantasy that he was going through. Getting over it rather quickly, he found a buyer just before the ranch market took a nosedive. Then ice dancing came around again in a big way and Rob, always *monied,* got fabulously rich.

"So anyway, about this Christmas trick of yours," said Rob. "Not paying for sex. What a completely subversive idea! How did that happen?"

"Well, he drove me back to my house and then we just sort of fell into it. Perfectly safe, of course, no gymnastics. Gorgeous, unbelievable black hair, about twenty-five or so and kind of . . . affectionate, I guess would be the word. I have his phone number."

"Well, I'll have to pop over and see a tape," said Rob. "I hope your cameras were running."

Brad hesitated. "Ah, no, darling, actually they weren't. I couldn't get away to turn them on. Maybe next time."

"Shame on you! Well, *I* have a new tape. Identical twin brothers fresh off the farm! They've worked up a little act with each other, a real pas de deux. Talk about affectionate. Once they started going at it, they completely forgot I was in the room!" said Rob with a raspy cackle.

Brad's thoughts were already wandering. He knew Rob's type well: stringy, pimply, and always under twenty-five. They came out of nowhere, this genetic strain, and were never in short supply.

Brad and Rob had been trading homemade videos for years. Some of the novelty had worn off long ago, but, still, they kept up the habit, for they were nothing if not disciplined. Their collections now numbered in the hundreds, with more than a few famous faces on many of the tapes. Brad didn't spend a lot of time watching them anymore, but he still liked to have a few fresh tapes from Rob on hand for trips to the airport or to concerts. Privately made porn was so much nicer than the canned stuff that came out of the Valley.

"Sounds fabulous," said Brad. "Listen, Rob, I'd love to chat but I gotta run. I need to return at least thirty calls this afternoon. Try me later."

Brad, still in his robe, hung up and then drifted into his office, perplexed.

He always shared tapes with Rob—that was a given, one of the terms of their friendship. But this time he just couldn't. The experience with Kevin had been . . . what? Special? Was that still possible?

From the moment Kevin reached up through the darkness and pulled Brad into the whirlpool, Brad felt himself become emboldened. They kissed while Kevin stripped Brad's clothes off underwater and they kissed some more on a mattress hastily pulled off a chaise longue. Finally, under the glowing coils of a heat lamp, with their skin prickly and sensitive from the chlorine, Brad decisively upended the rest of the bottle of the champagne onto Kevin's cock and *went to town*. (Kevin, of course, had no way of knowing that Brad was only using the alcohol for its sterilizing properties.)

Brad had not gone down on anyone for over a year, and he had almost forgotten how mind-blowing it could be: the head banging the back of his throat, the heat, the mechanical retracting of Kevin's swollen testicles just before the money shot. Even now, Brad could feel the fullness in his throat, the slight lingering ache. And the divine feeling of Kevin's hands holding his skull, his thumbs pressing into his temples!

Brad leaned back in his big leather swivel chair and put his feet up on his desk. He loosened his robe and peeked at his own swelling organ. It had received quite a workout last night, and Brad, touching it gently, thought it looked larger.

Oh, I'm in a tizzy, he thought. He wanted to call Kevin and tell him to jump in a cab and come back. He wanted to buy Kevin something, like a new car, or a truckload of expensive suits. More than anything else, Brad wanted to be held again. No one in recent memory had held him as Kevin had, except maybe his chiropractor, a guy with spotless offices in Century City (who looked into his eyes with such love—before flipping him over on his side and cracking his back).

Instead, Brad tightened his robe and put in a call to Corrine Landemann, his executive vice president and full-time majordomo at Magnet. It was a call he dreaded, but all these dreamy thoughts had to stop. Although he knew he would get a lecture about skipping out on the board meeting, to counter it he would simply remind her of the true purpose of her job: damage control.

She was at home with her husband, Dr. Richard Landemann, every Beverly Hills parent's favorite dermatologist. He did amazing things with stress-induced teenage rosacea.

Brad got right to the point. "Okay, Corrine, how fucked am I?"

"Oh, hello, Brad. Let's see, where do I begin? Much as I'd _like to_, I won't torture you. First off, I covered for you with the board."

"Good. That's all I wanted to know."

"I think I bought you a little time, but of course I had to tell the most outrageous lie. The official story is you're in Beijing, at a secret meeting that took months to set up, on stemming the tide of CD bootlegging in the Pacific Rim. I think they bought it, but when you didn't show up, that's all I could come up with."

"Perfect. That buys me a few more days."

"It was very upsetting, Brad. I took the call while I was up to my neck in mud at the Givenchy Spa, with cucumber slices over my eyes. And then I panicked and dropped the phone, which was ruined. I had to order a new one, but they don't make the model I like anymore, so I got this other one and it took me two hours to reprogram the entire index."

"Well, that's the fun of it, Corrine. And maybe I really will go to Beijing. That's actually a timely idea."

"The board went ahead and convened without you, Brad. This time it's serious."

"Hey, you did good, so relax. Don't bring me down."

"Brad—" began Corrine, but he cut her off.

"Stop, Corrine. I don't want to hear about it. Now look, I'm taking a short vacation and I'm leaving tomorrow. But keep it quiet. I'll only be gone a few days." He hung up the phone.

Corrine was a worrier, which was useful, but Brad was not ready to re-linquish his fragile good mood. Sure, she had reason to be upset, but they all did. Magnet stock had been downgraded on CNBC by an analyst from Merrill Lynch last week from "hold" to "neutral." But so what? He just needed to let the problems ferment in his mind a bit. He'd come up with a solution eventually, a solution that would please everyone. He always had.

He chuckled as he thought of Corrine stammering out her story about him and the Chinese.

Another ultraprivate line rang.

"Hello," sang Brad with uncharacteristic cheer.

"That pecan danish was disgusting. I was up all night with gas," said Brad's father.

"Oh, hello, Sy. Where's Mother?"

"She's here, where do you think she is? Listen, your mother wants to shop the sales. I can't go with her and your aunt Gilda isn't feeling well. Can you take her?"

"Dad, the stores will be crazy today. You don't have to shop the sales, anyway. How about if I send a car over next week so she and Aunt Gilda can make a day of it?"

"Oh, Mr. Big Shot can't take his mother out for an afternoon. You know that doesn't impress us. In fact, it's insulting. You didn't even stay for lunch yesterday, just ran out as soon as you could."

Brad sat up and tightened his robe.

"Look, I couldn't stay. I told you and that's that. Tell Mother I'll call her later this afternoon."

"Sure, sure, Mr. Big Shot."

Sy hung up. Brad pulled Kevin's number from his robe and once again considered calling him. Instead, he went to his laundry room and ejected the three tapes he had made of Kevin and took them into his media room. Before he allowed himself to view them, he padded barefoot out to the deserted beach and retrieved the champagne cork.

CHAPTER 4

Kevin slipped into black bicycle shorts, a midriff-baring Gold's Gym sweatshirt, and a pair of yellow construction boots. Leon, meanwhile, struggled into a faded pair of size-31 Levi's cutoffs, a Spandex T-shirt from the Undergear catalog, and Charles Barkley Nike high-tops. The boys showed an unseemly amount of skin, but for an afternoon at the Athletic Connection, they were dressed *conservatively*. Together they walked the short distance up the street to the club.

Inside, a crowded step-aerobics class was in full swing, the disturbing bass notes of Hanson sending everyone into paroxysms of demonic flailing. Kevin and Leon took their membership cards out of their socks and presented them to Greg, the front-desk clerk.

Greg was a butch number with a streaked ponytail. Because of his high self-esteem, he also sported a daring growth of facial hair. He took Kevin's card, ran it through a beige metal scanner, and then stared with great concentration at his computer screen. "You only have a week left on your membership, Mr. Malloy. Would you like to speak to one of our customer-service representatives about renewing?"

"Maybe later," mumbled Kevin. There was no way he could come up with the money it would cost to renew. Expenses had begun to pile up—the payments on the Miata, the rent, the Visa cards. Just that morning he had received notice that his car-registration fee was due. At the top, written in large pink letters, was a warning: CALIFORNIA HAS NO GRACE PERIOD.

Kevin was short for the month about six hundred dollars. He was expecting a check from an actor for whom he had done some head shots, and he made a mental note to stop by the guy's apartment later and collect. It was only for three hundred and change, but, clearly, now was the time to go in for the squeeze.

Patrick and Gina, his parents, were in Boca, and Kevin realized he might have to call them. He knew his mother would send a check, but only if she could conceal the withdrawal from Patrick. His father, retired now from the county planning commission where he had been the supervisor of parking policies and restrictions, was tight with a buck. What a geezer, thought Kevin. Patrick already collected about three government pension checks a month, and he had enough money to take advantage of every deduction within the law and then some. He and Gina, by virtue of living for a long time in a house they had paid very little for, were now rich. Not yet sixty-five, Patrick's senior-citizen discount seemed to bring him more joy than anything else in his life ever had.

Kevin's two older sisters were married and still living in Westchester County. The elder, Connie, was married to Ralph, a contractor who had bought up some old farmland in Yorktown Heights and then stuck seventy condos on it. Called "town homes," they were incredibly shoddy, yet sold for ridiculous sums. Connie and Ralph, now living in a stately tudor on the grounds of Westchester Country Club, had recently taken to saying that they were "fond of Bermuda in March."

Kevin hadn't spoken to them in years.

His other sister, Diane, the middle child, had married a townie named Eddie, and they lived in an apartment in Mamaroneck. Diane worked for Standard Foods in White Plains as an accountant and Eddie was a musician. They had a young daughter named Jennifer. Kevin knew although Diane was ready to wash her hands of the whole marriage, she was too proud to ask anyone for help. Connie offered her a little money, but Diane was so insulted that the two, observing an unwritten but strict family law, hadn't spoken to each other for months. And Patrick and Gina thought that Diane had made her bed and needed to lie in it for a while before they bailed her out. As good Catholics, Patrick and Gina felt all lessons had to be learned the hard way. They, of course, did not know that Eddie had hit Diane on more than a few occasions.

Kevin grimly wondered how his life had turned out like this, broke, thousands of miles from his fractured family, no real job, and alone. Such grim thoughts struck him more and more often nowadays. Oh, he had mastered a few adult tasks, but most of the time he felt like a fraud. He was a competent photographer, but he didn't have the killer instinct. He was insufficiently aggressive, he did not drive the latest sport "ute," and, most important, he found himself unable to schmooze the influential stylists and hairdressers. Shoots were supposed to be fun, but Kevin never bothered setting the tone or massaging the egos. He worked quickly and quietly, and at the end of the day, when no one felt like having unsafe sex or taking crystal, it was his fault.

Sometimes he would daydream about being back in New York, in his boyhood home, and tears would spring to his eyes. Kevin wanted to be back in his room, sorting through cassettes and cutting pictures out of *GQ*. He wanted to be playing hooky from school and sneaking into the city on the train with his best friend Anthony. He wanted to eat pizza again without having to spend an extra hour on the StairMaster the next day.

Kevin thought of Anthony as he and Leon climbed the staircase to the main exercise floor. Anthony Capozi—now that was a best friend. Kevin looked over at Leon and became depressed. He supposed Leon was his best friend now and wasn't *that* a sorry thought.

It had all been so idyllic. At sixteen, Kevin had his driver's license altered with a razor blade and got a part-time job selling men's hats and gloves at Macy's in White Plains. Anthony Capozi worked across the aisle in a department called Gentlemen's Jeans.

Anthony was a real fashion plate and all the girls in the store used to find reasons to pass through his department. He wasn't very tall, but he had a high-school football player's build that had everyone swooning. Since he worked in a trendy part of the store, he was allowed to wear jeans and he wore them as tight as possible. Pale hazel eyes and a distinctly Roman nose imbued him with an aura of royalty. When he sauntered through the employee lounge, elderly ladies from the children's department went giddy at the sight of him.

Kevin always hitchhiked home from work. One cold November evening he was standing in the road with his thumb out when Anthony appeared. Anthony was in his mustard-yellow MG convertible, a sixteenth-birthday present from his father. Sharon Jacobs, his girlfriend, who worked at Macy's in cosmetics, was by his side.

"Hi, you guys," said Kevin, shivering.

"I'd give you a ride, but we were just going to the WPD, that diner over there," said Anthony. "Want to come?"

Sharon, a glossy and sophisticated eighteen year old, opened her door. "Squeeze in." Kevin, excited to finally be meeting Anthony and Sharon, climbed in on her lap and clumsily introduced himself. They were the two most glamorous employees at the store, and for the first time in his life, Kevin felt touched by greatness.

At the diner, Sharon folded her coat neatly with the label out and placed it on the bench seat: CALVIN KLEIN. Kevin slid over by the window and Anthony sat down beside Sharon. Shirley, a black waitress who could have been forty or sixty, came over to greet them. "Hi, kids. Sharon, you look really fine tonight. Are those them Monet earrings you were talking about?"

"Yes," replied Sharon, beaming and batting her eyelashes with exaggerated pride. "Hypoallergenic. You know, I can get you a pair if you want."

"Are they expensive?" asked Shirley.

"Of course," said Sharon. "But I get a discount. I'll bring some in next week."

"You work at the store, too?" Shirley asked Kevin.

"Yeah," said Kevin. "Men's hats."

"That's nice. I need to get my son a hat."

"Come on, it's late," Anthony butted in. "I'll have a burger deluxe and a Coke."

"For a change," sniffed Shirley.

"Thanks," said Anthony. "*Surly!*"

"What did you call me?"

"Your name," said Anthony. "Shirley."

"That's right." She winked at Anthony and he winked back.

"Grilled cheese, no pickle, Tab," announced Sharon.

Kevin studied the large menu, scanning the prices. All eyes were on him. "Burger deluxe for me, too," he said. "And a Coke." Everyone beamed. Apparently he had passed the first test.

Anthony and Sharon were famous at the store for their cliquishness. They high-hatted *everyone,* even department managers. Sharon was a top salesgirl and she had completely clear skin so she could get away with anything. She also had one of the rare commission jobs and a lot of the older employees resented her for it. With her long auburn hair and a perfect button nose, courtesy of a talented and much-in-demand Scarsdale surgeon, she reigned supreme. Her entire salary went to her wardrobe.

Anthony was a senior at Fordham Prep, a Catholic boys' school. He had been accepted at Columbia and was looking forward to moving into Man-

hattan, everyone's dream in those days. Schools in Westchester always offered field trips to Radio City or Broadway, and afterward, as they rode toward home through the Bronx on a chartered bus, everyone felt hopelessly
suburban. When they got home, usually around five, they invariably
snapped at their parents.

"So how is men's hats, Kevin?" asked Sharon. "Pretty boring?"

"It's okay. I also have gloves, wallets, and belts. That breaks it up. But I
can't leave the counter or else Julius Manfredi freaks out."

"Julius, yecch," said Sharon. "Last year at the Christmas party he made
ambrosia."

"He's my manager, too," said Anthony, wading into the conversation.
"What a clown."

"And those cheap buckle shoes," added Sharon, rolling her eyes.

"They're very Plymouth Rock," said Anthony. "Definitely elevators. I
think he orders them from the back of the *Daily News* magazine section."

"My cousin works at Saks," Sharon said gravely. "They would never put
up with that."

Sharon and Anthony proceeded to pick apart almost everyone else who
worked at the store. Kevin didn't know most of the people they were talking about; he had only been working there a few months. Sharon did most
of the talking, with Anthony grunting agreeably. Soon they segued into
broader areas.

"Have you seen any new Broadway shows?" asked Sharon.

"Not yet," replied Kevin.

"Have you been to any of the new clubs?" inquired Anthony.

"No."

"Don't you go out in the city?" said Anthony.

"Not really."

Anthony and Sharon looked at each other, confused.

"How old are you, Kevin?" asked Sharon.

"Well, officially, at the store, I'm eighteen."

"Which means . . . unofficially?" prodded Anthony.

"Unofficially . . . I'm sixteen."

"Then how did you get the job?" asked Sharon. "You have to be eighteen."

"Well," explained Kevin, unsure of whether he should be sharing this
information, "there's a guy at school who fixes everyone's driver's licenses.

He charges five dollars. His father is some kind of printer, but I think he just uses a razor blade and a Bic."

"Wow, Sharon," said Anthony. "The years we've wasted. We could have been getting into the clubs a lot sooner."

"We were. Let's see it, Kevin."

Kevin pulled out his wallet, a purchase made with his first paycheck. Proudly displayed behind a little plastic window was the altered document. Kevin handed it to Sharon who studied it and then passed it Anthony.

"Whoever did this did a really good job," Anthony stated with solemn admiration.

Shirley arrived with the food and Kevin put his wallet back into his hip pocket. Anthony poured a gallon of ketchup on his fries. Sharon, having been to Europe on a Perillo tour with her parents, ate her grilled cheese with a knife and fork.

"You want more water?" asked Shirley. All three shook their heads and she walked away with a frown. She was subject to moods.

It was close to ten and a school night, so they all finished up quickly. Anthony, using a technique he had learned from his father, expertly signaled for the check. He paid for Sharon and then threw another five on the table.

"I'll get this," said Anthony.

"Your money's no good here, Kevin," added Sharon.

"Wow, thanks," said Kevin. "Should I leave the tip?"

"If you do, you can walk home," Anthony told him.

The three of them went out to the parking lot. It was cold and clear and Sharon put the collar of her luxurious navy coat up around her ears. She then reached in and pulled her hair out of the back of the coat and fanned it over her shoulders. It was a sleek and confident gesture and Kevin was mesmerized.

"How far from here do you live?" asked Anthony.

"About five miles up the road."

"If we take the top down, Kevin can sit sideways in the back," suggested Sharon.

"Oh, it's okay you guys, I can hitch," Kevin said. "It's just a straight shot, no problem."

"Don't be silly, Kevin," Sharon admonished. "Just get in. We're in charge."

Anthony unfolded the top and Kevin climbed in the back. Sharon got in and Kevin could smell her clean hair. As they pulled out of the parking lot her hair floated up against his face and he detected the rich aroma of apples and sodium laureth sulfide: *Herbal Essence,* he thought, during this, the most contented moment of his life, *the coolest shampoo ever invented.*

Feeling slightly charitable, but mostly just sorry for himself, Kevin put his hand on Leon's shoulder.

"You know, Leon, your breasts are looking absolutely superb today. I'm sorry I yelled at you before. I'm a little tense, as always."

"No big deal," said Leon, surprised to detect a note of sincerity in Kevin's voice. "You were right—I shouldn't have called Goldie Hawn like that. Pretty dumb, what with that new stalking law."

"Oh, well, don't get carried away, darling. I'm sure she didn't mind. I mean, nowadays it's more embarrassing if you don't have your own personal stalker. You probably lifted her spirits."

Leon did not know how to react to this kinder, gentler Kevin, so he changed the subject. "What do you want to do today? Chest or legs? The holiday threw our schedule off."

"I better do something about these tits," declared Kevin, "before my membership runs out. Things are getting a little tight lately. If I don't drum up some cash, I won't be able to renew my membership and the West Hollywood sheriff's department will be escorting me to the border."

"Well, if you're really desperate, I can loan you a little something to get you over the hump. I still have most of my game-show money sitting around."

"Wow, thanks Leon," said Kevin.

"Don't mention it."

Leon had tried out for a few game shows soon after arriving from Minneapolis. Although he had overheard a guest coordinator whisper "too fey" after one audition, he forged ahead, made the rounds and eventually managed to get on a second-tier show called *Vegas Windfall,* a summer pilot that did not get picked up. Leon was one of the the show's first contestants; all he was required to do was answer a few questions about the prices of popular supermarket items and then pull a lever on a giant slot machine. A brilliant coupon shopper, Leon got through the first round with ease.

After each successful pull, he was given a chance to double his money. Four nerve-racking rounds later, Leon walked away with $11,000. The audience, a few busloads of senior citizens dragged in from the desert, for some reason found it difficult to share in his excitement. When Leon's check was finally issued, it came with a stern warning about how the IRS closely watches game-show winners and to declare every single penny. Deflated, he parked the money in a savings account.

The show was dropped because winning was too easy.

Leon, however, had a knack with money. He worked at a glitzy kitchen-and bath-design shop on Robertson, and even though he went in only a few afternoons a week, he did well financially. He was good at convincing bored matrons that they needed brushed-stainless-steel subzero refrigerators and environmentally correct low-flush toilets. He shamed them into ordering Italian tiles that took ten weeks to deliver. He impressed upon them the need for Carrara marble or don't bother. If he had cared, he could have made a lot more, but the job wasn't—to his way of thinking—"show biz," so he spent as little time as he could at it.

Kevin and Leon warmed up at an incline press until, miraculously, a bench press opened up. They dashed over, and then silently began piling weight onto the bar, each taking an end. Kevin sat down first, with Leon standing behind him, ready to spot. Numerous couples around them were engaged in the same ritual, all of them deadly serious and determined. A few steroid monsters to their left were powerlifting, and their anguished grunts could be heard over the blasting techno music, like roars from a walrus cage at a city zoo. All this *right beneath* a framed "no grunting" sign, too.

Kevin and Leon worked quickly and methodically, conscious that the bench presses were always at a premium. Two guys, doctors who had worked out together since medical school, were already waiting, gazing at Kevin's artfully bundled crotch. Flat on his back, Kevin felt their stares. "Please guys," he chided, "go away and do some squats." They retreated huffily, once again discussing the need to find a more exclusive gym in Beverly Hills. But they never would, of course. They were in awe of West Hollywood boys.

Many of the men worked their chests at the expense of other body parts and had developed odd, bird-leg figures. Skinny, shaved legs and tiny asses supported jello-mold firm, cantilevered pecs. If one squinted, many of the physiques, in this loud, throbbing hothouse atmosphere, eerily conjured the silhouette of Jayne Mansfield.

When it was Leon's turn, Kevin got up and looked around at all the pinched faces. There were at least a hundred guys in this area of the gym. So many darting eyes taking surreptitious peeks at crotches. So many lewd costumes. And some camaraderie and hilarity, too. Here, the younger members could recapture the fun they were denied back in high-school gym class.

But today, under the hot lamps, everyone seemed all too pale and vulnerable. And much too far from someplace real. But what could be done? This was the white-hot center of it all, and who wanted it any other way? You want to take your shirt off at a circuit party and touch a stranger's chest? You want to hold your head high when you stand in line behind Bob Paris in the West Hollywood Koo Koo Roo? You want to be a *professional* homosexual? Well, this is where you paid your dues.

Feeling sadistic, Kevin forced a few extra reps out of Leon before taking the weight off him.

After their workout, Kevin and Leon went home to shower, for showering at the gym had become impossible. Guys with doughy faces and huge dongs lathered themselves for hours on end and the door to the sauna opened and closed with a horrendous bang every thirty seconds. It was a wonder the sauna ever retained any heat, what with all the traffic. Occasionally, management would put up a vaguely worded sign in an attempt to discourage hanky-panky, but it was always torn down. For the West Hollywood premium they shelled out, plucked directly from their checking accounts on the sixteenth of each month, the club members figured they had rights.

Entering the apartment, Kevin and Leon, out of habit, descended upon the answering machine. There was but one message.

Were they being alerted to a party? Or was it a creditor? Like opening the mailbox, checking their messages was an activity that no longer brought either of them any joy. The boys braced themselves. Leon looked over at Kevin, and Kevin nodded. Then and only then, did Leon hit the button.

"Hi, Kevin. This is Brad Sherwood. I just wanted to call and thank you for taking such good care of my address book. I can't believe I left it in your car, I was looking all over for it. Hmm, well, pretty stupid. Um, anyway, listen, I have to go to Maui for a few days and I wanted to know if I could see you before then. Like maybe even tonight if you're free. I think I owe you a dinner or something, so, um, give me a call. Here's my private number, okay? Got a pen?"

Brad read off the number and the machine stopped. Kevin and Leon, sighing with relief, continued staring at each other. Finally, Kevin folded his arms and headed for the kitchen. He opened the refrigerator and pulled out a gallon of distilled water. Then he took out two glasses and filled them. He handed one to Leon. Silently, they toasted each other.

"He's totally smitten," remarked Leon. "Past the point of no return."

"Yeah," admitted Kevin, "I think you might be right. Whew, I had no idea. It was just a poolside frolic, for God's sake. I thought I was too old for him. I mean, really. Oh, God, what should I do? A meal? Dinner? Food? Jeez, what's *that* all about?"

"He wants to see you again," said Leon

"Yeah, I get that part, Leon."

"It's called a date."

"Oh, God, don't say that. I did too many crunches yesterday. I may throw up."

"What the heck is wrong with you, Kevin? You slept with him and now he wants to take you out to dinner. It's supposed to go the other way around, true, but the hard part is over. Call him right now while I run you a bath."

"And lay out my trousseau, while you're at it. Oh, God, can't I just stay home and watch *Saved by the Bell?*"

"No," said Leon. "I'm afraid you can't. Brad Sherwood is probably the most influential person in this town. He's establishment A-list, not just gay A-list. Don't you get it? As your roommate, it's my responsibility to see that you don't squander your opportunities. Oh, God. But this is so much bigger than that. I mean, if Brad Sherwood calls, you just go. There is no other option."

There was a knock at the door. Leon went and peered through the peephole and then mouthed "Shane." Kevin raised his hand in an attractive papal gesture and nodded. Leon unlocked the door.

"Hi guys!" chirped Shane. "I heard you come in. I wanted to know if you wanted to come over tonight and have dinner."

"What are you making?" asked Kevin.

"Chicken with mushroom sauce. It's really easy. You just take a package of frozen parts from the Price Club, defrost them, and then take some Campbell's mushroom soup, no generics, and—"

"Shane, please . . . spare us," Leon broke in. "I'll come. But skip the sauce and just get some fresh broccoli and some rice or baked potatoes."

He turned to Kevin. "Well, these are your options for the evening, dear. I think your choice is obvious."

"Shane," commanded Kevin. "Come over here. Excuse me, but what the hell is going on with your hair? If you're going to go blond, you have to realize it's a commitment. How can you think about serving food with those roots? I should call the airline right now and have you grounded." Shane looked stricken as Kevin left the room.

"Don't pout, Shane," said Leon. "He only told you out of friendship. Kevin's got plans tonight, but I'll come over. I'll bring a movie."

"All right," said Shane. "Boy, he's in a bad mood. What did I say?"

"Absolutely nothing. He's just testy. I'll come over in a few hours."

"What sign is he?"

"Aries, I think."

"Oh, well, there you go, that explains it," said Shane.

"Yes, it does. Now go get some green vegetables. What kind of movie would you like to see?"

"Oh, anything's fine, as long as it's not foreign."

"I'll just look for something in the action section," said Leon. "Something with a sticker that warns of the possibility of male frontal nudity."

Shane left with hardly any prodding and Leon headed for Kevin's room.

"So," began Leon, "what are you going to wear?"

Kevin was lying on his bed staring at the ceiling.

"I haven't decided if I'm going."

"Listen, Kevin," said Leon. "Don't think I haven't noticed you moping around here for the last couple of weeks. What's the problem? You're young, and you're gorgeous. What's the point of living in LA if you're not going to take advantage of your opportunities? If Brad Sherwood wanted to go out with me I'd be ecstatic."

"Wouldn't you be just the teensiest bit embarrassed?" asked Kevin. "I mean, you know what these guys are like."

"No, I don't, but I'd like to. And he's not bad looking. His hair transplant is one of the best in LA."

"How would you know?"

"I've seen pictures."

"Pictures lie."

"Oh, come off it, Kevin. Stop wasting time. You know you're going.

Don't be such a snob. You have bills to pay and you know you can't do anything in this town without the right contacts." Leon grabbed Kevin by the shoulders and shook him. "This is the real world, Kevin! Besides, you might even have fun."

"Ugh, get off me. Listen, if I need to know about the real world, I can watch *The Real World*."

Leon was not amused.

"Okay, okay, don't be a haunt!" said Kevin. "Bring me a phone, Beulah."

Leon let out a whoop and ran out of the room.

Kevin sat up and caught a glimpse of himself in the mirror. He was struck by his own grim countenance. Fun. What was that? Merely another concept, one that had been just out of his grasp for a few years now. *God, he thought, the Irish in me is really taking over*. Kevin took a clump of hair between two fingers and pulled it down in front of his eyes. It was exceedingly greasy. He hadn't washed his hair properly in two days. His spirits rose a fraction. If he washed it tonight, it would come out really good. He might even blow-dry it a bit—but then that might overwhelm Brad. A little blow-drying, a little finger-styling, and a palmful of mousse—the total effect had grown men begging for mercy. *Oh well,* thought Kevin, *I've started this, I might as well finish it. I'll even use that cooling leg gel from The Body Shop*. Resigned to his fate, he got up and headed into the living room.

Leon had copied Brad's number off the answering machine. Kevin picked up their black Trimline and punched in the numbers.

"Hello?"

"Hi Brad. It's Kevin."

"Kevin," said Brad, sounding pleased. *"Hiii."*

"How are you?"

"Good . . . and you?"

"Fine. Thank you."

Kevin looked over at Leon, who was pretending to watch TV. *"Coming up at six, the Channel Nine Action News,"* blared an announcer, *"a complete, easy-to-understand look at the day's events."* Kevin went into the kitchen and withdrew a cigarette from a pack lying on the counter.

"So, I guess you got my message," said Brad.

"Yes." Kevin leaned down to light the cigarette on the stove.

"I know it's short notice," began Brad, "but I would love to see you. Are you free tonight?"

"I have another dinner invitation, Brad," Kevin replied, thinking of Shane.

"Oh, that's too bad."

". . . but I think I can get out of it."

"That would be wonderful! I think I told you I'm going to Maui for a few days and I'm leaving tomorrow and when I get back I'll be incredibly busy so, uh, well, I wanted to fit you in somehow."

"Perhaps that can also be arranged," drawled Kevin.

"What? Oh, okay, I get it." Brad tittered. "You are such a kidder."

"I've been called worse."

"I'll pick you up at eight," said Brad. "I already know the address. We'll go to Le Dome. Is that okay?"

"Okey-dokey," said Kevin. He hung up.

Leon was in the kitchen within seconds. "Where are you going?"

Kevin exhaled a long gray plume of smoke. "Le Dome."

"Of course," exclaimed Leon. "Wow. That's a classy place. Really high profile!"

"Yeah," Kevin snorted, "they put the pheasant under the glass for you and everything. Oh, God. I can't eat anything there. It's all game birds and carpaccio."

"You'll have to suffer; it's too late. You can order the vegetable plate if you have to." Every restaurant in LA offered a vegetarian option. Local law.

"No," sighed Kevin, resigned. "Tonight, I'll require a slab of prime rib, raw, swimming in aus jus, and a mound of horseradish. No vegetables. I want to go into total protein shock. I intend for this meal to exist in my colon forever as a souvenir of this momentous occasion."

"You are so gross," said Leon.

"Thanks," said Kevin. "Let's get ready. I believe you have a date with our young Shane, the pride of modern aviation."

And then the news came on. The lead story ("*Team Coverage!*") was about a girl on a bus whose ponytail was snipped off by a schizophrenic vagrant. She was suing the city for ten million. Kevin, watching the distraught, weeping girl, believed she deserved the whole amount.

CHAPTER 5

At 7:57, Kevin and Leon went out to the sidewalk to wait for Brad. Kevin had decided on a black Armani sport jacket (stolen from a shoot), a black viscose Sonia Rykiel T-shirt (stolen from a trick), black slacks from Yamamoto (bought at a discount at the Barneys warehouse sale after switching the price tags), and black high-tops from Patrick Cox (full retail at Fred Segal). His black hair playfully caught the light from the high-intensity, anticrime street lamp overhead. His mood? Black.

Leon, wanting to meet Brad, had thrown on a safari jumpsuit from International Male, the zipper open to the waist. He wanted Brad to see his magnificent rack. Maybe then he'd be more polite on the phone.

Kevin didn't mind the obvious ploy. Occasionally, he felt relieved when the focus was off himself for a few seconds.

Brad appeared, having driven himself to West Hollywood in his Range Rover. He kept the engine running as he got out to meet the boys.

"Hi," said Leon eagerly. "I'm Leon, Leon Delvalle. The roommate."

"Hi," replied Brad, forgetting to smile. He extended a hand and Leon pumped it. He turned to Kevin. "Shall we go?"

"Sure. Bye, Leon."

Kevin went around to the passenger side and opened the door. As he boarded the giant Tonka toy, he licked his lips and grinned lasciviously at Leon, out of Brad's view. Leon stood waving from the sidewalk until the immense land cruiser departed.

"Thanks for coming on such short notice," said Brad. "I suppose you got out of your other engagement?"

"Yeah, no problem."

"You look wonderful," blurted Brad.

"Thanks."

"I mean, you looked wonderful the other day, too, but, well, I didn't really expect . . ."

"I clean up really well," said Kevin, closing the subject.

Brad turned his attention back to the road. Kevin made no attempt to lob back some complimentary pleasantries of his own, preferring instead to trace the stitching of the beige leather of his bucket seat with his right forefinger.

Unable to tolerate the silence, Brad rushed in to fill the conversational airspace. "I have a few demo tapes that I need to hear," he said. "In fact, there is one I'd actually like to get your opinion on. Do you mind if we listen to it on the drive over?"

"No," Kevin mumbled.

"Just grab the one on top out of the glove compartment. I need to make a decision and I thought you might be able to help."

Kevin flipped the latch and pulled out a cassette. "'Soccer Moms on Crack'?"

"No. In fact, toss that in the garbage. No, the other one."

Kevin reached in again.

"'Tell That Girl Hi'?"

"Yeah, that's the one," said Brad. "They're supposed to be quite happening. Four girls, all about fifteen, from New York. They do a melodic rap thing. A new sound."

Kevin helpfully popped in the cassette as they waited at the light at Santa Monica Boulevard. There was a screeching wail, a whelp, and then a pounding bass note.

>Like dis y'all,
>Like dat y'all
>Ain't no gun in your pocket
>and I ain't got no time for dat
>Like dis y'all
>Like dat y'all
>Ain't no gun in your pocket
>Ain't no playing with my cat

"Well, so far they're pretty horrible," Kevin declared. "Where did you find them? Up in the Bronx?"

"Actually, they're from Syosset, out on the island," yelled Brad over the music. "But if we sign them we're going to say they're from Roosevelt. To give them some street cred."

> When you said you loved me
> I knew you had to go
> I saw you on the subway
> I thought, He just a ho

"Yecch, turn them off," said Kevin.

Brad switched off the stereo. "I like them a lot, but maybe I'm losing my touch." Brad took his eye off the road and looked over at Kevin.

A curtain of doubt fell over Kevin's features.

"I'll just call their manager and stall them," said Brad. He picked up his phone and dialed with his thumb.

Kevin shifted uncomfortably in his seat while Brad made the call. What kind of a date was this? He thought Brad was showing off. This was a social occasion and he could not believe that Brad was really concerned with his opinion of Tell That Girl Hi. Kevin cupped his chin and stared down at a car below theirs as they waited at another light. Three gay Latinos stared up at him with undisguised hostility from the open windows of their low-riding Plymouth Duster.

Brad finished up with his phone call. "Sorry, Kevin. Thanks for your input."

"I guess you do business round the clock."

"Well, not always."

Kevin looked at Brad and raised an eyebrow.

"Well, I do sort of do business around the clock, yes, but I'm in the process of rearranging my priorities. I don't want to keep up that pace. That wouldn't be good business. For example, take this new group, Tell That Girl Hi. I like them, but I'm not a teenager and I won't be able to predict what the kids will like to hear forever."

"Mmmhhh," Kevin grunted. "What do you care—it's your company. You like them, so what difference does it make? Go ahead. Make their dreams come true."

"Well, technically, it's not my company. I answer to my shareholders. My stock options are tied to my performance."

So are mine, thought Kevin.

The restaurant was on a glittery section of Sunset, and as soon as they pulled up, red-jacketed parking attendants lunged for their doors. The outside noises of traffic invaded the cocoon that was the Range Rover and the subject of performance was dropped.

As they walked the few feet toward the entrance, Brad leaned over to Kevin. "I know this is stupid, but I don't even know your last name."

"Malloy," mumbled Kevin.

"Malloy. Okay. Hey, that would make a good TV name," said Brad. "I wanted to know just in case I run into a friend so I can introduce you."

The maître d', slick haired and unctuous, showed off his new dental bonding as Brad came through the door. Noises, of the large sucking variety, were quickly made. Throughout the room, heads swiveled at warp speeds and nipples hardened visibly against sea island cotton. The room was a bit thin on famous faces tonight, and surgically enhanced jawlines had begun to wilt in despair. Now that Brad Sherwood was here, though, everyone could feel good about who they were, at least for a few minutes.

Kevin and Brad were led to a table for four in the epicenter of the room. Extraneous silverware and plates were whisked away with gratifying fanfare. Brad, in *peau de peche* Hugo Boss, was all grace and poise as a gilt chair was slid under him and a starched white napkin was laid across his lap. Kevin, no slouch himself in this area, took his seat with swift and sure moves and Brad felt a twinge of pride. Aware that all eyes were upon them, they were finally able to relax.

Pellegrino water, no ice, was poured into crystal goblets and embossed leather menus were presented. The waiter, handsome with TV good looks but foolishly sun-damaged skin, seemed anxious to begin his monologue. In his worldview, every human encounter was an audition.

"What would you like to drink, Kevin?" asked Brad.

This was the kind of moment that Kevin loathed. His teeth set on edge when anyone older than himself patronized him in this fashion.

"A bottle of Cristal," said Kevin. "To start. Later on we'll need to take a look at the wine list."

The waiter, pen in hand, looked at Brad for a sign of approval. Brad shrugged his shoulders and said, "Yes, that would be fine."

The waiter vaporized pleasingly and Brad reflexively scanned the room. A table of movie executives, four men in regulation Armani, caught his eye and, as if on cue, they all waved to him at once. These were little, cute waves, full of warmth; grade-A industry standard. Brad returned the wave with a commanding, five-fingered version and the men beamed—and then returned to their salads with renewed gusto.

"So," said Brad. "Here we are."

"That's what happens, wherever you go."

Brad paused. He was almost, but not quite, used to Kevin's oblique responses. No one in his world behaved that way. They would never get away with it. At work, Brad demanded, and received, a clear stream of pure information at all times.

"About the other night," he said. "I had a really nice time."

Kevin realized that Brad wanted to somehow sanctify their Christmas Day coupling. Since a waiter was charging toward them with the champagne, and a busboy was not far behind with an ice bucket, Kevin felt benevolent and generous.

"I did, too," he stated, gazing deeply into Brad's eyes. "In fact, I can't remember a more pleasant Christmas."

"Really?" said Brad. "That's great, because I wasn't sure how you felt."

"I thought I was pretty demonstrative in the whirlpool," Kevin told him, "and later on elsewhere."

"Yes, that you were. I was really taken by surprise. I haven't had many relationships because I've been really ambitious, of course . . . Oh, gosh. What am I trying to say here? I guess I just want to tell you right off the bat that I've neglected the personal side of my life. And I don't want to do that anymore." Brad paused slightly. "Neglect the personal side."

Kevin was used to having guys fall all over him. It was, in his life, a pleasing fact of everyday reality. The speech he believed Brad was about to give was one he had heard many times before. It usually went along the lines of wanting to settle down, wanting to grow old with someone, blah, blah, blah.

Kevin rarely believed it. These men were entranced with his looks, period. Beyond that, Kevin felt that his presence allowed the men to momentarily like themselves. Well, in this instance, he would play along; Brad Sherwood was not your typical lecherous Hollywood smoothie. He was a titan of industry, with tens of millions in stock options, some of them even marginable.

And Kevin Malloy—full lipped and green eyed, with million-dollar hair and a dense, silky cock—qualified for food stamps.

"What were you doing, Brad, in the parking lot behind Sunset Plaza? All the stores were closed."

"Well, frankly, I told my driver to pull in."

"Because you saw me?"

"No, actually. Since my phone company switched from analogue to digital, I just find that I get better reception there. And sometimes after spending time with my parents the calls pile up."

Kevin laughed and Brad, although what he said was not meant to be funny in the least, felt pleased. He joined in, just a regular holiday-maker himself.

"I wouldn't mind getting to know you a little better, Brad," said Kevin in a measured tone. "I, too, have neglected my personal life, although not with such spectacular results."

The waiter returned, thank God, for the conversation was veering too quickly toward the serious. Brad and Kevin watched him as he freed the champagne cork from its little cage. The bottle popped merrily.

All around the room, anxious diners wondered what Brad Sherwood was doing drinking champagne. (Insiders knew he only drank diet Coke. They *banked* on it.) They also wondered about his attractive companion. Was he one of the many beautiful boys passed around regularly by the velvet mafia, or was he, in fact, a new face?

"So," said Brad, "what do you do? I mean, for a living."

"Good. A New York question. Let's see. Well, at the moment I'm a photographer. A struggling fashion photographer."

"With your looks you should be a model," said Brad, unable to help himself.

"I tried that. It worked for a time, but I never really got the big jobs. The camera, shall we say, doesn't quite capture my mystery. Besides, it's kind of embarrassing, standing there in a pair of long johns for hours on end hoping you'll make the cut for the spring edition of the Banana Republic catalog."

"Did you go to college?" ventured Brad.

"Technically, yes. I went to NYU, God knows why. I liked going to the movies in the afternoon.'"

"You love movies? That's great," said Brad. "NYU is a good school."

"Yeah, I've heard that," Kevin replied. "I seem to remember watching a lot of old movies like *The Battleship Potemkin,* and I vaguely recall taking a class called 'The Oeuvre of Kenneth Anger.' But, you know, frankly, I wasn't much of a student. I was too busy running around the city at all hours, believing everything I did was important and interesting. God, I was impossible in those days. I didn't throw in a load of white when I did the wash, I threw in a load of black!"

"So nothing's changed," said Brad, with a glance at Kevin's black outfit.

"Right." Kevin took his champagne flute and toasted Brad but he was really toasting his own ability to charm.

The champagne, as always, went down easily.

"I'm not saying it wasn't fun. It was . . . well, it was what it was." Kevin stopped himself; he made it a rule never to discuss those disastrous days. "Anyway, how about you, Brad? Share with me the secret pain of millionaire media moguls."

"Secret pain? There is none."

"That can't be."

"I've always told myself, never be afraid of success. That's been my motto, and I've applied it to everything I do."

"Personally, I've always found roiling about in my own self-loathing to be much more rewarding."

"I hope you're not serious," said Brad.

"No," Kevin admitted. "Never."

Kevin and Brad polished off the Cristal, and it was past nine when they ordered their food. Kevin wasn't hungry but he ordered the prime rib anyway. He hoped later he'd have an opportunity to mix up a tablespoon full of psyillium husks into a glass of water before going to bed. "Death starts in the colon" was his motto.

Brad ordered the sole baked in paper.

A bottle of Pauilliac was sent over from Jason Priestley, and, after making a mental note to send the kid a box of Cohibas, Brad attacked his dinner with zest. Around them, other diners tentatively began to order champagne, or wine, or snifters of brandy, and the mood in the room elevated. It was, after all, the Holiday Season, and if Brad Sherwood was Drinking, then it was Permitted. Waiters bustled about and in the bowels of the restaurant, there was a mad scramble for the rarely used ice buckets. The maître d' could not believe how the night was shaping up. Restaurant patrons swilling booze with abandon was a rare sight indeed. No one in LA with a career could afford a DUI, especially with that harsh "three strikes and you're out" law. A tiny DUI, a little lewd conduct, and a few unpaid parking tickets and suddenly you were looking at three years in Pleasanton with some hard-timers. If one wanted to get drunk, and one of course did, one did so at home. Usually alone.

As would be reported all around town the next day, Brad could not take his eyes off Kevin. Kevin, responding to all the attention, became talkative. He told Brad a few stories about photo shoots, modeling, and even about how he sold his sperm during a particularly thin period.

"How could you do such a thing?" said Brad. "Do you mean to tell me that there may be a few little Kevins running around now?"

"Hundreds, perhaps," said Kevin.

"How did all that come about?" asked Brad.

"I saw an ad in the student newspaper. It was a great deal. You went in and for the first donation you were paid fifty dollars. They checked out your sperm, and if it was hardy enough, they invited you back for an interview. Mine was; good swimmers, all of them. At the second interview, they took your picture, gave you a short IQ test, and then asked a lot of questions about your heritage and background and so forth. If you passed that you were invited to come back up to three times a week and make a deposit. Twenty-five bucks a pop."

"My God, where was this place?" asked Brad.

"In the basement of an office building on the Upper East Side. It was very well organized. They had six cubicles off the waiting room and you could come in at any time before midnight, masturbate into a cup, and they'd cut you a check on the spot. For about two years, before the place got raided, I'd run in every time I went to Bloomingdale's. Which was often."

"I don't think I could do such a thing," said Brad. "I mean, I've heard of selling blood, but sperm? It doesn't seem right. Did they ask if you were gay?"

"No. I think it was a case of don't ask, don't tell. In the collection rooms, they kept a supply of *Playboy* magazines on hand, for inspiration, but not *Playgirl*. I was forced to use my imagination."

"If they had asked if you were gay," said Brad, "they could have made all sorts of genetic hypotheses for future research into the origins of homosexuality."

Kevin blinked rapidly. "I don't think they were interested in research, Brad. It was a quick buck for all concerned. The sperm was shipped all around the world. The receptionist told me once that they could barely keep up with demand. Back then, pure American sperm was all the vogue. Not anymore, of course."

"I don't know if I could live with myself, knowing that somewhere in the world, I was the father of a child. I love kids too much. Someday I'd like to adopt some."

"Really?" said Kevin. "Personally, I think kids are just the new gay accessory. We're slowly graduating from small-dog ownership."

"So cynical," clucked Brad. "At least, Kevin, you passed on a good hair gene. You have beautiful hair."

Kevin immediately became aware of the searchlight that was upon him. He had seen the same look before in the eyes of countless tricks.

"This is depressing," said Kevin. "Let's talk about something else. What was your first job?"

"Oh, gosh, now we're going back. Well, my *first* job was picking up golf balls at a driving range after school, when I was about twelve. Talk about depressing. The golfers deliberately aimed their shots at me. But it was a valuable learning experience. After I got hit a few times, I came to the conclusion that any job that took place out of doors *stunk*."

"So then what?" said Kevin.

"So then at fifteen, I started a mail-order film-poster business. That was pretty easy, and it paid for college. I had this dream that I would go to school in Boston. I thought it would be esthetically important for me to experience real snow in an authentic way. So then, while I was there at Emerson, I put together a little revue with a few friends and that kind of started the ball rolling."

"*Apocalypse Nude?*"

"Oh, God. You've heard of it?"

"Of course. I remember the protests."

"Well, *that* experience certainly put me on the learning curve. Who ever thought an X-rated Vietnam musical would stir up such a fuss? Funny, it all seems so tame now."

Kevin could see that Brad was relishing this nostalgic foray, so he encouraged the older man to recount other youthful triumphs.

"Anyway, I put some money in another show and it flopped and I was freezing my ass off, so I came back here to regroup. Then I met some people down in Laguna who wanted to make a movie, so we drove out to the desert and made one."

"*Freeway Bloodbath!*"

"Wow, you know that one, too? You're amazing. See, you did learn something at NYU. You know, we shot that in nine days."

"It doesn't look it."

"We wrote the script as we went along, at night, in longhand. And then, you know, I met some songwriters and I just said, hey, let's make an album.

I couldn't even begin to tell you how—we just did it. Nothing was planned in those days. We were a community of artists and we were all having fun."

Kevin briefly touched Brad's fingertips. "It sounds like it."

"Yeah," said Brad, his eyes moist. "And it seems like yesterday. One day I was getting stoned on the beach with a bunch of hippies and the next day I was back in New York explaining the finer points of punk rock to a room full of bankers. And then the money just got bigger and the rules changed and now I'm one of the suits."

"Sounds like all the joy has gone out of it for you, Brad. Maybe you should take back your company."

"Now *there's* an idea," responded Brad with a laugh. "I wish it were that simple. But I have too much responsibility now: to my artists, to my employees, my shareholders. Directly or indirectly, everything I do touches thousands of lives."

"Oh, please," said Kevin. "I'm sure you've made them all rich and they have no complaints. They'll survive. Excuse me. I need to go spend a penny."

Kevin, signaling a guarded promise of possible future clothing removal, held Brad's gaze for a fraction longer than necessary. Then he rose unsteadily from the table and weaved his way toward the men's room.

The waiter came over and presented the bill. "It was a pleasure serving you, Mr. Sherwood," he said.

Brad looked up and recognized the calculated proposition in the waiter's gaze.

"See that my car is brought around," Brad ordered, sobering up. He returned his attention to the check, adding exactly twenty percent for the tip. The waiter lingered a moment, reddened, and then scurried off.

Brad threw his napkin on the table and waited for Kevin to return. He thought about how Kevin was forced to sell his sperm in New York to put himself through college. Poor kid. Despite Kevin's air of carefree self-reliance, he couldn't have had an easy time of it.

Kevin returned and gave Brad's neck a fond squeeze. "Ready?"

Brad stood. There were more small waves, which in turn generated little bows from darker, Siberian corners of the room. Kevin felt as though he had just participated in a command performance. The maître d' was almost tearful when Brad and Kevin left. Their appearance had reconfirmed Le Dome's reputation as a hot place to be seen. Kevin engineered a sexy scowl. He felt cheap. It felt good.

The parking attendant had thoughtfully turned the heat on in the car, and by now it was a cozy spot for postprandial negotiations. Clearly, it was now Kevin's turn to take charge. Going back to his apartment on Westmount, of course, was not an option. Too shabby. That could be a turn on for Brad, but Kevin was not willing to take that risk. Back to Malibu? Too far. Anyway, Kevin did not think he had enough conversation left in him after that long dinner. While Brad fumbled for a tip for the valet, Kevin decided how the rest of the evening would proceed. He came up with a plan.

"Since you have to get up early for your trip, I guess you better take me home," Kevin said, his voice quavering with a hint of sadness.

"You're probably right," Brad agreed. He had been hoping that they could pick up Kevin's car so then Kevin could follow him back to the beach house. An hour's worth of maneuvering, but Brad was willing. Kevin, however, did not seem game.

Brad let a few cars pass and then turned out onto Sunset. The street was crowded with teenagers on their way to a concert at the Whiskey and Brad made a mental note to see if any of his staff were there. When business thoughts intruded, Brad could focus easily. But now, Brad wanted to prolong the evening. He found Kevin's company delightful, and was depressed to conclude that their date was coming to a thoroughly premature and ignominious close.

"Do you want me to listen to 'Tell That Girl Hi' again?" Kevin asked. "Maybe I missed something."

"No," said Brad quietly. "Always trust your first impression."

"Okay. That was a great dinner, Brad. Thanks."

"Sure."

"I'm not so used to eating red meat anymore."

Kevin reached down to the side of his seat and pushed a lever. His seat went back a few inches.

"God, I'm stuffed. Whew!" Kevin hit the lever again and this time he reclined the seat completely, all the way into the backseat. The chair had now become a sleeperette.

"I'm just going to loosen my belt," said Kevin. He undid the buckle and reached into his pants to undo the two buttons that held the waistline closed. He then dragged the zipper down four inches. The elastic band of his white Calvin Klein underwear, and a triangular patch of cotton, was now tantalizingly visible.

"Ooh, that's better," whispered Kevin. "Shouldn't drink so much."

Kevin put his hands behind his head, yawned like a kitten, and then shut his eyes. He was glad he had worn underwear. His balls felt snug and cozy. Any minute now he hoped they would be given an airing. He had no urge to check on Brad to see what this lewd display was accomplishing. There was no need.

Kevin arched his back and his shirt inched up a bit. Now, along with the steamy patch of underwear, Brad had a view of taut stomach muscle to contemplate. Pleased as always with his own physique, Kevin felt the stirring of an erection. Raising his hips imperceptibly, he willed it into being. He needed his cock to lie flat and then systematically stretch in the direction of his navel. His dick, understanding the gravity of the situation, cooperated.

By the time they arrived at Westmount Street, the head of Kevin's turgid unit was poking out from underneath the elastic waistband of his underwear. The blue and green dashboard lights illuminated it luridly. Kevin, keeping his eyes closed, pretended to doze. For added effect he let his lips part and he did not lick them. He kept them dry, innocent looking.

Brad pulled the parking brake. "Ah, Kevin," he said, his voice barely audible. "Wake up. You're home."

"Already?" said Kevin, his voice that of a sleepy little boy. He opened his eyes slowly.

Kevin sat himself up and shook his hair out. In the process, his pants moved three more inches down his legs. Now Kevin's inner thighs were exposed, although, really, it was an accident. And if a boner had popped out, after driving over all those potholes, who was to blame? The mayor?

Kevin noted with satisfaction that Brad's hands were trembling. Wonder and lust distorted Brad's features.

Excellent.

"Thanks again for dinner," said Kevin. "How about a good-night hug?"

Brad loosened his grip from the steering wheel and welcomed Kevin into his arms. Kevin wiggled a bit and his pants came down even further.

Brad tried not to notice. He wanted to provide Kevin with a bit of tenderness. He believed that Kevin, underneath that tough shell, was just a wayward innocent.

Kevin pulled back and provided him with an angelic and healing smile. It proved too much. In this area alone, Brad lacked an iron will. Bending forward, turned on by his own guilt and lust, he greedily went for Kevin's cock—a salty staff more enticing than any Triscuit.

CHAPTER 6

At 6:15 the next morning, Brad groggily emerged from the Malibu house carrying a steaming mug of coffee. He wore neatly pressed jeans, a white cashmere sweater, tennis sneakers, and a pair of Persol sunglasses.

Jeremy sensed the boss wasn't in the mood for small talk as he held the car door open. After they mumbled dutiful "Good mornings" to each other, Brad settled himself onto the chilly black-leather banquette.

"If I ask you to pick me up on a cold winter morning like this, Jeremy, please be sure the cabin of the car is heated up."

"Sorry, Mr. S."

Brad switched on the TV. The host of *A.M.L.A.* was interviewing a young sitcom sensation whom Brad had once met at a network convention in Vegas. It had been one of those *long* nights. The kid, reeling around nude in Brad's suite at the Mirage, seemed to have an abnormally unquenchable appetite for crystal meth. Brad, in the thick of a deal, regretfully had him removed.

"I can't wait to be a father," said the actor, giving a line reading more convincing than anything he ever mouthed on his show.

The audience burst into applause.

Brad turned the volume down and picked up one of the four newspapers that Jeremy had placed in the car before they left. Feeling a twinge of remorse, Brad grabbed the intercom again.

"Thanks, Jeremy, for getting the papers."

"No problem, Mr. S."

Brad scanned the headlines. A rebel uprising here, a coup there. Brad took out a pad and made a note to touch base with the manager of one of his Latin acts. He then turned to the business section and read an article about a friend of his in Detroit who was in the process of turning a car company around. The man was fighting for his job and the board of directors seemed supremely indifferent to his pain. Brad, sympathetic, made another note.

Rob was waiting just inside the door of his Tara-like mansion on Rexford Drive when Brad's limo pulled up. Jeremy got out and helped Rob with his small Vuitton flight bag, the two of them engaging in some easy servant-to-master banter while Brad, still skimming the papers, waited in the car.

Brad and Rob had shipped their resort clothes to Maui the day before, via Federal Express. It was a habit left over from the days when they used to fly commercial. (Both of them had given up on the airlines; along with growing a mustache, or buying an American car, standing around a baggage carousel for ten minutes or more was, in their crowd, quite unthinkable. Also, it saved time to have their clothes unpacked, pressed, and hanging in their closets when they arrived.)

Rob liked Jeremy, but then Rob adored servants of all kinds. He was especially fond of nude servants, and over the past twenty years he had employed no other kind. Nude boys vacuumed his carpets, cleaned his drapes, and scrubbed his toilets. When he gave a dinner party, he used nude waiters; when he needed a trim, he went to a nude hairdresser. For a cheap ticket up to San Francisco, he once patronized a nude travel agent out in Thousand Oaks. His pool cleaner was a young guy who didn't work for a proper nude pool-cleaning service, but Rob persuaded him to strip down one summer day for an extra fifty and the kid was happy to oblige. If he hadn't, Rob would have had no choice but to fire him.

He piled into the car, full of energy. "Before I show you my latest tape," said Rob, as he settled his bulk into a seat across from the TV, "I want to know all about last night. I spoke to Elinor Graham this morning and she told me you were at Le Dome last night with a gorgeous boy, drinking champagne. I've never, in all my born days, heard of anything so naughty!"

Brad, slightly hung over, carefully folded his *USA Today* and rolled his eyes.

"Elinor Graham is a gossip," he said wearily.

"True, and an extremely reliable one," retorted Rob. "So tell me, who was the boy? And why am I always the last to know?"

Jeremy was sitting in the front, listening avidly to the conversation. Brad picked up the intercom. "We're ready whenever you are, Jeremy. The plane is at LAX today."

"Uh, okay, Mr. S. It's hangar eight, right?"

"Yes, Jeremy. Go directly to the south side of the airport and then just follow the signs to Garrett Aviation. Stay off the freeway." Brad sent the sliding window up with the push of a button.

Elinor Graham was a Beverly Hills doyenne and well known as a local tastemaker. She and Rob had been friends since childhood, and he often squired her around town, usually to black-tie events held at department stores. She had called Rob at 5:30 in the morning with her news. They both had been up, rambling around alone in their gracious mansions.

"I told you all about him," Brad said peevishly. "He was the boy I met on Christmas Day up in West Hollywood."

"Elinor reported he was quite dishy," said Rob. "Is he the one who came out to your house?"

"Yes," replied Brad, wondering already how much he wanted to share with Rob. "He's a nice kid."

"Oh, now I remember, you forgot to turn the cameras on. What a pity. Well, I for one have not been so lax in my duties," Rob reached into his carry-on bag and pulled out a tape. "Here they are, just off the bus. Those identical twins I was telling you about. Wait till you see the corncobs on these two!"

Rob leaned over and popped the tape into the VCR. Regis and Kathie Lee vanished and there was a moment of static and snow. Rob grabbed the remote off the built-in teak media shelf and hit the play button.

The interior of Rob's poolhouse came into view. There was a large pink couch, a fake silver palm tree, and a pool table. Rob's voice could be heard off screen.

"Come on in, boys, and get out of the sun. Settle yourselves on the couch and relax. You boys deserve it."

There was some unintelligible garble from Rob, the words "more coke," and then two stringy boys who looked to be about twenty dumped themselves onto the couch. They both had long, greasy blond hair. One of the brothers wore overalls; the other wore tattered jeans and held a ping pong paddle. The one in overalls leaned over to the other and whispered something. Then they both guffawed.

Brad watched, his stomach feeling slightly queasy. Still, he could not look away. The boys were mirror images of each other. At one point, they both even picked their noses simultaneously. Fascinating stuff!

Rob's voice could be heard again on the tape. "You two look so uncomfortable in those dirty old jeans! Why don't you take them off and I'll get you some nice crisp tennis shorts."

The twins looked at each other, shrugged, and then started peeling off their clothes, piling them in a commingled heap. They stripped down to their underwear and then stopped.

"Should we take it all off now, Mr. Erickson?" the one with the Ping-Pong paddle asked.

"Or should we wait?" added the other.

"Just do whatever comes naturally, boys," instructed Rob, his voice suddenly deep and businesslike.

The limo made a turn onto La Cienega. There was a slight traffic tie-up as cars attempted to squeeze through the twin butt cheeks of the Beverly Center and the Beverly Connection. Brad briefly took his eyes off the TV and looked out the tinted window. Crowds of postholiday shoppers thronged the streets, anxious, even this early in the day, to hit the stores. Brad guiltily thought of his mother and his Aunt Gilda; he had neglected to arrange a shopping day for them. He guiltily thought of Corrine holding down the fort. He guiltily thought of Kevin.

"Turn it off, Rob. Save it for the hotel. I really don't care to see porn this early in the morning."

"Darling, it's not porn. They're brothers!" Rob sniffed a bit and then hit the stop button. "You're right. All in good time." Rob, too, looked out the window. "Oh dear, the traffic. I hope we don't lose our takeoff slot!"

A pristine white Grumman Gulfstream IV, glistening with early morning dew, awaited them on the general-aviation tarmac. Brad's initials were on the tail so that other moguls could see he was in town. Off to the right he saw a white 737 with NEWSCORP printed on the side. Brad made another mental note: "Call Rupert."

All the media darlings had planes, but Brad's personal GIV was legendary—*there was a window in the bathroom!* It was absurdly expensive to maintain, but if the money wasn't spent, it would all go to taxes. Having a jet at his disposal, therefore, wasn't really a luxury at all. It was vital for his image, and since America's relevance to the rest of the world was largely about selling and packaging entertainment these days, he was expected to spend extravagantly. And if on the off chance Brad wanted to hear a new band from South Carolina, or fly a movie star acquaintance to Texas to visit her parents, or go to New York at two in the morning, it was all possible— it could all be *arranged.*

After greeting the captain perfunctorily, Brad and Rob climbed aboard. Bagels and lox from Barney Greengrass, chilled shrimp cocktails from Gladstone's, and desserts from the Cheesecake Factory had been provisioned in the tiny galley, along with coffee and a full bar. Unlike flashier moguls, Brad did not usually take a steward along. They listened too closely to his calls, and unless there were a few more passengers, they were generally a nuisance.

For takeoff, both Brad and Rob naughtily declined to put on their seat belts. As soon as the wheels were up, Brad decided to warm up with some easy work. Get the ball rolling again. Tidy up some loose ends. He pulled a script out of a bag and then dialed a producer in Brentwood. They had a two-picture deal that was about to expire.

"What the fuck kind of crap are you sending me, Monty? This script, for example, *How to Rent a Human Shield,* On the third page the detective says, 'We may have to drag the river.' Hello? This takes place in LA, right? Well if you knew anything, you'd know that the LA River only has four inches of water in it! It's a major plot point! This is the best you got? Are you trying to waste my time on purpose?"

Rob shushed him and Brad disconnected the call. "Can you believe the nerve of this guy? How dare he send me this kind of junk. Creep. I think he wants more money. *Suspicion of Doubt,* the prequel to *Harsh Intent,* opened three weeks ago and already it's headed toward fifty mil. Now he thinks he's talented."

Brad, seething, started dialing again, calling the producers of *Stray Bullet, Executive Prerogative,* and *Baby Makes Ten* to congratulate them, and to confirm weekend grosses. Then he called a few agencies to suss out which stars (preferably Arnold—*always* Arnold) had slots open. If he had to, he'd have the script rewritten, cut Monty out of the deal, and then just make the lousy picture himself.

Rob put on headphones and read the *Star.* He had little interest in the slate of films being developed at Magnet—he thought them all dreadful, although, somehow, they always made a ton of money. Rob would go to screenings with Brad and try to make sense of the plot, but after ten minutes drift out into the lobby and start a conversation with the teen at the concession booth. The concerns of the people who populated Brad's movies—terrorists, district attorneys—evaded him completely. The idea of a bomb going off on a bus if it went under fifty miles an hour—Oh, puh-lease! What were those people thinking? Why didn't they just take their cars?

Brad put in some more calls, ranted for another hour, abruptly lost heart, and then passed out.

He dreamt of daytime running lights.

He dreamt of a train going into a tunnel.

He dreamt of all the alterna-hunks that got away.

CHAPTER 7

Leon had gotten up at eight after having spent a pleasantly dull evening with Shane. It had been an evening marked by a lassitude of almost heroic proportions, even by West Hollywood standards.

First they watched a Jean-Claude Van Damme actioner. Then, after they had wound and rewound the naked-butt scene several times, they turned it off and downloaded a few naked pictures of Brad Pitt on Shane's PC. After that they strolled up to Santa Monica Boulevard and had a decaf at Starbucks. Around eleven, they considered going for a drink, but then realized they had left their ID's at home. Even though they both looked much older than twenty-one, they knew there would be no point in arguing with the doormen at the clubs. So, after a soulless debate, they headed over to Circus of Books and rifled through a new shipment of glossy Dutch porn. Finally, around one, they walked home through the leafy backstreets, cruising desultorily. There was little action, and they arrived home dateless and exhausted.

After Leon had met Brad out on the sidewalk the night before, he began to think about how tiny his life had become. Dinner with Shane confirmed it. Unbeknownst to Kevin, Leon had actually read the book Shane gave him on healing the inner child. One chapter talked about "rescue fantasies": seems that a lot of gay men put their lives on hold while they waited for a mythical father figure to save them. They never took charge of their lives, because that would mean they were grown up and would have to give up the fantasy.

In another chapter, the author, a New Yorker, posited the notion that growing up gay in America was "a deep trauma that one had to recover from." Only then could one "dare to dream." Well, Leon believed he was ready. Kevin might think a date with Brad Sherwood was no big deal, but Leon knew it was nothing less than a life-changing event. He also knew that the Brad Sherwoods of the world did not pursue the Leon Delvalles of the world. It was the oldest of problems, one that never attracted the proper attention from Washington. There just weren't enough sugar daddies to go around!

It was close to noon when Leon heard a low moan come from Kevin's bedroom. He put on a fresh pot of coffee, tidied up the living room, and waited.

Kevin stumbled into the kitchen wearing just a pair of white Calvin Klein briefs and a terry-cloth robe. The sash was missing. He wended his way toward the coffeepot but only made it as far as the kitchen table, throwing himself in a chair and plunking his head down. A few minutes later, he peered out from underneath a crusty eyelid.

"Mama . . . is . . . hung," he groaned.

Leon opened a cabinet and removed a large mug. He poured Kevin a cup of coffee, black, and put it in front of him. He then went to the refrigerator and took out a carton of orange juice and some B vitamins and set them down. Kevin whimpered and then drank directly from the carton. The juice, enriched with calcium, tasted chalky and bitter, but it seemed to revive him. He shakily extracted a vitamin from the bottle and washed it down.

And then he lurched into his bathroom to throw up.

Leon opened the window in the living room. The gossip would have to wait. After a moment of consideration, he picked up the phone and called his boss at the design shop.

"Brian Jennings, please . . . Hi, Brian, it's Leon. Yes, merry Christmas to you, too. Listen, remember Mrs. Shotwell in Brentwood? Well, she and I did the tiles in her daughter's bathroom a few months ago and she mentioned she was thinking about some new fixtures for the wet bar off her screening room. Well, I have some ideas and I wanted to ring her up, see if she's still interested. I need the number. Uh-huh. Uh-huh. Well, I figured she was so easy to work with it would be dumb not to call her. She was such a nice lady. Yeah, I'll hold, thanks."

Leon's boss was shocked. Leon was a reliable-enough employee, but he rarely took initiative. Although once he started a project he usually became enthusiastic and clients liked working with him, he wasn't one to go out drumming up new business. This aspect of Leon's work habits had kept him from making the important contacts that led to the truly interesting money.

Brian came back on the line and gave Leon the number.

"Maybe I'll stop in later and look through the books, get something together to present to her," said Leon.

"Oh, dear," Brian responded. "Now you're really frightening me."

Leon heard the shower running in Kevin's bathroom and decided to make another fast call.

"Mom? Merry Christmas. Sorry I didn't phone . . . No, everything's okay, really. I had a quiet day. How are you and Dad?"

Leon's mother launched into a lengthy description of all the holiday goings-on. The turkey was a little dry, his brother's youngest daughter had the sniffles, his father did the entire tree himself this year on account of her shoulder and it was lovely. The celebration got a little out of hand when the next door neighbors, the Bullards, brought over some Christmas cheer: blackberry brandy, made in Oregon. Leon's mom put it in the microwave for a few seconds, served it, and everyone got a little tipsy. The caroling around the piano got so loud that the neighbors on the other side finally came over, and everyone was up till ten-thirty.

Leon, lulled by his mother's small, cheerful voice, savored her stories. Vivid childhood memories of snow and holidays still showed up frequently in his dreams. He never wanted to live in Minneapolis again, despite the presence of a vast and randy gay college crowd. But Leon could no longer stomach the thought of putting chains on his tires just to drive to the gym.

While he listened to his mother, he took a saucer from a kitchen cabinet and put it over Kevin's coffee to keep it warm. When he heard a series of squeaks, he knew Kevin was through with his shower so he gently told his mother he had to run. He was dying to know how Kevin's date with Brad had gone.

Kevin emerged from the bathroom with a Coach belt holding his robe closed, looking marginally fresher around the gills. He lifted the saucer off the coffee and took a tentative sip. "Ugh, red meat. Never again."

"Talk to me, baby," said Leon.

"He went to Maui this morning. I don't know how he got up. He probably didn't get home until two in the morning."

"So tell me," Leon asked, "is he still smitten?"

"I would say so."

"Well, are you going to see each other again, or are you just the latest casualty? I mean, what's going on?"

"It's hard to tell. Brad is all business. It's not like he asked me to come to Maui with him. Everything in his life is scheduled down to the last second."

"Did he want to do it with you again?"

"Oh, God, yes, of course. We did it in the car. I must admit I had to really work to make it happen. He gets into the spirit of the thing once you get him going, but jeez—so much maneuvering on my part! I've never worked this hard."

"In the car?" said Leon.

"Yeah, it's kind of my specialty. Besides, how could I bring *Brad Sherwood* in here and do it on the floor of the living room? It would have lacked tone. So we did it right outside, right under a street lamp. Quite public, actually. I recommend it. Unfortunately no one happened by."

"You are a tramp," Leon chided. "You should have gone to a hotel. The Peninsula is five minutes from here."

"Oh, no, darling, that would have completely ruined the mood. Brad secretly craves a bit of raunch. And now every time he gets in that car, he'll think of me. I came on the passenger seat. I left a huge stain on the Corinthian leather. My aim was impeccable."

"Very rude," declared Leon, impressed. He got up and went for the coffee pot.

"Any nails left?" asked Kevin.

"Coffin nails? Yeah, here're some." Leon took the pack of cigarettes that had been on the counter since the night before and tossed them to Kevin.

"Want one?"

"No," said Leon. "I'm swearing off. Don't want to get addicted."

"They're still a legal substance, last time I checked," said Kevin, lighting up. "So are we going to the gym?"

"I don't think so," Leon replied. "I'm checking in at the design shop today to see if anything is happening. I haven't been there in ages."

"Oh, my, how ambitious," said Kevin. "I suppose I should take care of some of these bills today and try to get something going myself."

"Call your parents," suggested Leon. "It's Christmas."

"Yeah, you're right. I didn't find a check in the mailbox. I'd better remind them."

After Leon had showered and left for Wishbone Kitchen and Bath (wearing wrinkle-free Hilfiger khakis and a crisp Brooks Brothers button-down), Kevin dug his address book out of a messy drawer in his bedside table and looked up the number for his parents' condo in Boca Raton, Florida. Gina answered on the first ring.

"Hi, Ma, it's Kevin."

Gina began to weep. "Oh, Kevin . . . Oh, my baby . . ."

"Ma, Jesus, what's wrong? Stop crying."

"Your father and I are taking a plane back to New York tomorrow. Eddie hit Diane on Christmas Eve and she left him. She and Jennifer are with Connie and Ralph. She wants a divorce. Your father is furious and we had a big fight. All the flights are booked and we have to pay the full coach fare, but I told your father we must go, we must. Diane is upset and no one is there to take care of Jennifer. Connie and Ralph are going on a cruise." Gina blew her nose and dried her tears. "Oh, everything's just gone to shit, Kevin. I wish you were here."

"Me, too, Ma. God, Eddie turned out to be a real jerk."

"Connie wants to come live at home but your father is planning to sell the house. He thinks it's a good time what with all the new tax laws, or something, I don't know. He wants to live in Florida full-time, but I'm not ready. He's become an old man, Kevin. We don't know anyone down here and I can't get good sausage."

Kevin was hating this call. There was always a drama at home, always over some petty nonsense. And his father was turning into a real crank.

"Ma, listen, I'm sorry about all this but somebody should have helped out Diane sooner. At least now it's all out in the open."

"Come back to New York, Kevin."

"You know I can't, Ma."

There was a long moment of silence at the other end.

"Ma, are you still there?"

"Kevin, I've been thinking. Maybe that business with the Capozis has all blown over by now."

"I don't think it would be in my best interest to find out," said Kevin.

"You should never have taken the money. You should have stayed and tried to work it out."

"You know I had no choice. You, of all people, should know how those mob ginzos think."

"I know," said Gina. "That bastard! Every day I give him the *malochio*. I wish him dead!"

"Me too, Mom, me too. Just keep praying."

"Kevin," Gina blurted suddenly. "Have you heard from Anthony? Are you sure he knows where you are? Maybe you should try to contact him."

"Forget it, Ma. They know exactly where I am. They both do. They have my social-security number, everything. If I make a move, they'll know, believe me. Look, it's not so bad. I'll just sit tight. You know how it is. It's a waiting game . . . we shouldn't talk about this stuff on the phone."

"Kevin, listen to me. I pray for you every day. And once you stop this whole gay thing, everything will be all right, I know it. Father Murphy told me in confession that you need to see the error of your ways. And they have programs now that can help you change."

Oh, God, thought Kevin. *Here comes that old speech.* She made it every time he called, if he stayed on long enough. She blamed herself, she blamed Patrick. If only they had paid more attention to him, if only they'd been stricter.

Kevin held the phone away from his ear for a few seconds. When he listened again, he could hear Gina launching into the second half of her usual argument.

"I've never told your father, Kevin. He's not understanding like me, but he's a good man and it wouldn't be fair. He never got over you running off to California the way you did. He never says anything, because that's not his way, but I know what he's thinking."

"I got to go, Ma. This is long distance. Stop blaming yourself."

It hadn't always been like that. Talking to his mother got Kevin thinking about the good times, the best times, really, when every day was new and thrilling. When new and thrilling were gonna last forever.

Kevin, Anthony, and Sharon had become an inseparable threesome at the store. They always took their fifteen-minute breaks together, and their lunch hours, too. Anthony would cross the aisle from Gentlemen's Jeans over to hats and gloves, collect Kevin, and then the two of them would ride the escalator to the second floor where Sharon held court at the Clinique counter.

All three of them were part-timers, seventeen and a half hours a week. After work on Saturdays, the three of them would change their clothes in the employee lounge and then go out. Manhattan was a thirty minute drive.

The first event the three of them attended together was a David Bowie concert at Madison Square Garden. They had driven into the city in Anthony's MG. When Anthony Sr. found out, he grounded him. The next week, as Anthony was getting ready to go to work at Macy's, his father came into his room.

"You going out after work?" he asked.

"Yeah," said Anthony sullenly, pulling on his jeans.

"Going into the city?"

"Maybe."

"Take the Caddy," said his father, tossing him the keys. "It's safer."

Anthony Capozi Sr., a.k.a. "Tony Hot Tip," liked the fact that his kid had a straight job. The two of them had not always had a lot to say to each other since Anthony's mother died ten years before, but they were respectful of each other. Anthony Sr. had never remarried. He spent a lot of time in Jersey with his girlfriend Janice and was planning to move to Atlantic City as soon as his son was settled in at Columbia.

Anthony didn't really understand what his father did for a living, and he didn't want to know. At times, Hot Tip called himself a "contractor," at other times he was a "builder." Officially, he was "involved in cement." One day his father told Anthony to go out to the car and empty his trunk. Anthony did as he was told. Inside the trunk were twenty canvas bags filled with quarters.

"What do you want me to do with them, Pop?" asked Anthony Jr., fourteen at the time.

"Put 'em in your room, just get 'em out of my sight. I can't be driving around with a bunch of quarters in the trunk. People will think I'm a schmuck."

Anthony took his friends to a video arcade every day after school for about six months. His popularity, while never in question, soared.

Anthony Sr. was a vain man. Every morning he got up and drove into New Rochelle to see his barber. Eventually, he even bought the shop for the guy, laying down only one condition: Every morning, at eight, Hot Tip Capozi would be coming in for a shave and to get his hair washed and styled. And the place better be open. Hot Tip didn't like how his hair came out when he washed it himself, so this was how he solved the problem. That was how he solved most problems: a little money and the slightest hint of menace. If the shop wasn't open, explained Hot Tip, there would be *consequences*.

The man's wife took care of Hot Tip's nails.

Anthony Sr. was a snazzy guy and he liked his girlfriend Janice to look a certain way, too—stand-out pretty, but not too flashy. She had been a change girl at Caesar's when they met; because she worked at night her makeup was always a little heavy, but Hot Tip changed all that. Halfway through her transformation, seeing that she was coming along nicely, he asked her to quit her job, which she was only too happy to do. As a reward, he gave her a day of beauty at Georgette Klinger in the city.

"Now do what they tell you," he advised. "Learn from 'em. I want you to look like class when you walk out of there."

Janice complied, and years were lifted from her face. Her confidence soared, and her disposition, kind of sunny to begin with, blossomed into radiance. Hot Tip felt proud of her, and his own stock within his organization climbed.

Anthony Jr., when he started dating Sharon, behaved just like Hot Tip. Anthony often went shopping with Sharon, although he would hang back a bit, acting as if he were uncomfortable being in the ladies' section of a department store. The truth was, however, that he loved it. As a full-blooded Italian, he had very definite ideas about style. Once, he saw Sharon eyeing a pair of red high-heel shoes.

"Sharon," he exclaimed, genuinely alarmed, "those are really low class. What do you want? To look like a ginzo?"

Anthony and Sharon were in love. In a few weeks, they would be going to the senior prom together. Kevin had been hearing about the preparations for months. Sharon had bought a dress and Anthony rented a black tux. A lot of couples were going in on limos together, but Hot Tip gave his son a car all his own. Sharing limos was for schmucks, father told son, and besides, Sharon was a classy girl and she deserved the best.

The week before the big night, Anthony called up Kevin after school. "Hey, do me a favor," he said. "I got to go pick up my tux at this place in Hartsdale. My father knows the guy. Come along for the ride?"

"Sure," said Kevin.

"I'll be over in twenty."

Kevin had been in his room, listening to a Dead or Alive album while doing his homework. His mother and sisters were shopping at the White Plains Mall, so it was a perfect time for Kevin to sneak out of the house—he felt cooped up and kind of antsy. He wondered if Anthony was bringing Sharon, and he was a little unnerved to discover that he hoped Anthony wasn't.

He took off his school clothes and put on his new Calvin Klein jeans and a fringed vest. It didn't go so he tried another shirt and put a sweater over it, but that didn't work either. For some reason, he wanted to look especially good and it wasn't happening. In the end, he went with just the jeans and a white T-shirt, on instinct.

When he heard Anthony's car pull into the short driveway, he pounded down the stairs two at a time. It was a spring day, great for goofing off. Since the sun was, as Anthony's grandmother would say, "eating up the clouds," Anthony had the top down. Halfway into Hartsdale, in Mamaroneck, they pulled over for an emergency slice of pizza.

After they picked up the tux, Anthony asked Kevin if he wanted to ride back home and drop it off. Since he was meeting Sharon later, Anthony didn't want to leave it in the car. Kevin didn't object. His homework was sort of done, and he loved tooling around in Anthony's MG. It was about four o'clock when they arrived at Anthony's house, a split-level ranch, meticulously landscaped and freshly aluminum sided. As usual, no one was home.

The maid, an ancient Italian woman who was distantly related to Anthony Sr., had just left for the day. Anthony threw the tux down on a couch and then led Kevin over to a glitzy stand-up bar. It was covered in tufted red leather, and behind it were glass shelves, mirrors, and a large assortment of bottles. It was an impressive, professional-looking setup, similar to one Kevin had seen when his family went to a wedding reception at a catering hall in Yonkers.

Anthony pulled on the door of a mini-refrigerator and brought out two Cokes.

Kevin, feeling cool, settled onto a bar stool. He loved coming to Anthony's house. In his own house, a TV or radio was always blaring.

"What's that?" Kevin asked, pointing to a tall bottle filled with yellow liquid. The bottle stood on the floor and the base was covered in straw.

"Galliano," said Anthony. "It's a liqueur. An after-dinner drink. My father likes it."

Kevin pointed to another bottle. "And what about that one?"

"Anisette. Tastes like mint cough syrup."

"And how about that red one?"

"That's Amaretto. My father says the moulies drink it with Coke. I think it's made with cherries. No, wait. Almonds—that's it. Want to try some?"

"Sure," said Kevin. "Why not?"

Anthony took two ornate, gold-rimmed tumblers down from a shelf over his head and set them on the bar. He then pulled an ice tray out of the freezer and twisted it. A few cubes popped out and Anthony dropped them into the glasses. He then took a jigger from another shelf and carefully poured out two shots of Amaretto and topped them off with Coke. After grabbing two cardboard coasters from a pile at the side of the bar, he set the drinks down with a flourish.

Kevin took a sip. It was a sickeningly sweet mixture, but it went down easily. It wasn't like drinking alcohol at all. Kevin had tasted his father's beer a few times and hadn't liked it.

"Sharon won't show me her dress, so I didn't want her to come when I picked up my tux. She doesn't even know it's black, but I figured it would match. I told her she should wear apricot. She looks really good in pastels."

"She could wear anything and still look hot," said Kevin.

"Yeah," Anthony agreed. "Come on, let's go up to my room and call her. Take the drinks."

Anthony put the coasters on the bottom of the pile and checked to make sure everything looked untouched. He grabbed the tux and they headed upstairs.

Anthony's room was a shambles. Closets were open, and comic books, trophies, ties, belts, and assorted teenage paraphernalia, already unimportant and forgotten, spilled out. Clothes from Macy's, still in their bags with the price tags on them, littered the high-pile carpet. Next to the window, which looked out over the gated driveway, was a cassette deck and a stack of tapes. Kevin started flipping through them.

Anthony threw the tux over a chair and grabbed the phone. "Hi, Sharon, I got it! . . . Yeah, Kevin and I just went. I'm not telling you what color . . . Okay, black . . . No, I didn't try it on. I'm sure it's fine. The guy's a friend of my father's, so you know he did a good job . . . All right, I'll try it on and make sure. What time am I picking you up? . . . Okay . . . Bye. I love you, too."

Anthony sat on the edge of the bed and kicked off his shoes. They flew in opposite directions. Then he stood up and started pulling off his jeans. They were, as always, tight, and he struggled.

"Don't kick over your glass," said Kevin.

"Oh, yeah." Anthony picked up his glass and drained it. "You know, these are pretty good. I wonder why only the moulies drink 'em? Hey, what the fuck, why don't you go down and make us two more?"

Kevin finished his drink and then took Anthony's glass.

"Don't mess up the bar, okay? And refill the ice tray."

Kevin left the room and as he headed downstairs, he heard the opening strains of Madonna's "Like a Prayer."

Kevin felt weird behind the bar, almost as though he were performing in a miniature theater playing the role of jaded bartender. He found the bottle of Amaretto, but his stomach heaved when he unscrewed the cap. The sensation, a combination of nausea and excitement, gnawed at the lining of his stomach. It was a sensation that had been coming upon him on and off all afternoon, and he couldn't shake it. He somehow knew, though, it had nothing to do with the pizza.

Kevin mixed the drinks, pouring more than a shot in each, and spilling a little on the bar. He wiped it up with a towel and then unsteadily carried the cocktails upstairs. When he got to the door of Anthony's room, he found Anthony dressed in the tux, shooting his cuffs.

"Hey," he said, "it fits perfectly. What did I say?"

Anthony went to one of the Macy's bags. "I got these shoes, too," he said. "My father said I should buy them, even though the place rents shoes for an extra two bucks. He told me it was okay if I rented the tux, since I'd probably outgrow it, but that I should buy the shoes new. Only lowlifes rent shoes."

Anthony opened a box and brought out a pair of gleaming patent-leather loafers wrapped in tissue paper. He tossed one to Kevin. They had thin leather soles and across the front was a fancy grosgrain ribbon.

"I'll probably never wear these again, but what the fuck, you know?"

Kevin handed the shoe back and Anthony slipped it on over his white athletic socks. He then picked up his drink and admired himself in the full-length mirror on the back of the bathroom door.

"You should slick your hair back," Kevin told him. "Like in *GQ*."

"Yeah," said Anthony, "that's a good idea. I wonder what they use to keep it wet-looking like that?" Anthony handed his drink to Kevin and then went into the bathroom to run the water. He cupped his hands and doused his soft, wavy brown hair. It slicked back easily.

"Man, I look tough," Anthony boasted, staring at himself. And he did. His shirt was starched just right and the crease in his pants broke perfectly across his instep. The collar of the shirt wrapped his thick neck elegantly. He looked like a teenage pit boss.

With the Amaretto swirling in his bloodstream, Kevin stared at Anthony, a *GQ* model in the flesh.

Anthony, transfixed by his new sophisticated look, remained in front of the mirror.

"What time are you meeting Sharon?"

"About eight," mumbled Anthony, not taking his eyes off himself.

"So are you just going to stand there sweating up that shirt till then?"

Anthony laughed and pried himself from his image. He took the jacket off and then unclipped the cummerbund. He reached back and unclipped the bow tie. He took off the shoes, using the toe-to-heel, sure-to-ruin-them method. He pulled the pants off and threw them over the back of a chair. He unbuttoned the shirt but left the studs in, lifting the whole assemblage off over his head. He found a hanger and wedged the shirt into the closet.

Now wearing only underwear and socks, Anthony jumped onto his bed and stuffed a pillow behind his neck. His well-packed crotch, straining the thin white cotton of his underpants, loomed large.

"Hey, play that last song again," he said.

Kevin got up, relieved to have a task.

"It's going to be a great night," declared Anthony. "We got the limo for eight hours. I'm horny just thinking about it."

"I wish I was going," mumbled Kevin dully. He turned around and saw that Anthony had one arm behind his head and one hand in the waist band of his underwear.

"You guys are doing it, right?" said Kevin, this personal question coming out of the blue. Had Anthony been more sensitive to the nuances of speech, he would have detected a low-pitched note of jealousy.

"All the . . . ," Anthony began. "Oh, shit, I can tell you. We haven't gone all the way. She's saving herself for the prom."

Kevin turned away and looked out the window. The sight of Anthony, lying spread-eagle on the bed with his hand in the band of his underwear, destroyed Kevin. He now knew what he had been feeling all afternoon and the realization made him feel ill, like a total perv. Anthony, however, seemed oblivious to his anguish.

"She can't wait either," said Anthony hoarsely. "Hey, Kevin. I got a big one. You know how I know? A priest told me when I was in the sixth grade!"

Kevin could not turn around. His palms were sweating and he was getting, to his extreme and ultimate horror, a boner. He fixed his eyes on the gravel driveway outside the window and tried to think of his grandmother in a negligee. The image always worked for him whenever he popped one in math class.

"Hey, Kev," said Anthony. "You got a big one?"

Kevin continued staring at the driveway. "Yeah, I got a big one."

"Big like this?" Anthony, using both hands, outlined a hard-on through his underwear.

"Yeah," gulped Kevin when he turned around. "Big like that."

"Bullshit."

"Fuck you."

"Ten bucks," said Anthony. "Ten bucks says mine's bigger."

"Fuck that, that's chump change," Kevin countered. "Forget it."

"Loser."

"Fuck you, man."

"So prove it. Whip it out."

Kevin went over to the side of the bed and started undoing his belt buckle. But it was all false bravado. He stopped abruptly when he saw a brittle glint in Anthony's dreamy eyes.

"Come on," said Kevin, "that's no contest." Kevin laughed and started closing his buckle again.

"All right. I'll make it a real contest," Anthony said. "Whoever loses has to blow the winner."

"That's sick, man," said Kevin, this time his voice a whisper.

Anthony stared him down coldly. "Come on, Kevin, who knows? You might win."

Kevin's hand went to his zipper. He pulled it down. Then, with his eyes still on Anthony, he peeled his jeans and underwear down slowly. His hard-on sprung free.

Anthony looked at it critically.

"Not bad," said Anthony, "not bad at all. I knew you were hiding a stiffy. You've been hiding it all afternoon." Anthony stretched a hand out and cupped Kevin from underneath. Kevin shivered at the touch, almost ejaculating right then. His teeth began to chatter.

"Good heft," Anthony went on. "Pretty. But nothing like this." Anthony pulled his legs up and then stripped his underwear off completely. His gargantuan penis, a rigid dirigible, flopped around a bit and then settled on his stomach, too top heavy to wind up anywhere else.

"I win," he said.

Kevin knew from hanging around Anthony that one didn't welsh on a bet. Not with Italians.

"Okay, so you win," whispered Kevin. He felt stupid and humiliated standing next to the bed with his hard-on still raging, but he couldn't move. How had this little game gone so far, so fast? He felt the forbidden sensation of air touching his swollen penis and he felt like crying. He felt like pulling up his pants and running out of the house.

Anthony smelled Kevin's fear and in this respect, too, he was just like his father. He relished it. "So what are you waiting for?"

"You got to be kidding. I'm not a homo."

"Who said you were? It's still a bet."

Anthony reached down and grabbed the base of his own cock, lifting it with superhuman strength until it was pointing straight up. "Come on, loser. Fair is fair. Hurry up."

Kevin awkwardly got down on his knees. "Okay. Just for a second."

He steadied his hands on the edge of the bed and opened his mouth. With his heart and soul converging in his throat, Kevin inhaled the humid mustiness of his best friend's crotch. He closed his eyes and bent forward and when his lips and tongue made contact, his entire body twitched and convulsed like Frankenstein's monster at the first jolt of lightning. Possessed, he blew Anthony with instinctive expertise, feeling, for the first time, the miracle of finally inhabiting his own body.

CHAPTER 8

At the Royal Wailea, Brad had reserved the Queen Lili'Ouokouolani Suite. Rob took the unnamed suite across the hall, which was only slightly less grand. The rooms had, of course, a tropical motif, featuring greens and beiges. There were also large tiled balconies with splendid ocean views. Off in the distance, one could see Molokini, a discreet volcanic island crater. Since it was whale season, a pair of binoculars had been thoughtfully provided by management.

Brad and Rob decided to go to their separate quarters, relax, get a massage, and then meet down by the pool for cocktail hour. Included in the two-thousand-dollar-a-night room rate was a complimentary welcome mai tai that they both wanted to take advantage of.

Brad's clothes were already unpacked, pressed, and hanging in his closet when he arrived. He decided to have a quick shower, change, and then attempt to do some more work. He had a backlog of scripts, a few books in galley form, a dozen contracts, a stack of earnings reports, and a rough draft of a proxy statement to look over.

But before he delved too deeply into the pile, he allowed himself to ponder an image of Kevin.

The tumble they had last night in the Range Rover had been amazing. Kevin got naked fast and Brad, thinking what the hell, climbed on. It was all so unplanned and thrilling, and Kevin's skin seemed particularly delicious. At one point, Kevin turned over on his side, and while Brad licked the perfect white globes of Kevin's ass, Kevin's cock and balls pressed right up against the window. Someone strolling by could easily have seen everything.

Brad was impressed; the kid knew what he was doing. When it was all over, Kevin gathered up his clothes in a bundle, kissed Brad at length, and then walked nude across the street to his apartment. Taking a cue, Brad drove his sticky self back to Malibu, wearing only his unbuttoned Armani shirt.

With the Pacific trade winds rustling his papers, Brad came out of his reverie, at least one decision made: he'd give Tell That Girl Hi the big push. Kevin hadn't liked their song, but Brad decided to continue trusting his own instincts. It was a sexy song, perfect for teenagers who ate fast food and groped around in cars. After last night, Brad felt he understood them.

He forced himself to concentrate as he scrutinized their contract. He then called Alan Levy, one of the lawyers at Magnet. Alan told Brad that one girl's father had some objections concerning the rights to the songs.

"We don't have to do this deal at all," Brad sighed wearily. "Tell him I can make those girls very rich this afternoon or I can sign someone else."

"I told them," replied Alan. "But the father is being a real pain in the ass."

"Give me his number," demanded Brad. "Maybe I can make him see the light of day."

Brad hung up on Alan and then called the meddling parent. "My only concern is that the girls are happy," said Brad, in sincere Hollywoodese.

"Well, to be honest, it's not so much the rights I'm concerned about," admitted the father. "I just don't know if Magnet is the place for them. It's like a big factory these days, and, frankly, I'm afraid they'll get swallowed up."

"But I, personally, will oversee their careers," Brad told him. "However, if you believe, in your heart of hearts, they won't be happy with us, I'll simply make a great deal for them anywhere else they want to be. I adore them that much."

"Look, let me be straight with you, Mr. Sherwood. I'm just not convinced Magnet is truly the most wholesome environment for them. Morally speaking—from the top on down . . . well, let's just say I've heard a lot of wild stories. They're just kids, you know. Teens!"

What was this guy insinuating? Brad struggled to remain cool. "Contrary to what you may believe, sir, our record division is a family. I admire the girls—they have a huge talent—but if they're not happy with us, well, then we have a dysfunctional family."

"Mr. Sherwood, I'm not interested in any of your California psychobabble. We're looking at other offers and we'll get back to you." The father hung up.

Brad grabbed a heavy ceramic seashell ashtray and sent it flying over the lanai toward a palm tree.

What was happening? Magnet was renowned worldwide as a haven for talent, a safe place. Everyone wanted to be on board! If word got out Brad was slipping, there could an executive power grab or, worse, a mutiny among the artists. Jesus. Didn't this asshole realize there was nothing Brad Sherwood didn't know about corporate rock?

Rob, having changed into a roomy silk caftan, hung about in his suite contentedly making a few calls. The first was to Bonn, Germany. The grosses were in on last night's "Fantasies on Ice" performance at the Stadt Rink and Rob was pleased; another sold-out show. The tour manager told Rob that the receipts had already been electronically transferred to a bank in Luxembourg where Rob had set up a nice, slushy private account.

Rob then put in a call to Elinor Graham, just to say hello. His masseur, a large Hawaiian, arrived shortly thereafter. Rob was disappointed—he'd been hoping for a quiveringly demure exotic. He felt achy, though, so he allowed the masseur in and climbed on the man's table without removing his caftan. The masseur immediately began kneading Rob's suety flesh.

At 5:30, Brad and Rob met down at the pool, which was situated directly in front of the ocean and featured an island in the center with a lone Palm tree surrounded by sand. Off to the left was a swim-up bar. Around them, several families lingered in the water before going up to shower and dress for dinner. Two groupings were Japanese, one was French, and another was either Swiss or German.

Brad chose a shaded table and the two of them sat down. A waitress crept over on silent feet and took their order: two mai tais.

A cute island boy in a pareo ran around lighting tiki torches.

"I can't imagine what the poor people are doing right now," mused Rob, "but the sad part is, I have no desire to know. This is the life."

"Just be grateful you live in a country that rewards debt rather than saving," said Brad grimly. "It's the only reason we're here."

"Okay," Rob said. "Here's to the American way." He took a long pull on his mai tai.

"It's all an illusion anyway," snapped Brad.

"Well, at least it's a pleasant one," replied Rob, his eyes trained on tiki-torch boy.

"You won't think it's funny when we go back on the gold standard! You know, at the rate this government prints money, we'll be selling apples on street corners if we don't watch our backs!"

"Oh, Brad, enough," chided Rob. "Just stop it. You've been watching the History Channel again. See how you are? We just got here and already you're being a churl. Well, I won't tolerate your moods. I won't. I'm warning you. Try and enjoy the moment for God's sake."

Brad took a sip of his cocktail, tossed the paper umbrella, and then finished it off. He slammed the glass down and signaled for another. Then he stared menacingly at Rob with his meanest face—the face he had been terrorizing peons with for as long as anyone could remember.

Rob only laughed, and Brad did too.

They'd been friends for over twenty years. Rob was a chorus boy in a smash Broadway musical revue that Brad had invested in when he was about twenty-two.

Back then, Rob was a famous boy beauty. He had a dancer's build, a flashy head of blond hair, chiseled features, and a high-stepping style both on and off the stage. One summer on Fire Island, Rob, quite high on pot and wearing only a tiny yellow Speedo, stood at the end of a diving board. Famously limber, he slowly raised one leg straight up and out, eventually managing to tuck it behind his neck, all the while maintaining his balance. He then jumped into the pool in this position and a photographer at the party immortalized the moment on film. The picture made the cover of the next issue of *After Dark,* and from then on, Rob's place in the pantheon of gay celebrities was assured. Oh, Rob was a star in those days, the toast of every A-list party. His twinkly blue eyes were always roving and he was loved by all for his uncanny ability to jump-start a dull orgy.

Back then, Brad Sherwood was just a pimply kid. He was painfully shy, his hair was already thinning, but he was shrewd. He knew he would need a glamorous friend like Rob if he were ever going to get on the circuit and meet the really exceptional boys.

One night, at a small cast party at Joe Allen's, Brad cultivated Rob by flattering him and buying his drinks. The next night Rob offered to take Brad to Studio 54. It was a big thrill for Brad to be invited; he ordered a limo for the occasion. A huge crowd was outside, but Rob was there almost every night and the velvet ropes parted easily for them. Once inside, Rob shoved a bottle of poppers under Brad's nose and the rest was disco history. After a magic night of dancing—Liza, Bianca . . . Bjorn Borg!—they went back to Brad's apartment on the Upper West Side. Three juicy Puerto Rican busboys, wearing only black-satin hot pants, trailed behind them. The doorman did not even look up from his racing sheet. Great days.

Years of frenetic partying had taken their toll on Rob's face, but he was still handsome in a gone-to-seed kind of way. His nose was now host to a freeway of broken capillaries, but that problem was easily remedied with a bit of concealer. Booze had bloated his jowls, but he had them liposucked regularly. The skin hung heavy over his twinkly blue eyes, though that was only because his doctor canceled his last blepharoplasty appointment on him, to appear in court over something that was not really his fault at all.

And while his capped teeth were much too youthful and white for the rest of his face, to the indigenous peoples of Beverly Hills, they looked completely natural. His body sagged and his blond hair had dulled a bit, but these problems were all fixable as well. He'd just been a bit inattentive of late.

"Oh, darn," said Rob. "I wish I had brought my binoculars down from my room. Maybe we'll see some migrating whales while we're here!"

Brad looked over at Rob and smiled. Rob had a persistently cheerful outlook. As the sun began to set, Brad, however, began to feel melancholy. He didn't have much in common with Rob anymore, not really, but the unspoken truth between them was that they were the survivors. They fit the profile, but were not chosen. It was as if they had come through a plane crash together and woke up to find themselves shaking hands in the middle of a corn field.

Nevertheless, it was a bond neither wanted to dishonor with words. Instead they carried on, acting brave for each other, secure in the knowledge that they didn't have to.

A delicate Japanese couple, on their honeymoon, wafted past their table.

"What's happened to Hawaii?" hissed Rob. "I only come here to fulfill my sailor fantasies. Where are they all hiding?"

"Maybe in Honolulu," said Brad. "I see already that you are forgetting the point of this vacation. We're here for the spa treatment, remember? We're going to get tan, lose our spare tires, and start the new year off right for a change. Healthy food, a little sun, and a few quick dips in the Pacific."

"Father knows best," grumbled Rob. "Okay, we'll stick to our diets. We should make a deal, though. I won't cause any scandals and you won't spend all your time in your room making calls. I'm getting a sinking feeling that you have a lot on your mind. Normally by now you'd be telling me to bring on the boys."

"Well," said Brad, "I came here this year because I needed to be somewhere anonymous."

"Okay, Brad. Let's have it out. What's bothering you?"

"The stock hasn't moved in months, and I'm in trouble with the board. They think I don't know what the public wants. They think I've lost my touch."

"Sounds rather serious."

"It is. They want to push me out, Rob, I know it. I can't go on this way. I have to make a big decision. That's why I needed to come here. I didn't want to run into the usual faces."

"Always a horror!" shrieked Rob. "Remember that time you dragged me to Aspen? I still haven't forgiven you. And thank God you didn't bring along any of your assistants. That one from Yale never put my calls through and he had dreadful skin."

"Oh, he's gone," Brad said. "He gave terrible head."

Brad went back up to his room. He was a little drunk, mildly depressed, and not yet sleepy. The call with that girl's father still rankled.

Just then, Brad heard a rustling under the door. It was a hotel envelope containing an expertly rolled joint and a short note.

"I just popped down and bought this off the bellman. Maui Wowee. Have it before breakfast. Sweet Dreams, Rob. P.S. NO CNN!!!"

Brad found some matches and lit up. Then he picked up a legal pad and drifted out to a chaise on the lanai. He decided he needed to calm down and just think about the larger picture.

He leaned back and looked up into a sky filled with a billion night stars.

After a few minutes, his chair began to wobble, and his head started to pound, so he got up and took a few aspirins as well as a tiny football-shaped capsule filled with Ativan. For a moment he contemplated suing the hotel—for using cheap rum in their mai tais.

What am I doing here? he thought. *Alone, spinning my wheels, falling apart, still hanging out with Rob, every minute getting scarier.* Out in the main room of the suite, a huge box of documents had just been delivered and Brad knew that he would have to go through it all, process it, and then send it back into the void with the hope that he'd done the right thing. It had all become so legal, so life-and-death. He'd sacrificed everything—relationships, his youth, his hairline—in getting Magnet off the ground, and now it was out of control. Across the ocean, an entire race of ambitious scumbags were conspiring at this very moment to take it all away from him. The tail wagged the dog, and Brad could only wonder—what had he ever done to deserve this? What had he ever done to make all these people want to destroy him?

He went into the bathroom and splashed lukewarm water on his face. That was the trouble with these resorts in Hawaii—the water coming through the pipes was never cold enough or refreshing enough. He wondered what the board was really thinking. Had they been discussing a successor?

With his head over the bathroom sink, sweating, Brad suddenly remembered Kevin's words at Le Dome: *"You should take back your company, Brad."*

Brad brought his face up to the mirror and stared dizzily into his tired, bloodshot eyes. What a ridiculous, naive idea.

Or was it? Brad had seen what happened to others. Moguls, big players, *Titans of Industry*—they had all vanished without a trace. Years later, they would turn up in Palm Springs, selling swamp coolers or working for auto window–tinting concerns. They were the walking dead, and they were everywhere. Brad dried his face and then lurched into his bedroom. Maybe it was time to make something big happen while he still could.

There was an investment banker who specialized in takeover deals in New York at the white-shoe firm Levinson and Co. His name was Fenny Atkinson, and all the moguls had his number because he was the one you went to. He was the one to call. But was Brad ready? Was he willing? The more he thought about it, the more he knew he didn't have a choice. Talking to that phony producer was proof. Talking to that smug father of the singing group was proof. And then Brad recalled how the board had convened without him. That kind of affront only meant one thing: It was war.

Brad dug his address book out of his bag.

It was early morning on the east coast but who cared? A call from Brad Sherwood still meant the ground under a mountain of money was in the mood to shift. Knowing that pleasantries were not for people like themselves, Brad put the call through and slurred straight to the point.

"Fenny, this is Brad Sherwood. I have an idea I want to discuss."

Fenny Atkinson, in his double-wide East Side townhouse, jumped out of bed. His wife, used to such calls, did not even stir.

"You're not hearing it from me," said Brad, "but how feasible would it be to take Magnet private?"

"Hang on, let me wake up and go plug into Bloomberg." Fenny trotted into his office and turned on a powerful computer that was hooked into a vast financial-information service. While the computer cranked up, he rang for coffee from his butler.

Fenny noted with wonder and glee that his hands were shaking. This was a call he'd always dreamed of. *No one* was immune to the glamour of Brad Sherwood.

He entered the code for Magnet and scrolled through pages of stories and figures. Peering at the blinking colors on the screen, Fenny giddily concluded that the numbers had a ripe odor.

"Now could be the time, Brad. The stock is flat, so are sales, and expenses are up. And there is a lot of shareholder discontent. But I'm also sensing there is some cash on hand."

"Wanna do it with me?"

"Whoa, boy, hold your horses! Let me just make sure I'm hearing this correctly. You want to take over Magnet? Go private?"

"Yeah," Brad responded. "Why not?"

"Well, for one thing, you'd be breaking a lot of balls. That would be the fun part. But there is also a great deal of personal risk. There's a slim chance you could actually get away with it, but most likely you'd just end up invalidating your golden parachute."

"I know all that. Give me a better reason not to do it."

"Okay," said Fenny, his head clear now, his focus sharp. "First tell me why you want this, Brad. Is it the money?"

"Well, it's always the money, you know that."

"But you'd be bucking the current trend. Why not a merger or an acquisition? That's the latest fad. Consolidate. Get bigger."

"Been there, done that. And, frankly, at this stage of my life, I don't want that kind of scrutiny. Who needs all that filing with the SEC and all those quarterly reports? I have those hassles already, and they certainly haven't added any richness to my life."

"You have a point. You may be on to something, and I think a privatization scheme might just be the way to go. There's no privacy in the world anymore and none of us can withstand that kind of microscopic examination. Everyone knows everything about everyone."

"Look," said Brad. "Don't fuel my paranoia. Let's just say I'm tired of working for a living. If I'm going to go on I want the whole shebang."

"I'm not surprised. You don't really have a choice these days. If you don't want everything, then you get nothing."

"That's always been the rule out here."

"It's the golden rule. You know, there's another thing to consider. When the government begins privatizing social security your shares will be worth millions."

"I don't want any part of that America. If the government privatizes social security, I'm betting we go back on the gold standard within five years," said Brad.

"I'm with you on that," Fenny agreed.

"So I'll need to be prepared. Let me tell you a story. The other day I ran a yellow light. I was on the car phone, you know how it is, it wasn't my fault. Well, a few days later I get a summons in the mail. An electronic surveillance camera had taken my picture. Now guess what? I have to pay a huge fine and then spend eight hours in traffic school. So I call a judge I know in Beverly Hills and he tells me I can't get out of it. Do you think that's right?"

"That's fucked."

"The DMV has a picture of my face! This is the world we now live in. No one is safe."

"It's scary."

"That's why I think now is the time to cash out. I may be wrong, but why should I continue worrying and guessing? I'm ready to leave the party now."

The butler came in with a silver coffee service. Fenny waited until he left before continuing. "There is only one way I would structure this kind of deal for you, Brad. You would have to be absolutely sure this is what you want. This game is all or nothing. There's no room for cowardice, hesitation, any of that. No attacks of middle-class conscience halfway through."

"It's what I want, Fenny."

"Okay. But it will have to be an all-out assault. Are you up to it? Are you in good health? Are you gonna have a heart attack on me? Are you gonna get in a stupid helicopter crash over Sun Valley halfway through?"

"How do I promise that?"

"You say it and you make me believe it. This is not a game for mortals. I know how to do these deals. You're the wildcat factor, not me."

"I'm up to it, Fenny."

Five thousand miles away, fingering a box of Cuban cigars and sipping a Sumatran blend, Fenny contemplated his decision.

Brad, on the edge of his soft hotel bed, waited.

"All right," said Fenny. "Count me in. I'll put a few things together and fax them to you. Give me all your contact numbers."

Brad gave him the Royal Wailea numbers, and six others.

Later, gazing out over lapping moonlit waves, Brad thought about what he had just done. He had set in motion a chain of events that would snowball with entropic inevitability. Even if he changed his mind now, the gossip alone would crush him. Fenny Atkinson would only have to say a few words. *"Got a call from Brad Sherwood in the middle of the night . . . ooooweee, these Hollywood types and their fancy notions . . ."* There would be immediate consequences. The gauntlet had been thrown and Magnet would go into play.

He should have been terrified. Instead, he felt exhilarated.

He called down for a massage and another burly Hawaiian arrived a few minutes later with a folding table.

"I just want a quick massage; neck, back, legs, and only for twenty-five minutes. There's a clock over there by the TV. Keep your eye on it, okay?"

The burly masseur nodded.

". . . and don't be offended, but no talking please."

The buyout could pave his way to becoming an elder statesman. For too long he'd been coasting, and he needed to shed the open-shirted, serially tan image. If he could pull this off, he promised himself that he would henceforth be known as a Hollywood benefactor. A developer of talent. A fearless champion of class-A projects.

Perhaps Kevin could play a role in these plans. If they were in a stable relationship, Brad could be a role model for the young gays who had not been so fortunate.

The massage invigorated him and Brad suddenly realized how stunning a coup it could be, especially in this overheated era of megamergers. The hairs on his arms tingled. He felt sharp, focused . . . horny, really. He stripped off his towel. Before he could give his image a complete overhaul, he'd need to be a ball breaker one last time.

CHAPTER 9

Despite the much-vaunted exclusivity of the Royal Wailea, the grounds were crawling with honeymooners, noisy families, and rich oldsters from the Midwest who came for the golf. Almost immediately, Brad and Rob concluded the hijinks of the past would not be so easy to start up—which was a shame; the balmy island breezes and the bland luxury of the hotel ignited the familiar itches.

Brad, however, was full of renewed purpose. He appreciated the quiet of the hotel and even had to admit he was relieved the waves were set far back from his suite. The endless crashing, the walls of water that were his constant companion when he was alone in his house in Malibu, sometimes scared him. Smoking joints in bed with a hustler, Brad would sometimes hallucinate that a tsunami, personally dispatched from the Ring of Fire by a vengeful Japan, was coming right at him.

But here, in a sunny, tranquil environment free from distractions, Brad seemed to go into a Zen-like state of higher mogul-consciousness. As the idea of the buyout took hold, his natural killer instincts kicked in, and he felt renewed. On closer inspection, the deal seemed fresh. Timely. And breathtakingly ruthless.

Reams of material, more than expected, streamed out of the fax machine. Calculator in hand, Brad quickly realized that Fenny was going to refashion the standard eighties plan. A smile spread across his face. It was all so obvious, no one would see it coming.

First, they would hire an accounting firm to do a report called a "fairness opinion" so that it would seem the deal was fair to the stockholders, employees, and anyone else who had an interest. Then actuaries would be called to crunch the numbers so that they would favorably impress the board members. Finally, Fenny would shop the company around.

Actually, this was the most delicate aspect of the entire process. Fenny was obligated by law to alert any qualified parties that Magnet was in play, but somehow he just would never get around to it. Meanwhile, he instructed Brad to keep his mouth shut and do some major hiring. After the deal went through, Magnet would do a massive layoff. That last bit was Fenny's signature twist and why should they keep it out of the equation? Why should they deprive themselves?

The sun was setting and bathing the room in a gorgeous crimson glow. This is ridiculous, thought Brad. He'd been working in his room for seven straight hours; his vision was blurring and his stomach was growling. Rob was right. Here he was was in Hawaii, on vacation, and there was no reason he shouldn't be having fun.

Was there time to fly a hustler over from Honolulu? Maybe he could make that a project for Rob. But Brad was really not in the mood. He'd done that hundreds of times and while he usually enjoyed the diversion, the instant gratification, the release, he wanted to get away from all that. Hustlers and masseurs had been taking the place of genuine lovers for too long. Their touch, a little too professional at times, a little hurried, was not connected to anything. He wanted to be with someone who had thoughts, interests, *plans*. Someone who could *hang*.

And maybe that person was Kevin. Why not send the plane for him? He pulled Kevin's number from its hiding place.

"Brad," said Kevin, after screening for a few moments. "What a surprise. I was in the shower."

"Hi Kevin. I've been thinking about you. I . . . well, I miss you, I guess."

"Really? I imagined that you were whooping it up at a luau every night. No thoughts of me at all."

"No, that's hardly the case. I've been forcing myself to relax."

"That's good news. It must be hard to relax on Maui."

"Very hard!" blurted Brad.

"Well, you're not missing anything here. Bring me back some lava."

"Would you like to join me? It would just be for a day or two but I think we could have fun. I could send the GIV."

Kevin, two thousand miles away, was shaken. It was too early for all this, and too grand. Sexless. No, the timing was off. Kevin, in the way of all good liars, immediately cobbled together a plausible excuse.

"I wish I could, Brad. But I'm in a fix. I think my sister is getting a divorce and I have to stick around."

"Oh, that's awful. I wish I could help."

"You already have."

"I wish you were here."

"Me, too."

"But I understand. It's a family thing."

"In fact, I'm expecting a call from her now. Can we talk later?"

"Of course."

Brad's estimation of Kevin's character grew. But he hoped Kevin wouldn't be dragged down by family problems; he suddenly wanted Kevin by his side during his upcoming corporate battle. After all, Kevin, in a cosmic way, had given him the idea of the buyout in the first place.

Brad became momentarily distracted by a devastating memory of Kevin's curving, indolent cock outlined in the golden light of the street lamp on Westmount. His concentration blown, he got up, stretched, and took a guava juice from the refrigerator. He decided to put a call in to his own parents.

Midge and Sy were at home in the condo that Brad had bought for them. Sy was watching *Jeopardy* and Midge was making her special potato pancakes.

"Hi, Mom. Just calling to say hello. What are you and Dad doing?"

"We're making your favorite dinner and if you were here you could have some but you're not so it's your loss. No skin off my nose. Aunt Gilda is stopping by."

"Sounds good. I wish I were there, Mom," said Brad. And this was true. Brad was not looking forward to another evening of bland hotel food. "But I'm taking a break. Rob and I are doing the spa treatment."

"You tell Rob to come over soon, too. I'll make a nice meal. But you can't fool me. I know you're working hard. You sound terrible. When are you coming back? Your father wants to see you. He says he wants to ask you about his investments but I know he misses you."

"I'll take him to lunch next week. He can come to the office and say hello to everybody and then I'll take him over to one of the studios for a screening."

"Good. He'll enjoy that."

"So, Mom, I'm almost finished here, do you want to come to Maui for a few days?"

"No, we're perfectly happy right here. You just come home soon."

"I'll send the plane! I could have a car pick you up in half an hour."

"Oh, pshaw. Such talk. Don't waste your money."

Brad's parents did not like to think too much about his wealth. In fact, they ignored it, and that was one of the things he loved best about them. His Aunt Gilda, now she was another story. She adored the idea of Brad being a big *macher* and she lovingly searched the trades for articles about him. She would never ask, but she especially loved when Brad arranged for her to go to premieres. One of his secretaries kept her up to speed, and she always got her tickets in advance. If you can't make an old aunt happy, what's it all for?

"Okay, Mom, I'll be over next week. Take care of yourself. I miss you."

Kevin, smoking cigarette after cigarette at that kitchen table, hoped he'd played Brad right. Although it might have been fun to fly off to Maui, Kevin sensed it probably wasn't the right move. It would weaken his position, and he had no plans to do that. These rich guys—they all bored so easily.

And the fact remained that a massive pile of bills sat unopened and un-paid in front of him. Kevin realized his present financial situation needed some immediate attention. Unfortunately, his mother had such a litany of complaints and was so weepy and anxious over Diane's problems, that he had forgotten to hit her up for some money.

That meant he'd have to go and collect the head-shot money from that actor, Dan Evans. It would be enough to help only a tiny bit, but what else was there? Kevin spied the green frog piggy bank. Moving quickly, he put it in its box. This must be worth at least thirty dollars, he thought. It wasn't much but it *was* gas money, and that was a crucial consideration. Without a car, one simply did not exist. Kevin wrapped it up.

A plan for his day was forming. He would return the piggy bank to the Beverly Center, get the cash, fill the tank, and then zip over to Dan's apartment and collect his fee. After that he would pick up some food and go to the gym.

Inappropriately influenced at too tender an age by a picture book called *Looking Good* that he found at a garage sale, Kevin pondered his wardrobe. He decided he needed to look enticing. Dan was all image, so Kevin knew he'd be in a better position to wrangle money out of him if he wore something smutty. With a sense of resignation, he pulled on a pair of white Lycra bicycling shorts. Attention would be drawn to his crotch, true, but that was part of the price of admission to the game. As the rest of the outfit was now rendered irrelevant, Kevin threw on a sweatshirt, black Timberland boots, and, over the entire ensemble, a bulky black leather jacket. Just another day at the Beverly Center.

Kevin knew from working at Macy's all those years ago that returning an item to a store was easy as pie. He and Anthony used to shoplift items at discount stores and then return them to Macy's, where they would pocket the retail difference. His only worry was that the shop would try to give him store credit. *Nothing* irritated him more. He examined the sticker on the box. "Reflections." Kevin knew precisely where it was: third level, to the right of the escalators. They sold stationery, cards, gift items, paperweights, all of it made by children in China and all of it marked way the hell up. He didn't think he'd have a problem.

Before he left the apartment, he dug out the actor's address. Dan Evans, 412 Spaulding. It was off Melrose and close to the Beverly Center. Full of renewed purpose, Kevin set out, a man of action, with places to go, seizing the day.

The exchange at Reflections went off without a hitch, and Kevin netted forty-seven dollars and twelve cents. He was a bit stunned that Shane, with a flight attendants' salary, had spent that much on him, so he reminded himself to be nice to him. Maybe he'd ask Shane to come over and have a cup of coffee later, and then appear at the door shirtless. That would make them even.

Melrose Avenue was crawling with skinheads and punks, all looking for a cheap bit of silver jewelry—something in a death's-head broach, perhaps, or a new nose ring. Kevin, finding them filthy and disgusting, felt contemptuous as he drove past Johnny Rockets, their favorite hangout. He turned onto Spaulding and found a parking spot in front of Dan's faux-Moorish building, looking over his shoulder to make sure no knife-wielding homeless junkies were lunging toward him as he locked up. While ringing Dan's grimy doorbell, Kevin decided he would need to go home later and fit another shower into his jam-packed day.

"Hey man, good to see you," said Dan. "Come on in."

Kevin spied warped floors, a couch, a futon, and a coffee table with a glass bong on it. An elaborate stereo system set on cinder blocks was tuned to a country station.

"Want a bong hit?" yelled Dan over the radio.

"No, thanks," answered Kevin. "I'm here on business."

Dan went over and turned the music down. "You want your money, right? Well, you're in luck. I just got a check for that Lever 2000 commercial and I'm starting on a soap next week. My shit is really coming together, so I'm celebrating."

"Wow," said Kevin. "I guess those head shots were even better than I thought."

"Actually, for the soap I used my old ones. Want a drink or something?" Dan picked up the bong and a lighter and prepared to take another hit. "I have La Croix mineral water or Arrowhead."

"Some mineral water would be fine." Kevin, relieved that he was getting his money, took a seat on the futon.

Dan was about six-foot-two and had wide shoulders, a thirty-one-inch waist, blue eyes, and thick blond hair. He was from Canada and had arranged to stay in the U.S. by paying a girl with a mild heroin habit five hundred dollars to marry him. Now, armed with a green card, Dan was all set to pursue his Hollywood dreams. His plan? The soap, a nighttime series, then movies. Not the most cutting-edge road map to stardom, but not unrealistic, either. No Shakespeare in the Park for Dan, no matter what he told that lady from *Soap Opera Digest*.

Dan came out of the kitchen with two bottles of Tynant and plunked down on the futon. He wore standard Melrose biker drag: black cowboy boots, 501's, and some sort of ribbed T-shirt universally recognized as "actionwear." Oh, thought Kevin, the touching pretensions of these newcomers.

"Yeah, those pictures you did were great, but I didn't get them back from the lab in time," said Dan. "Made no difference in the end. So what have you been up to?"

"Oh, you know, working here and there."

"Looks like you've been going to the gym a lot."

"Yeah, well it's the key to everything, isn't it?"

"Yeah, it is. It's in my contract that I have to keep my body in shape or they can write me out at any time. There's a whole raft of shit in there, public-morals stuff too. The queen who hired me told me the tabs would be on my ass if I had any vices, so I better keep them really quiet or they'd give me the ax."

"Is speaking exclusively in clichés actionable?" Kevin wondered aloud.

"What, man?"

"Nothing."

"I *know*," said Dan sagely.

Dan was great looking, but Kevin found sitting around his apartment soul-destroyingly dull. He had had narcissistic, one-sided discussions like this with actors a hundred times before, and he was simply not in the mood. And how come success was coming so easily for this twenty-two-year-old hick from Winnipeg, while he, Kevin Malloy, was having to struggle for every dollar? It didn't seem fair.

"Listen, Dan, congratulations, but I got some stuff to do this afternoon and I'm kind of in a hurry."

"Hey, relax, take a bong hit. This is great weed, and I deserve to party. News like this doesn't come along every day. I'm going to be working overtime soon and I want to have a little fun. Don't worry, I got the cash in my bedroom."

Kevin had no argument prepared so he acquiesced. He leaned forward and took a tiny hit. Like all the new stuff going around, it was incredibly strong. He immediately felt dizzy.

"You know, man, that day we took the shots I was pretty nervous," said Dan. "I couldn't figure out why."

"You should learn how to stand still," advised Kevin, already regretting the hit. "It's a skill that comes in handy."

Dan took a sip of water. "That wasn't it at all. I got turned on by you taking pictures of me. Maybe we could do another session some time."

"Sure." Dan's eyes, Kevin could now see, looked small and glassy.

"A little racier this time though."

"What about your morals clause?"

"Shit, it's not really a morals clause. You know, just some beefcake shots. No one would object to that. Maybe we could do a poster or something."

Kevin considered the request. Through the gritty haze of the pot, the idea did not seem unreasonable. It might work out to be a tidy little afternoon's work.

"I'm getting some great definition in my abs," said Dan. "Hell, I'll give you a preview." He stood up and peeled off his T-shirt. And then he unnecessarily broke upon the top button of his Levi's. "My legs are really coming together too, man. Maybe you could do a poster of me in a toga. It'd be real Fabio kind of shit, but it could work."

"Yeah," Kevin agreed, "that would be great. Listen, Dan, I gotta go, but give me a call man when you want to pull this together."

"Hey, all right already. You want your money? Just take it easy. I'll go get it. It's in my bedroom."

Dan weaved off, so Kevin drank the rest of his imported mountain spring water. He then examined a few dust motes that were visible in a ray of sunlight near the kitchen. He checked his cuticles and found them without flaw.

The signals were always there. Kevin knew his role, and, as always, the only question was whether or not he would play it.

"Hey, Dan," called Kevin, projecting his voice. "I'm in a hurry."

There was no response from the bedroom. The country station played a lengthy commercial for a mortgage product and Kevin listened to every word.

"Shit," whispered Kevin. This low-level photography gig had so many strings attached. Was he going to have to go in the bedroom now to get his lousy fee? As the seconds passed, he knew he would. Kevin, his head clearing, considered walking, but then knew he'd never come back. Dan would be insulted and make him grovel for the money.

Had a day in Kevin's life ever gone according to plan? The second Kevin came up with an itinerary, forces swooped in and waylaid him, ruining his fragile notion of a schedule. So why not just have it off with Dan for a half hour or so and be done with it? Dan was undeniably a number. Heavily, Kevin got up off the couch and drifted over to the door of Dan's bedroom, his action-man resolve gone.

Dan, not a stitch on save for his cowboy boots, lay face down on his mattress. Properly art directed, it could have been his poster pose.

Kevin stood in the doorway, which, he noticed, was slightly off center, probably from the earthquake. He decided to take it slow and easy.

"Man, if I only had the time . . ." said Kevin, oozing regret, "but really, I got an appointment."

Dan turned his head around and smiled. "That's cool. I just felt a little woozy. I made out the check. Mmmhhh. Now where did I put it?"

Dan cradled his head in his arms.

"It's around here somewhere. Man, I'm sacked out."

Kevin drifted over to a pile of papers stacked on a radiator.

"I think I may be lying on it," said Dan helpfully.

Kevin pondered the task before him and decided not to make a big deal of the whole thing. He smiled. "Maybe you can check for me, Dan."

"Or maybe you can, Kevin, my boy. I'm too stoned to move."

Kevin moved toward the bed and reached under Dan's hard stomach. Dan made no move to shift. Kevin felt nothing but the coarse texture of cheap cotton-poly sheets. He wedged his hand up further.

"Wrong direction," said Dan.

The sleazy novelty of this game was working slightly for Kevin and he reconsidered his actions. What the hey. He slid his hand roughly down along Dan's ribcage until he discovered a wiry texture somewhere below Dan's navel. He fished around in a calculated, lingering fashion. Dan moaned softly.

"That's it, man. Pull on it."

While Kevin complied, his eyes happened to fall on a framed picture of Dan and his wife. They had, apparently, undergone a drive-through Las Vegas ceremony. Both grinned tightly from the front seat of Dan's Mitsubishi truck.

It soon dawned on Kevin that there was no check waiting for him anywhere underneath Dan's taut body, and probably not anywhere else for that matter. He withdrew his hand as if burned and immediately lost his temper. "All right, enough of this shit. Just write out the check."

Dan flipped over, his eyes wide and alert. "I thought we could have some fun first, man. Don't be so uptight. Come on. Keep choking my chicken. I know you know how."

"Look, Dan, I told you. I don't have the time. Gimme a check, will ya? I'll come back tonight."

"Hey, Kevin," said Dan. "Want to know a secret? I'm a bottom. But don't tell my publicist."

Kevin got up and started to walk out, but as he approached the door Dan leapt up and caught him in a bear hug. Dan then spun them both around until they crashed onto the bed. The cheap mattress plunged.

Dan drew his face up to Kevin's. "Relax, man, I'm versatile. I thought

you were a top. It's not on my resume, but I can be one too, in a pinch."
Dan pinned Kevin down with a knee and then grabbed both of Kevin's
wrists at once and held them against the headboard. He then leaned down
and took a hard bite of Kevin's nipple. "You Americans are too hung up
about sex."

Kevin struggled. Although he and Dan were the same height, Dan was
at least thirty pounds heavier. Dan thrust his hand down Kevin's white Lycra shorts.

"Man, you are sweet," said Dan. "Put out or no check. Come on, you
know you want to. I'm gonna be on TV!"

Kevin forced himself to breathe easy. "Well, give me the check first."

"Nah, that would be no fun. Do you like to wrestle?"

"No. You're too heavy."

"I'll let up a little. It'll be fun."

"Okay," said Kevin.

Dan loosened his grip a fraction and then rubbed his hands all over
Kevin's stomach. Kevin, acting like one of those human curiosities who
find the strength to tip a car over in an emergency, pushed Dan off.

But then Dan lunged. He grabbed Kevin's arm and broke through the
skin with a fingernail. Hanging on to each other, they rolled into the living
room and smashed into the coffee table. Bong water spilled and Dan, livid,
hurled Kevin onto the couch. Kevin slid along a greasy cushion until his
face hit the corner of the coffee table with a sickening crack. He touched
his cheekbone and found it slick with blood.

"This is how I like it," said Dan, panting. "I like it when the girl puts up
a fight. I got some toys, too." Dan reached under the couch and pulled out
a dusty two-headed dildo. "Pretty little fuck face," he snarled crazily. *"Show
me your mangina!"*

With his Lycra shorts halfway down his hips, Kevin summoned all his
remaining strength and careened over to the front door. He ripped it open
and bolted.

Dan stood nude in the doorway, laughing, his teeth bared, his cock a lev-
itating iguana. "Come back any time for that check, Kevin. You're *special*. I
like you."

An old Russian couple, part of the onslaught of refugees that had been
taking over the neighborhood in the last few years, gaped from the sidewalk. Before going back inside, Dan made sure to give them the finger.

CHAPTER 10

Rob tried mightily to appreciate the charms of the Royal Wailea Resort, but the appalling and unforeseen absence of nubile young boy-flesh troubled him deeply. Standing alone in his bathroom, rubbing cortisone cream into his elbows, he tried to make the best of a bad situation.

How to occupy himself—that was the problem. Television was out; he never watched. He'd already had a facial as well as a shiatsu, too. Ditto colonic hydrotherapy. He thought it might be pleasant to just go out on the lanai and read *Palimpsest,* a book Elinor had given him, but he'd stupidly loaned it to one of Brad's pilots.

And Brad was holed up with a DO NOT DISTURB sign on his door. Rob couldn't think of anything else to do, so, on a whim, he decided to make a stab at purpose and discipline: he would wander down to the hotel gym and get on the Lifecycle.

The fitness center, a small but state-of-the-art affair with new Cybex equipment, was located at the bottom of a stairwell near the conference ballrooms. Rob crept in.

A lithe young man of blooming virility sat in a pool of soft light behind a white, seashell-shaped desk. He wore white slacks, no belt, and a white T-shirt, and had straight yellow bangs that hung into his eyes and plump arm muscles covered in fine, downy blond hairs. His eyes and lips were droopy, but somehow managed to be darling. Best of all, he was working that exceedingly clean surfer look, a look no one seemed to bother with anymore these days, especially surfers.

"Goodness," Rob gasped under his breath.

The vibrant and dewy creature at the desk looked up and smiled. One of his front teeth crossed over to slightly overlap the other, and it gave him the low-wattage look that Rob always found particularly winning.

"Are you here for a workout, sir?"

"Indeed I am, young man."

"Well, you've come to the right place. If you'll just sign in, we'll get you all taken care of."

The boy spoke with an unusual accent. He had a gurgling, singsong voice that sounded mildly British.

"You're Australian!" exclaimed Rob.

"You got it. I'm Kim. I'm one of the private fitness consultants here. Would you be interested in a personal training session?"

"I think that would be splendid," said Rob, as the boredom and anxieties of the earlier half of the day suddenly receded.

Kim stood up, all youth and smooth movements.

Rob came alive. "Ah, Mother Australia! You know, Kim, I'm quite fond of Australians. Sydney Harbor, the Great Barrier Reef, the opera house . . . Oh, the whole country just inspires me!"

"I'm a Perth boy, myself," said Kim. "The whole country is just a big rock as far as I'm concerned. I'm glad to be off it."

"But such history!" Rob cried. "When I think about those convicts crossing the Tasman, the conditions on those ships, the scurvy. What proud stock you come from. Such hardy souls, forging their way in a new world, arriving in . . . chains!" Rob seemed almost tearful. But then he gathered his wits and signed in.

"If you'll just sign this release, sir, we can get you started on some of the strength-training machines."

"Of course. Wonderful. A little strength conditioning might be just the ticket. I'm a bit out of shape, but I trust you completely. And, please, call me Rob. I abhor formality."

"The locker rooms are right this way," said Kim. "I see that you've already changed, but I'm afraid you'll have to wear our workout clothes. House rules."

"Oh?"

"It's a Japanese thing."

Kim handed Rob a pair of shorts, a sweatshirt, white socks, and sneakers. He also turned over a lock and a key with an attached safety pin. Kim then led Rob down a carpeted hallway.

"Now, sir, when you're all ready, meet me back here and we'll get you all fixed up. Normally, we require an appointment, but it's slow today. Most of the hotel guests are Japanese; between you and me, all they really want to do is sit in the steam room. They sit in the steam room and smoke. Can you believe it?"

"Oh, my," Rob said. "Well, not me. This is an active vacation. I think I shall require an appointment every day."

"Great," replied Kim. "I'll set up a schedule. I'll do a body-fat analysis, a blood-pressure test, a fitness test, and then we'll draw up a goal plan."

"I'd like to lose a little flab," admitted Rob.

"Well, then we'll have to do some aerobics. Do you swim?" Kim asked.

"Oh, yes," Rob told him.

"Well then," Kim went on, "we'll need to get you some goggles. We can do that tomorrow. Let's get to work."

"I have goggles," Rob said.

Rob took to his new trainer with enthusiasm. Every day they met in the little gym for back-to-back appointments. Rob felt as though he were back in training, just like in the old days, when he was known in certain exclusive circles as "The Queen of the Frozen Stage."

Rob had a bit of German blood in him and he relished the discipline. He monopolized Kim's schedule and tipped him lavishly. He held his head higher, and breathed properly for a change, pushing his stomach *out,* lipo-scars be damned. He called Elinor Graham, raved about the Maui onions, and told her he was thinking of becoming a vegetarian. Kim even made him try meditation.

Rob's newfound diversion dovetailed perfectly with Brad's rabid new in-room work schedule. They would eat breakfast together in Brad's suite on the terrace at six A.M. and then, disguised in big sunglasses to avoid industry types, they took a two-hour walk on a path that threaded along the beach in front of all the garish hotels. As they strolled, they chuckled and reminisced about parties in the past, talked solemnly of encroaching middle age (which, of course, didn't really apply to them), and threw clumps of sand into the ocean for no reason at all. After that, Brad swam a bit and then went to his suite to work. At two, they would meet for a lunch that was dietetic yet filling: cottage cheese in a pineapple, a piece of grilled fish, or a fruit salad. Following lunch, they took long naps, both of them astounded by how easily the sleep came.

Tucked away in bed by 9:30, they fell asleep with gift-shop paperbacks on their chests. The faint tunes of the local Hawaiian crooners, old men with surf-logo stickers on their guitars who performed nightly down by the pool, knocked them out.

"You must come down for Mardi Gras in Sydney one year, Mr. Erikson. It's the largest party in the world." Kim and Rob were resting a moment before Rob's laps in the pool. "It's really unbelievable. Last year there were eighty thousand people."

"Oh, my dear Kim, you can't imagine that I haven't already been. You underestimate me unconscionably. I adore Mardis Gras in Sydney; I've been attending for years. I rode on the Qantas float. I've been to every recovery party on Oxford Street. I slip down, check into the Regent, and just let myself go. In fact, it's one of the mainstays of my travel schedule."

Rob began to rhapsodize, one of his less endearing habits, but hardly a crime. "From now on, Christmas on Maui, Mardi Gras in February, Paris in the spring, and late summer on Mykonos. Oh, wait . . . I forgot. A weekend, of course, just one, on Fire Island, in July, as an homage. How could I forget that! I sit on the beach at night and all my dead friends come by and we have a chat. It's an all-night affair, believe you me. And, by the way, they're fine! Soooo relieved and chattier than ever. But then, none of them ever could shut up, especially the dancers. You should see Fire Island, Kim. It's the wellspring."

"I want to."

"Deer everywhere. Watch out for ticks. Oh, and then I always do a strenuous New York theater week, followed by a few days in LA for business, a millisecond in Palm Springs—*why, I have no idea*—and Miami in the fall. For the White Party at Vizcaya."

"Mr. Erikson, you are a total circuit queen," said Kim.

"And I couldn't be happier. It's taken me a long time to perfect my yearly travel schedule. Of course I tinker with it—I'm *still* trying to get back to Cape Town—but I've really seen almost everything. I have more frequent-flier points than God. I bet you didn't know that every year I get a signed Christmas card—*from the chairman of Iberia!*"

And it was true that Rob, as he stood in the shallow end of the pool, seemed calm and spiritual. His roving blue eyes always had a twinkle, plus he had that rare genetic coding that predisposed him toward mirth and joy. And that, of course, was his real secret for success with the boys.

"Well, when I grow up I want to be just like you," teased Kim.

"Cheeky bugger! You Australians lack couth."

"Yes, but we're hung like horses," sallied Kim.

"Not all of you," replied Rob. "Trust me on that one."

"Okay," Kim conceded, "that I believe. Now, are you going to do your laps or just stand there?"

"You're in charge," said Rob. He put on his goggles and prepared his feet so he could kick off from the wall. But first he drifted toward an area free of glazed-out honeymooners.

Kim, stopwatch in hand, and not unfamiliar with a variety of pharmaceutical hallucinogens, suddenly experienced a dim chemical flashback to a huge Mardi Gras dance party. The sight of Rob in his goggles reminded him of a drug-saturated moment down in the bowels of the main pavilion. In a stadium-sized men's room, a crowd had gathered after a particularly moving Kylie Minogue number.

A gaggle of men, smoking, drinking beer, and repairing their costumes in the lone mirror, began to drift toward the dark end of a forty-foot-long metal urinal. Kim, wearing a feathered headdress and a pair of see-through plastic shorts (having painted his genitals an abstruse denim blue), pushed his way along as well as he could. Upon arriving at the front of the queue, he was startled to see a man, dressed in rubber, lying in the metal trough. The man grinned and reached out as three or four revelers peed on him, and the expression on his face was nothing less than beatific. His hair, sparse and slightly greenish in the dim lighting, was soaked and continued to be soaked, for hours. To protect his eyes, he wore goggles.

The gay newspapers dubbed this individual "Troughman," and he was an instant celebrity. No one, however, bothered to find out his identity and his mystique grew larger each week. It was analyzed that his presence *made* the party. He was certainly discussed over coffee a great deal more than Madonna's live video greeting that played on six huge screens at four A.M. Even though it had rained during the week of the festival, everyone agreed it was one of the best Mardi Gras parties ever. The presence of Troughman added such a touch!

Just as thousands claimed to have been at Stonewall for the riot, far more people claimed to have encountered Troughman than actually did. "Yeah, I sprayed all over him," the young children would say, and who could dispute their story? *"He loved it!"* It was said that Troughman had lain there for ten hours, that he was gorgeous, that he was a horror, that he was a cabinet minister from Melbourne. The rumors took on a life of their own and soon "Troughie" became a mythic hero.

The straight papers took up the story, resulting in a flurry of editorials. "As a country," wrote Mrs. Anouka McElhaney of Potts Point, "we have become nothing but a playground for the devil." "My knickers are in a twist," declared one Blinkie Hallam. Jim O'Hare, a ferry captain, mourned "the loss of decent tourists."

But their words carried no weight. The Gay Mardi Gras brought in too much money and created too many jobs. Jumbo jets and restaurants and hotels filled to capacity and oceans of Foster's beer were consumed.

Kim watched Rob do a flip turn with grace and accuracy. *No way,* he thought. Kim remembered joining the line. He remembered he felt bad about peeing on the obviously demented man, but then, no one put a gun to the poor bloke's head now, did they? The guy was having his idea of a good time and who could object to that? For weeks, like everyone else in Sydney, Kim was consumed by the mystery of Troughman.

Rob swam steadily, turning his head for a breath of air every few strokes. As he came to his final laps, he flipped over and transitioned gorgeously into a skillful backstroke.

Kim leaned over the edge of the pool and considered the way the water streamed over Rob's forehead. It seemed familiar in a far off way. Was it possible? Could Rob be Troughman?

Dripping wet, Rob hoisted himself out of the water and Kim met him with a towel. When he pulled off his goggles, Kim felt less convinced. No, the idea was ridiculous. I got to stay away from the Eccies, he thought.

"Splendid!" said Rob, vigorously drying off. "Now, what's next?"

"We're through for the day. I have a client at four, but we'll meet again tomorrow, same time."

"Oh, what a shame. I guess I'll go work on my tan then, before dinner. Perhaps you'd like to join us? I'm here with my friend Brad and we're a bit tired of dining alone. We could use the company."

"I'd like that, Mr. Erikson, but there's a rule about fraternizing with the guests. I could get fired."

"How barbaric! And America calls itself a democracy. The hypocrisy of it all. But I'm sure it would be okay. My friend Brad has the Lili'Ouok-ouolani Suite! It's Brad Sherwood, for goodness sake."

"Well, maybe I can sneak up for a few minutes for a cup of tea. I'd like to meet him. I'm thinking of moving to LA, you know."

"Well, then, you must come tonight before dinner. We'll talk all about it. If you come to LA, I can be your first client. I think you've done wonders the past few days."

"Great," said Kim. "I'll come up after I do this Taiwanese businessman's wife."

"I don't give a damn about the shareholders!" Brad yelled into the phone. He was standing in his suite, wearing a tiny bathing suit and having an argument with the friend who was turning the car company around in Detroit. Now that Brad had a top New York investment banker whispering in his ear, he felt entitled to give free advice.

"You can wipe your ass with that offer," said Brad. "And don't implement any cost cutting now. That's always a mistake. Forget the board for a minute. Give in to them and you'll be holding your dick in your hand on the unemployment line, especially if they start talking about employee stock-ownership plans." Brad paused to listen for a few seconds and then let out another stream of obscenities. "Unions? Who gives a flying fuck about unions? Don't talk to me about unions until you've ordered yourself a new GV. Spend! You've already sold your soul; it's too late to grow a conscience. God, Christmas in Detroit must really suck."

His friend was a gray-haired lifelong executive whose wife was a tireless Democratic Party fund-raiser. She and her husband also liked to make small investments in theater, and had backed two of Brad's shows back in the early days. They were modest churchgoing people who were in way over their heads. Brad, bristling with frissons of supermogul pleasure, continued ranting. He heard a knock on the door but ignored it.

"More is at stake than you realize! And don't talk to me about this year's lineup. I went to the auto show. What were you thinking? Find someone to write a bullshit speech about electric cars. In fact, why don't you make a decent one already? That's all anybody wants in Southern California. We're all suffocating to death. Happy New Year!" Brad slammed the phone down and went to the door.

"Brad, you look flushed!" said Rob, who was back in his roomy caftan.

"I'm getting overexcited," Brad admitted. "I've been on the phone all day."

"Tsk. You're incorrigible and you broke your promise." Rob scanned the room and saw that the effluvia of Brad's wheeling and dealing was everywhere. "In fact, you're out of control. Your blood pressure must be soaring. Did you even get a swim in today?"

"No. I got too involved. It's so pleasant to meddle in a car company's affairs. It's such a nuts-and-bolts kind of thing. Really restful, actually."

"Well, now I think a little conventional relaxation is in order. I'm going to put that phone to some really good use and order up some ice. Don't say a word. You owe it to me. You've been ignoring me, so I've invited my personal trainer, Kim, up for cocktails. He's a bit cheeky, but I've grown quite fond of him. And I might as well tell you now—he's thinking of moving to LA and I'm thinking of sponsoring him. Don't look at me like that! He's *quite* an eyeful."

Rob went back to his room to change out of his caftan—it was comfortable, but so ridiculous looking. Brad put on something loose-fitting and gauzy. Kim arrived at 6:30, still in his gym clothes: running shorts and a tank top. Rob had not yet returned, so Brad let Kim in and offered him a drink.

"Nice to meet you, Mr. Sherwood. I've seen you on *Entertainment Tonight.*"

"Have you?" said Brad. "Take a seat. What can I get you to drink?"

"Um, a beer?"

"No problem." Brad procured a Kirin from the minibar and opened it. He took a Diet Coke for himself and then settled on the couch opposite Kim. Kim sprawled and the left leg of his loose shorts gaped open. Brad, amused but not aroused, thought fleetingly of a line delivered by a sorority girl in one of his early movies: *"But, Dean Weinstein! Those computer nerds were brazenly shooting pickle!"*

"Rob tells me you want to move to Los Angeles."

"Yes," said Kim. "I'm getting a bit of island fever and I want to better myself."

"Hmm. What is it that you do?"

"I'm a personal trainer. But I need to get a certificate. I already have a certificate that can get me a job teaching aerobics."

"Good for you," Brad said. "You know, my friend Rob could help you very easily. He thinks highly of you. I hope you think highly of him."

"I do," said Kim.

"He's an old friend of mine. It would behoove you to be very nice to him."

"I will."

"Very nice," Brad said again, losing his patience.

Kim sat up and closed his legs.

"I've been extremely busy on this vacation," Brad continued, "and I haven't been spending as much time as I would like with Rob. But I'm glad he's found you to spend his afternoons with. We only have a few more days so I hope he continues having fun. Do you get my drift?"

"Um, I think so," Kim said, not getting it at all. He genuinely liked Rob already.

Rob knocked on the door and Brad looked at Kim long and hard before he went to answer it. When Brad finally released him from his gaze, Kim took a deep pull on his beer.

Rob came in, all in a tizzy. "Always a crisis! One of my star skaters had to go home to his mother. Poor boy, she lives in England. I never knew. She contracted mad cow disease and now she's got *brain fever!* I had to wire some money to a place called Hampstead Heath. Oh, well. It's an opportunity for someone in the back row. Oh, Kim, you made it." Rob turned to Brad. "This poor boy is risking life and limb to sneak up here. It's all too exciting. Brad, could you find it in your heart to fix me a small vodka and soda?"

"I don't think your new trainer would approve, Rob. How about a nice pineapple juice instead?"

"Oh, just give me a glass of water. Everyone, I see, including my best friend, has it in for me today," sighed Rob.

"Listen, you guys," said Brad. "Can I ask a favor? I need to make one last call. Why don't you go over to Rob's suite and I'll meet you there in half an hour. Then the three of us can go out to dinner. I'm starving, and I think it would be good if we got out of the hotel."

"Half an hour means forty-five minutes," said Rob, rolling his eyes. "Fine. I have water in my suite, thank you very much. Come on, Kim. I've learned over the years that with my friend here there is no use in arguing. Please hurry, Brad."

After Brad closed the door behind them, he dialed Fenny Atkinson.

"Hey, Brad old boy, I'm glad you called. That stuff you sent me is great. And just in time, I'd say. Looks like the board is getting ready to fuck you without lube."

"Yeah, I know that."

"But don't worry. They won't know what hit them."

"Is there anything else you need to see?"

"Let me digest some of these figures. Meanwhile, enjoy your vacation. It's in my hands now. I have to compliment you on the work you've done. I'm very impressed with it so far. You've brought me a very doable deal here. Don't be nervous."

"I'm not," said Brad.

"Good. Gotta go, partner. Gotta be up at four for a run and then I have a breakfast meeting at six. Sleep tight, babe."

Brad had a good feeling about Fenny; he could sense the guy was hungry for a life-changer. Oh, sure, if all went as planned, Fenny would probably make an easy leap onto the *Forbes* 400, but there was more to it than that. This deal was about self-respect. It was about redemption. It was about freedom. It was about horseback rides with Ted and Jane. If Fenny didn't fuck this one up, he'd be seen as a visionary, not just another bloated dealster.

Yeah, the guy was ready. Fenny was the perfect man for the job.

Brad changed his shirt, looked at his watch, and trotted over to Rob's suite.

Kim, completely nude, cracked the door.

"Um, hi, Mr. Sherwood," he said, blushing.

Rob came up behind Kim. "Brad," he said, "I thought Kim might be more comfortable if he got out of those evil, constricting shorts. He seems more comfortable, don't you think?"

Despite himself, Brad laughed out loud. "Yes, he does."

"This is a vacation, darn it. I won't be drinking water. It has no taste. Kim, please get that white wine out of the fridge. I think we all deserve it."

Kim, padding across the carpet, complied. The moon outside, a full one, was no competition for the luminous moon where a Speedo had once clung to Kim's terribly perky butt.

Brad, happy to see his best friend up to his old tricks, magnanimously made the following announcement: "I'll open the wine, Rob. Why don't you go down to the lobby and see if you can rustle up some more pot."

CHAPTER 11

Coming back home, Kevin slammed the front door. It was just a hollow plywood thing, so it was a not very satisfying gesture.

Leon, feeling the plasterboard walls shudder, thought it was another aftershock. He came tearing through the small living room.

"Goddamn fag actors!" yelled Kevin.

He flung his heavy leather jacket on the floor, hitting a neat pile of CDs. They scattered into the kitchen, where they picked up speed on the linoleum. Donna Summer's *Greatest Hits* skitted under the refrigerator, never to be seen again.

"What the heck are you talking about?" asked Leon.

"I just went to get some money from that tired queen Dan Evans and he . . . well, he didn't give it to me and he just got a job on *Sudden Storm,* the bastard. It's only three hundred dollars. He tried to get me . . . into bed."

"Dan Evans? He's hot. I'd do him in a heartbeat."

"Fuck off, Leon."

"All right, sorry. What happened? Didn't he have the money?"

"No, he had it."

Kevin stormed into the bathroom and examined the gash on his face. It was not a deep puncture, but the area was already swelling and a greenish tinge surfacing from underneath would undoubtedly turn black and blue. Kevin, who never had so much as a pimple, tried to stem a rising tide of panic and hysteria. It was a shock to look in the mirror and see a face he would think twice about before cruising.

"Come and look at my face!" he shrieked.

"What is it, a bruise?" said Leon.

"Yeah. The bastard hit me. Will it scar?"

"Kevin. It's nothing. What's wrong with you?"

"Do I need to dress it? Should I put some Polysporin on it? Or should we just go to the emergency room at Cedars?"

"Get real, Kevin. You can't afford Cedars."

"Oh, you're no help. Get out!"

He turned back to the mirror. By all outward appearances, Kevin looked relatively normal. His crotch bulged obscenely, his hair was glossy and moving, his lips were plump with vitality. But his perfect face was undeniably marred, and his panic gave way to white anger. With shaking hands, he put a Band-Aid over the cut and then stormed back into the kitchen.

"What do you know anyway?" he screamed. "By the way, I called my parents, as per your brilliant advice, and, boy, was that a mistake. They were all pissed off about my sister's husband, who also is something of a complete asshole and . . . and . . . and they haven't sent me any money for Christmas and, well, I'm really fucked and someone has to pay!" He slammed his fist down on the counter.

Leon laughed.

"What the fuck do you find so funny?"

"I'm just amazed that you find it so shocking when everyone you meet wants to throw you down and examine your willie up close. You should be arrested for wearing those bicycle shorts."

Kevin calmed down immediately. It was a great relief to hear Leon voice his awareness of Kevin's superior beauty.

Leon continued. "Now listen, I've made a study of this. You know those ads they have everywhere now for porno actors? Well, they only ask for two out of three things: Big dick, pretty face, hot body. You've got all three!"

"Your point? Anytime before my AARP card arrives will do."

"Well, those are are not respectable things. Flaunting that grotesque organ of yours in Dan's face. Really. What else did you expect?"

"Ugh. That fucking hick. Do you realize he'll be making, like, five thousand a week? Do you think that's right?"

"Mmm. Yum. He sounds just like my type."

"This is way too much work for a lousy three hundred dollars," muttered Kevin.

"Oh God, stop worrying," said Leon. "I can give you a loan. Like I told you, I'm starting a job after New Year's that is really going to pay."

"Oh, that's not it," Kevin said quietly. He slumped into a heap on the floor. "I'm not making it, Leon. I'm twenty-eight. What kind of life is this?"

"Oh, lighten up, Kevin. My offer still stands. If you can't renew your gym membership, I'll have to go alone and that would be a drag."

"Jesus, Leon, don't you get it at all? I'm not supposed to be here. *This is not the life I'm supposed to have.*"

Leon shook his head sorrowfully as he ducked into his bedroom for his checkbook.

"Look," said Leon upon his return. "This job in Beverly Hills is really going to change everything. Originally, I was just going to sell this lady some faucets, but now she wants to rethink her entire wet-bar area. You have no idea how much that can cost."

"Oh, but I do, darling."

"Just take it easy, kiddo. Count your blessings. It's all gonna be fine."

Leon wrote out a check, placed it on the counter and then busied himself picking up the CDs.

"Prancing around on *Sudden Storm*," muttered Kevin to himself, "acting like Madame Lasagna."

"Huh?"

"That's what my mother call people like him."

"You and your expressions. I never know what you're talking about."

Kevin watched Leon fuss about for a few moments and then got up and opened a fresh pack of cigarettes. "Okay. I'll borrow a little something to tide me over."

"Good. Why don't we go get a frozen skinnychino at the Coffee Bean to celebrate my success. I'll buy."

"Let me just go clean up."

Kevin went into his dark, messy room, stripped off his white Lycra shorts, and threw them in the garbage. They were nothing but a girdle!

What kind of scene had he wandered into? Suppose he had gone to bed with Dan—where could that have led? As he examined his face in the mirror over the dresser, he began to shake. Had he narrowly escaped a rape?

This was all so totally wrong. Hollywood was a joke, and dangerous things only happened on the six o'clock news. Violence came to Asian math students in El Monte, to gang bangers in Bellflower, to liquor-store owners in West Covina. Not to him. He'd never even been carjacked!

Sick bastard. It was time for a little revenge.

Kevin put on soft, faded Levi's, a button-down shirt from a thousand centuries ago, and a pair of Vans sneakers. Then he grabbed the pile of phone numbers that he and Leon had copied out of Brad's address book and stuffed them down his shirt front, once again a man with a plan.

"I'm going out," he said to Leon, nonchalantly. "I'll be back in a little while."

"What about that skinnychino?"

"I'll just be half an hour."

"Hey, I have an idea. Let's skip the skinnychino and go have a nice dinner somewhere. I'll treat."

"Yeah, that'd be good."

"Hey, Kev. You're okay, right?"

"Oh, yeah," said Kevin, with his wide, gorgeous grin. "Crazy town."

"You got that right," Leon agreed.

"Yeah, well, whatever." Kevin started to choke up, so he bolted.

He sped up to Santa Monica Boulevard and headed east. Now, if he stayed on this road he would eventually find himself in Silver Lake, which was where a lot of people who hung in too long ended up. Too weakened by rejection and carpal tunnel to escape to Santa Barbara and open up a bed and breakfast, too devoted to irony to move to San Francisco, they scraped together a down payment on a one-bed/one-bath Craftsman fixer-upper, on the off chance that they still might get *the phone call*. The patient waiting, fueled by the crack high of futile longing—no wonder the neighborhood was clogged with so many leather bars.

This famous road offered other attractions, too: It was the premier route for picking up boy hustlers, ever since they cleaned up Selma over by Hollywood High back in the seventies. All along the road, lounging at bus stops or hanging out at Astro Burger, were lanky youths of all races bebopping along, trying to appear purposeful but peering into every passing car window with a frightened look. Their jeans hung low on their skinny hips, and on hot days, their shirts were stuffed in their back pockets. There was never a lull in the traffic.

Kevin admired them as he drove along. These kids were doing a better job of it than he was. They were surviving on nothing but car fumes, half-eaten pastrami tacos, and the occasional fifty, for which they had to whip it out in the bucket seat of a midsized, late-model leased Saturn.

On the fringes of old Hollywood, across from a Trader Joe's, Kevin slammed on the brakes. He had found what he was seeking.

A strip mall.

Like thousands of others, it had everything: a nail salon, a dry cleaner, a Beef Bowl, a Mailbox Center, and a liquor store. "VISIT OUR WEBSITE!" implored a tattered banner flapping in the breeze out front. Kevin parked his car, and then leggily tooled into the Mailbox Center.

"You have a fax machine?" he asked the attendant behind the desk, a thirty-five-ish leftover punk.

"Right behind you."

"Can I borrow a piece of paper?"

"Are you going to give it back?" snarled the guy, all attitude and acne scars.

Garage-band dreams die the hardest, thought Kevin, and laser resurfacing can only do so much.

"No."

"Then it's twenty-five cents."

"Fine."

"I need a deposit."

Kevin languidly handed over his last twenty and the aging punk slapped down a letter-sized sheet of paper. Kevin bought a pen as well, and then ambled over to the fax and started composing a message.

"DAN EVANS," he wrote, in large block letters, "WHO IS NOW APPEARING ON SUDDEN STORM, IS NOTHING BUT A BIG QUEEN."

Big queen, thought Kevin. Was that insulting enough? Well, that's all he really was, in the end. There were other words that hurt more, and Kevin began to remember the taunts he had once endured. The classic was fag, but homo was popular, too. And fudgepacker! *That* was a refreshing variation. It was uncanny how the other boys knew the score about him in sixth grade, way before he himself did.

"ALL DAN THINKS ABOUT IS HAVING COCK UP HIS ASS," Kevin continued. "HE IS A BIG FAG AND HIS MARRIAGE IS A SHAM. HE HAS NO RIGHT TO APPEAR ON TELEVISION. SIGNED, ANGRY."

The words were stupid and hateful, but they had to be. There was no homophobia like internalized homophobia, as Kevin knew all too well and as Dan was about to learn.

Kevin pulled out the numbers he had copied from Brad's address book and began flipping through them. He saw the number for a big entertainment manager. He punched in the fax number and inserted the paper. While the connection was being made, he browsed through some other numbers.

He found another name, Lainie Mazzer, a celebrity journalist. He inserted the paper again and faxed a copy to her. Then he faxed the message to a publicist over at Sony Studios. After that, he faxed one to a number at an accounting firm, just for the hell of it. A slew of them went to CAA. And one to another journalist. And then one to a ruthless junior velvet-mafia type at Disney whom Kevin had actually tricked with. Finally, he sent a few to New York, just to cover the East Coast.

He turned back to Mike Brazier. Brazier was a well-regarded agent who represented a lot of highly visible talent—which was what Dan was on his way to becoming. *Oh, no he wasn't.* Kevin decided that this fax could be the most damning, the fax that could stall Dan's career before it went any further. It was common knowledge that Mike was a closet queen, and everyone knew that they were the most venal of gossips.

All Kevin could imagine was revenge as he blithely sent off another fax. And then a few more. He found the whole process gratifying and therapeutic. Kevin felt quite in control, as if he were finally correcting a whole lifetime of imagined slights. As his glee was mounting, he turned around to see if the punk rock clerk behind the counter noticed his excitement. Nah. The guy was in the back making copies of somebody's pathetic script. Kevin punched the start button a final time.

At long last vindicated, Kevin paid his bill and got back in his car. He sped along as well as he could, feeling better, looking forward to dinner and happy that he had finally taken some action. He knew it was all rather silly and childish, but at least now that $300 cosmic debt wouldn't gnaw at him.

It was ultimately, Kevin decided, a purely Italian thing. People out here in this phony city, this big suburb of nothing, would never understand that. You have to tweak your enemies, just to keep them on their toes. He had not spent all those years with Anthony Capozi for nothing.

He imagined the faxes shooting out of machines all over town and knew when they were read the rumor mill would go into action.

It was not a wasted day after all.

As he drove along, he ripped up the copied phone numbers and tossed them to the wind, vowing never to drive east of Fairfax again.

CHAPTER 12

A battered, hastily wrapped package came for Kevin the next morning. His mother had sent a Cassatta, a homemade Italian cheesecake. More important, wedged in the box was an envelope with a check for $100. So now, along with the money from Leon, he felt a little better prepared to temporarily assuage the mercurial feelings of Citibank Visa. It was only enough to cover the minimum payment, but, for a month anyway, reprieve was his.

The cheesecake was beautiful, and Kevin, inhaling its aroma, became drunk with nostalgia. It reminded him of high-school football games that he never attended (but drove by), Greek diners with endlessly rotating cake refrigerators, Sinatra, the smell of burning leaves in autumn, and Anthony Capozi. Of course, he could never permit himself to eat it, but he set it on the counter and allowed himself to look at it.

Kevin would deposit the money after he renewed his gym membership. Feeling pardoned, he decided to clean his room. And with remarkable insouciance, he also decided to listen to a little music. Why not? He put on a pair of cutoff shorts and, for extra fun, he wrapped a little do-rag on his head to attain that humble "I am just a maid in a cheap motel" feeling.

He wanted Leon to think his money went to a worthy, industrious person, so he scoured his tub and then, while still a little gritty, went to work on the shower stall in Leon's bathroom. Catching himself in Leon's bathroom mirror, he saw that the cut was healing beautifully.

· · ·

Next door, Shane was at loose ends. He had caught his favorite soap at two and it was now three. The *TV Guide* said that Maury was having an international sexiest-fireman contest, but that was at four. As a daytime talk-show connoisseur, Shane, in the meantime, flatly refused to subject himself to an hour of Maureen Hogan. Shane's pride came from only watching the quality shows. That meant Oprah, Rosie, Ricki, Montel, Geraldo, or Jerry Springer. He refused to watch Jenny Jones, Gordon Elliot, Leeza, Maureen Hogan, or Sally Jessy Rafael. To watch the lesser chatfests, in his mind, was an affront to his dignity. He rarely watched Maury, but today he would make an exception; he saw on a commercial break that there would be men in bathing suits.

And why shouldn't he plop down on the couch and spend the day in front of the TV? He had already vacuumed. He had already consumed a Lean Cuisine lunch pack. His closets were faultless and his uniform was pressed. He was fully prepared to work his flight tomorrow, and he had plenty of time to kill. He was about to pop in a porno tape and have a go at himself, but just then he heard the thwack of a refrigerator door through the thin walls. Could Leon be home? Shane brightened and leapt off the couch. He had an idea. He would *drop by*. Leon was always fun and he always had such sensible advice.

Of course, that meant *getting ready*. He had taken a shower at eight-thirty, after enjoying a large bowl of Honey Nut Cheerios. This breakfast triggered a need to take care of a whole host of personal-grooming actions, which took over an hour and culminated in a thorough and scalding blow-dry. Shane had managed to stretch those personal-care moments until ten, and he thought he looked good. But perhaps Kevin was right. His roots did seem a little dark. Maybe he would do a quick touch-up with a supermarket product tonight. But only if he felt like it.

"Shane, darling, come in."

A trickle of sweat sparkled like a jewel in Kevin's deep pec cleavage. Kevin's chest was breathtaking to begin with, but for some reason, today his nipples had an especially inspiring jut. Shane went weak in the knees. Slightly on the shortish side, Shane could have stepped forward and licked those nipples, no problem. But he was not one for bold gestures. Instead, he just swooned.

Kevin generously rescued him. "I'm just about to put on some coffee,

Shane. What perfect timing. I've been cleaning all day. And guess what? I baked a cheesecake for you last night and now I can give it to you."

"Really? I can't believe it. Thanks."

"Don't mention it."

"Is Leon here?" Shane asked.

"No," said Kevin. "You have me all to yourself."

Kevin guided Shane to the kitchen table and sat him down. He then put the Cassatta in front of him and wished him a merry Christmas. Kevin felt odd making Shane so welcome, but now he no longer felt guilty about returning the ceramic frog to the Beverly Center. In Kevin's opinion, giving the cake to Shane, along with appearing shirtless, paid off all outstanding and future debts.

Kevin readied the coffee and then joined Shane at the table. "So how is our glamorous young stewardess?" Kevin inquired thickly and confidentially. "Breaking hearts from coast to coast?"

"Well," said Shane, "it's not like that, anymore. The flights are so full today and the people are just mashed into the seats. There's hardly any time to talk to the passengers and make them feel special."

"You do look terribly harried, Shane. Why don't you take a vacation? You can fly for free, can't you?"

"Yes, but I never know where to go."

"That's ridiculous," said Kevin. "Why don't you gussy yourself up and go to Miami?"

"Oh, there are too many queens there," Shane replied.

"There are too many queens everywhere," Kevin retorted, "but that is our lot in life. Embrace it. One month in the gym, a quick touch-up of those roots, a good cut, two days in a tanning bed, some new clothes, and you'd be beating them off with a stick."

"But I want them to know the real me!" declared Shane, vehemently.

Kevin pulled his head back theatrically. "What a horrible thought. And believe me, there is no time."

The coffee was ready and Kevin, wallowing in his servant role, got up and filled two mugs. "How do you take it?"

"Cream and sugar," said Shane.

"My, how indulgent," Kevin commented. "You can't go on this way. I had no idea you were in such a rut. Since I baked this for you, you can have a slice, but tomorrow we are going to start you on a program."

Kevin leaned over and viciously pinched Shane's midsection. "Just as I thought! I can tell you have a body-fat percentage of at least twenty-four percent. That's disgraceful."

Shane was mortified and blushed deeply. Kevin ignored his discomfort and plunged his hands into Shane's hair. "My God, the damage! Don't you ever condition? You're blow-drying yourself into the grave. I think this will all have to come off and we'll have to start from scratch. You live in LA now. Haven't you noticed there is no moisture in the air? Not to mention oxygen. You're falling apart right before my eyes!"

Shane felt alarmed. His day off, which had started out so well, had taken a nasty turn. He had watched Oprah earlier, and she had had a feature on children with debilitating diseases. Afterwards, Shane felt grateful just to be alive! But now he was feeling all wrong.

Kevin, enjoying the makeover possibilities, continued: "Yeah, we'll start with a nice crew cut. It will butch up your act considerably. Later on, we'll go into a goatee—but I'm getting ahead of myself."

"But I don't want to look like a clone!" moaned Shane, rigid with fear.

"Yes, dear, you do. You just don't know it yet. The combination of a butch cut with your baby face will have them running for the exits. It will be tremendous."

Shane caught sight of the clock on the oven and nervously began to re-alize that the Maury Povich show would soon be starting. He longed to be in his apartment alone so he could watch the sexiest-fireman contest in peace. But Kevin was tugging and pulling the dry hair at the front of his scalp.

"I'm going to call the Three Melrose Place salon," Kevin was saying, "and see if I can get you an appointment with Jerry. He's a genius. Bruce Weber won't even rent a trampoline without calling him first. I mean, he's like a guru to that crowd. He just sort of stands around, one hand in his pocket, the other holding a pair of construction-paper scissors, and the next thing you know, you're walking out of there looking like Marcus Schenkenburg. He's that mellow!"

"How much does he charge?"

"I have no idea. He does me for free. Now, do you belong to the Athletic Connection?"

"No."

"Well, do you have a credit card that isn't maxed out?"

"I have a Bank of Hoven MasterCard, but I keep it only for emergencies."

"Well, this certainly qualifies. It's worse than an emergency. Thank God you came over."

"But the Athletic Connection is expensive," Shane whined.

"Everything is expensive, Shane. But I think they're running a 'New Year, New Body' special, so you're in luck. Give them my name when you join and they'll take extra-good care of you. In fact, I'll take you over right now."

Kevin did not add that they would give him three free months on his membership for referring a new member. There wasn't a reason in the world for Shane to know that.

"And in a month, I'll take some shots of you. I'll even give you a five percent discount off my normal rate. You'll look incredible and you'll thank me when you're old. You'll have some pictures to pass around that will prove that once, for one brief shining moment, a long time ago, you were an irresistible beauty."

Shane's afternoon had taken a sharp turn and he was not sure if he was happy about it. He had planned to watch Maury and then walk up to Koo Koo Roo to treat himself to a chicken pot pie. After that he was going to pack his suitcase for his trip and enjoy a relaxed evening of masturbation, having neglected that task earlier. But Kevin was persuasive. And Shane did feel inspired. He had never spent this much time alone with someone so desirable.

"Okay," said Shane. "I'll join the gym. If you think I should. Will you help me learn the machines?"

"Oh, all new members get one free session with a personal trainer. They'll teach you everything. I can't believe you've gone this long without a gym membership."

"I do all right," said Shane, his tone vague.

"Yes, I'm sure you do, but hon—that ass of yours, which is now pleasingly plump, could blow any day now. One day you'll find yourself buying Dockers if you don't pull out of your denial."

"Okay, I'll join!"

Leon came home at that moment—perfect timing, because now the sale could be closed in front of a witness. "Leon, I've just persuaded Shane to join the gym."

"Well, thank God."

"We're going to go over now and sign him up. Do you want to come?"

"No, I'm just here for a minute to make a call, and then I have to drive out to the Valley and get these tiny halogen replacement bulbs for Mrs. Shotwell, and then I have to buy some Polaroid film and, oh, some other piddly little detail things."

"When are we going to work out?" Kevin asked him.

"Can we go tonight?"

"Then we'll have to fight the crowds."

"It can't be helped."

"Shit. Okay. Shane, why don't you go home and change and get your credit card. Come back in fifteen minutes and we'll go over together."

"Okay. Oh, and Kevin: *Thanks.*"

With his work finished for the day, Kevin refilled his coffee cup and lit up a cigarette. Leon went into his bathroom and saw the bucket full of soapy Ajax.

"Wow, my shower looks great. Thanks, Kevin. I can't believe this."

"Well, I'm sort of crawling out of my funk. Did I tell you Brad Sherwood called the other day from Maui and invited me to drop everything and come out? He said he would send his plane for me."

"Wow! Why aren't you packed?"

"Oh, of course I'm not going. He can get any twink to fly out there. I think I'm going to play this one a little slower. Besides, I'd rather be here for New Year's Eve. Before I marry myself off to Brad I want to have some fun. I have a stack of invitations."

"Really?"

Kevin went over to the dining area and picked through the bills and mail. "There's an underwear party, a benefit pool party at that surgeon's house, some grueling Jeffrey Sanker extravaganza, and a foam party, dignified by the presence of numerous multinational corporate sponsors. Hmmm. It's not really a stack, but it will have to do. Oh, here's something in Palm Springs that sounds not at all intriguing. A DJ direct from Manchester. 'Trance Dance.' Well, that's kind of gross, but no matter. What do you think? Personally, I think the foam party is our best bet."

Leon was sorting shirts in preparation for a quick trip to the dry cleaner. "Actually, this year I think I'd prefer something a little more high minded. Something intimate, like a nice dinner with close friends."

Kevin harumphed. "Don't you think it's a little late in the game to be cultivating friendships, Leon? But if that's what your heart is set on, I suppose a few hits of Ecstasy could resolve that issue."

Finished sorting his wash, Leon went to his desk and began looking through a stack of design magazines. On the floor were catalogs for kitchen and bathroom fixtures. He had a small pad of Post-it notes at the ready to attach to the pages with designs that caught his fancy.

Kevin came in and flopped down on Leon's tightly made bed.

"At work already?" he asked.

"Well, I probably won't use any of this stuff, but I guess I should act like I'm prepared. This is really kind of a big test for me. Normally, this would be a job that Brian would handle, but he told me to go with it."

"It's not really showbiz though," Kevin remarked. "Why get so worked up?"

"A girl's got to pay her rent," said Leon. But then he felt a surge of resentment. "And so what if it's not showbiz, anyway? It's work. It'll keep me occupied for a few weeks, and that will feel good. I don't want to spend the rest of my life going to underwear parties, Kevin. I need to get real."

"You are real, Leon. Horrifyingly so. I'm just saying that maybe it's too early to give up your Hollywood dream. I thought you wanted to get a job on TV—what happened with that? You certainly have more than enough talent."

"That's true and that's why I'm happy about this job. It's exposure. Mrs. Shotwell's husband is a producer with two shows in syndication. I've been going about this all the wrong way. I just need to get some work under my belt. Word will get around."

"Oh. So let me get this straight. You're going to do it the old-fashioned way?"

Leon turned around in his metal office chair. The casters protested loudly as they turned in the gluey pile of the old carpet.

"Yeah, I think I am, Kevin. Meeting Brad Sherwood the other night forced me to realize some things. Did you see how he ignored me? I may have stopped hearts in the Land of a Thousand Lakes, but here I'm just average. Well, I'm above average, but I'm not twenty-five. Shit, I'm not even thirty. That was two years ago. This whole system we love is based on youth. And the new children are coming up right behind us."

"Oh, you're bringing me down, Leon. Just get a chemical peel with that wet-bar money. You look fine."

"I look okay, for my age."

"Well, so what if you're not young? The point is you *pass* as youthful. Besides, adolescence doesn't end until twenty-eight. It's true. A therapist told me in the bathroom at the Mother Lode. At your age, you still qualify as a young adult. Thirty-two just ain't what it used to be, darling."

"Well, even if it's not, I'd still just be putting off the inevitable. And I sort of don't mind taking myself out of the game. Maybe I'll even find a boyfriend. It would be such a relief."

"Such talk!"

"What are you going to do, Kevin? That's the real question."

"Well, I'm certainly not going to go out and get a job. I've done that and it's for schmucks. Don't worry. I can drum up some head-shot business or something. Maybe I'll do some test shots next week and start dragging my portfolio around again. It's been so long, I'll be a new face again. And if I want, I can always assist on the big catalog jobs. It's humiliating, but all I have to do is change the cameras every few minutes."

But Kevin knew himself well enough to know that he was not about to start calling the big LA fashion photographers for work anytime soon. The pay was good, but Kevin hated the whole scene. Models didn't appreciate his dry comments, which became sarcastic as the day wore on. And getting up at five was a hassle. Oh, there were plenty of reasons not to work, not the least of which were the schedules. If a job lasted four or five days, there was never any time to squeeze in a visit to the gym. To maintain their fantastic physiques, Kevin and Leon needed two hours of solid gym time each day. Such was the price of a thirty-one-inch waist after twenty-five.

"If I were in your shoes," said Leon, "I would marry Brad Sherwood. He could take you out of West Hollywood and you would never have to look back. I saw the way he looked at you. You're the boy of his dreams."

Kevin knew this. He didn't need to hear it from Leon. That phone call from Maui clinched it. But Kevin had already made up his mind. Kevin decided it was time to do it the Jackie-O way. The first marriage is for love, the second for money. And the third, well, that one you didn't even have to bother with—that last stab was all about companionship, for having someone around when you fell in the shower and broke your hip.

Well, thought Kevin, he had already done the first. Of course, he bungled it, tragically, but now he would make a fresh start. It was time to go for the second.

CHAPTER 13

Mike Brazier liked to get to his office on Wilshire around six A.M. All of the other agents worked out their own hours as well, but Mike preferred a little solitude before all the high drama of the day began. These hours also made his home life run smoother; he could creep out of bed before the wife and kids woke up.

His good looks had paved his career path, but now he was a recognized force on his own, a solid citizen of Hollywood. He had broken out of the ranks of minor agentry when he championed a comedic actress from New Zealand for a pithy supporting role. Surprising everyone, the woman went on to win a Golden Globe. She then replaced, on a fluke, a finicky actress on a sci-fi actioner on the first day of shooting, and the movie went on to gross two-twelve worldwide. Since then, all the ladies thought Mike had a touch. He had a way of reassuring actresses of a dangerous age that they could get out there and compete with all the up-and-comers. He lavished them with attention, bombarding them daily with gifts of flowers, books, stationery, picture frames, and perfumes.

Mike, wearing a hands-free headset, was on the phone to New York when his assistant Portia came into his office with a new phone list, his meeting schedule, and a pile of recent messages.

"Oh, and I just thought I'd show you this strange fax before I sent it over to security to be put into the database," she said.

These days, most celebrities kept a record filled with information culled from their fan mail, most of which contained requests for autographs. Often in the fan mail, especially if they received a lot of it, was a significant amount of cash for return postage, usually more than was necessary. A few celebrities actually sent this money *back*.

Next came the requests for personal appearances, which were examined and weighed for their publicity value. Good diseases, meaning anything involving children, preferably leukemia, headed the list. A star by a hospital bed—wearing a Sundance baseball cap, the absolute minimum of makeup—made everyone look good. Mall openings were to be avoided. The crowds were just too hostile and unpredictable.

But then, always, the fan mail also contained missives from the obsessed fans, the crazies. The ultimatums, the declarations of eternal love, the misspelled suicide notes. More and more of them each year. This information was tracked and discussed with the private security companies that provided bodyguards, or, if direct threats were involved, with the FBI.

Portia handed the fax to Mike.

"Who is Dan Evans? Is he a client of ours?"

"No," said Portia. "I've never heard of him. I don't know who represents him, but I could find out."

"Well, do that and then I'll make a call. It's strange this came to me. It looks like a prank. Whatever. Okay. What's next? Anything come in from legal about the HBO special for Ellen?"

"Just came."

"Great. And did you leave a message for Marisa on the set to tell her to call me tonight?"

"I'll do that now."

"Goddamnit! All right. Just forget it. I'll do it myself." (For this actress, Marisa, Mike had a special gift, the gift that all the stars coveted: a high-paying TV commercial . . . *that would run only in Japan*.)

Mike sent Portia off with her tail between her legs and then dug around for a copy of *TV Guide*. He flipped through it and saw that *Sudden Storm* came on at one, and he decided to tune in and check out Dan Evans. Maybe that would offer a clue as to who sent the message.

When *Sudden Storm* came on, Mike sat back with the volume turned off and tried to figure out which of the obscenely pulchritudinous young men on the show was Dan. He began to hope it was the one with his shirt off, the strapping blond with the gigantic shoulders, playing the hospital administrator.

Mike was a standard-issue Hollywood bisexual. He had a wife, two kids, the great career, and had come to boys rather late in the game. The desire had always been there, but he was able to sublimate it for a time. In LA, though, why bother? When Mike arrived from the University of Arizona seventeen years ago, he was shocked to discover that a lot of people who worked in the industry were openly gay. He might have gone that route himself, but by then he had already married his college sweetheart.

Now pushing forty, Mike still could not quite fathom the idea of two men living together. He liked having a woman's touch in the home, a frilly bedroom, and all the comforts and securities a good woman provided. He also adored his kids and wanted to protect them as much as possible. He privately believed raising a child in California was nothing less than outright child abuse, but because of all the money, it could not be avoided.

When Mike let it slip to his wife that he was troubled by thoughts of men, they immediately went into couples counseling. There they came to an agreement: As long as Mike didn't act upon those feelings, the marriage could hold together. Mike decided he could live with that. He loved his car, his beach club, his house in the Palisades, and, after all, the family had come through an earthquake together, so they could survive this, too. Like most Hollywood couples, the Braziers rarely slept together anyway and the arrangement was, as the therapist pointed out, not at all uncommon.

"Relax, kids!" he proclaimed. "You're normal! By the way, I have a house in Big Bear and the skiing is great this season. And all my clients get a special discount on the weekly rate. Weekends slightly higher. Just clear it through my secretary."

The psychologist diagnosed Mike and his wife with seasonal affective disorder; the insurance covered everything.

And the dalliances continued, under the heading of experimentation. Oh, and Southern California, the ninth-largest economy in the world, was rife with opportunities—to experiment, to explore, to discover, to grow. Opportunities abounded not only at the gym, but also at the video store and on the freeway and in restrooms at the airport and in the customer lounge at the Lexus dealership, and so on and so on forever. So now and then Mike discretely indulged, no one the wiser.

"Everybody free, feel good," as the song demanded, goddamnit!

Mike liked the look of Dan, if that blond one was indeed Dan. He turned the volume up, and as he watched *Sudden Storm,* he realized the kid did a good job of passing for straight. He decided to study the show further and see what Dan was all about.

It was a professional decision. His roster was short on men, and male actors commanded much higher fees than women did.

It was New Year's Eve. Kim knew that Rob and Brad were clearing out of Maui soon. The thought depressed him: Hollywood had crash-landed into his life and he was transformed. A paradigm shift had occurred, and the idea of staying on at the hotel, such a magical place just last week, now seemed dreary and colorless.

While Rob put on his caftan, Kim, holding on to his power and privilege for as long as possible, remained pointedly naked. Like a spunky catamite, he put his feet up on the coffee table, no longer worried about getting caught in a room with a guest. So what if they fired him?

"So, Rob," inquired Kim as the torrid sun hovered sumptuously at the edge of the horizon, "what do you and Mr. Sherwood have planned for tonight?"

"Well, we had thought about doing the midnight five-K, but we're not really mixing too well with the other hotel guests. And Brad has been so preoccupied. I can't get him out of his room. Oh, well, he's always been that way. I can't let it it spoil *my* good time. Shall we have a wee daiquiri? I'm parched."

"Sure, I'll make them." Kim sprung from the couch.

Rob watched contentedly as Kim's various body parts to-and-froed. "That would be heaven. You know, I thought the crowd here would be a tad more congenial. But they're like creatures from another planet. So all the festivities are just kind of . . . not for us. I only have time to do the circuit holidays now, anyway."

"Like Mardi Gras," Kim suggested.

"Oh, yes—that, of course, is my favorite."

Kim took a blender from a closet and then started choosing fruit from a wicker basket. "Is there such a thing as a papaya daiquiri? I think it could work."

"Well, you could give it a try. If it's horrible we can just order up from the bar."

"Oh, no. This is more fun."

Kim put together a hefty cocktail and ran the blender. The ice jangled and banged, reminding Rob of a million Fire Island afternoons. He was glad that he and Brad were leaving in the morning. Meeting Kim was lovely, but Maui just wasn't gay enough.

Kim brought the drinks over to Rob, and after toasting each other, they took tentative sips.

Rob shook his head. "Yecch. Take this away. I've reached my limit for all this tropical-drink silliness. Back to the bar, young man, and come back with the vodka. Dump these."

"Good idea." Kim retrieved a bottle of Absolut, two fresh glasses, and a bucket of ice. He set them down in front of Rob.

"Oh, this is vastly better," said Rob, an expression of deep contentment on his face.

"So, you're really leaving tomorrow?" said Kim sadly.

"Yes," replied Rob. "Now, be sure to call when you get to LA. You can stay in my guest house until you get settled. But you'll have to continue training me."

"That's fair. I really appreciate this opportunity."

Rob waved a hand dismissively. "No, it is you that is doing me the favor, Kim. I suppose you'll have to give notice to the management and take care of some other macabre, gruesome little things like that, the kind of things that just suck all the youth out of your bones. But keep me informed. I'll give you all my private numbers."

"Okay," Kim said. "Thanks."

But Kim was still troubled. He was not getting paid for another four days, and the money he would receive would not be enough for a plane ticket, anyway. Who knew how long it would take to raise that kind of cash? He sipped his vodka, realizing that all was well and good now, but he wanted a stronger commitment. By the time he would be able to get it together, maybe Rob would be off in Miami or Ibiza or some other gay mecca and they would lose touch. So much could go wrong.

"Are you planning on Mardi Gras in February again?" he asked.

"Oh, yes. I had the most wonderful time last year."

"It was fabulous last year, even though it rained," agreed Kim. "But I'm thinking that maybe my Mardi Gras days are over."

"Oh, don't say that! The wonderful thing about Sydney is that they welcome everyone, young and old. In the U.S., one tires of the ceaseless ageism—not that I've ever experienced it. Some of my friends have, poor dears."

"That's true. All tastes are welcomed." He paused a moment, then continued. "Rob, can I ask you a question? I've been wondering about something. Now don't take this the wrong way, but I keep having this feeling that I've met you before. Like at last year's Mardi Gras."

"Why would I ever take that in the wrong way?"

"Well . . . by any chance, were you in costume?"

"But of course."

"I know this is crazy, but was this costume, by any remote chance, made of rubber?"

Rob put his drink down. He took a moment to gather his thoughts, and since this was so rare, one could, all at once, see the intelligence that percolated behind his perpetually twinkling blue eyes. This mental acuity was the real reason he and Brad had been best friends for so long; only Brad knew Rob was terribly smart.

"A rubber costume," he said. "How intriguing. Perhaps you could describe it?"

"Black rubber, like a wet suit, but tighter."

"Mmm . . . and wherever did you encounter this vision?"

"In the men's room. You know, the giant one. There were about five hundred people in there."

"Yes, I remember," Rob drawled. "Perfectly."

"Are you . . . well, I was wondering, were you . . . are you . . . Troughman?" Kim stammered.

"*Troughman.* I like that. Is that what they're calling him?"

"So it *was* you!" exclaimed Kim.

"What if I were? What would you think of a man who lies in a trough?"

"I don't know. Who cares what people do?"

"Well, that's a polite notion, to say the least. Albeit a tad naive." Rob leaned forward to freshen their drinks. "*Troughman.* The *names* these children think up! By the way, Kim darling, if you're going to spread a rumor, you should at least get the story straight. It was latex, not rubber."

"Oh, my God," Kim shrieked. "It really was you! Do you realize you made the party? Everyone was talking about you. You were the hit of the whole week!"

"It was a wonderful experience," conceded Rob. "I had gotten the idea the year before. We don't have bathrooms like that in the U.S., bathrooms that foster that sense of community and good feeling. I was so worried I was going to have a problem at customs with that suit, but the inspector didn't say anything. In fact, he seemed rather encouraging. Oh, the magic of that night. Total bliss."

"I hope you're going back next year. They would give you your own float!"

"Would they? Such charming people. No—next year, I shall find my jollies some other way. And that's the key to happiness, my child. Find your jollies. It was a beautiful experience, but I know by now that one can rarely re-create magic twice. Of course, my ice show does it every night, but that's a different thing altogether. Oh, Kim, you should see the tears of the little children streaking down their grubby little faces!"

"Does Mr. Sherwood know you did this?"

"Ah, no," said Rob. "I don't want him to worry. He's got enough on his mind. In fact, no one knows but you, I'm afraid."

"So you want me to keep this a secret?"

"Yes, I would prefer that. Of course, if it got out, who would care? But I'd rather it didn't."

"Okay. I won't tell anyone," Kim promised with a long face, "even though it's probably the most irresistible piece of gossip I have ever heard."

"I can see how it would be. But I'd really prefer that it doesn't go beyond this room. Just let the myth feed on itself and let that be that. It's ancient news as far as I'm concerned."

"How will you ever top yourself?"

"The most shocking thing I could do would be to settle down and start dating. Which I have no plans to do. Life is much too short and I have too much love to share."

"Coming from anyone but you, Rob, I would say you were crazy. But somehow that makes perfect sense."

"Oh, dear, now, no one has ever said that to me. You're a good lad. Thank you. Now what can I do for you? You have made this dreary diet vacation into a most splendid and wonderful, ah, thing."

"Well, I am very serious about coming to Los Angeles and I promise I will. As soon as I can."

"Oh, good. It will be a pleasure. But life, like I said just a lost moment ago, is too short. Why don't you break out of this mausoleum and come on the plane with us? I know there's room. It sleeps eight."

"I was praying you would say that! I have to admit that for a moment there I was going to try and blackmail you, once I found out you were Troughman. But I lost my nerve."

"Cheeky little blackmailer! I adore your spunk. Besides, I was planning to ask you anyway."

•   •   •

Brad, Rob, and Kim, with a great sense of relief, took off out of Maui together the next day. All agreed that Maui was one of the most spoiled places on earth, totally plastic, lacking in action, deadly boring and horrid. They vowed never to return. At dinner the night before, there had been some talk of popping over to Honolulu, for all of them in their day had scrounged up plenty of perfectly satisfactory tricks at Fusion, but it didn't seem worth the trouble. Instead, all New Year's Eve hotel activities were skipped and they went to bed early. Brad alerted the pilots, who were staying at the nearby Intercontinental, to be ready to depart at 5:30, and to make sure there was plenty of hot Kona coffee on board.

Brad, especially, was eager to get back home. He was anxious to see Kevin again. Their relationship existed solely in his imagination, but now he wanted to get things rolling again. If something significant was going to happen, he wanted to know right away.

From the plane, he called a florist in Beverly Hills and ordered up a huge arrangement of roses.

The flight took only four and a half hours. Brad dozed while Rob and Kim enjoyed the video of the identical twins. As the jet banked over Catalina, the smog over the Santa Monica Mountains, a sludgy brown strip of greasy particles that never truly disappeared, came into view.

The pilot dropped the landing gear. Blocks of tract homes appeared, then grids of streets choked with traffic. One could only imagine the carjackings and the gang wars. The stickups, the pit-bull attacks, the eighty-car freeway pileups. The sinkholes. The rampant elder abuse. The utter despair. Home at last!

PART TWO

"AND A HAPPY NEW YEAR"

CHAPTER 14

Back on his home turf, Brad released an internal hormone that gently returned him to his most natural state: straight-for-the-jugular, take-no-prisoners, megamogul-of-death mode.

"Magnet headquarters, Jeremy."

"Yes, *sir!*"

The night before, Brad had come up with another fresh plan, one that he was anxious to implement.

Magnet maintained a corporate apartment on the Wilshire corridor, picked up one afternoon in a fire sale. It was a showy, trilevel penthouse with salmon marble floors and a private elevator. Brad had originally bought it for his parents as an anniversary gift but they didn't like it. It was too imposing and ornate for their tastes, so Brad decided to keep it for guests. Four other homes that he owned were currently rented out.

He had been thinking about offering the penthouse to Tell That Girl Hi as a further incentive to sign with Magnet, but it came to him in a flash that if he were going to be seeing more of Kevin, the drive out to Malibu would become tedious. So he decided to move into the apartment himself, at least for the rest of the long, harsh LA winter.

"Keep the engine running; I won't be upstairs long," said Brad as he jumped out of the car at Magnet, still in his vacation outfit: sandals, linen slacks, cashmere Armani T. He looked tanned and fit—his short vacation had rejuvenated his appearance.

With nary a greeting, he bounded past the receptionist, an exceptionally cute and preppy-looking boy fresh out of Harvard. The kid looked like a model straight out of an Abercrombie and Fitch ad. Normally, Brad would have given him a short course in intimidation therapy, but he was in a rush today. He found Corrine, his majordomo, in her scarlet-red office.

Corrine was a woman who wore reading glasses on a chain but dressed only in the most up-to-the-minute clothes. Today she wore a black-and-white Issay Miyake pantsuit that looked as though it were made of wadded-up newspaper, but it wasn't, of course—it was made of silk. It should have been hideous; on Corrine, however, it worked.

Brad gave her a direct yet cheery peck on the cheek and she, in turn, favored her boss with a warm and crinkly smile.

"Happy New Year," she said.

"Oh, right, New Year's Day, I forgot. Are you the only one here?"

"It's just me and Matt downstairs. Everyone else took the day off. Most of them were at that big party at Elton John's restaurant last night." Corrine, of course, had not attended. "I certainly didn't expect to see you here today."

"I can see that," said Brad. "How long has that kid downstairs been working here?"

"About three months now. He started as an intern, but we hired him on as a temp."

"Did he come in today on his own?"

"Yes, as a matter of fact. I think he went to the party, but he was here before me today. I found him waiting on the curb."

"He might have the stamina to stay up with rock stars all night, holding their heads over the toilet. It's very good training."

"Do we still have anyone like that?" mused Corrine. "Everyone on our roster just pretends to do drugs. All of them pretend to smoke. The truth is they're all in bed with books by ten."

Brad threw up his hands. "God, this business has gotten boring. They all used to beg me to get them some good blow and now they all beg me to set up meetings with accountants. They love a meeting with an accountant."

"And they all love to pick stocks at home on their laptops. If their fans only knew."

"Times change. Well, I'm glad you came in. Tell me something. Is the apartment on Wilshire vacant?"

"Yes."

"Get a maid and a cook in for me. I want to use it for a while. I need to be close in."

"Sure. I'll go over myself this afternoon and set it up."

"Great. And if you could, call old Bill at Neiman's and tell him to put some new suits and shirts in the closet. He'll know what to buy."

"A simple phone call. Anything else?"

"No, that's all. I trust you have everything running well. Which is good. I'm in the mood to tear some new assholes this year. Fasten your seat belt."

"Very exciting, Brad. I was beginning to think you were never coming back to the office. Where were you, by the way? You seem really positive."

"Maui."

"Oh. I'm sorry."

On the way out, Brad stopped in the lobby and greeted Matt, the new receptionist. The kid was reading through back issues of *The Hollywood Reporter, Billboard,* and *Variety.* After skimming the articles, he copied the names in a notebook. Brad came upon him silently from behind. "What are you doing?"

The kid nearly flew out of his chair.

"Oh, Mr. Sherwood. Sorry. I was just copying down some of these names. Just to know who's important when a call comes through."

Brad had known exactly what Matt was doing. He was trying to figure out the hierarchy, getting to know the players. The kid was doing his homework. Brad took in Matt's golden skin tone and decided to call Rob . . . to tell him that Magnet *finally* had someone cute at the receptionist desk.

"Good," said Brad. "I'm sure you'll find out soon enough. There are only a handful. How was the party last night?"

"Really great. Maybe a little stiff at first. But then Marcia Clark showed up."

"If you like staying out all night, you're in the right business. Maybe we could get you working in talent coordination soon. Some of our people need a lot of hand-holding."

"I would love that."

"I'll tell Corrine." And with that Brad was back out the door. Total time in his office: seventeen minutes.

Kevin and Leon had spent New Year's Eve at Prod. It was a last-minute decision that appealed to them more than the other, more commercial events.

Prod, a place to dance in a nondancing town, was simply an old standby. The guys who went there were what Shane would call serious gym queens. The bodies, the drugs, and the gropings were all predictable and comforting reminders that you *can* stop the music. It was the land that time forgot, and that was its chief appeal.

Kevin, especially, thrived on the hopelessness and romance of the place. It was here, and at other sanctuaries like it, where a solitary voice confirmed his entire belief system: *In my beauty, I am safe.* Unfortunately, this voice only offered up its wisdom when he was half undressed on a black dance floor being groped and pawed by similarly hollowed-out strangers.

It was a pattern that took hold at seventeen, and it imprinted an indelible worldview that he clung to, even though it was rendered obsolete by the flag-waving young muscle queens of today. For Kevin, the language of the dance was all furtive signals and secret glances—not that he didn't learn the ropes soon enough. It only took one long shift at Macy's before he finally understood the power that was his.

Kevin had been daydreaming behind his counter. It was springtime, and no one was in the mood to buy hats and gloves.

Business was also slow over in Gentlemen's Jeans. Anthony was supposed to be straightening up piles of designer denims, but instead he lounged behind his cash register with a copy of the *New York Post*. WALL STREET DEATH PLUNGE, was the headline.

Upstairs at the Clinique counter there was a little more action. The Dramatically Different moisturizer was flying off the shelves. Sharon casually dropped that it was a miracle product—and the customers fervently believed her.

At seven, the three of them were scheduled to have a fifteen-minute break. Anthony put his *Post* in a drawer and walked over to Kevin's counter.

"You're still pissed, man," said Anthony. "What's the big deal? It was just a bet that got out of hand."

"You tricked me," Kevin replied.

"Come on, let's go take our break. I'm sorry. But you could have backed out."

Kevin turned on Anthony. "Oh, really? Welsh on a bet with a Capozi? That would have been smart. I'm half Italian, too, you know. You would have beaten me up."

Anthony laughed. "Yeah, so what? What's a little beating between friends? I was drinking that moulie drink so I got a little crazy."

"Let's just forget it."

They had reached the wide escalator and the two of them boarded it together.

"Yeah, fuhgeddaboutit!" said Anthony, with broad good cheer. "It'll never happen again." The escalator climbed higher. At the top was the Clinique counter. Sharon saw them ascending and she broke into a grin. Here were her boys. But just as they were about to step off, Anthony leaned over and whispered into Kevin's ear: "*Unless you want it to happen again.*"

"Come on you two," said Sharon, brightly. "I'm dying for a Tab."

After their shift, the three of them settled into their regular booth at the WPD. Shirley came over immediately, and Sharon broke out the prom pictures. Shirley cooed and clucked and told Sharon she looked beautiful. She also allowed that Anthony looked all right, "Almost like a decent human being."

At the counter, two cops yelled to Shirley for more coffee, but Shirley didn't even turn around. They called again, this time more raucously. She spun on them quickly. "Get out there and clean up the streets. You've had enough of my fresh coffee!" The cops laughed.

Only Anthony noticed that Shirley wasn't joking. Like his father, he hated cops. Hot Tip always called them pigs, "Always on the take." One of them got up and went behind the counter and fetched his own coffee.

Shirley's good mood returned. "Well, Sharon, these are beautiful. You look like a real princess in these pictures. You deserve a boyfriend who treats you like gold."

"I do," protested Anthony.

"My foot," Shirley retorted. "At least you deserve someone good-looking. Like Kevin here. You're too quiet, Kevin."

"I'm shy," said Kevin.

"My son is shy. You sure are handsome, though."

Kevin did not yet know how to receive a compliment, although this was a lesson he would learn soon enough. He was basically a charmless teen, but then he had no early role models. Who ever does?

Anthony and Sharon quickly became engrossed in a discussion of their college plans. Sharon had been assigned a dorm at Tufts, while Anthony's father was working on getting him an apartment in the city. Kevin, slumped at the edge of the booth, felt left out. Finally, he just threw some money down and said he had to go. Anthony offered him a lift, but Kevin said he'd hitch.

Is there anything more wretched than a teenager on a dark stretch of road with a thumb out? In short order, a white Lincoln Continental, driven by a thoroughly grandfatherly businessman, slowed down. Gravel and aluminum pop-tops crunched under American-made, steel-belted radials.

"Where you headed, son?"

"Just a few miles up the road."

"Hop in."

The man, a New York City ad exec on his way to his country house, could not believe his good luck. The gods had deigned to send him this archetypal vision of teen-flesh at the precise moment he had been grimly anticipating a boring weekend with his aged and incontinent Irish setters. "What do you think of the Mets this season, son?"

Kevin, having absolutely no concept of what the man was talking about, automatically switched into sullen mode.

"Not much," said Kevin, certain as soon as the words left his lips that he had said the wrong thing. He had no knowledge of sports talk, had never heard his father talk the talk, and it was a real barrier to developing friendships. Anthony could talk about sports with conviction, but with Kevin, he never bothered. They talked about other things: in public, cars; in private, clothes.

"I have a nephew about your age," the man said. "Getting ready to go to college?"

"I'll be a senior next year."

"Great! Enjoy it. Got a girlfriend?"

Kevin could have said yes, for that would have been easier. But his curiosity about this man was growing.

"No."

"Well, then I bet you break a lot of hearts."

Kevin did not respond. Twice in one day, first from Shirley and now from this old guy. Something clicked.

"What do you mean?"

The man, hangdog with lust, became flustered. "Well, I mean you're a good-looking kid."

"Yeah?" said Kevin snidely. "How good-looking?"

"You're . . . gorgeous. Sorry, I mean, you're . . . handsome and . . . lovely. Come to my house."

"Okay."

"*What?* Listen . . . forget I said that. Where should I drop you off?"

"We still have a ways to go. But really, why do you want me to come to your house? What would you do?"

"I don't know." The man pulled a silver flask from his suit breast pocket and unscrewed it. He accelerated slightly as they approached a short incline. "Scotch," he said to no one.

Kevin grew impatient. "Can I ask you something? Are you a homosexual?"

It was the first time Kevin had ever said the word aloud and it freaked them both. The man gritted his teeth and pulled the car over. "Get out of here. Are you trying to get me arrested?"

"Are you?" repeated Kevin. "I think you are. I need to know."

"Get out. You don't know anything! Wash your mouth out!"

The man sped off.

Kevin wished he hadn't. He wanted to talk some more. He had, however, gotten confirmation on one concern; he now understood in his bones why people stared at him. And it was not because he was a weirdo. It was not because he was a freak.

Kevin walked the rest of the way home, a billion night stars having no impact whatsoever.

Deciding to ring in the New Year properly, Kevin and Leon did a little Special K at Prod, but it backfired around three and they briefly went into mini K-holes. They emerged only when the DJ put on a remix of "No One Gets the Prize" by Diana Ross. But even the old music failed to rouse them. The mood just didn't hang right.

Leon was feeling morose, but he brightened after receiving a straightforward blow job out back behind a garbage dumpster. Afterward, he found Kevin and dragged him into a cab.

"That kid you were making out with on the dance floor," Leon exclaimed as they drove off, "was gorgeous! Why didn't you take him home?"

"Was he?" said Kevin. "Right now, I don't think I could pick him out of a police lineup."

"The last one. He was so tiny and pretty. The blond."

"Oh, wait, now I remember. The one still in high school. Poor thing. He told me he couldn't get any Roofies, so he was snorting his own Ritalin."

"I never, ever, get those really young, tiny, pretty ones," said Leon.

They woke up on New Year's Day with disappointingly mild hangovers. Around two, a messenger came with a colossal bouquet of roses.

Leon read the card: "I'm back from Maui and waiting to hear from you. Let's make the New Year about us if we can."

Kevin, in the ripped underwear he'd been wearing the night before, the special pair he always wore on big nights, snatched the card, peered at it closely, and then picked up the phone and punched in Brad's Malibu number. He got a machine but was undeterred.

"Hi, Brad, it's Kevin Malloy. Thanks for the flowers. I'm really glad you're back. I thought about you a lot and I have to admit I missed you. You sort of swept in and swept right out and, uh, left me breathless. So call me when you can."

While Kevin was never one to woo, he *could* turn on the charm when needed. And he was about to. If Brad Sherwood was going to pursue him in a big way, Kevin was ready to cave in. He was prepared to live in that big house in Malibu, or get a new car out of the deal, or *something*. But he was determined not to go on living like this. He was not going to end up like all those overbuilt dinosaurs on the pitch-dark dance floor at Prod. He wanted maids, he wanted lap pools, he wanted imported-parquet floors. He wanted . . . *Burmese-teak plantation shutters!*

"I've never been more proud of you," said Leon, wiping away an imaginary tear. "My only daughter, sold to the highest bidder."

"Shut up, Leon. Don't be coarse. This all must be handled very delicately."

"I'm just jealous."

"Well, don't be. I need to do this, before I lose my luster. I only have one problem in my life, one that I never even dreamed of, and I think maybe this is the way I can fix it."

"How dare you have a problem." Leon rolled his eyes.

Kevin, now truly addicted, lit up a cigarette. "My problem is I don't have anywhere to go. I can't go back to New York, and there's really nowhere else for someone like me. This whole country terrifies me. Where could I go? The South? Phoenix? Seattle? This is a nation of rednecks, and I'm

afraid California is the only place where they don't hang depraved cock-
suckers such as ourselves."

"Jeouo, Kevin, why do you always have to say negative things like that?"
said Leon. "It gives me a creepy, uncomfortable feeling—"

"—which I'm sure you already get from your underwear."

"Ugh, you're impossible. Get with it. Gays are accepted now."

"I don't know where you ever got that idea, but it's irrelevant to our discussion."

"Go to San Francisco," Leon suggested.

"No," said Kevin, biting a fingernail. "I don't think I can be around all
those lesbians in plaid. Ugh, sitting around, forced to watch *Home Improve-
ment* while waiting for the fog to lift? All that leather? *No way.* No, I think I
need to let Brad Sherwood take care of things for a while. This life we've
been living is too hard."

"Oh, please. It hasn't been that bad."

"Well, maybe not for you, darling. But you forget . . . I'm from New
York."

Kevin flounced off. Now that he had made up his mind, he was only
waiting for Brad to make the call. With the confidence that supreme good
looks confer, he knew he would not have to wait long.

Seconds later, the phone went off.

"Look," began Brad, "I'm not going to make a big deal out of this. I
thought about you a lot in Maui and I really would like to see if we can
make a go of it. My feelings for you are really strong. I want to be with you.
So now the ball is in your court. I need to know."

"So I'll be right over," said Kevin.

Wasting no time, Kevin jumped into his Miata and sped off to Malibu.
He gave Brad, as he would tell Leon later, the screw of his life. He used
grunts and groans to excellent effect and ensured a good time was had by
all. He posed, he showed his muscley butt, and he ran around the bed so
that his cock gained swinging momentum. He left Brad as he had
intended: wrecked, spent, turned inside out; all those things that one
reads about in the better magazines. His erection never faltered, and he
poked it into Brad's sides, he poked it into Brad's ear, and he insistently
poked it into Brad's mouth. He planted wet kisses in hard-to-reach nether
regions and pinched Brad's tender nipples till they were chapped and sore.
He yelled, he slapped thighs, he yipped. It was a bravura performance,

completely without spontaneity, but there would be time for that later.

Brad had known sex could be this good, but that was a long time ago, when he used to do poppers. With every lick, Kevin suffused Brad's limbs with a renewed sexual confidence. There was heat, passion, pockets of springy moisture, glistening drips of preliminary ooze and wholly unexpected moments of serendipitous good timing. There was drool. Kevin's hair got messed up and it looked incredible. Their gratification was instant, the best kind, and they felt it in their thoroughly sucked toes. Afterward, depleted of electrolytes, they rose from the bed with red faces and exhausted tongues.

It was sort of understood, after they completed this act—this third manifestation of what is often called physical love—that something was going on, and Brad could not have been happier. He felt deliciously carnal as he padded out to the kitchen, nude, for the postsex Triscuits. He felt like he could take back Magnet that afternoon, just by waving a pinky.

Kevin, enjoying himself as well, in the way that one can on a set of two-thousand-dollar sheets, followed. He also remained nude, and Brad wondered if he would ever tire of the privilege of looking upon Kevin's steely flanks, his pendulous balls, his sculptured torso. He didn't think so. Kevin's flesh was so tender, so intoxicating.

He grabbed the chilled champagne. (*Their* drink, now.) Then he opened the cabinet.

There were no Triscuits. Brad's personal nutritionist had banished them. There was very little to eat that didn't require cooking, but after their strenuous workout, they were ravenous. So they swigged champagne from the bottle, passing it back and forth, grinning at each other until Brad decisively called out for Chinese. Slurring his words, he demanded they bring over a complete dinner, *now!*

Rather than showering, Brad and Kevin jumped into the lap pool. There was playful dunking and some very photogenic joshing and splashing. Happy gays cavorting in their joy at living! The promise of youth extended! Then they lowered themselves into the hot tub. After that, they finally put on robes—but Kevin kept letting his fall open, just to keep the atmosphere lewd.

The food arrived promptly, and the chef had obviously dropped everything to outdo himself for Brad. Soon the kitchen table was covered in creamy-white wrapping paper. Brad and Kevin, eating greedily out of the cartons, each found themselves silently relieved the other could use chopsticks.

"Do you want to go into the screening room and watch an old movie?" Brad asked, after they had stuffed themselves.

"Sounds like heaven," said Kevin. They took their fortune cookies with them as Brad led Kevin into a dark room over the garage.

It was furnished like an old theater, except in miniature. A shimmering movie screen hung between red damask curtains. Near the bottom of the amusingly sloped floor stood an original antique upright player piano. Facing the screen was yet another vast and plush couch and six fringed armchairs. Overstuffed hassocks lining the western wall were available if needed.

This was a room Brad used only for special occasions. He did his serious media watching in his office, where he had four monitors that were always on.

While Brad fiddled with the knobs that controlled the lighting, Kevin wandered around. In the projectionist's booth, he discovered over two thousand tapes and laser discs: movies, concerts, entire TV series, all stored and cataloged in alphabetical order.

"Anything you want to see, just name it. A curator comes in once a month and keeps everything up to date."

Kevin put his arm over Brad's shoulder. It was a gesture that delighted Brad more than any of the energetic gymnastics of only an hour before. Brad pushed a button and the cabinets spun around with a discreet whir.

"This is really sort of fabulous," Kevin commented. "I could shut myself up in here forever."

"When I first set it all up I used it every night. Go ahead, pick anything."

Kevin pulled out *The Women,* a George Cukor film from the thirties. "I once bought a term paper about this movie from an ad in the back of *Rolling Stone.*"

"Nineteen thirty-nine. What an amazing year. I love that movie, too. They keep talking about remaking it, but we just don't have stars like that anymore."

"Hollywood today is a disaster," said Kevin. "I hate special effects. I hate them even more now that they're practically undetectable."

"I'm afraid the rest of the world does not share your opinion. That's why Stallone still gets twenty million a picture. The world never tires of American action heroes blowing things up."

"Now who's being cynical?" clucked Kevin.

"Oh, I'm not cynical at all. If that's what the world wants, it's fine with me. A long time ago I decided to embrace the world the way it is. I decided that everything is happening exactly the way it is supposed to be happening."

Kevin put his arms around Brad. "What is happening?"

"Well, I'm here with you. This morning I was on Maui and I couldn't have been more depressed. But this has turned into a truly perfect day."

Brad kissed Kevin and then inserted the tape into the VCR.

"Movies like this made America great," Brad declared. "That is why LA, the laughingstock of the nation in some ways, is really the only place left that counts. Certainly more important than Washington. And, although it's a secret, vastly more important than New York."

"I don't think it's a secret anymore, Brad. Even my mother in Boca can tell you the weekend grosses."

"Really? That's terrible. Average people should not know those things."

Kevin bristled but then climbed on to the couch and decisively lolled his head on Brad's shoulder. He felt snug, tucked away in Brad's screening room. It felt so much safer than his dank apartment on Westmount.

The opening credits of *The Women* came onto the screen and they hunkered down into the couch. As Kevin watched the movie unfurl, he felt amazed as always at how Hollywood could put these perfect worlds up on screen, these worlds that felt more real than real life.

Kevin had originally thought that Brad could somehow get him some work. But now he felt more ambitious. He would play it all by instinct and allow himself to be protected by Brad's great wealth for a while. Worrying about gym membership fees was a problem that was too awful for Kevin to deal with. Not to mention car registration fees, gas, food, rent, phone, and cable. And those were just the bare minimums necessary to survive. Forget health insurance, vacations, or actually saving for the future. That all took real money. Since Brad was in thrall of him, Kevin decided he would just be who Brad wanted him to be. He would make this love affair work out, and if he could hang in for at least six months, he could hire an attorney and get some palimony.

•   •   •

Brad had never brought a hustler into the screening room. He had never wanted to, as this was his sacred refuge. This was where, at times, his innocence and wonder could be rekindled. There were only three phones in this room.

Momentarily at peace, Brad stopped thinking about his impending takeover. He loved having Kevin beside him, and the thought of having a boyfriend that could travel, who could talk, who was *presentable,* was an idea that titillated him to no end.

This cozy little movie-sharing experience would be the foundation. Look at us! We're romantic, we're good! We could pose for IKEA and who could snicker? Brad almost wanted to call Rob and tell him to come over so he could show off his prize. (Normally, of course, he would just show him a tape.) But Brad had greater ambitions now. Gazing at Kevin from the corner of his eye, he began thinking that he could show off Kevin not only to Rob, but to all Hollywood.

CHAPTER 15

Corrine whizzed through that Wilshire penthouse, and within hours it was spic-and-span and ready to be inhabited by two camera-ready Hollywood lovebirds. All Brad had to do was pick up a set of keys at the front desk.

That next morning, Brad surprised Kevin with the news that he was going to be closer in and Kevin reacted with joyful noises that were positive and encouraging. Then, to save time and do their part for the environment, they showered together.

The penthouse unit came with four parking spaces. Brad slipped his Range Rover in one, while Kevin parked his Miata right beside it. There was an elevator court just steps away. They rode up one floor, collected the keys, and then rode up to the thirty-ninth floor in the private elevator, kissing mushily the whole way.

The views were colossal, breathtaking, out of this world. On one side, the ocean. On the other, America. Straight down? Oblivion. But if one felt terrified near the floor-to-ceiling windows of the main salon, one always had the option of retreating in safety to one of the many inviting and impeccably designed conversation areas.

Brad and Kevin made the kitchen the first stop on their tour. Brad was pleased to see that the refrigerators and freezers had been stocked with a variety of low-fat gourmet items. There was a separate refrigerator for wine, which Kevin yanked open. Inside were over a hundred bottles: chilled champagne, row upon row of Cristal, Dom, and Veuve Cliquot. Kevin pulled out a bottle of Dom. "A wee toast to your new digs?"

"Why not?"

Kevin opened the champagne as Brad produced a pair of Baccarat flutes. They took their glasses with them as they toured the rest of the apartment.

"I forgot how big this place was. This is only the second time I've ever been up here. But I think it's really going to work out," Brad observed as he and Kevin wandered through the spacious rooms.

Corrine had seen to every detail. There were exquisite cut stems in crystal vases, towels on heated towel racks; even the bed in the master bedroom had been turned back. There were scented candles lining the bathtubs, wooden matches close at hand, for soothing aromatherapy sessions. There were full tubes of toothpaste of many varieties in all the medicine cabinets. Every imaginable amenity, down to the German-engineered toenail clippers that Kevin found in a drawer in each bathroom, had been anticipated.

The suits Brad had ordered were hanging in a closet and they were perfection. There were five pairs of carefully selected matching shoes, too. Brad knew everything would fit. Old Bill at Neiman's had been buying his clothes for the past fifteen years. His commissions on Brad's purchases alone had allowed him to build a small dungeon in his house in Silver Lake, complete with manacles, chains, pulleys, harnesses, and a rack. But then, Bill worshiped Brad. He sent Brad a new Hermès tie now and then, for free, just because he liked him and because Brad was the perfect customer.

Kevin surveyed the room and felt a ripple of excitement. Still, his intrinsic cynicism pushed to the fore and he could not help but make a comment. *"Inhuman."*

"You could stay here, Kevin. I would like that."

"Maybe we could get a dog or something. To warm it all up."

"It has a dog." Brad pointed to a life-size greyhound, carved in jade, that sat in front of a built-in air purifier. Seeming to know that it was a bit of leftover corporate chinoiserie, the inanimate dog conveyed an expression of extreme plaintiveness.

"Hmm," Kevin murmured noncommittally.

"All right, I'm moving a little fast. But that's just how I do things."

"No, no, that's not it. In fact, that's one of the things I like most about you, Brad."

"I'll have a key made for you, and you can move some stuff over today."

"No," said Kevin. "Let's take this back to DEFCON three if we may. I have a roommate, an apartment, all that stuff. It's only a ten-minute drive from here. I need to get my life in order before I can consider it. I need to work and all that. So hang on."

"Oh, yeah," said Brad. "How's the work going?"

"I get a job here and there. Now and then."

"It's photography, right?"

"Yes," Kevin replied, tightlipped.

Kevin was momentarily shocked to realize that Brad did not clearly remember what Kevin did for his altogether tenuous and meager living. The question hung in the air as a warning; when dating moguls, one's life came second. Kevin's tiny career, so glamorous and sassy on paper, carried little weight in Brad's world. A fashion photographer—so what was that? A hired hand for advertisers. But what about supermodels, catering trucks, exotic shoots in Africa? Well, that was not his world, but that was the idea behind the job, anyway. It was just that Kevin had never been that driven. He had never made all those things happen.

"I could get you some work if you want," said Brad. "In fact, I could get you an assignment this afternoon, now that I think of it. It would just take a phone call. Which reminds me . . . can you excuse me for a second?"

Brad went into the office off the living room while Kevin pondered his newfound status as a decorative boyfriend with an "interesting" career. He swallowed a few lumps of hurt pride and then looked out the window. Who knew there were so many golf courses nearby? Clearly, the world of the LA rich was increasingly well hidden. One could struggle along for years and have no idea.

Kevin could hear Brad yelling into a phone. He drifted into the kitchen, feeling a bit shaken and out of place. The romantic mood, so all consuming and significant a few hours ago at the beach, dissolved in the sterile environment of the penthouse.

So he marched into Brad's office.

This room, too, was a triumph. French country highboys had been reproduced to conceal office supplies, fax machines, scanners, photocopiers, and monitors.

Kevin examined a switch on the wall by the door. A polished brass plate above it read FIREPLACE. Kevin flipped it and the French-limestone clerestory fireplace roared to life. Kevin imagined that Brad had lived for quite some time now in a world where wall switches activated ultrarealistic fireplaces, and were Kevin to move into this world, he would have to get used to it, too. He looked around the room and spied a pair of pale-green curtains. If he were to live here, Kevin knew, one day very soon, he would find a switch, or perhaps a remote, that would electronically open and close those heavy drapes.

It would not take long to get used to such absurd luxuries.

And then he understood. Kevin felt as though he was let in on the secret. It was life imitating the movies. The LA rich were *acting* their way through their lives, as opposed to merely living them . . . and it made them *happy*. Well if *they* could, so could he.

He wanted to go home and ponder it all, but, gauging Brad's mood, he knew it was crucial to forge ahead and close the sale.

Kevin sauntered over to Brad's vast, polished desk and climbed on top of it. He then unzipped his pants and extracted his fat, rubbery prize. Kevin, lying back, was in the throes of a lolling semi when Brad finally turned around.

Brad, engrossed in conversation, immediately found the precise words necessary to wind up his call.

"I want you out of your clothes," said Kevin. "Right now."

Brad became wild-eyed and grabbed for his belt.

"You're so beautiful, Kevin."

"*Ssh*. Close the curtains."

Brad, his pants around his ankles, lunged for a remote. The drapes closed dramatically.

Kevin climbed down off the desk and then buttoned the top button of his pants. For all intents and purposes, his voluptuous cock hung out now just like the big black one in that important Mapplethorpe photo.

He sat down on a burgundy leather couch. "Take your clothes off, Brad. You've been very bad, keeping me waiting like that."

Brad, not sure of what was happening, became erect. Truly stiff. He shuffled over to Kevin.

Kevin gently bent him over his knee.

"Oh, I see," laughed Brad. "Are you going to spank me, little Kevin?"

"Yes, you've been very bad. I think I need to spank you very hard."

"Well, if you have to," Brad tittered.

"This will hurt me more than it hurts you," said Kevin, borrowing a line from an old porno movie he'd seen at the Spike.

Brad looked into Kevin's eyes and suddenly understood that Kevin was going to give him a real wallop, not just a play love tap.

"Now this will hurt a bit," Kevin warned him. "I'm sorry. If you cry, I'll understand. But after, I'm going to take you in my arms and give you a big kiss and everything will be okay."

At that moment, salty tears stung Brad's eyes. Kevin was right. He had been a bad boy. It all made sense.

"Come on, be brave." Kevin reached between Brad's legs and found a quivering, red tuning fork. "Oh, this does not look good. You are a very bad boy, Brad Sherwood."

"I'm sorry."

Kevin, in the role of the disillusioned priest, shook his head. "I am, too. Stand up. I didn't want to have to do this, but now I'm afraid I have no choice. Face the wall. Spread your legs."

Brad stood up and now the tears were streaming down his face. He knew he'd been out of control lately. His buyout was morally wrong, he knew that, but he had to do it. He had felt so desperate, so afraid. He was tired of keeping up the front.

"Spread your legs wider now."

Brad, achingly engorged, complied.

Kevin separated Brad's cheeks and began probing and inspecting with methodical detachment.

"Oh, this is not good. It's worse than I thought. You've been keeping a secret, Brad. A very dirty secret."

Brad gasped and a great bark of anguish escaped from his throat.

"Okay, that's enough," said Kevin. "It's all out in the open now."

Brad, thoroughly humiliated, nodded.

"I'm so disappointed," Kevin continued, as he took off his Kleinberg Sherrill alligator belt. "I thought a spanking would be enough. But I was wrong. Please get down on all fours now. Yes, that's right, like a dog. Stop crying. Be a man for once, Brad."

Brad was absolutely floored. He had never—not once—cried in therapy. He didn't even cry in the sweat lodge on that men's retreat, even though he and seven other top executives had all been trapped in that hut for eight hours. He felt love for Kevin. And great relief. Kevin was going to punish him. But after, if that time ever came, all would be forgiven.

That was the drill.

"Are you ready?" Kevin asked.

Brad nodded.

With a great snap, Kevin rapped the belt across Brad's bare buttocks. Brad's narrow back flinched. The sting was sharp, instant, and it reverberated throughout his whole body. After a few seconds, a red welt surfaced.

Brad felt as though he had just completed an entire course of Scientology. For an instant, he felt *clear*.

But then the pain began.

Kevin swept Brad's limp body up into his arms. Then, with his hand covering Brad's sore bottom, he set him down on the couch. Brad looked up and saw the louche eyes of a corrupt angel. When Kevin, as promised, kissed him, Brad squirted a copious load of mogul-come involuntarily, like a pissing newborn, in a great and joyous arc.

With Brad grinning goofily along the way, Kevin carried Brad into the master bath and deposited him in the shower. Kevin then went into the kitchen and poured himself a fresh glass of champagne.

Kevin had not planned on the spanking, but he had once spoken to a hustler at the gym about how it was a regular industry request, and Kevin thought he'd try it out. It could have backfired but now was not the time for half measures. It was unpleasant but it had to be done.

Brad came in, sparkling clean, wrapped in a white robe. "Guess what? I signed Tell That Girl Hi! Their manager just called. They decided to go with Magnet even though everyone was all over them. I don't mind telling you, but it was all a little touch and go there for a while. This is fantastic!" He alighted briefly on a Philippe Starck barstool but then thought better of it. "You know, I think I want them to record in New York. I don't think they should come out here. They're too pure and untouched. But I'll line up Propaganda to produce the video. And I need to call some directors. I can't have some grizzled old hack on this." Brad went over to Kevin and held him. "That was fun. Thank you."

"Listen, Brad," said Kevin, pulling away, "I really do need to go take care of my own life for a few minutes. I'm going to take off now and do some chores and go to the gym." After all his hard work, Kevin wanted to return to his homely life on Westmount. He wanted to see Leon, and even Shane. Things were moving so fast; he needed a moment to ground himself. He wanted to dip back into a world where he was the undisputed star.

"There's a gym here in the apartment," Brad offered. "Come on, it's upstairs."

"I'm sure there is," said Kevin, "but I still should go. Besides, I can tell you're dying to get back on that phone."

"Don't be scared, Kevin. I've never felt this hopeful. Great things are happening, and I want you to be a part of it. Everything is going to be so fantastic, I promise."

Kevin smiled shyly.

Brad put his hands on Kevin's square shoulders. "Okay, I understand. I'll call you later and we can meet back here tonight. I want to sleep in your arms."

"Me too."

"We can go out to dinner if you want, or eat in, or get on the plane and go to San Francisco. Anything you want, do you understand?" said Brad.

"No," Kevin replied, "anything *you* want." Kevin orchestrated a sexy yet poignant upper-lip tremble. "I better leave now, Brad. I think I'm falling in love with you."

As Kevin whizzed out of the subterranean garage, he came to the conclusion that life in the world of the ultrarich involved a lot of long, silent elevator rides. His ears had popped on the way up to the penthouse and they had popped again on the way down. These are the very good problems of the obscenely rich, he thought as he jiggled a pinky in his ear.

Now, back out in the appalling glare, Kevin felt vulnerable in his low little car. Everything around him seemed all too lifelike. The feeling wore off, though, after he tuned in to Howard Stern. Soon, his aggressive New York driving skills took over, and by the time he crossed over the border into West Hollywood, he was back to running yellow lights, passing in the right lane, and cutting people off with ease.

On Westmount Street, he found Leon fresh from a workout. Leon wore red bicycle shorts, under which the arc of his thick midwestern farm tool was damply outlined, held in place, and on full display. His top, a tank made of threadbare cotton, was soaked and molded to his V-shaped lats in a way that heightened their perfection. The total effect, however, was curiously uninviting: Leon packaged himself in a way that was lewd, which was the goal, but he just came off looking regular. Like who shops at Bijan, it was a phenomenon that could not be explained.

He could almost pass for straight, thought Kevin.

"Welcome back, Miss Thing," said Leon.

"Thang, to you."

"I'm totally starving."

"So am I," said Kevin, after lighting a cigarette. "Should we go to the supermarket?"

"Sure," Leon replied. "You can tell me what's gone down on the way. Since you didn't come home last night, I think you must have sealed some sort of deal with Brad. I'm really depressed about it, of course, so pardon me if I don't beg for the usual blow-by-blow right away."

"I gave him the screw of his life," said Kevin. "And I'm *exhausted*. You know the drill. Spanking, the foul language. *Oy vey!*"

"Why do all those studio execs want to be spanked? I never got that," Leon said.

"Oh, it helps them be better bastards in the morning, I suppose. At the last minute I used my belt. I didn't want to hurt my hand."

"Gross." Leon winced. "I think I'll have a cigarette with you."

"Good," said Kevin. "Is there any coffee?"

"Yes, but there's no milk."

"I take it black, or have you forgotten already? Like my female vocalists."

Kevin changed into a trampy outfit. They were going to Pavilions, the scene of some of the heaviest cruising in the world, and it was obligatory to dress appropriately. Shoppers lingered there for hours, in a trance state, before settling on a Lean Cuisine, a single can of Diet Coke, and a pint of rum. Pavilions was where most guys went after the Athletic Connection if they didn't get sex in the sauna. It was the next logical place.

Shopping carts slowed and lingered or simply followed Kevin around. Leon secretly hoped the strangers they passed, guys they had seen around town forever, would think that he and Kevin were lovers. It was as if the connection would raise Leon's own stock.

They selected some protein and carbohydrates with extreme care, knowing every morsel that went in their bodies would affect their muscle mass, the shininess of their hair, their skin. (The skin, of course, being absolutely everything.)

A combative discussion of gastrointestinal-tract conditions arose, so they decided to split up and go on separate search-and-destroy missions: Kevin sought out the spinach juice, while Leon hunted down the papaya. Then they backtracked through the produce section, both believing that their hair was crying out for the fat lipids that could be found only in avocados. Nothing was chosen for taste.

"Look, Leon. Tomatoes. Great for the prostate." They bagged up twenty.

"Kevin . . . asparagus? I don't know what it does for you, but it makes your come smell really foul."

"Throw them in."

In the bread aisle, Leon examined a package of organic-wheat dinner rolls.

"Darling, put those down," Kevin clucked. "Wheat is packed with naturally occurring estrogen."

"We're not quite there yet, are we," agreed Leon.

"Far from it."

When they returned to the apartment, they ran into Shane. In a huddle, it was decided that Kevin and Shane would go to the gym while Leon fired up the salad spinner.

Shane, delighted to be included, raced to his apartment to change.

"I met with a personal trainer yesterday, and he showed me a few things," said Shane as he and Kevin walked companionably up to the club. "But I still don't know what I'm doing."

"It will all become second nature, dear. And not a minute too soon. But you'll be fine. I know you'll be thrilled with all the new changes."

Shane signed in with his temporary card. Kevin's card registered the extension on his membership; he was once again restored to the status of a member in good standing. Only a week before he had been so close to losing this crucial connecting thread. Chilled, he pushed the memory from his mind.

"Now, Shane . . . ," said Kevin, as they entered a great hall of mirrors, "you're about to become the you you never were supposed to be. Are you ready?"

"I think so," said Shane, "but I'm not sure. I went home to Chicago the other day and I saw my parents. They said I looked weird and that I've gotten skinny."

"You? Skinny?"

"I was always the skinniest one in my family, but I guess that isn't saying much. My brothers and sisters are all a little overweight."

"I shudder to think what that means in the Midwest."

Shane ignored the insult and continued, for he was struggling to express a new insight about his life. Of course, he didn't come from a place where personal insights were particularly valued, so the words did not come easily.

Nevertheless, he plunged courageously into the murky depths, his hands out in front of him, feeling.

"You can never go back, can you? I always thought Chicago was my real home, but I really don't like it there. I don't like going to the mall anymore. Everyone is so fat! I like being around good-looking people, which is something you get used to here. I'm so confused. I love my parents, but I didn't know what to say to them. I asked them to come visit, but they said they didn't want to be around all those snooty people. It's crazy. They've never even been here!"

Shane, in his blundering way, struck a nerve. Kevin's parents never came to California either. They said the fares were too high, and that he didn't belong out there anyway. Oh, sure, they had once talked about going to Vegas, and then driving to the Grand Canyon, but those were places you visited if you were a decent patriotic citizen. They would not, however, consider venturing further. To visit California struck them as un-American. "Too many Democrats," his father would say, "Democrats" being his all-purpose code word for blacks, for Jews, for Asians, for gays—for any group he feared.

"Well, that's sad, Shane, and all the more reason to work on your triceps. Let's try and not be too dreary about this."

Kevin, out of the goodness of his heart, took Shane on an extended tour of the gym.

Shane had never been out in public with Kevin, and the experience was a revelation. So many men were brazenly gawking at Kevin. Shane, not used to being in anyone's reflected limelight, became utterly self-conscious. Just before Kevin was about to explain the proper form for a lat pull-down, his anxieties bubbled over. "Kevin, don't you see all these people staring at you? I've never seen anything like it. You could have any one of them in a minute. You must feel like John Kennedy Junior when you walk in here. Guys are practically following us around."

Kevin looked up lazily and caught several men gaping at him. They turned away quickly. "They are following me around, I know. I just try to ignore them. If I catch their eye, the bolder ones will try to speak to me. And if I let that happen I would never get my workout done. It's a problem I've had to deal with almost all my life."

"I should have such problems," sighed Shane.

Kevin was wearying of this conversation. He was sinking into his own murky depths, pondering the secret thought that Brad Sherwood—media darling, supermogul extraordinaire—was in love with him.

Even though Kevin loved coming to the gym, and he loved the attention he so skillfully ignored, and he loved the bodies in motion straining around him, he knew that this phase of his life would soon be ending. Brad's world was about personal trainers who came to your house and worked you over in your own custom-built home gym. And then rushed off to do the same for Meryl Streep! Kevin, if he so chose, could have all of that and more.

He suddenly became acutely conscious of the shabbiness of his surroundings. There was a tear in the vinyl on the Roman chair next to him. There was a greasy ball of dust clinging to the air-conditioning vent over his head. And there was paint chipped off the Smith machine to the right of him.

A crowd of men were hunched over a contraption tucked away in a corner. "What's that over there?" asked Shane.

"Darling, that's a glute buster, and it would be totally irresponsible of me to subject you to it at this time. You're far too pure of heart. To even look upon it will rob you of your soul. Come on, let me show you the free-weight area and then let's get out of here and eat. Oh, that's very important, too. If you're going to eat, make sure it's in the one-hour window after your workout. Your body is still burning calories during that time and you can eat as much as you want. No fat, of course. Actually the best thing is to restrict yourself to six small meals evenly spaced throughout the day."

Shane nodded, a bit dazed, not quite understanding the concept, but finding himself agreeing. If Kevin said it, it must be true. Kevin did not have the most overbuilt body in the gym, but it certainly was the dreamiest. And the obscene way his crotch bulged! Oh, it was all too much.

After Kevin left the gym, there was always increased activity in the locker room downstairs. Doctors became frotteurers, real-estate salesmen frantically clutched themselves in the showers, and nude hairdressers dropped their blow dryers into the wet sinks under the changing-room mirrors. And it was all because Kevin had come in, lifted a few weights, and then, upon leaving, demonstrated to all his expertise in that most cutthroat of Olympic events—*the tossing of the hair.*

CHAPTER 16

That night, after dinner with Leon and Shane, Kevin returned to Brad's Wilshire apartment. That night and every night afterward for the next two weeks. And soon, the weeks stretched into months. The relationship gained a momentum all its own, propelled and greased by the excitement and newness of the sex and the dovetailing of their own separate agendas.

Kevin's photography career prospered like never before. One morning, Brad made a call and set up an impromptu backstage shoot with a Magnet band at the Universal Amphitheater. Then he arranged for Kevin to shoot publicity stills on a set, the results of which generated more work. As it became known that he was Brad Sherwood's lover, Kevin found doors opening for him all around town. Anytime he wanted to schedule a shoot at Smashbox, the extra-fabulous photography studio in Culver City, he could—no problem. Brad would make a fifteen-second phone call. It was that simple.

But Brad did not want Kevin working too much. When he looked up and saw Kevin enter the apartment with a bulky Filofax one afternoon, he curtailed the jobs so that Kevin worked no more than two days a week. Kevin objected, but then Brad bought him a filmless video camera and Powerbook.

Brad, too, was busier than ever. In constant contact with Fenny Atkinson, he finally learned one day that their plan to do a leveraged buyout of Magnet Entertainment was about to come to fruition. Soon, Brad would become an owner-manager of his company. The value of his shares, now worth millions, would approach a billion. *Ten units.*

"Keep the red tape flowing and spew out a lot of the current management jargon—then you can do whatever you want," advised Fenny during one of their now-regular early-morning chats. "Think only in the short term. And relax. I'm taking care of everything. Go form a task team. No, wait. That was last year. Go form a quality circle."

"I'm amazed at how easily this is all coming together," said Brad.

"The best deals always do," Fenny explained. "In the end, though, it's only about keeping on top of the details. Speaking of which, Brad, while I have you on the phone, I might as well tell you about this strange fax that came in a while ago. I have no idea what it means, but it came through on a number that hardly anyone but you uses. Maybe I'm just paranoid—"

Brad, eager to be involved, interrupted. "Tell me what you got."

"I don't know, that's why I'm checking it out with you. It says, 'Dan Evans is—' Oh, hell, I'm just going to fax it to you right now."

Seconds later, the fax was in Brad's hand.

"Who the hell is Dan Evans?" asked Brad.

"Besides being a 'big queen,'" said Fenny, "it seems he's an actor on something called *Sudden Storm*. Now, I traced the number, and it came out of LA, from somewhere in Hollywood. It's probably nothing, but it really got on my nerves for a few days."

"This disturbs me," said Brad. "I don't know anyone named Dan Evans."

"Are you sure?"

"Of course I'm sure!"

"He's not a leading man in one of your upcoming movies? You know, some actor who's just about to hit? 'Cause if he's starring in a film made by Magnet, this kind of propaganda could create a disaster at the box office—which would, in turn, affect the stock price."

"Fenny, if he were a star of one of our movies, don't you think I'd know it?"

"We can't have anything fucking with the money flow, Brad! I agree, it's probably nothing, but you have to understand. It was just so sinister—since it came from LA."

"Look, Fenny, if he's a good actor, it doesn't matter if he's gay."

"Hey, I know. I'm cool. My wife, she's got an uncle or something that's gay. Met him at a wedding. So don't worry about me. I'm down with all the gays."

"Fenny, just take care of the Wall Street end of things and I'll worry about Hollywood," Brad said before hanging up.

God, what did the East Coast know, anyway?

Brad returned to the bedroom where, after that annoying phone call, he was grateful to see the naked, angelic form of Kevin sprawled sideways across the king-size bed. The sight immediately soothed his frazzled nerves.

Of late, Kevin seemed particularly stunning. He'd been letting his hair grow, and it was now just touching his shoulders. Brad wanted to shower him with kisses, but he had a special chore to do this morning and could not afford the time. A message had come in late last night on his personal line: "*Back in town, sweetie. Stop by when you can!*"

It took less than six minutes to get over to Rob's house in Beverly Hills. So trusting was Rob's nature, the front door of his mansion was unlocked.

Brad found Rob in the patio off the breakfast room, doing sit-ups. Kim was there too, struggling to hold down Rob's ankles.

"Oh, Brad, thank God you're here," said Rob, springing from the floor. "Now we can end this torture. Kim, put on a fresh pot of coffee. The great Brad Sherwood has deigned to make an . . . er . . . appearance."

"Hi, Kim. My, you've worked miracles on our friend here."

And he had. Rob glowed. Numerous muscle groups had been reinvigorated. His eyes were clear, his nose looked not at all bulbous, and he simply radiated health.

"I take all the credit," said Rob. "I'm the one doing all the work."

"Well, you look great," said Brad.

"I do. But what brings you here this early? Not that I mind. I'm thrilled you've interrupted my workout. Torquemada over here has evolved into a rather sadistic taskmaster."

"I wanted to talk to you. Do you have an hour? In private?"

"Absolutely. There's a lot to talk about, I should say."

"Let's have coffee with Kim and then go for a ride."

"Aren't we being mysterious? Okay. I'll go change out of these dreadful clothes."

Brad went into the breakfast room and Kim smiled at him. Brad smiled back easily and then accepted a cup of coffee. "So, Kim, how are you enjoying LA?"

"I love it. The people are really nice and the TV has about a million channels and I went to Disneyland with Rob and we did all the rides. Then I saw an ad for a water park in San Dimas and Rob took me the next day. And then from there we drove out to the Nevada border and went on that new roller coaster that drops you off in the casino and guess what? I won sixty dollars!"

"Great."

"But then Rob had to go to Europe and since he was so into his program he asked me to come with him. So we went all over, and, God, it was freezing. I hate Europe. But on the plane home he told me he would get me a green card through the ice show, so it was all worth it."

"Wow, so you've been having fun. That's good. But here's a question. Why aren't you naked?" Brad knew Rob's demands as an employer better than anyone.

"I was," Kim admitted, blushing, "for the first few days. But Rob told me that since I was a guest he would allow me to wear clothes. I guess I'm not really his type."

"Oh, he likes you a lot, I can tell. But Rob was never one to settle down. Anyway, you've really got him disciplined. He looks great."

"Thanks. Anyway, he's got a nude pool boy who is absolutely gorgeous, and then this other guy comes in to clean nude every day and he's even more gorgeous. So maybe he gets his fill. Since I've been working with him he's lost over a stone—which is about fourteen pounds."

"Talking about my weight loss?" Rob asked, entering in head-to-toe white Versace. "Really. Oh, well, it's on everybody's lips these days. I look divine. Thanks to our young Kim."

Rob and Kim beamed at each other, as Brad thought about how fun it would be to introduce Kevin to Rob. Perhaps the four of them could squeeze in a weekend in Guana, that secluded island in the Caribbean where everyone was heading this year. Brad imagined Kevin and Kim playing a game of nude Frisbee on the beach. Rob grilling shark steaks on a hibachi. An afternoon of parasailing. All of them getting their hair cornrowed. He would set it up after the buyout went through.

"Well, I guess your workout is ruined for the day," said Kim. "If you don't mind, I'd like to have a swim."

"Spring is in the air," Rob trilled. "Okay, run along. My wicked sister and I are going to rehash some old times."

Kim left and Rob poured himself a cup of coffee. He sat down with Brad and they both looked out at the pool and the tennis court beyond. It was a serene, meticulously tended setting.

Neither of them would ever leave LA, despite the crime, aftershocks, fires, home invasions, carjackings, and lowered bond ratings. So what if the schools had to have metal detectors? If you were rich enough, the town was heaven. For Rob, there was but one obstacle to his everlasting contentment: he had never been able to find an appropriate nude gardener to nourish his hydrangeas.

"Drink fast," ordered Brad. "Suddenly I have an overwhelming desire to go to the Farmers Market and have the blueberry pancakes."

"It's not part of my diet, but I won't tell Kim if you won't," Rob said. "Let's go."

After some deliberation, they decided to ride together in Rob's canary-yellow Rolls Royce.

"So," began Rob from behind the wheel, "I've been hearing it all over town, but I need to hear it from the horse's mouth. I called you from Germany, I called you from Hungary, I called—"

"You are aware that I run a public company in my free time, aren't you? In my few spare moments?"

"Oh, please. That company runs itself. Just tell me you're not still with that Christmas trick."

With anyone else, Brad would have taken great offense. Brad knew, however, that he had been neglecting Rob of late, so he let the strong remark slide. "Excuse me, Rob. You're the one who's been out of town for months."

"That's true. I finally had to go over to Europe and crack the whip. The show was getting sloppy. And then on the way back, the LA flight canceled so we got the last two seats on American to JFK and Kim, of course, had never seen New York, or *Cats* for that matter, or Chelsea . . ."

"Oh, Rob. I can't tell you how wonderful it's been."

Rob came close to rear-ending an Infiniti, so he pumped the brakes twice and then got into the right lane where he belonged. "Oh, dear. All right, Brad. Tell me all about it."

Brad took a deep breath. "For the first time in my life I really think I'm in love. I mean, I just can't wait to start the day, you know? Waking up with Kevin beside me is just a dream."

Rob arched a carefully plucked eyebrow. He took this new development very seriously. "Well, that's wonderful, Brad . . . so very *au courant* of you. I would hate to see you hurt, of course, so as long as he's not a gold digger, I'm happy."

Brad laughed. "God, Rob, *gold digger*? I guess that's an expression that never goes out of style. No, he's not a gold digger, but even if he were, I wouldn't care. He's so good looking he has a right to be."

"I'm only thinking of your happiness."

"I know. You fax me your schedule and I'll fax you my schedule and we'll arrange a dinner. He's completely changed my life. And he's so much fun. You know what we did the other night? We went up to Yamishiros in Hollywood, up by the Magic Castle, and had daiquiris. He knows all about movies and he loves all the old Hollywood stuff. And when I pointed out to him the apartment that Marilyn Monroe and Shelley Winters used to share! You should have seen him. He got so excited. He was so into it."

"My goodness. It's rare these days for the young children to appreciate anything. I adore him already. You know, perhaps I should throw the two of you a little coming-out party," said Rob, instantly enthralled with the idea. "A full-on Hollywood-style affair. It'll be like the old days."

"I'll have to talk it over with Kevin."

"Good heavens. Well, it's your debut; I'll let you decide. But we should do something big. It's been ages. Do you recall that party I gave that year in New York?"

Brad chuckled again. Of course he remembered that party. By the end of the evening, Rob had thirty people playing a new parlor game he had invented: Musical Rim Chairs. (Rob had the convertible chairs hand-made in North Carolina. The factory still had the pattern on file.)

"I could do something like that," suggested Rob.

"I think something tamer would be more appropriate," Brad replied.

"Whatever you say. I'll start interviewing event coordinators."

The Farmers Market, a ramshackle collection of wheezy buildings, was one of the few LA landmarks that never changed. Across the street was the Farmers Daughter motel, a convenient trysting place for consensual sex between adults involved in television. Brad and Rob went into the local restaurant, Kokomo's, where they were lucky enough to find an empty table.

Brad recognized a few faces at one table, probably people who worked across the street at CBS, he thought. They eyed him hungrily, but since he couldn't place them, he didn't wave. Brad Sherwood could not afford to squander waves on just anyone.

Rob and Brad ordered the pancakes and then settled in for some serious gossip. Rob's ice-dancing troupe was always a source of amusement to Brad, so Rob fed him a few late-breaking stories: a prima donna fell on her ass and walked off the ice; a new Zamboni resurfacing machine disappeared off a train in Hungary; a dancer in the "Pixies and Faeries at Midnight" number no longer trusted her partner after he dripped hot candle wax on her breast during sex.

Following that, they carted out a whole Rolodex of Hollywood names and went over what they were working on, who was sleeping with whom, whose house had dropped in value, and who had decided to go gay—*at the last possible minute*.

It was the most relaxed morning Brad could remember. Around eight, the restaurant started filling up and the waitress, who obviously did not recognize Brad, baldly told them to get a move on; they were taking up prime space. Rob treated and they split.

Their short excursion into the land of the "regulars" made them anxious to get back to their real lives. The traffic in this part of town was horrendous, and Rob's huge Rolls attracted a great deal of hostility. They got in, locked the doors, flipped down the visors, put on their sunglasses, and fastened their seat belts.

"I used to go to Kokomo's with my father when he worked at the studios," said Brad. "Seems like yesterday."

"Now don't get all maudlin on me just because we visited the old neighborhood."

"Sorry." Brad momentarily became distracted by the sight of an armless man holding a cigarette between his toes. "God, this area has changed. It's a brave new world out there. Which leads me to the real reason I wanted to see you this morning, Rob. How much stock do you have in my company?"

"Since the last split, about eighteen thousand shares."

"Do you? Who knew you had such faith in me? Well, I'm only going to say this once and then I'm not going to say another word."

Rob paid close attention and said nothing. When it came to discussing money, Brad and Rob dropped all the breeziness.

"Some things are about to happen," said Brad, "that I haven't told you about. I did this for a reason. Now, in a few weeks, you'll know everything and you may be offended that I didn't let you in on it. But just keep in my mind that I left you out of the loop on purpose. Don't worry. This deal is big but I promise, somehow, you'll be a part of it. I don't quite know how just yet, but

for now, don't buy or sell any more shares. Everything hinges on absolute se-
crecy, and there must be no suggestion of impropriety. Just sit tight and don't
ask me any questions, okay? We've never had this discussion."

Rob crossed Doheny, and now that he was back in Beverly Hills, he felt
free to let his wrist dangle out the window. His wafer-thin gold Patek
Philippe wristwatch sparkled like a deep-sea fishing lure in the airstream.

"What discussion?"

Brad returned to the penthouse and found Kevin in the kitchen drinking a protein shake, wearing an old pair of Brad's boxer shorts. Brad pulled
them down and gave Kevin's left gluteal a good-morning kiss.

"We're out of cereal," Kevin mumbled, half awake.

"I just ate," said Brad, pulling the boxers back up. "I went to Kokomo's
with Rob. What an adventure."

"I don't like to see you taking risks like that," Kevin chided. He kissed
Brad directly on a new hair plug. "I think you should have bodyguards."

"Well, in about a month I may need some."

"What's that supposed to mean?"

Brad held Kevin and considered cluing him in to some of the details of
the buyout. But at the last second, Kevin wriggled out of Brad's arms and
went to the refrigerator. The moment passed.

"Just kidding," said Brad.

Kevin smiled, gave Brad another kiss, and then picked up a newspaper.
"'Senate Hearings on Obscenity in Rap Music Drag On.' Did you see this?
This article might interest you."

Brad felt touched so he skimmed the article. Of course, he already knew
about the senate hearings; he had originally planned to testify, but then decided to lay low and hope the gang leaders attending the East Coast–West
Coast rap summit would work it all out with a minimum of gunplay. Besides, he believed the whole issue was just another political smokescreen.

"God," muttered Brad. "It's worse than the days when they wanted to
ban Elvis for gyrating his hips on *The Ed Sullivan Show*."

"Huh?" said Kevin, turning to the horoscopes. "By the way, did you
know the drain in the powder room off the foyer is running slow? I think
we should call the super."

But by then Brad's attention was caught up in the article. "It's so pitiful
how these politicians try to justify their existences. I mean, instead of

blaming everything on rap, why don't they just come out and say they plan to cut Medicare? Or that forty percent of every tax dollar still goes to service the interest on the national debt?"

"Don't let it bother you."

"You're right," said Brad. "Let them yammer on. I can't let my blood pressure go up. I should be happy. Senate hearings are free publicity."

"Sounds like a philosophy learned at the knee of Andy Warhol," said Kevin, with a well-practiced gaze of adoration.

Brad kissed Kevin's forearm. "You know, maybe I'm getting old, but I really find all this stuff so disheartening. I mean, there are huge problems in this country, and all they want to do is legislate morality. They won't let gays marry, they kick them out of the military, they want to take back control over women's bodies—the list goes on and on. It's insane. None of it makes any sense. I should get more involved."

"You should, Brad. Don't you know by now you can do anything? You're just one of those people."

"Oh, God!" Brad exclaimed, scanning another article. "Look at this. Porn on the Internet! Imagine caring about such a thing? Don't these people have lives? What about gun control? That does it. I'm gonna go in there and break some balls."

"Grrrrr!" said Kevin, in his best *Beavis and Butt-head* voice. "Break balls! Break balls!"

Brad stopped the nonsense with a kiss.

After a few minutes, it was Kevin's turn to become reflective. "You know, where I grew up, around all these New York Italians, there was only one truly unforgivable sin: making a watery sauce."

Brad laughed. "And around here, I know a father who stopped speaking to his son for ten years. You want to know why? The son bought a house. *At the top of the market.*"

Brad picked up another newspaper. "Prayer in the schools," he muttered to himself. "How about *math* in the schools?"

Kevin decided to bolt. "I'm off to the gym. I have a completely free day. I'm going to stop off at my apartment, give the rent to Leon, have lunch, and be back around four."

"Lucky you," said Brad, glancing up. "Hey, why don't you go see old Bill at Neiman's and get some clothes? The poor guy lives off my commissions, so you'd be doing me a favor."

"Okay," said Kevin. "If you think I should."

"Yeah, it's time you met him. Bill's like a living symbol of the old days. Even my father remembers him. Years ago, Bill knew everybody. You'd see him in pictures dancing at the Mocambo with Cyd Charisse."

"He sounds great."

"I'll call him and tell him you're coming in." Brad took a generous lick of Kevin's nipple, and then held him. "You know, Kevin, I don't see why you still maintain that apartment. I like having you around, you know."

"I would feel bad leaving Leon in a lurch like that."

"Who's Leon?"

"My roommate, remember?"

"Well, just pay him off. There's petty cash on my desk in a manila envelope. Really, Kevin. Life's too short."

"He's an old friend."

"I know. But sometimes when your life changes, you have to cut the cord. It's better for everyone. That way no one gets hurt."

"I actually think I know what you mean. Someday I'll tell you all about it," said Kevin. "Oh, Brad. Are you always right?"

"Yes! Now, I have a meeting at my office. I'm bringing in some image consultants to work with Tell That Girl Hi. Something's not quite jelling there. The lyrics are way too intelligible. Anyway, I'll see you tonight. Do you want to eat in or out?"

"You decide."

"Let's stay in. I don't feel like sharing you with anyone."

Kevin was in an unusually upbeat mood, so he dressed quickly. When he arrived at Neiman's in Beverly Hills, he handed his Miata over to the valet instead of parking in the self-serve lot; he planned to do a lot of damage and didn't want to have to carry his packages too far.

Kevin revered department stores. They reminded him of the days in New York when life was simple. He loved the heavily painted girls in the makeup departments, the layered scents of all the rip-off perfumes, the rumbling escalators. He loved the lighting. Department stores were sexy and he loved to drift through them, fingering and judging the clothes. He loved the thick paper bags.

Brad told Kevin to go find Bill before he did anything. Kevin spied an old guy leaning against a rack of suits and knew that had to be the man.

Once a pretty boy, now gray and stooped, Kevin pegged him as a lifer retail queen—and adored him immediately.

"Excuse me. Are you Bill? Brad Sherwood's friend?"

"Oh, hello!" said Bill. "You must be Kevin. I just got the message that you'd be coming in. How fabulous to meet you."

"And very fabulous to meet you, too."

"Brad never comes in any more. I suppose he's busy." Bill stepped back and took a long, critical look at Kevin. "So you're his 'friend.' Oh, that Brad . . . now I understand everything! He's a very bad boy, wouldn't you say?"

"Yes, I would have to agree," said Kevin, smiling.

"I thought you would. Now, I've known Brad since he was a little pisher and I'm so proud of him. But he's neglectful, wouldn't you say?"

"Very."

"Well, then, he deserves to have his account plundered, don't you think? What do you need?"

Kevin smoldered a bit. "Well, Bill, what do you think I need?"

"Sweetie, you don't need nothing and you and I both know it. Oh, boy, is this going to be fun. You and I are going to do our absolute best to bankrupt Brad Sherwood this very afternoon."

"I think it's what he would want," whispered Kevin.

"Definitely," said Bill. "Now let's get to work. Shall we start with a few suits?"

"Oh, I think more than a few . . . sweetie."

"Oh, Kevin, that's just the attitude. You know, in my day, I was just like you. None of this polite stuff. If those old studio bosses wanted me, there was no dithering. Only the best. I have an Hispano Suiza in my garage that's worth a fortune and I'm going to sell it soon. I'm going to sail around the world on the *QEII, twice,* and then buy the biggest house I can find in Palm Springs and have a party every night."

"Sounds fabulous," said Kevin.

"Promise you'll visit. I like your style. Now follow me. All this stuff right here is crap, but I can tell you knew that."

Bill, moving lightly on tiny feet, led Kevin deep into the hushed environs of the men's suit department. "You've come at the right time. Thank God Barneys took up shop down the street. Before that, we were the only game in town, and all you ever heard was Armani, Armani, Armani. So boring, but then nothing ever changes. Of course, he still has the best cut. But with your figure, which I must say is luscious, we can really go with anything. Why don't we get the basics out of the way first."

Kevin circled around a rack and then turned to Bill. "I need to look expensive," Kevin told him, honestly.

Bill cocked his head and clasped Kevin's wrists. "Darling. Trust me. How old are you? Twenty-eight?"

"And a half."

"I thought so. Not a second to spare. Although I must say you've preserved yourself beautifully. Don't worry. Now, let's start with a few conservative things. See this Armani suit right here? It's perfect for you. Let me show you something. Under these lights it appears to be charcoal. Very power, very *now*. But if you step back a bit, and squint, you'll see just the slightest suggestion of laurel. And that's the genius! It's a trick of the eye, almost as if you're imagining it."

Kevin squinted until he could see what Bill was talking about. "Power," he said, "but with a faint wisp of youth. I'd say it would take off about three years."

"Exactly," Bill replied. "It will give you a little more time, this suit. I think you should get it."

"I agree," said Kevin. "Okay, put it aside. Show me some more. In fact, hon, let's stop screwing around. Why don't you go in the back and get a rolling rack."

"Oh, that's a good idea," Bill chirped. He practically skipped away. By the time he came back, Kevin had already pulled down three more suits.

"Oh, those are excellent," pronounced Bill. "Just what I had in mind."

"I know a little bit about what I'm doing," said Kevin. "In another life I worked a counter at Macy's."

"No! Oh, you are *too* darling. A boy after my own heart. If I didn't respect Brad so much, I'd snatch you up myself and lock you away in my little playroom."

"Well, you were too slow, Bill. Your loss."

Kevin began to have some serious fun. He pillaged the Armani and then raided the Rykiel. He fingered some Calvin, ignored the Ralph, then nosed his way through most of the Hugo Boss. He started to think mod so he sniffed out Paul Smith. On the way to the changing room, he grabbed a DKNY vest.

"These designers need to go down to their sweatshops and teach everyone how to sew a button on," Kevin muttered, returning it to the rack.

"Oh, so true," agreed Bill. "But it doesn't matter how much you pay for anything these days . . . the buttons always come off."

It was time to get fitted, but Kevin, pleased with all his new purchases, decided that Bill, who had been staring at him all afternoon with faraway, nostalgic lust, deserved a treat.

He sent Bill off for the tailor and then slipped over to the men's furnishings display area and grabbed a pack of 2(X)ist briefs. On the way back, he helped Bill push the rolling rack.

"Okay, Bill," said Kevin. "It's time to earn your commission. Help me out here." Kevin selected a walnut-paneled changing room and went in. "Now we'll do this like an assembly line," he instructed. "Keep the merchandise moving."

Bill started with the charcoal Armani. He waited a moment and then knocked on the louvered door.

"Are you decent?"

"Yeah, just come in and out, otherwise this will take forever."

Bill lightly pushed the door open.

Kevin, pale and lanky under a recessed pin spot, had stripped down to his T-shirt and underwear. He held up the packet of briefs. "Tell me, Bill. What do you think of this 2(X)ist line?"

"Well, it might not be for you, but we'll have to see, won't we? It all depends on what you are trying to say."

"Well, I think that I deserve the opinion of a professional," said Kevin, handing Bill the packet. "Help me in them."

Old Bill's mouth dropped.

"Don't make me go back to Brad and tell him how lazy you were, child."

Bill's yellow eyes glittered with disbelief. His old fingers shook as he attempted to open the box.

"Let me help you." Kevin ripped through the thick plastic and unfolded the white briefs.

Bill took them and regained his composure. "Well, the customer is always right, right?"

Kevin peeled off his T-shirt and then leaned back against the mirror. He glanced down at himself. "Just help me out of these."

"Yes, sir," said Bill. Bill peeled Kevin's briefs down and Kevin stepped out of them. After a long reverential moment, Bill, holding the new underwear, looked up at Kevin. "May I?"

"It's your job."

Kevin raised a foot and Bill held out a leg hole for Kevin to step into. Then the other.

"Now, do you really think they work, Bill? You might have to adjust them. Make sure. Take your time."

Bill slipped his hand around the leg holes professionally, checking the fit. "I think so, sir."

"Well, Bill, make sure. Go ahead. Check the front."

As proud as a father with his firstborn son, Bill smiled up at Kevin. And then he allowed his gnarled, arthritic fingers a full exploration of Kevin's moneymaker, in what he would remember as the single most memorable moment of his long and distinguished retail career.

"They fit, sir," Bill proclaimed, his rheumy eyes moist with gratitude.

"Good. Go grab ten pair and put them aside."

Bill left and Kevin got down to work with the tailor.

"Well," said Bill, returning after his heart rate went down, "I think you've done well. But I have something here I think will really knock you out."

Bill held up a creamy, black leather blazer from the house of Hermès. Both of them gazed at it reverently for a moment, speechless. It was beyond exquisite. When Kevin saw the cashmere lining, he almost fainted with joy. It was no less a garment than the shroud of Turin. On the spot, right there in Neiman's Beverly Hills, Kevin felt like he was receiving the stigmata.

"Oh . . . my . . . God . . ." said Kevin. "Heaven."

"We've been keeping it in the back," Bill explained, "holding it for Spielberg. We didn't want the hoi polloi fingering it. But you know what I say? Tough toenails!"

"That's what I always say!"

"I want you to have it."

"It's perfection. It's life itself."

"Little Stevie will just have to find one in Paris," said Bill. "It was made for you. You deserve it."

Kevin, exhilarated, loaded up his bags, but instead of heading back to Wilshire, he sped over to Westmount Street. Leon and Shane always wanted to hear the latest events from Kevin's glamorous new life: the weekends at Twenty-nine Palms for the mud baths, the tenth-row aisle seats at the Grammys, the Monday nights at Morton's. They would crowd around the kitchen table while Kevin filled them in, behaving as though he had just returned from the war.

"And this is the platinum card Brad gave me," Kevin would say, passing it around. The only things missing in his life were a prenup and an engagement ring (Kevin had his eye on a platinum model from Bulgari), but he felt certain those little trinkets would soon be forthcoming.

Leon was dressed for the gym when Kevin arrived. "Oh, good. You can come to the Athletic Connection with me and Shane. I guess he's my new workout partner since you left. He's totally into it now."

"Well, darling, you know I have a private gym."

Leon let loose with a giggle. "Oh, you bastard. Coming down to West Hollywood just so you can lord it all over us poor working stiffs."

Shane came over and Kevin, who had an eye for such things, saw that Shane's visits to the gym were paying off. Shane was thinner now around the middle, weightier in the shoulders, and his chest showed an unexpected whiff of promise. But the most shocking change was his hair, which had been completely rethought. Shane had given up the blond highlighting and was now working a stiff, dark brush cut. The transformation was dramatic; Shane no longer looked desperate.

"All my friends from the old days," said Kevin, "all in one room. The stewardess and the decorator."

"And what does that make you, Kevin?" Shane inquired, with an edge that had never been there before.

"Nothing but a high-priced hooker, I guess. Which is far more respectable than what you two do."

"I agree," said Leon. "We're so proud." Leon, appalling everyone, gave Kevin a hug.

The three of them then settled in for coffee. How their lives had changed in the span of just a few brief months! Leon was doing his magic on kitchens and baths all over the west side, and was now the star salesman at Wishbone. Shane, looking tougher and more clone-like, had become addicted to his gym routine and was turning down dates right and left.

"Well, this is the day," Kevin announced, after showing them the Hermès jacket. "I'm moving in with Brad for good."

"I've been preparing myself for this," said Leon. "But I suppose it's all for the best. I can turn your room into an office."

"How heartless. Well, I'm only ten minutes away. Anyway," said Kevin airily, "the Wilshire apartment is so convenient, we probably won't open up the Malibu house until June or July."

Leon and Shane looked at each other, both of them shocked to hear such "couple" talk burbling out of Kevin's mouth. How easily Kevin had slipped into the domestic role.

"But of course, I'll still visit West Hollywood now and then," Kevin continued.

"Well, I don't mean to bring you down," said Leon, "but your mother left a message this morning. She wants to know why you haven't called. Your parents, by the way, have sold their house. They're going to live full-time in Florida."

Kevin's mood crashed. He had been avoiding his parents' calls. He checked in with them, but hadn't yet told them about Brad. Kevin found it extremely difficult to be open about his gay life with his parents, and they, of course, never brought it up, either.

He decided he would tell them he had been working more than usual, and that he'd been extremely busy. Since they were organizing their big move to Florida, he didn't think they would ask him for details. Kevin, always sentimental about New York, found it all too depressing.

"So what about your stuff?" asked Leon. "Are you going to take it with you?"

"Let me go see what's in there." Kevin hadn't been in his old room in some time. It needed dusting. The blinds were closed, and Leon must have made the bed some time ago. It was a room from another life. He opened the closet and plunged his hands in among the mouldering T-shirts. He then pulled out his best suit. Fingering it, Kevin already felt that it was passé and dingy-looking.

On the floor of the closet, his shoes were lined up so neatly that they almost seemed to be apologizing for going out of style. Kevin spied a pair of Timberland boots and tried to remember the last time he had worn them. It was kind of sad to think how these shoes had once brought him so much pleasure, how they made him feel so cool. Even proud. But now they just made him feel old. Foolish.

And there was a black cap on a top shelf, impulse-purchased at a surf shop in Venice. The words NO FEAR were inscribed across the front. Kevin pulled it down, and, for a moment, considered keeping it in his glove compartment.

Leon drifted in and stood in the door frame.

"*Some* fear is more like it," said Kevin, holding up the hat. "You want this?"

Leon shook his head. "It's more you than me."

Kevin tossed the hat into the trash.

"I better not take any of this stuff. I mean, can you imagine me trying to wear any of these getups on Brad's jet?"

"Kevin, are you sure you want to move in with Brad so soon? Because if this is all moving too fast, I can keep your room the way it is for a little longer. It's really no problem."

Kevin shut the closet door. "Thanks, Leon, but no. You go ahead and make it into an office. Get rich, and then buy a house next door to Brad's. I'll sneak over in the mornings with a gin bottle in the pocket of my housecoat. We'll watch *I Love Lucy* reruns together."

"Kevin, be serious for a minute."

"Leon. *Relax.* I know what you're getting at, but he's just another guy. A really great guy, in fact, and maybe I even love him, but for now let me keep pretending he's just an ordinary guy."

"But he's not, Kevin. He's Brad Fucking Sherwood."

"I know," mumbled Kevin in reply. "No one ever lets me forget it."

"He's a strange one," said Leon. "It's almost like, to him, being gay comes *second.* You know what I mean?"

"Look, let's not overanalyze the situation. I have to go. Do me a favor and just take whatever you want in this room and then send the rest to the Salvation Army."

Kevin pulled out a wad of hundred-dollar bills. They were crisp and powdery, difficult to count. Finally he just dug a fingernail into the stack and slapped a hefty clump into Leon's palm.

"What's all this?" asked Leon.

"The rent."

"But this is way too much," Leon protested as he painstakingly separated the bills.

"Oh, take it," Kevin insisted. "I know it's all too awful, but really, it's just Monopoly money now. Backed by the Bank of Magnet."

CHAPTER 17

As Kevin drove away from Westmount Street, he admitted to himself for the first time ever that LA really wasn't such a bad place. The sun was still out and he had a jacket meant for Spielberg in his trunk. Kewl! Feeling accomplished, he decided to head home and take a bubble bath. And home, he realized, was with Brad, especially since hearing his parents had sold the house he grew up in.

Kevin loved the Wilshire penthouse. At night, when the central air conditioning kicked in with a discreet hum, he felt like he was back in New York.

He would be especially loving tonight with Brad. He would cook Brad dinner maybe, Italian, or stop off and get some kind of kinky sex toy that they both could laugh over and then use later with deadly seriousness. Or he could rummage around and find something obscene to wear and have it on when Brad came home. Or he could ask him a question about show business. Oh, he had plenty of tricks up his sleeve, but, of course, he would do none of these things. There was no need.

The doorman took the Miata and Kevin strode through the lobby like he owned the place. On the ride up the elevator, he thought about how much he was looking forward to the summer. Summer! That's what it was all about around here. Blond hair, golden sunsets . . . *rinsing the sand out of your Speedo.*

Maybe he could convince Brad to let Leon redecorate the Malibu house. Or if too many tourists were clogging up the PCH, maybe they could open up one of the Bel Air properties. Would Brad be willing to forgo the $10,000 a month rent he had been charging for the past few years? Probably. The tenants had been getting a bargain for too long.

All he had to do was ask.

Kevin let his baggy 501's fall to the floor. One of the maids, Minerva or Innocencia, would pick them up later and whisk them away to be cleaned, fluffed, and folded. How did he ever live without daily maid service? It was a very natural thing, and not at all excessive. No more piles of sweaty gym clothes everywhere. A fresh towel every day. No more cleaning out the disposal, or finding toothpicks left in the communal building washing machine by that out-of-sorts, not-very-communicative retired postal worker back on Westmount.

Oh, for a month there, maybe they'd gone a bit overboard; Brad had hired an English butler, but the guy had too little to do and the sight of him shuffling around, looking for silver to polish, made both Kevin and Brad feel old. Kevin asked Brad to fire him, and Chester, a really rather sweet war vet (the Falklands), was gone that afternoon.

He landed on his feet, though—Jackie Collins took him in.

Padding around nude, Kevin luxuriated in the afternoon warmth. Insouciantly, as he mixed foaming moisturizer into his bath, Kevin also concluded that he deserved a short nap. He'd been working out extra hard lately and needed to let his muscles truly relax so they'd be spurred on to extra growth.

A phone rang but Kevin did not even attempt to answer it. In Brad's life, there were so many different phones, so many different ringing sounds, that Kevin never knew which extension to pick up. It didn't matter. The calls were always for Brad anyway. Only sometimes did all the ringing become irritating. Half the time, it wasn't even a phone call at all—it was just a phone ringing on a sitcom playing on TV in another room.

Lying in the tub, looking out the picture window as planes flew by practically at eye level, memories of New York flooded back. Nothing, of course, could ever equal those great days with Anthony.

The high times really began when Hot Tip Capozi bought his son a two-bedroom in that gleaming new co-op on Central Park West. It had parquet floors and glorious eastern exposures.

Anthony had been stunned when his father handed over the keys.

"I had a good year. But more than that, I'm proud of you. You're the first Capozi to go to college."

Anthony was also put on a generous allowance.

"I want you to spend all your time studying. I don't want you to have to work, or nothing. You get good grades and go to law school and then one day you'll take care of me. That's just how things work."

Anthony took the apartment without guilt, as was his right as an Italian-American prince. Hot Tip then gave the Westchester house to a cousin and moved with Janice to a gated enclave near Atlantic City. Whenever he wanted to visit his son, he hopped on a helicopter.

Anthony fell easily into the college routine, and even though he affected a rough way of speaking, he was an excellent student. Sharon came down from Tufts about once a month, but as they each became more involved in school, these visits became more and more sporadic. The camaraderie they shared with Kevin that last year in Westchester faded as their days filled up with new faces and activities. No longer playing football, Anthony took up running in Central Park to keep in shape.

Kevin's senior year of high school dragged along until the day he got an acceptance letter from NYU in the mail. When he showed it to his parents, they rejected the idea out of hand; if he wanted to keep going to school, they said, he should go to the community college nearby and live at home.

But Kevin had caught *Fame* on the midday movie and knew he needed to be in New York City where there were other people like him. Luckily, his older sister Connie dropped by one day and announced she was getting married to Ralph. Patrick and Gina objected to that idea, too; they thought she didn't know enough about life. But Connie Malloy was tough and she laughed when she told them she wasn't asking for their approval, she just thought she'd let them know. When Patrick and Gina met Ralph, and saw that he was getting somewhere, they began planning the wedding. In the resulting hysteria, they gave in to Kevin's crazy NYU idea too, just to have a little peace.

Kevin and Anthony had let their friendship dwindle, but one day Anthony called Kevin's house and invited him up to see his new apartment. On the train into the city, Kevin told himself he was just going to see an old friend, no big deal. He had learned how to sweep feelings away by assuring himself that his life had not yet started. He was just in a phase, a time of life that didn't count. Images of naked men would intrude upon his thoughts, okay, so what? Maybe a time would come when he wouldn't want to do those things. Then his real life, whatever that would be, could begin.

Anthony greeted Kevin like nothing had ever happened between them, and as he showed Kevin the apartment, they both began to think that everything was going to be all right. In fact, since Kevin was going to be attending NYU, it finally dawned on them that their New York City dreams had actually come true. They spent the day tearing up the streets, just like they used to with Sharon, only this time they felt like they belonged.

When Kevin returned to Westchester that night he felt more hopeful than ever that his life was going to work out. But when he turned the light out in his room, he grimly realized that his lust for Anthony had not dimmed.

Anthony, however, hadn't seemed interested. Hailing a cab, or running into a deli to pick up some meatball sandwiches, Anthony already seemed like a real city slicker. The whole afternoon he had talked about Sharon and about other girls he had met. Kevin could not hope to catch up. For one thing, he would not be living in a beautiful apartment like Anthony's. He'd just received notice he'd be in a dorm, sharing a room with twin beds.

Spring didn't happen that year, only summer. Kevin continued toiling away, finding himself unable to get out of bed before noon on weekend mornings. He didn't attend his graduation or buy a class ring. His sister married Ralph in a big, gaudy ceremony, and that was the only topic of conversation at home that year. When it came time to move Kevin into his dorm that fall, his parents seemed relieved to have two out of their three kids out of the house. After they dropped him off, his father declared that it was the last time he was ever going to drive into Manhattan.

Kevin's courage faltered when they sped off. His dorm room was dark and cramped. The dirty windows faced a brick wall close enough to touch. Tiny scribbles of graffiti were penned into the cement between the cinder blocks.

He called Anthony from a pay phone in the lobby.

"Get your ass up here!" Anthony commanded. "There's a subway stop two blocks away."

On the packed uptown train, a yuppie-ish guy of about thirty, in a pinstripe suit, carrying a briefcase, and wearing wing tips, kept backing his ass into Kevin as they swayed and rocked along the tracks. Kevin became hard and the man, noticing, finally just settled his butt right up against Kevin's crotch, getting comfortable for the rest of the ride.

At Forty-second Street a group of commuters got off and another, larger group got on. Kevin and the yuppie were pushed deeper into the car. Forced to turn around, the yuppie adroitly placed his cock against Kevin's. Observing an instinctive protocol, neither looked at the other, and when the wheezing train started up again, jerkily, there was an exquisite friction.

With his eye on the man's wrist, where it clutched a metal strap, Kevin made a decision. He detached his own hand from the bar—and plunged it straight into the yuppie's pocket.

The pocket was deep, damp, and pilled. At the bottom were keys and some loose change. Kevin glanced briefly at the yuppie and saw that he seemed completely unfazed.

Kevin grabbed a handful of yuppie cock and held on. As the train gained speed along a straightaway, Kevin massaged and squeezed, tighter then looser. Finally, after one particularly rude yank, hot jizz seeped through the thin cotton.

Which was perfect timing because they had just arrived at Seventy-second and Broadway, Kevin's stop.

The yuppie followed Kevin up an odorous stairwell and out to the bright street. In the middle of a windy traffic island, with crowds swarming around them, he finally spoke. "Hey, kid, you made me miss my stop."

"Sorry," said Kevin.

"I was on my way to Penn Station. I live out on the Island. Want to come back to my place so's I can finish you off?"

Kevin noticed that the man's suit did not hang well; the arm holes were too tight. And a few tufts of hair poked out of the back of his shirt collar. Then Kevin looked down and saw that the man's wing tips were battered and unpolished. The soles were cracked with old winter street salt.

"No."

Kevin turned and joined a crowd crossing the street. The yuppie hesitated, but then chased Kevin down just as the light was changing.

"Hey, why not? You seemed into it."

"Yeah, well, I'm not." Kevin started walking faster.

"We could go to your place," hissed the man. "I could fuck you!"

A few pedestrians hurrying by heard this and threw interested glances in their direction. Kevin felt a mixture of scorn and horror. How could anyone's need be so base? No way was he going to have anyone witness this. He broke into a run.

• • •

Anthony, barefoot, greeted Kevin at the elevator with a frozen margarita.

"You ever had one of these?"

Kevin, upset about the business he had started on the subway, shook his head, but gulped down half of it anyway.

"Tequila," said Anthony. "Made in Mexico. Come here and look at the fucking bottle."

They went into Anthony's large kitchen.

"That shriveled-up little thing at the bottom is a fucking worm," Anthony told him. "Can you believe that shit? You're supposed to eat it."

"What for?"

"How the fuck should I know? I ain't no damn crazy Mexican. Hey, wanna try one of those Mexican places over on Columbus Avenue? There's a new one on every corner."

Kevin had never been to a Mexican restaurant. His family didn't eat out. Why go out when you can get better food at home for a fraction of the cost, his father would say as he ate dinner on a tray in front of the TV.

In Anthony's living room, a long window framed a twilight view of Central Park. The sun was setting, and lights were coming on in the grand buildings across the park on Fifth Avenue. Monstrous gray clouds sped cinematically through a smoky-pink sky.

"Can you believe this view?" marveled Anthony as they settled onto leather couches in the living room.

"It's beautiful," said Kevin. "You're so lucky."

"Well, Hot Tip came through, as always. Most people live like animals in this city."

If Kevin hadn't accepted another margarita from Anthony, perhaps he wouldn't have had the courage to bring up their oldest piece of business. Or perhaps he would have. The grope on the subway, combined with the now-purple sunset and the greenish drinks, had left Kevin feeling raw, randy, and wanting to be touched.

He got up and stood in front of Anthony. "You have this whole place to yourself and a lot of new stuff and, you know, that's great. But I've never forgiven you for that day, Anthony."

"What are you talking about? That's all in the past."

"Not for me."

Anthony considered Kevin's words. "So that's what all this shit has been about? That's why we stopped hanging around together?"

"Yep," Kevin answered. "And maybe you don't remember, but you said you would do me. Well, it's time."

"You little perv," said Anthony, a grin creeping across his face. "Why didn't you want to do it back then?"

"I didn't think it was right. I was thinking of Sharon. She's always been really nice to me. And if you don't want to do it now, that's okay. But I don't think we can be friends if you don't. I mean, it's no big deal. You live up here and I'm down in the Village—we'd probably never see each other anyway."

"God, you make a big deal out of everything."

"You might even enjoy it," Kevin suggested. "I think those were your words."

"I get it. Now I understand. You're a homo."

"Yep," said Kevin. "I am. I wish to God I was anything else, but I can't help myself."

"Well, fuck, then maybe I am too," said Anthony. "I guess it's time I found out."

Anthony took the drink out of Kevin's hand and put it on the coffee table. "How do you want to do this? You've been waiting for this a long time, so you call the shots."

"It doesn't matter."

"Oh, yes, it does matter. I want everything to be the way you want it," said Anthony. "The truth is, I've wanted this to happen for a long time, too."

"But you're not a homo, Anthony. You can't be."

"Why the fuck not? You are."

"It's not right. I mean, you're a jock, you're going to be a lawyer, and you have Sharon."

"I love Sharon. But I think about that day all the time. To be fair to her, I should find out what it means."

"God, Anthony. I didn't know."

Anthony got up and gazed out at the awesome blackness of Central Park. Taxis were speeding south, heading for the theater district. Soft, muffled honks could be heard over the hum of air conditioning.

Kevin joined him and looked down at the street scene below. The window was cold to to the touch.

"I met a homo on the subway," Kevin said dully, "right before I came up here. This city is crawling with them. Why don't you go with one of them?"

"I don't care about them. I can't do it with just anyone. When I think about it, I only think of you."

Kevin had always believed that Anthony was special. He had a sports car, lots of money in his pocket, a father who gave him anything he wanted. Well, if this is what Anthony wanted, he was going to have it and it was going to be offered for free. Kevin wanted Anthony to see how easy it was to give up, how completely without value it was. Kevin unbuttoned his shirt and pulled it off. He removed the rest of his clothes in a completely matter-of-fact way, and when he was finally naked, he neatly folded his pants over a Maurice Villency morris chair.

Across the way, over on Fifth Avenue, a man with a high-powered telescope came upon the scene and focused in. Through the plate-glass window he saw the completely nude Kevin and the fully dressed Anthony. He marveled at his good fortune. His seven-hour vigil was about to pay off. Too bad Kevin had other plans.

"I think I'll go into the bedroom."

Anthony, still sipping his drink, watched Kevin depart. He was no longer a kid in a hurry, a jock on the go.

The last time Sharon had come into the city, they had made love expertly, but Anthony did so with a sense of detachment, as if he were observing the act from above. Afterward, Sharon raced out to catch her train. All that night, Anthony's heart splintered and cracked with loneliness.

Kevin pulled the down comforter off the bed and then lay flat on his back, splaying himself like a human X. When Anthony opened the door, a thin beam of milky-white light traveled across Kevin's smooth chest.

Anthony took off his clothes and then slipped onto the cold sheets, careful not to touch any part of Kevin's body. He looked down at Kevin's pale flesh and tried to figure out a way to begin. After a time, he picked up Kevin's cock with two fingers and guided the tip into his mouth.

Kevin responded immediately. Blood filled his thick penis, and as it expanded, it bounced up and tapped Anthony lightly in his face.

Anthony, intent on discovering the secret of himself, stared at it with wonder.

"Suck it."

Anthony looked up and saw that Kevin's head was thrown back and his eyes were tightly shut. His mouth was clamped into a grimace and his hands gripped the sheets.

Anthony flicked the tip of Kevin's cock and then licked underneath. Pulling on wet hairs with his lips, he discovered tastes and textures he had never before imagined but knew he'd been seeking. He became entranced by the feel of Kevin's skin. He became deeply involved in the mystery of Kevin's vulnerable pubic bone.

"Suck it!"

Anthony did not understand what the rush was. He believed these things were done slowly. Still, Kevin was in charge. He had set the terms and Anthony believed this act was for Kevin's pleasure, not his own. With a mounting sense of wonder, he placed Kevin's cock back into the groove of his tongue.

Kevin's hands shot up and clamped on to Anthony's shoulders. Egged on, Anthony hunched up on his knees so that he could burrow in deeper. When he felt Kevin's hands on his stomach, Anthony's gargantuan cock twitched threateningly. Almost by accident, he moved it over Kevin's face.

Kevin took it in his mouth and a feathery sensation rippled along Anthony's stomach and ass. Soon, every inch of his skin felt charged and electric. They discovered a rhythm and their bodies became warm and slick. At one point, Kevin gagged, but when Anthony tried to ease up on him and give him some space to breathe, Kevin drew him in even closer.

Their torsos straining, they began to feel a gathering from deep within, but they did not let go. Mauling each other, each eviscerating the other's throat, they discovered there was no turning back. Life as they knew it was ending. As they willingly dropped themselves over the side and into the void, they held on like two sleek animals, each suffocating as he devoured the other, knowing it was their only chance to forge a rebirth of their souls.

Kevin, with hot pre-come searing his lips, wanted to weep at the horrible rightness of it all.

Anthony went for Kevin's tongue and tried to own it with his teeth. Kevin, struck by the brutality of two men kissing, swirled his own tongue madly. Out of breath and defenseless, he caught sight of Anthony worshiping him with his eyes. At that moment, their misaimed, fibrous loads exploded between their stomachs.

But their exploration was far from complete. They needed to feel each other's face with every part of their bodies. They needed to tangle their legs up until they were bound in a knot. They needed to make each other know who they really were. They separated only once, and only for a second—to turn a light on, and so they could witness themselves in each other's eyes.

They came again and again, first Anthony, with Kevin watching, and then Kevin. Finally, withdrawing themselves from the dream, they rolled off the bed and stumbled into the kitchen, where they swilled tequila directly from the bottle. The effort weakened them and they slid into an embrace on the chilly floor.

"I love you," said Anthony. "I always have. You are the one."

Kevin, slumped against the cold metal door of the dishwasher, his face twitching with secret smiles, looked up—just in time to see the worm in the tequila bottle complete a slow-motion back flip.

CHAPTER 18

Shane had taken to the gym with a vengeance, and his efforts were *totally* paying off. His physique became toned, but then he embarked on a weight-gaining regimen, trying out all the different muscle powders. Eventually, even Greg, the desk attendant at the Athletic Connection who rarely spoke to anyone, took notice.

"I see you're taking your routines pretty seriously," Greg commented one afternoon after observing that Shane had been to the gym eight days in a row.

"I think I've plateaued," said Shane. "I can't seem to put on any more mass."

"I know how to fix that," Greg stated. "I have a guy who gets the best stuff from Tijuana."

"Protein powder?" asked Shane.

"No, you dizzy queen, steroids."

Shane looked wide-eyed at Greg and leaned across the counter. "But aren't they really bad for you?" he whispered.

"Nah, they work great. I used to be smaller than you. Everyone used to kick sand in my face."

Greg engorged his neck with blood and then flexed each of his fat tits in a herky-jerky, left-right motion. Then he held an arm over his head and pumped a bicep. Shane saw that Greg's arms were huge, what the magazines called "big guns."

"I can set you up if you want," Greg told him. "It will cost you, but it's worth it. You'll be gigantic in four weeks. You may throw up a little at first, but when you get used to it, you'll crave it. The stuff I use is really pure so you don't have to worry about 'roid rage."

A few months ago, Greg would not have even talked to Shane—and now here he was sharing confidential body-building secrets. Shane felt like he had finally been welcomed into the club.

"And after a few weeks, maybe we could arrange a private pose down," Greg continued with a promising leer. "Just the two of us."

So Shane withdrew some money from his credit-union account and Greg, after taking a hefty profit on the deal, invited him over to set him up with the works. Shane was thrilled when they arrived at Greg's one-room apartment in Hollywood. Ornately framed pictures of bodybuilders hung on each wall.

On the bed was a black Cabbage Patch doll.

"This is Cinnamon," said Greg, holding up the doll. "Now watch, it's really easy. Just take this needle and jam it in my ass. See how I'm doing it with Cinnamon? You do me and then I'll do you. Just find a spot you like."

Greg handed the hypodermic needle to Shane. He then pulled his pants down. His ass featured a mealy collection of pock marks.

"Hey!" snapped Greg, twisting around, his big ass hanging out. "Pay attention! Just jam it in as far as you can. But be careful. It has to get through the muscle. If you do it wrong, the needle could break off. I hate when that happens."

Shane put his hand on Greg's left cheek and steadied himself.

"That's right, good technique. Come to Papa."

Shane plunged it in, getting it right the first time, thrilled to discover he possessed a skill.

"OOOH," yelled Greg. "Yeaaaahh!"

Greg hopped around a bit and then pulled up his pants. "That is it, man, better than sex! 'Roid rage!" he screamed. "Now your turn." Greg unwrapped a fresh needle.

Shane was nervous but tried not to show it. He sheepishly pulled his workout shorts down a few inches. "Not too hard," he implored.

Greg got down on his haunches and then yanked Shane's shorts down around his ankles. Greg then took a deep, unnecessary slurp up Shane's crack. "Virgin flesh!" he cried.

Shane, shocked by Greg's gesture, turned around, but before he had time to ponder the deeper meaning of the lick, Greg jammed the needle in hard.

Shane screamed.

Greg's neighbors, not unfamiliar with random, piercing screams (although normally in the middle of the night), found themselves impressed—by the volume, the pitch, the sheer *timbre* of Shane's wail. As screams in that neighborhood went, this one expressed *true agony* and surely merited a score of eight, quite possibly a nine, on the neighborhood scream meter.

"Beautiful ass, man!" Greg exclaimed. "Just beautiful!"

Shane kept up this ritual for a few weeks.

Oh, at first he was horrified to discover that sometimes there was a little problem with blood in his stools, and sitting down was a bore, but Greg told him not to worry about it. As a bonus, Greg threw in some glycerine suppositories, no charge. And as for liver scarring, well, it was a small price to pay, wasn't it?

Shane was bowled over by all the new attention he received at the gym. Skinny doctors and lawyers moved out of his way, and huge guys who made porn out in the valley asked him to spot. He felt deeply honored.

His neck gained three inches and he had to order all new shirts for his flight-attendant uniform. On the plane, he could no longer work in first class—he found himself too clumsy to navigate the tiny galley. So he gave up and became a "coach roach." And since the people in the back didn't pay much for their tickets, he felt free to abuse them.

"I know I ordered a special meal," said one harried passenger, a stressed-out marketing consultant in her mid-thirties, "but I'm really starving. If you have any chicken left over, I'd really appreciate it if I could have one. There was so much traffic on the way to the airport!"

"You ordered a fruit plate and that's what you're getting!" yelled Shane, slamming it down.

The flight attendant on the other side of the cabin ratted on him to his supervisor after the trip, saying he was rude to the passengers.

So Shane went out to the employee parking lot and slashed her tires.

Shane became obsessed with his looks, spending hours in front of the mirror, examining every muscle group. He shaved his body hair and oiled himself before going to bed at night. He could not get his crew cut short enough, so one day he just completely shaved his head. All he cared about was muscle, and his new friend Greg cheered him on every step of the way.

But as his body became more and more grotesquely proportioned,

Shane found more fault with it. He worked out even harder. He power-lifted in an attempt to jump-start new growth. He met with Greg regularly; they could not wait to shoot each other up. Once inside Greg's apartment, they would rip down each other's pants.

Shane began to have insomnia and he would lie in bed at night thinking only of deltoids, calf muscles, and pecs. When he felt high, he would dream about the great life he could have on the bodybuilding circuit.

And when he felt low, he would recall the words spray-painted across his high-school locker: TONGUE MY SHITTER, FAGGOT.

He would then run to the mirror, paranoid that he hadn't worked out hard enough.

He kept his TV on twenty-four hours a day. One night, having abandoned his old values, he tuned into Maureen Hogan. She was interviewing men who had undergone plastic surgery. The last guest she brought out was a man in a curly black wig and dark sunglasses.

"So tell me," began Maureen in her rabid way, "what have you had done?"

"Maureen, last year, after my divorce, I decided that in today's environment, I needed an edge in the dating world. So I went to a doctor and had a penis enlargement."

There were gasps and groans from the audience.

"I added two inches in length and an inch and a half in girth."

The man introduced his teenage fiancée to the audience and a question-and-answer segment ensued. Shane sat riveted until the credits rolled and then raced into his bathroom. Standing on top of the toilet, he pulled down his Chicago Bulls pajama bottoms and looked critically at his own penis in the mirror. Now that his legs were huge, the insides of his thighs chafed and were red and sore. His penis, nestled snugly and compactly between them, was the only aspect of Shane left that was still perky.

On the spot, Shane decided to get the operation. He would find out where to get it and just do it. He would get the airline to pay for it! It would make him a better flight attendant. Shane went to bed that night and slept well, thinking that he had finally found the last detail that would make him okay.

CHAPTER 19

"So it's decided," said Rob, from the phone in his pool cabana, "the fifteenth, a Saturday night, an old-fashioned party. It will just be about fun, and I'll make that clear on the invitations. No networking, no suits, or you'll be thrown right out."

"Okay," Brad agreed. "That will coincide nicely with the announcement. Everyone will know by Friday morning. MSNBC will have it first."

"Oh, then maybe I should host a sit-down dinner before for Midge and Sy. And I think I should invite Elinor Graham and a few others. I owe them. Then we'll ship them out by eleven, strip all the waiters down, and move the party outside by the pool. Oh, God, the details. I'll really have to rush to make this happen. I'll get Kim to bring in a few new faces from the gym and then we'll supplement those with a few strippers. I could fly in that really famous one from Miami! The upper-management velvet-mafia types will appreciate that. Oy, these up-and-coming youngsters work much too hard."

"Okay," Brad said, putting his feet up on his desk in the Wilshire penthouse. "We'll bring back the old days."

"Some of my backup skaters will be in town, too, so I'll invite them. I can show them a little benevolence and at the same time write the whole thing off. It's so crucial that a party work on multiple levels."

Brad got off the phone. He had not told Rob that his privatization plans were coming together, but Rob, an old shrewdy, had figured it all out from just a few clues.

Brad leaned back in his chair and clicked off the remaining details in his mind. There were only one or two items left, but those would be taken care of by Fenny Atkinson. Soon, his life would be completely his own. He would never have to answer to a board member. The truly powerful of the world would take his calls. He could call on the president of the United States if he wanted, and Brad would.

Money *does* buy happiness, Brad decided as he surveyed the terrain, the Santa Monica Mountains enshrouded in smog, and whoever said that it didn't was the biggest con artist of all time.

Brad got up and roamed around the vast apartment, on a safari for Kevin. He heard water splashing in one of the spa-sized bathrooms. Brad cracked the door and saw Kevin in a shower cap, luxuriously soaping his broad chest under the heavy jets. A few months before, Brad would have felt compelled to strip down and join him, but now he just took a few moments to watch. It was an amazing and beautiful sight.

My lover is taking a shower, thought Brad, and he felt as though another item on his list could be checked off. Everything was in place. Every second of his life had been refined so this moment could happen. With wonder at his own ability to plan and execute, he realized that one of the high points of his life would be when he introduced Kevin to his parents. Brad had found someone to be with and that was all they wanted. They really didn't give a fig about the rest of it.

Brad knew Kevin could spend hours in the bathroom, so he didn't disturb him. After scribbling off a short note, he took off for Magnet headquarters.

He rode down in the elevator carrying only his phone and his address book. Other than the occasional bottle of water, he rarely carried anything else. His passport was kept locked in a safe, as was his driver's license. When his plane landed at foreign airports, he was given a "courtesy," which meant he never filled out a customs form, never had his bags searched. He got the same VIP treatment when he returned to America.

There was never any need for him to step out into air that was not rarefied and, now that he had his edge back, he believed life could only get better and better. So, as the elevator descended, he made a snap decision. He dialed the phone in the apartment that he had installed exclusively for Kevin's use and left a message.

"Hi, it's me . . . I left you a note but I just had a thought. I know you're busy today, in fact I think you have a shoot, but I miss you already. I'm going into my office but I want to ask you a favor. I don't like the idea of you driving that Miata anymore. If you go out today, take the Range Rover. Spare keys are in a bowl on the console table in my office. And free up tomorrow morning. We need to buy you a new car. I want you in a Hummer, now that you're mine. Does that Miata even have air bags?"

By now Brad was striding into the limousine. Jeremy knew that when the boss was on the phone he shouldn't speak. But when he heard the word Miata, he knew Brad was talking to Kevin. Jeremy slammed the car door a little too forcefully.

Brad, jarred out of his buoyant, lovesick state, noticed that the dividing window to the front seat was open. A frisson of irritation visited him. "All right, now I really have to go. Oh, and one other thing. My friend Rob wants to give us a party. We just decided that it will be on the fifteenth, so that's to give you a little warning. And you'll finally get to meet my parents. Okay. Have a beautiful day."

Brad ended the connection and then seethed a bit. Jeremy was getting to be a pain. He seemed even more temperamental and possessive than usual. He was a slavish employee, and that was a good thing overall, but what did he expect of him? Had Jeremy asked, Brad would have found him a new job, something with some career potential, but he never did. Maybe it was time to ease him out. He was tired of his eavesdropping and disapproving glances.

"The office, Jeremy."

"I know, Mr. S. I've had the car ready for over an hour."

Brad looked at the back of Jeremy's head. Jeremy had been around for too long. You're history, thought Brad. And then he flipped through his address book and made another call.

CHAPTER 20

Kevin had always been competent enough as a photographer, but his new work was, for the first time, actually beginning to show a creative spark. Since Brad got him the assignments, and the money didn't matter, Kevin could do and say what he wanted. Imperious and full of attitude, everyone soon recognized Kevin as cutting edge. On the set, he became more confident, and soon he was in the lovely position of being able to turn down jobs—which, of course, only made him more sought after.

Kevin liked his new life, too. He loved the views from the apartment. He loved the twice-weekly delivery of plants and flowers. He loved the private jet—though he didn't like traveling in it so much as he loved the fact of it. The ceiling on the GIV was fine for Brad, but Kevin thought it was too low.

Even though Brad had offered Kevin a beautiful weekend in New York, Kevin had no intention of going. It was too risky. Maybe Hot Tip Capozi still had a contract out on him or maybe he didn't, but the whole situation was a scab that Kevin did not want to pick at. He would tell Brad all about it soon, though. Kevin, like everyone else, had come to believe that Brad could fix any problem.

Kevin never did adjust to life in a college dorm. First of all, his roommate was from Bangor, Maine, of all places. Kevin instantly, and altogether unfairly, pegged him as a hick. The guy was not good looking, so Kevin didn't care whether he was straight or gay, but when he found out that the guy was majoring in *German,* and wanted to be a *teacher,* Kevin simply stopped speaking to him.

Campus life, such as it was, did not suit Kevin either. He and Anthony had become completely involved with each other, and the city served as a back-drop to all their good times. With Anthony's allowance, there was always a fantastic time to be had. They held court at nightclubs, went to all the new restaurants, and joined a gym together because that seemed the thing to do. Hot Tip gave Anthony a new car, a Beemer, and paid for a garage two blocks away. He wanted his son to be able to get out of town now and then.

Anthony asked Sharon to come down to the city. He needed to tell her something and didn't want to do it over the phone. Over dinner at Mary's in the Village, Anthony told Sharon he was gay. He was proud that Kevin was his lover, and he wanted her to know. Sharon was rather floored, but told him she appreciated his honesty. Flush from a Psych 101 class, she found Anthony's admission somewhat fascinating, so she was able to hold back her tears until she was safely tucked into a cab.

Sensible and no-nonsense, Sharon would not pine over Anthony; he was her first love, though, and it had been real. Privately, however, she began to worry. She didn't think Anthony would have an easy time of it—and God help him if Hot Tip ever found out.

Hot Tip was always around. He would drop by Anthony's apartment whenever he needed to come into the city, and would often find Kevin there. The three of them would then hit an expensive Italian restaurant on the Upper East Side. Hot Tip was well known everywhere. Kevin loved getting into a limo with him and hearing about his latest grapplings with business partners. There was always a lot of talk about unions, casinos, horses, and the cement trade. The city was experiencing one of its periodic building booms and Hot Tip had a pipeline into all the product necessary to raise the new skyscrapers.

The days when Hot Tip would give his son a bag of quarters were long gone; he had moved up into the big leagues. Now Hot Tip scheduled lunches downtown with politicians, cavorted in the Caribbean with financiers. Once, while Kevin and Anthony were having dinner with him and Janice, Kevin heard a man at the next table whisper to his wife: *"That guy is the number-one influence peddler in the tri-state area."*

After these dinners, Hot Tip would pull out a thick roll of bills and slip them to Anthony. "Here, take some walking-around money. Keep up your studies."

Hot Tip believed in friendship, so he took an interest in Kevin's future, too. He tried to tell Kevin to focus on school, to get good grades, and to start planning for his career before he graduated. He asked Kevin what his father thought he should do.

"My father says I should just graduate and then he'd try to help me pass the civil-service exam, because that way you never starve," said Kevin between mouthfuls of veal.

"Well, your father has a point. But you need to be in a position where the government money comes in regular. That way you can do people favors. Otherwise it's a big waste of time."

"My father sells handicap-parking stickers on the side," said Kevin. "Does that count?"

"Small potatoes," scoffed Hot Tip.

A week later Kevin went home to Westchester on the train and had dinner with his family. After they ate, his father went into the living room to watch TV.

"Come into the kitchen and talk to me while I do the dishes," Gina suggested to Kevin. She wanted to make a decision about all the leftover sauce. "I could give you some to take back or I could just freeze it," she said.

"I don't want to carry it all the way back into the city on the train."

"Next time you come with Anthony and I'll fill up the trunk of his car."

"Sure, Ma."

"How is Anthony?"

"He's good."

"Tell him he's always welcome here. It was so sad that he grew up without a mother."

"He does okay. Hot Tip watches out for him."

"So you call him Hot Tip to his face? That's not respect."

"I respect him."

"Well . . . be careful. You're half Irish and you never know with the Irish."

"Jeez, Ma, what's that supposed to mean?"

"The Irish have a temper," explained Gina. "They do things without thinking. My life would have been easier if I had married Italian. Not to say your father isn't a good man. But I wish that my children were full Italian. It's my only regret. But I was young and your father was so handsome."

"Full Italian," Kevin repeated, rolling his eyes. "Come on, Ma. That kind of thing doesn't matter."

Gina ripped off a sheet of tinfoil. "Family is everything to an Italian.

And now your sister is married to an Irishman and the line will be diluted even further. It's all my fault." She collapsed into tears.

"Jeez, Ma, I have to get to the train station."

Gina tore herself away from her pots of sauce, her ladles, and grabbed him. "Take care of yourself in the city, Kevin. It's not the same place it was. It's not safe. I don't like the thought of you being there. The other day I watched the Puerto Rican Day parade on the news. Who ever thought such a thing could happen!"

"I got to go," said Kevin, untangling himself from his mother's hug. He went into the hallway and poked his head into the living room. His father, reclined on the couch with his hand on the remote, was watching a rerun of *Hart to Hart.*

"Okay, Dad. I'm going."

Patrick took his eyes off the TV for a moment. "Let me just see the end of this show and I'll drive you to the station."

"Dad, the last train is at eleven, so I have to leave now."

"You'll make it in time. That reminds me—I have to fill the gas tank on the way. I always go to the Power Test station in Port Chester now. They have bootleg gas, so it's a lot cheaper. Comes in at night from Connecticut."

Patrick seemed deeply absorbed in his program. Kevin was anxious to be back in the city, walking the dark night streets. He had plans to meet up with Anthony. They were going to a private party at a club called the Tunnel. He wanted to get back to Anthony's apartment, change, and have a smart cocktail before leaving. That was their routine. With any luck, they'd arrive at the club by two.

"I'll go now, Dad. I'll hitch."

"Just wait a few more minutes," said Patrick.

"Nah, I'll go now." Kevin went out the back door, closing it quietly.

Finished with her kitchen chores, Gina went into the living room with a tray of cookies.

"Where's Kevin?"

"He left."

"Couldn't you drive him to the station?"

"I just wanted to watch the end of my show. He couldn't wait."

"So you let him hitchhike?"

"Yeah. It's okay. He's grown up now. He's gonna do what he's gonna do."

"Well, I'll go after him. He can't have gotten far."

"Let him go, Gina, he's grown up now. Stop worrying. When I was his age do you think anyone ever gave me a ride?"

"Your family didn't even have a car!"

Hot Tip Capozi was a man not to be trifled with. Everyone knew this. In Hot Tip's world, cement shoes were not a joke; they were an integral aspect of doing business. No blood, no DNA, no hassle, and, really, no drama. Just plop 'em over the side. No muss, no fuss—the way everyone liked it.

Now, as is often the case with these hard guys, they keep a soft spot reserved for family. There was nothing Hot Tip would not give his son, and there was no one of whom he was prouder. He was so impressed that his son got good grades. His colleagues in the cement world, in Atlantic City, and in "the families" were impressed, too. They had kids who had watched *The Godfather* one too many times and wound up dealing crack. The families knew Hot Tip had a son who was studying to be a lawyer and they all respected that. God knew there was always room for another lawyer.

So anything Anthony wanted, he got, and he always shared with Kevin. In the old days, when they were just a couple of working teenagers at Macy's, they were sort of on equal footing. But there was no pretense anymore. Hot Tip, getting up there, felt Anthony Jr. deserved "the whole cannoli cake." Every week, more and more money, always cash, in *bundles,* was sent over. One of Hot Tip's goombah minions dropped it off.

Kevin, always at Anthony's side, was swept up in the grooming process. There were lavish meals, limos, the latest electronic equipment, clothes, and orchestra seats to all the shows. Kevin made no new friends. All his free time was devoted to Anthony, because that was the way Anthony liked it.

But Kevin still didn't like living in his dorm. His roommate was a slob who seemed never to do a load of laundry. Kevin finally told Anthony he wanted to move in with him, full-time.

"I want you to live with me, you know that," said Anthony, "but I think there could be some problems."

Slumming, they went to have a slice of pizza at Ray's on Bleecker.

"Come on," said Kevin, "we don't have to tell anyone."

"Shut up a sec and listen," Anthony retorted. "I got this cousin. I never see him, but they just found out he's gay and he's totally fucked. They don't trust him any more. He's been cut out. I don't think he's going to last, either. He's scared shitless and knows too much."

"How do you know all this?"

"My father told me a few weeks ago. We were having dinner on the East Side with some of his people. My cousin Petey, he was always a little *schtoonod,* always with the pinkie rings. Well, it all came out. Dumb fuck—he was shacking up with some waiter."

"No one is going to find out about us," Kevin said. "We don't act like fags."

"I wouldn't care if they did. But it might create a problem for Hot Tip. That's why you can't move in with me. It's okay to hang around, but you just can't move in."

"I don't see why I should have to pay for a dorm if I never sleep there anyway."

"Listen," Anthony replied hotly. "Don't ever think like a small-timer around me. That dorm legitimizes our whole setup. You go to school downtown, I go to school uptown, and ain't it nice—two friends from the old neighborhood. This is not about playing house, you know!"

"All right," said Kevin.

"Everything I have I owe to my father. Don't forget it. And don't use that word *fag!* That's not what we are. I'm proud of who I am, and who I sleep with is nobody's fucking business. I don't answer to anyone. So don't talk that shit around me."

Wow. Anthony had called him a small-timer. That stung.

Now that they both knew the score, Kevin and Anthony adjusted their arrangement so they could keep living life on easy street. They acted straight, and the bags of money kept coming in regularly. The years of school flew by, no one caught on to anything, and Anthony made a seamless transition to law school. To celebrate, his father rented a yacht so Anthony could invite a bunch of friends for a tour of the Caribbean. He and Kevin and a few others flew down and spent ten days cruising in style. They brought along some cool girls for the sake of appearances.

When Kevin graduated, Hot Tip came through for his son's best friend and found him a rent-controlled apartment in SoHo. It was the deal of the century. No one would make any money on it, but it was an apartment that people would sell their flimsy little souls for.

"Yeah, if you're going to be some kind of creative type," Hot Tip declared, "this is the neighborhood you need to be in."

"This is incredible," said Kevin, after signing the lease, "I can't thank you enough."

"It's nothing. Just a favor for a friend of my son. Don't even think about it. We'll move you up into the two-bedroom on the top floor as soon as the old guy up there kicks."

Kevin's rent was less than eighty dollars a month. The whole thing was a joke. It was like living for free, and it was in a fantastic location. He was surrounded by art galleries, hot new restaurants owned by movie stars, and crowds of fascinating, beautifully dressed sophisticates.

Sometimes Anthony would drive down to SoHo from the Upper West Side and he and Kevin would get a frantic urge to get out of town. The easiest place to go was to Atlantic City. Anthony didn't like to gamble, but if he and Kevin drove into Atlantic City and dropped a dime, it was a favor for his father. Spreading cash around always looked good, so he and Kevin took trips there every other month or so. They'd play a few tables, not caring if they won or lost, and then go take a steam bath. Later, they'd order up room service and watch movies on Spectravision.

This was their favorite time. They'd lounge around the room playing TV keno between frequent bouts of sex. When the maids came to clean, Anthony would go for a three-mile run. Kevin would remain behind, finding it oddly soothing to sit off to the side and watch the maids strip the beds.

Hot Tip's ladyfriend Janice had an aunt and uncle down from Buffalo for a few days. Wanting to get them out of his hair, Hot Tip drove over to the Emperor's Retreat Hotel one Saturday morning, hoping to palm them off for the rest of the weekend.

As always, Hot Tip asked for the manager, and a Mr. Colabella quickly appeared. "An honor, Mr. Capozi, an honor," he said, effusively. "How may we be of service?"

"Well, I have a client that I wanted to introduce to the hotel, and I was hoping we could set him and his wife up in a suite for tonight."

"Of course. That can be arranged immediately. Will they be needing transportation to the property? A limousine? A helicopter?"

"No, I'll take care of that."

"Fine, Mr. Capozi. Let me just check on availability in our new computer."

Mr. Colabella entered a series of keystrokes and came up with a record of recent Capozi gaming activity. There had been some slot play at 5:47 and at 9:12 the night before, and then half an hour at the blackjack table. There was also an hour at the roulette wheel. It was an amateur's evening, hardly enough play to warrant the comping of the suite, the limo, and all the room service, but Mr. Colabella was not about to tell that to Hot Tip.

"I see here that your son is currently occupying the Hadrian Suite, Mr. Capozi. It says that he will be checking out tomorrow."

Hot Tip had not been aware that Anthony had come to Atlantic City for the weekend. What good luck. The weekend would not be a total loss if he could see his son.

"Yes, my son is upstairs. Can you put my client in another available suite?"

"That should not be a problem."

"How's my son playing?"

"I am happy to report that he is slightly ahead of the house."

"He don't like to lose, my son. You know, why don't you give me a key to his room. I think I'll take him out to breakfast."

"Okay. Let me just finish putting in the reservation for your client and then I will cut you a key to your son's suite."

"Fine."

Hot Tip hadn't seen Anthony in a month and was looking forward to catching up. Janice and her hick relatives could wait. Let 'em linger over the Entenmann's coffee cake at home for another hour or so. Hot Tip was pleased to see Anthony taking advantage of the suite. And he was even more pleased to hear his son was beating the house. Anthony had some levelheaded ways—stepping away from the table, quitting while he was ahead—astonishing behavior in the son of a don.

Hot Tip knew the Hadrian Suite was on the top floor, at the end of the hall. Ionic columns made of plaster, in a state of faux-advanced decay and lit from underneath with red and yellow lights, framed a double-width doorway wide enough to slide a grand piano through. It was a room that was too good for Janice's hick relatives from Buffalo, but it was the right room for the son of Hot Tip Capozi.

Hot Tip knocked a few times, wondering if Anthony was still asleep, wondering who his son might be with, if he was with his old half-Irish friend Kevin, or maybe the two of them had some girls over. Anthony hadn't brought a steady girlfriend around since he stopped seeing that smart girl Sharon. Hot Tip often wondered why she was out of the picture. She was a classy girl. He knocked again, a little louder, and then decided to use his key.

The block-out curtains had been drawn. All was quiet in the cavernous suite.

"Hey Anthony," Hot Tip yelled. "It's your old man. You in here?"

"Hang on a second," said Anthony in a groggy voice. "I'll be right out."

Hot Tip switched on a few lights. He pulled back the thick drapes and saw that a hot and muggy day was shaping up over the famed Atlantic City boardwalk.

"I thought we could have breakfast," said Hot Tip. "I'll meet you in the coffee shop."

"Okay, Pop," Anthony replied. "I'll be down in ten. Me and Kevin."

"I'll go get us a table."

Hot Tip felt uneasy. It was too quiet in the suite. Something was wrong, something he couldn't put his finger on. As he made his way out, he noticed the door to the second bedroom was ajar. Touching nothing, Hot Tip peeked in. All he saw was a bed—and it was still made.

At first, Hot Tip did not let his curiosity get the best of him. When the boys came down for breakfast, they all bantered like nothing was the least bit out of the ordinary, like nothing was the least bit untoward. But a week later, Hot Tip, back in the city again, remembered the unmade bed and decided he could not ignore what it meant. He had to dig further, if only for his own son's safety. One balmy afternoon, he cabbed it up Central Park West to Anthony's building.

"Excuse me," said Hot Tip to the liveried doorman smoking a cigarette out on the sidewalk. "I'm Anthony Capozi Senior."

The doorman promptly tossed the cigarette.

"I just need to ask you a question," said Hot Tip, "if you have a minute." The corner of a fifty dollar bill peeked out from between two fingers.

"Yes, sir, how can I help?"

"My son's friend, Kevin Malloy. When is a good time to catch him?"

"Oh, he's always around," the doorman responded in a phlegmy voice. "He and your son, they go out at night, you know, they're in and out. They go out on the town."

"So are they usually together?"

"Yeah, pretty much. But everyone likes your son. The other one, he don't even say hello when he come in."

"But he's always here?"

"Yeah. I would say every night. Is there a problem?"

"No, no. Thanks for your time." He slipped the doorman the fifty.

Hot Tip was not pleased to learn Kevin was staying full time at the apartment. It was not right, especially since he had given Kevin his own apartment downtown.

The whole situation had a bad smell.

CHAPTER 21

"So, Leon, this old queen friend of Brad's is giving a party and I thought I would invite you. It's on the fifteenth of this month and it's going to be wall-to-wall industry scum, so I need you to be there. Besides, I think you could fit in, now that you're a big decorating maven. So call me back on my private number. Tah, motherfucker. I'm off to Rodeo Drive to buy a new jock."

Leon switched the machine off.

It was the middle of a weekday. Sometimes it seemed that all of West Hollywood was home during the day, and this was one of those times. The parking lot in the building was full, and daytime talk-show applause seeped out through every window. Shane, hanging around next door with nothing to do, heard Leon's answering machine and decided to drop by.

"Do you think I'll get an invitation?" he asked Leon.

"I'm surprised I got one," said Leon evasively. "You know I haven't seen Kevin in a few weeks."

Shane went over to a mirror and started to pose down.

"Shane, must you? It's too gross. Do that at home."

"I have to go to the gym," said Shane dully.

"Get a life already. Have you had any dates lately?"

"No. No one ever approaches me. It's because my arms are so skinny." This was ridiculous. Shane now had the biggest arms on the block. Almost every part of his anatomy had been puffed up.

"I guess I'll go," Shane said. "I know when I'm not wanted." Shane thought he should go home and at least watch *Oprah,* but he doubted he would be able to sit through it. He was always jumpy these days. He was anxiously waiting till five, when he could return to the gym. He and Greg were doing intensive, split workouts now, twice a day. In between, they went home, swallowed a carton of egg whites, and then lay down, a certain amount of midday rest being part of the regimen.

"Don't be so touchy," said Leon. "Maybe I'll see you at the gym. Take care."

Shane went back to his own apartment. The mailman had just left, and Shane was relieved to see that the information he had requested from the Beverly Hills plastic surgeon had come. He plunked down on his high-tech black couch and ripped open the envelope.

"*Congratulations,*" stated the bearded Dr. Williamson from the cover of his glossy brochure, "*you have taken the first step in reinventing your Total Image!*

"*Penis Enlargement Surgery is now the Number One most performed elective surgery in Southern California. Join hundreds of satisfied men who have taken control of their lives and increased their confidence in both the Board room and the Locker room. As you will see on the next few pages, we create results that will leave you and your partner completely satisfied.*"

Shane flipped through the brochure and closely examined all of the before and after pictures. All shapes, sizes, and hues were represented. Shane then read about the details of the procedure.

"*Inside the body, there is up to four inches of unextended penile shaft. We free this part of the penis from its prison by making a small incision below the pubic bone. This incision cuts across what is known as the penile web. Trapped inches, literally falling out of the body, are gained. To add girth, we then take purified fat from the inner thigh and reverse micro-lipo it directly into the shaft. It is the simplest of procedures and we have obtained excellent results.*"

On the back of the brochure, there was a list of other available options: breast augmentation, breast reduction, pectoral implants, nipple reconstruction, calf implants, gluteal cleave redefining, laser tattoo removal, ear contouring, and twelve different kinds of face lifts. Shane wanted it all.

He lunged for his phone and dialed. The operator informed him that there was a waiting list; he would not be able to get in for ten weeks. She would, however, call him if there was a cancellation. She sounded doubtful.

He switched on *Oprah*, but the theme of suburban child snatchings failed to engage him, so he put in a fresh porno tape. This too failed to quiet his thoughts.

Shane wondered why Kevin hadn't called to invite him to the party.

Shane wanted to go. He had lived in West Hollywood now for almost two years and still hadn't been invited to a real Hollywood party.

Dan Evans was about to move to a new house in the hills. Strange fans, many of them disheveled and almost all of them overweight, had started hanging around in front of his apartment, and it was ruining his concentration. He was *definitely* over the funkiness of Melrose. His new place was secluded and absurdly expensive, but, as the realtor patiently explained, *it was near the Brad Pitt compound.* Dan wrote out a check for the deposit with great speed.

His career had taken off. Still, he had been surprised when Mike Brazier called out of the blue to set up an appointment. Dan would dump his current agent in a second to be represented by someone like Mike. Mike's agency represented all of the up-and-comers—the unshaven actors, the angry writers, and the radical directors who, if they all hung in long enough, would eventually become the entrenched establishment.

Dan drove over to see Mike Brazier after a rehearsal of *Sudden Storm.* Mike had told him it would be just a casual meeting, to drop by so they could discuss a few projects, see if they were on the same wavelength, that sort of thing.

Mike was at his desk, sifting through contracts when Dan strode in, all woodsy lankiness. Only two weeks before Dan had stopped wearing his cowboy hat; everyone on the set of *Sudden Storm* thought it was an annoying affectation. Still, he missed it. He liked to finger the felt brim during table readings.

"Mike Brazier," said Mike Brazier.

"Dan Evans." They shook hands, immediately sizing the other up. As always, the first question to consider was whether the suit was gay. Dan, spying a heavy silver slave bracelet, assumed he was.

"I admire your work," said Mike with a direct stare. "I've grown quite addicted to *Sudden Storm.*"

"Thank you, Mr. Brazier." Now Dan had his answer. The stare confirmed it. The only question now was how soon it would be before he would have to step out of some of his clothes. He hoped it wouldn't be long. He needed to get home. He was having a wide-screen Mitsubishi TV delivered that afternoon.

"Can I get you a drink? Water? Something soft?"

"I'd like a root beer," said Dan.

"Root beer," Mike repeated, "*I like that*. I think we could do things, Dan. You have a quality. And that quality is what we need to talk about, to bring out."

"I mean, I really would like a root beer," Dan said. "Basically, I've been rehearsing all day."

"Of course." Mike buzzed his assistant. "I need a root beer in here!" He let his finger go.

His assistant buzzed right back. "We don't have that. I'll have to run out and get it."

"So do it, goddamnit! Send an intern."

"She quit."

"Just make it happen, Portia! I don't want to hear anymore about it! Sorry, Dan, my apologies."

"No problem," Dan replied with a slight smile and a lick of his lips.

Mike started to play with one of the executive toys on his desk, a scale-model putting green.

"Now, talent is a rare thing," Mike began, but he could not go on. Dan's left hand was very gently caressing the thick denim over his bulge with almost imperceptible, circular swirls.

"I'm listening," said Dan.

"Yeah, like I was saying, talent is a rare . . . thing. There's damn little of it in this town, so when you spot it . . . it's like discovering oil! I think you have a raw talent, Dan. I can see it in your performances."

"Thank you," said Dan.

"About your name. It's a little boring. Would you be willing to change it?"

It was obvious to Mike that Dan was now good and hard. But whose move was it?

"I already did. My real name is Peter Johnson."

"I see. Oh, well. None of that crap matters. I'll let you in on a little trade secret, Dan. In this business you either have it or you don't!"

"Oh, I have it," Dan stated. It took only the slightest pressure, using only his left pinky, for the top button on his jeans to pop. "The question is, do you want it?"

It was two A.M. and Brad and Kevin were desultorily making love, such as it were. Brad found himself lazily blowing Kevin while Kevin held the remote to the TV, bouncing back and forth between infomercials. There was a road-to-wealth segment that involved placing thousands of tiny classified ads in hundreds of papers across the country, a celebrity hair-care discussion group, a Kenny Kingston Psychic Hotline presentation, and some sort of show promoting a meat defroster that had been developed by NASA but was now available in the home for three easy payments of $49.95 each.

Kevin was light-years away from coming, so he asked Brad to nibble his ass for a while.

Brad was okay with this idea. He was keyed up, and Kevin's butt was always a reliable distraction. He shifted around and got down to work, but then the bedside business line rang.

"It's so close, Brad. I feel like my nuts are in a vice," said Fenny Atkinson.

Brad spread Kevin's legs apart and cradled the phone between Kevin's thighs, so he could talk and take an occasional nip at the same time.

"Okay, Fenny, calm down."

"We shouldn't be talking on the phone. In fact, this should absolutely be our last call. It's that serious. I'm having a very weird feeling."

"What's wrong?" asked Brad.

"Probably nothing, but I'll tell you when I see you. Let's just say I've been sleeping with my briefcase."

"Where do you want to meet?"

"Here in Bedford. Joanna is in Paris at the collections. How soon can you get here?"

"I can get my pilots out of bed and the plane can be ready to take off at, let's say, by five," said Brad. "That should put me in White Plains by one in the afternoon."

"Fine. I'll be there. I'll pick you up out front. Call me only if there's a problem."

"There won't be." Brad hung up and jumped out of bed.

Kevin remained leaning against the tufted headboard, his legs still spread, his moneymaker a throbbing flagpole. Brad ignored it and called his pilot on the speed dial. Kevin, totally engrossed in the hair-product infomercial, finally noticed he no longer had Brad's full attention.

"Hey, what about this?" he said, pointing at his slick member.

"Ssshhh," Brad hissed, cupping the phone. "Get up, boys. File a flight plan to White Plains, New York. I want to take off at five. I appreciate this. Take a couple of rooms at the Arrowhead Conference Center and bring your golf clubs."

Brad hung up the phone again and looked down at the sprawled figure of Kevin.

"If I had your face, and your hair, and your skin, I never would have worked a day in my life. But I don't. So I have to go to New York."

Brad had recently handed over to Kevin the keys to a new 500-series Mercedes convertible. But as he looked down now at Kevin's miraculous display of cock, balls, thighs, and stomach, he knew the car was nothing. Kevin's body, so silky and responsive, turned him on like none had ever before.

Kevin curled himself up in Brad's arms, knowing that it was an appropriate gesture. A new Mercedes. A dazzling penthouse. It was such a *healthy* lifestyle.

"What's going on?" said Kevin.

"Big show-business happenings." Brad gently cupped Kevin's chin. "Get dressed and come on the plane with me."

Kevin tensed up. He and Brad had talked about flying to New York many times, but there was no way Kevin would actually go. And especially not to White Plains, so close to where he grew up. It was part of the deal he had made with Hot Tip Capozi. God, he'd been such a stupid kid. An all-too-familiar feeling of self-loathing and remorse washed over him anew and he felt sick.

"I can't," Kevin told Brad, trying to keep his voice under control. "I have a shoot tomorrow with the cast of *Beach Rescue.*"

"Look, don't take on any more work. I need you by my side. Sometimes I have to move at a moment's notice and I want you to come with me."

"Well, you got me the job," said Kevin. "I can't cancel now."

Kevin, of course, could cancel now and it would not matter in the least. The photos would be taken by someone else, it would all be rescheduled. The giant Hollywood machine, the endlessly sucking maw, would not, for one split second, register Kevin Malloy's absence.

They both were aware of this fact but would never speak of it. It was too embarrassing. Brad knew Kevin needed to maintain the thinnest veneer of respectability, even though there was no chance Kevin would even be allowed on the closed set of *Beach Rescue* unless it had all been pre-arranged. After all, Brad owned the company that produced the show.

Brad pulled an Etro weekend bag from a closet and started throwing in folded shirts.

After Brad left, Kevin pulled the sheet over his now-oozing limpness. He couldn't sleep. Screw this. He fished an Ativan caplet and a full-strength Normison out of a beside drawer and swallowed them with water kept in the bedside mini-fridge. Kevin, suddenly sweaty—and actually emitting armpit odor!—wanted codeine wishes and Lorazepam dreams.

But after half an hour, he was still wide awake. He considered taking off for West Hollywood, or even to Prod.

He could not tune out memories of Anthony. He didn't even know if Anthony still lived at the same apartment; the one time he tried to call there, one of Hot Tip's goombahs had answered with just a "Yeah? Who's this?" and Kevin hung up immediately.

It was smart that he hadn't said anything. Maybe Anthony himself would have come after him.

CHAPTER 22

One wet day in New York, Kevin came bounding out of his SoHo apartment only to immediately step into a huge pile of black slush. He was about to go back and change, but then remembered that most of his shoes, and almost all of his clothes, were up at Anthony's. Actually, he didn't really mind the wet feeling; it made him feel like a real New Yorker, someone who put up with a million inconveniences for the privilege of living in the greatest city in the world.

Although the streets were covered in slush, and there was another garbage strike looming, and budget cuts had turned thousands of mental patients out on the streets, Kevin felt happy as he headed for the subway. He and Anthony were going to a party at a chic new hotel that night.

He had only returned to the apartment because he needed to pick up the invitation, sent to him by a swell Eurotrash-type guy who had turned an old Murray Hill mansion into a hotel for all his globe-trotting friends. It was an exclusive event and Kevin felt pretty cool. Usually all the important invitations were sent to Anthony, but this one was addressed to Kevin Malloy . . . and guest.

Across the street, Hot Tip Capozi was waiting in a stretch Caddy. When he spotted Kevin, he lumbered out, shuffling toward him slowly, so they would run into each other on the corner.

Hot Tip had a black wool coat draped over his shoulders and wore a felt homburg. His slow gait and lugubrious demeanor cut a wide swath that impressed the bedraggled day-trippers who were clogging up the sidewalks. As they saw him approach, they stopped yammering and moved aside.

Kevin felt proud to know him. "Hey," he yelled, "Mr. Capozi!"

"Kevin, you half-Irish hooligan," Hot Tip greeted him, smiling and kissing Kevin on the cheek. "How are you? How are your parents?"

"I'm good, they're good."

"Say hello to your beautiful mother."

"I will."

"So where are you off to?"

"I'm going uptown. Anthony and I are going to the opening of the Lotus Hotel."

"Good, good," said Hot Tip. "Say hello to all my cement for me."

"That's your cement?" Kevin said. "That is so cool."

"Yes, it is. They did nice work. It was a wonderful project, with quite advantageous tax breaks. And I understand it's already booked solid through New Year's."

"Well, it's the place to be tonight," said Kevin.

"Have a good time."

"Thanks. I guess I better get going. Anthony's waiting, and you know how the subways are."

"No, I don't, thank God," Hot Tip said. "Kevin, I wonder if you might have a minute to come with me to a small social club that I sometimes visit when I'm down here. I would appreciate the company and then I'll put you in a cab."

Kevin, wearing a fashionable but not very warm Commes des Garçons overcoat, shivered. "Sure," he answered. "That would be great. I just stepped into some slush and my right foot is already freezing."

"We'll have an espresso."

Hot Tip led him around a corner and they went through an unmarked doorway. Inside were folding chairs and card tables. The place was empty, but when Hot Tip came in, an ancient man appeared from behind a curtain near the back. He waved and then disappeared.

He returned with two minuscule cups of espresso. Kevin was impressed. He was getting the full wop treatment, which was, in New York, as glamorous as any opening night. Hot Tip thanked the man respectfully and the old guy just shuffled off.

"So, how do you like your new apartment?"

"It's the greatest. I can't believe what a good deal it is. I'm really grateful you found it for me."

"It's nothing." And to Hot Tip, it really was nothing. Just a few cramped rooms with low ceilings. Unlivable. Still, the arrangement had required calling in a favor.

"And how do you like the neighborhood?"

"I love it down here. I think I'm more downtown than uptown, you know? This is where it's all happening."

Hot Tip nodded. "Well, this neighborhood's changed a bit over the years. It was a lot nicer in my day. But hey, that's progress." Hot Tip leaned across the table and stared into Kevin's eyes. "Some of my associates still live down here. They make a very good living with the gay-bar trade. Just a fortune."

Kevin took a sip of his bitter coffee. He did not know what to make of that remark.

"There's a lot of art galleries down here, too," he replied, hoarsely.

"Do you know of a bar over on Sheridan Square? It has a blue neon light outside. I can't remember the name of it."

"I think I've passed it," said Kevin evenly.

"Yes, what is the name of it?"

Kevin knew what it was called. He had been in there, at all hours of the day and night, probably fifty times. The bartenders gave him free drinks.

"I don't know," he lied.

"Oh, now I remember," said Hot Tip, leaning back. "It's called the Bunk Room."

Kevin drained the last of his coffee, getting a mouthful of grounds.

"Yeah, I've heard of that place."

"Ever been in there?"

"No."

Kevin was sweating now, and the gangsterish atmosphere suddenly struck him as too clichéd for words. He tittered a bit and flashed a smile. He was dying to look at his watch, but Hot Tip would not release him from his gaze.

"Yes," Hot Tip continued. "The Bunk Room. It's run by a very old friend of mine. Quite respectable in its way. There's a piano in the back."

"Really. Maybe I'll check it out."

"It may not be to your liking," said Hot Tip. "It's frequented solely by homosexuals."

Kevin did not know where this game was leading, but he knew that he was being put to the test. And he suddenly had the feeling that running into Hot Tip had not been an accident. *Shit*. He wished Anthony were here. Anthony could tell him what to say, how to play this.

Stalling, he stammered, "Well, then I probably wouldn't go in there. Not that I have anything against fags . . . I mean, you know . . . Greenwich Village, USA!"

Hot Tip did not laugh.

"That's good," said Hot Tip. "Now here's a question. I don't really know how to ask it, of course, but I need to know." Hot Tip leaned across the table until his face was just a few inches from Kevin's. "Are you sleeping with my son?"

Kevin's eyes watered and his stomach turned over. So this was the real purpose of the meeting. Jesus, how did the old bastard find out?

What would Anthony want him to say? This was a situation they had not anticipated. But what was the big deal, anyway? Who could fault Kevin for loving Anthony? Everyone who met Anthony fell in love with him.

"All right, I see where this is heading, Mr. Capozi. So. The truth. Okay. *Yeah*." Kevin wrapped his coat around himself. "I *am*. So now you know."

Hot Tip's expression did not change. After a few long moments Kevin sensed that perhaps the crisis had passed. But there was no way he was going to say anything more.

"Well, this changes things," said Hot Tip finally. "All right. Thank you for your honesty." Hot Tip got up from the table. "Let's walk, Kevin. It's getting stuffy in here."

Kevin hesitated, so Hot Tip lifted him under one arm and pulled him out of his seat. He held on to Kevin's arm as they stepped out into the street. It had started to snow.

"This is all rather unfortunate. I did not expect you to make such an admission. In the old days, people who turned out like you, well, they just never admitted such a thing."

"Yeah, they just offed themselves. But times have changed."

"Hmm. Yes, maybe they have," Hot Tip agreed. "But let's not speak of this subject any more than necessary. Right now it is making me feel too sad. When Anthony's mother died, some part of me died, too. I have known all the sadness I need to know for one lifetime."

"It's not the worst thing in the world," Kevin said. "You'll see."

"Come. Let's go back to your apartment."

"Um, I can't, Mr. Capozi," Kevin protested. "I'm meeting Anthony, re-member?"

"No. I don't think so."

Kevin shivered with fear.

"Come along," said Hot Tip, moving quickly now. "Here we are. Give me your keys."

Kevin swallowed hard and then handed them over.

"Okay, go inside. I know this building from years ago. Everyone in it was Italian. Fine families. They all worked hard, and then, one by one, they all moved out to Long Island. Well, good for them. The city has turned into a cesspool."

Hot Tip knew which apartment was Kevin's and which key opened the door. He walked directly into Kevin's small bedroom. "Get in here!"

Kevin almost crumpled to the floor, but he obeyed. He found Hot Tip looking through a closet. Hot Tip stared briefly at him and then went over to the bed and pulled back the zebra-stripe Perry Ellis coverlet. Kevin would have fainted, but then he saw Hot Tip reach under the bed and pull out a hard-sided, light-blue Samsonite suitcase. It had been Kevin's mother's.

"I'll give you two options," Hot Tip told him. "One: You leave town. I'll give you one hour to pack. Do it carefully. Take all your pictures of your fam-ily, any mementos that are important to you. Anything you can carry out."

"What do you mean?"

"I mean, this is it. You are no longer welcome. You can no longer live in New York. And call your parents. Tell them you're in a lot of trouble. Tell them why. Tell them the truth and they won't suffer as much."

"I could never," said Kevin.

"You have to. If you don't, your mother will never understand, and you have no right to do that to her. This is a problem you brought on yourself."

"Where am I supposed to go?"

"That's up to you. But the farther the better."

"What's the second option?"

"I mess up your face. Don't test my patience, Kevin. It wouldn't be the first time I've done it. You corrupted my son with your perversion. It would be a pleasure."

Kevin, wide-eyed, tried to fight back the tears. This was all too incon-ceivable. Where was Anthony? Why was this happening?

"If you choose the second option, you would probably lose your sight.

Which would be a blessing. Then you'd have to go in for at least six operations on your jaw alone. For your mother's sake, I recommend the first option."

Kevin began to sob.

"Oh, Christ," snapped Hot Tip. "Look, it's going to be fine, it's going to be okay. You're young. You'll get over it. But it can't be any other way. It's not safe for Anthony."

"It's not like you think," said Kevin.

Hot Tip grabbed Kevin by the lapels and pushed him against the wall. "Start packing."

"No," whispered Kevin. "I don't want to go."

Hot Tip flung Kevin across the room. "You two, you're both young and stupid! Don't you realize everything I have is in Anthony's name? It's all his. If I get indicted, they don't come after me, they follow the trail right to him. So I got to spend the rest of my days protecting him. I'll never let him get sent up. If you care about him at all, you'll get lost."

Kevin saw it all clearly now, for the first time, and he knew Hot Tip was telling the truth.

"Listen, just go out to California, or some place like that, some place far away where nobody knows nobody. I have money to give you, don't worry. It will be a new life for you and in time you'll see it's for the best." Hot Tip reached into the pocket of his overcoat and pulled out a thick white envelope. "Ten thousand in cash. That should be enough to get you a plane ticket somewhere and start you out in a new town. Now give me something with your social-security number on it, like a bank statement. That way I'll always be able to keep track of where you are."

Kevin took the envelope from Hot Tip.

"Don't call Anthony. Pull yourself together and get on a plane tonight. If I ever find out that you've come back to New York, even for a visit, there will be a problem. And not just with you. I know where your family lives."

Kevin knew there was no point in arguing. He accepted the envelope. "I'll do what you say," he said. "But I know Anthony and I know this is not what he wants."

"Be smart, boy. Hate me all you want, but just remember, one word and they go after Anthony. They can't touch me."

Hot Tip took off his hat and wiped his forehead with his palm. "One hour. All this other stuff—don't think about it. Tomorrow it goes into a landfill."

CHAPTER 23

Brad's GIV touched down a few minutes ahead of schedule.

Fenny was waiting outside the entrance to the small White Plains airport parking lot. Brad spotted him immediately, but they did not speak until they were safely seated in Fenny's anthracite Viper.

Fenny, still high-school-wrestling-team wiry at forty-seven, wore a beige fishing hat low over his forehead and hid his eyes behind sunglasses. He didn't want anyone to recognize him, for this was yet another unholy alliance on a list that stretched back ten years.

"So this is where we're at," said Fenny, foregoing any greetings. "The board has agreed to sell at a premium price of fifty-one dollars per share. That's twenty percent above the market price. They're not happy about it, but they haven't really grasped the situation so I had to tell them the Japanese were coming."

"Oh, God, how did you get them to buy that?" asked Brad.

"Well, here's the profile of your board. Ten men all over the age of sixty, one white woman, and one black man. It's a Pearl Harbor thing with them. Besides, all those guys are on at least four other boards, and they're not entirely averse to the idea of cashing out. Mrs. Siminoff and Mr. Jackson's opinions don't count because all the old white guys vote together. You know them: it's the last gasp of the old order."

"A bunch of right-wing foot soldiers."

"Exactly," said Fenny. "Which, of course, works in our favor."

"I don't think they were too happy at the last shareholders meeting.

They didn't expect Snoop Doggy Dogg to perform. They were all terrified for their lives."

Fenny had stopped listening. He was gunning the engine in an attempt to merge with the traffic on Route 684.

Brad felt natural being on a freeway, although he had spent enough time in New York not to call it that. These people insisted on calling it a turnpike. East Coast versus West Coast, as always.

"You know, the stock at fifty-one is still undervalued," commented Brad. "I know I don't have to tell you how much money is in the entertainment industry these days."

"Do I ever! This is the sweetest deal I've ever come across. I may have to move out to Hollywood myself. The figures are just breathtaking."

"Well, it's our little secret. As long as the rest of the country keeps believing we're all a bunch of leftie pinko flakes, I think we'll be safe," Brad said. "And from here, it can only get bigger, you know. What else do we have to offer the world?"

"Microchips, telecommunications, cars . . . nothing but a lot of low-margin crap. Nothing recession-proof."

Fenny pulled off the highway and turned on to a narrow road. He navigated slowly around a group of teenage girls on horseback who were heading toward a bridle path. Then, after another mile, he made a left.

From there, a winding driveway led to a stately colonial-style house. White Shetland ponies grazed untethered on the lawn.

"Let's go around back and have a drink," suggested Fenny. "We'll deal with your bags later."

Behind the house was a pool, a barn, and a paddock, all of it surrounded by weeping willows.

"My grandfather lost this place in the crash," Fenny told Brad. "I bought it back a few years ago, thus redeeming my ancestors. Bunch of drunks. That old WASP thing of fiddling while Rome burns. Had to gut the place completely."

"Wouldn't a tear-down have been easier?" asked Brad.

"We don't do tear-downs out here in Bedford, Brad. That would be too nouveau. We like to keep everything just a little shabby. You know, leave the butter out all night on the kitchen table kind of thing."

"Oh," said Brad. He had no idea what Fenny was talking about.

A pitcher of fresh lemonade and two glasses had been set up on a table under a gazebo by the pool.

"Okay, let's do it. Oh, shit, let me get my laptop out of the safe." Fenny trotted lightly off toward the house.

Brad took a deep breath of the humid air and tried to relax. The setting was beautiful, but he could not enjoy it. He would enjoy life only after this deal came through. Then he could relax. Then he'd whisk Kevin off to Fiji.

A mosquito happened by and Brad swatted at it wildly. *Okay,* thought Brad, *Think Cool Thoughts.* A therapist had taught him that. "Imagine a quiet lake," she'd say, from the center of a feeling circle. Brad closed his eyes, but then opened them angrily a second later. There was a perfectly bucolic setting right before his eyes! There always was!

For the millionth time, Brad questioned himself—was he doing the right thing? Lately, he felt a constant need to reassure himself that the deal was a positive one, fiscally as well as karmically.

Well, clearly, the buyout was the next logical step in his reinvention. Besides, if the company were not taken private now, it would become a sitting duck for any number of hostile-takeover artists. Magnet Entertainment's problem was it simply had too much raidable cash on hand.

For the past few weeks, Fenny had been expertly fanning the flames of paranoia, spreading breathy words of misinformation up and down the street: A refrigerator and microwave-oven company was interested in getting into media, as was a large insurance concern. So was a Swiss chocolate-and-powdered-soup conglomerate, a rapacious Dutch consortium, and, of course, the always-inscrutable Japanese.

The Japanese bid was, by now, patently nonexistent. Brad had met with a contingent of them over golf a few years back, and although they cagily professed what seemed like genuine interest at the time, the deal made no progress. They had already made a number of highly publicized forays into the Hollywood game and had been burned badly, just like they'd been burned with New York real estate.

Still, they all came around—to sniff. Magnet was a glamorous target. It was Brad's uncanny knack for signing up groundbreaking new groups that kept them coming back. For twenty years, Brad had foreseen almost every major musical trend and there was no demographic market he did not know how to exploit. How he did it was a mystery to everyone.

Except to Brad. Sneaking off on a solo cross-country drive, he discovered the malaise rampant in the nation's trailer parks, so he hurriedly signed up a score of mournful country artists. When suburban teenagers started turning to fey grunge artists, Brad, with deep pockets, set up quirky festivals that sought to recreate Woodstock. Then, after reading an article in *USA Today*, he had the idea to bring aging bands out of retirement and force them to sing their tired hits from long ago. The stadiums, swollen with disillusioned boomers, were not a pretty sight up close, but, oy, the deafening *ca-ching!*

These days, while the content of their lyrics was being debated, Brad was stocking up on rap groups. Meanwhile, the Latin salsa machines, the techno remixes from Manchester, the classical department with its emphasis on esoterica—these divisions, too, were thriving beyond all expectations. And, of course, he loved the pocket change that came in from the Evangelical Christian Spoken Word division. Those shekels had a poetic beauty all their own.

But none of it really was enough. Because it really wasn't just about money. Brad wanted to be accountable to no one. He didn't want to have to speak politely to stockholders who held five shares of Magnet—those pain-in-the-ass cranks with too much time on their hands who pulled up SEC filings off the Internet. He had a GIV, but now he wanted a refitted commercial jet like an Airbus, or perhaps something larger. He wanted to dictate policy in Washington. He wanted to be feared.

Brad wanted action, and if he just had more money, he would be in a position to get it. He could then jack up his contributions to AIDS research and also find a way to get the same-sex marriage ball rolling again. He could meddle around in Detroit and get them to finally build a realistic zero-emissions vehicle for the masses. He could endow universities, receive honorary doctorates, manipulate currency markets, and make uplifting films about dull people with small lives. It could all be possible. Yes, this deal was a positive one, and it could not get pushed through fast enough.

Fenny, letting a screen door slam, came bounding out of the house.

"There's been a few leaks," he said, sitting back down, "and any day now we could be facing a hostile bid by more than a few of my pals on the street. So we have to move now."

"I think we're out of the woods," Brad stated calmly.

"Not yet. Now, I trust you, Brad, but to protect us both I did a background check on you. Not the standard kind. I'm talking CIA-quality. But don't worry, I didn't find anything out of the ordinary. I already knew it was pretty sleazy, what with boy hookers and what have you, but believe me, I couldn't care less. It's just that neither of us can afford to have any ASAMs popping up as we enter the home stretch."

ASAMs. The acronym struck terror in their hearts. It stood for Automated Search and Match, and it was the federal government's most powerful weapon against insider trading, a computerized list of all the registered stock representatives in the country with every possible cross reference of who might have told a secret to whom. It listed all country-club memberships, religious affiliations, college-roommate information, relatives—anyone and everyone who might benefit from an illegal stock trade. The government did not make compliance absolutely mandatory, but anyone who wanted access to the markets knew that this was one area where you didn't screw around with Uncle Sam. Fenny, as a registered rep, could not be too careful. He had once visited a friend who was resting up in a "country club" minimum-security prison and could not, much as he tried, appreciate the facility's amenities.

"There are no hookers, Fenny. That's not the way my life is anymore," said Brad.

"All right," Fenny replied. "At this point I have no choice but to believe you, so let's not get ourselves spooked. I've been a nervous wreck ever since I got that sinister fax. But we'll forget that and move on. Right now I need you to concentrate on the name change. After the deal goes down, we'll need a ton of distracting publicity while we sell off all the individual divisions. Then you'll need a lot of layoffs to falsely inflate the value of your shares, followed immediately by a blizzard of fresh mission statements."

"Wait a minute. Did you say change the name of Magnet?" said Brad.

"Yeah."

"But it's a great brand name in American entertainment."

"So? It has to be done. There needs to be a million distractions. But don't hire a consulting company. There could be leaks. Just pick anything. It doesn't matter what it is."

"Okay," said Brad slowly, "if it's for the good of the company."

"Stay with me, Brad. We have a lot to cover."

"Sure." Brad sat up and collected himself. "You know, Fenny, you and I both know this isn't the most kosher deal to ever come down the pike, but it's going to be a good thing, and not just for you and me. I'm going to make a difference. These are strange times. The government is morally bankrupt, the markets are spinning out of control, and a deep cynicism is permeating American life. I'm going to go in there and demand some action. It's my civic duty."

"Civic duty," said Fenny, "that's a good one." He laughed heartily. It was the first time he had ever heard Brad tell a joke.

"Kim, dearest, now help me. I can't do everything myself, you know," said Rob. A tiny pair of reading glasses, purchased at the Beverly Hills Thrifty for six dollars, were perched on the end of his nose. He was going over the guest list for Brad's party.

"What would you like me to do?"

"Well, all these people in this column are coming to the dinner, and all these people in this column are coming after. Brad just faxed me these from the plane. Now, here's my problem: How am I going to clear out all the straights by ten o'clock?"

"How many straight people are coming?" asked Kim.

"Tons! So far, four to the dinner and zero to the after-hours party. It's just dreadful."

"Why are you doing this to yourself? Just have a barbecue."

"That would be lovely," said Rob, "but this isn't Sydney, Kim."

"Well, then do the dinner at a restaurant."

"Now there's an idea. A quiet dinner at L'Orangerie and then Brad's parents can go home and we can we can all come back here for the real festivities. That would be much simpler. But then you can't come to the dinner. I'd need you to stay here and make sure the caterers are on time and the DJ and all that. Would you mind in the least?"

"Not at all," said Kim. "I'll take care of all that and you and Mr. Sherwood just have a good time."

"You are a treasure. That's a gorgeous solution. Now I can concentrate solely on the party."

Kim looked down the list of guests. So far, there were about seventy names.

"So all these people are gay?" Kim inquired.

"Of course."

"Don't you know any straight people?"

"No!" Rob asserted. "Well, Elinor Graham; I think she's straight. And I presume my parents were. And there was an uncle . . . felled by a Komodo dragon on a small island in Indonesia. Let that be a warning! *It wasn't the bite, it was the saliva!*"

Kim backed off and helped himself to a glass of nonfat milk from the fridge. "Well, do you need me to stick around now? Because otherwise I can go to the gym for an hour. The bodies in this town! I feel positively emaciated."

"Yes, the tyranny of the body culture," said Rob. "It's ruthless. Those boys just get meaner looking every year. But as you know, I just go with the flow. Why don't you round up a few of the cruelest-looking ones and invite them to the party. The more the merrier."

"Sure."

"Now, *normally,* I'd call an escort service and just have them send over a dozen or so boys and put the whole thing on my credit card. That way I'd get the frequent-flier miles. But the authorities are really cracking down. Imagine! Those poor boys, thrown out of work. Oh, well, I can call around. Of course, we can't re-create the old days, but I think we can come close. God, these are vulgar times!"

Kim took Rob's white Lexus to the Athletic Connection and parked on the street. He was about to jaywalk across Santa Monica Boulevard, but then remembered Rob's warning about tickets and the absolute ruthlessness of the LAPD. So he walked out of his way to cross at the corner. A black Jeep Cherokee filled with joyriding supermodels was waiting at the light. What a great town!

Inside, Kim made his way down to the changing rooms and fluffed himself unnecessarily before heading upstairs into the main rooms. He did a few stretches, then found an open StairMaster and set the computerized timer for thirty minutes. It was a good spot to case the room.

Now Kim, just a darling lad from Perth, thought that the Athletic Connection was heaven on earth. American boys were so sinewy, more so than even the Dutch or the Germans. Kim didn't think he'd ever want to leave America. He and Rob were even thinking about taking a railway trip to the Hoover Dam!

The StairMaster finished the warmup segment of the exercise and Kim was forced to pump harder. When he began to feel a rush of endorphins, he suddenly found himself locking eyes with the kind of guy that really got his juices flowing. The guy returned the stare, looked away, and then stared again.

Kim's heart raced and he pumped the pedals of the machine faster. The guy had a lean, regular face, V-shaped lats, and a massive tool loping along one thigh. "A nice lunch" is what his mates would have said back home. The guy also had good pecs, bowling-pin calves, and straight teeth. Americans are *too* healthy looking, thought Kim, and he stared harder.

Across the room, Leon saw a really adorable number on the StairMaster giving him the eye. The guy had well-muscled thighs, wavy, blond surfer hair, and just the merest suggestion of a snaggle tooth. He actually looked like a real blond, and in LA, that was an opportunity that could not be missed.

Leon dropped the thirty-pound dumbbell that he was using to do curls and leaned against a pillar. He crossed his legs in a way that bulked up his package. Kim, from across the room, nodded his head appreciatively.

"Don't take a break now," said Shane, who was working out nearby with Greg on an incline press.

Leon ignored him, scooped up his towel, and strode over to the row of StairMasters. He climbed aboard the one right next to Kim. It was not something that made sense, of course. The StairMasters were for before or after a workout, depending on your program. But Leon was bored and feeling adventurous.

"I was hoping you'd come over."

"Normally I wouldn't. But I wanted to meet you. My name is Leon."

"I'm Kim."

Leon was grateful that Kim did not make a mean crack about his name. Kim's stock soared. Now, a lot of midwestern boys, including Leon, often went the Latin route as soon as they hit LA, for the ease-of-useness of it all. But Leon was a bit homesick for Minneapolis and was ready to go back— to blonds, that is, not Minneapolis.

"Are you almost finished working out?" Kim asked him.

"I am now."

Leon had tricked with enough Qantas stewards to recognize an Australian accent. "Are you a trolley dolly?"

"God, no," said Kim. "I'm a personal trainer. I live here now."

"Would you like to go get a wheat-grass juice or something after your workout?"

"Why don't we just go now? I don't have a lot of time."

"What about your routine?"

"I don't think I'd be able to concentrate," Kim admitted, frankly checking out Leon's massive pecs.

"I live right around the corner."

"Pardon the living room," said Leon. "I have a couch on order." He pulled Kim against him and they immediately went into a shockingly soulful kiss. Kim felt Leon's solid frame and began massaging and exploring. Leon did the same, and after a few minutes, they peeled off each other's shirt. Leon then tried to drag Kim down onto the carpet.

"Let's go into the bedroom," Kim whispered.

It had been a long time since Leon had been with anyone in a bed. He was so used to just doing it on the floor or behind a garbage dumpster in the alley outside Prod. But now that Kevin was gone, Leon believed he could bend the Rules.

"Sure. *Yeah.* Why not?"

They went into Leon's heliotrope room, pulled back the sheets, and eagerly hopped in.

Both were delighted. Each felt they had moved up in class.

Their tongues intertwined in a complementary way, and they drew this aspect of the act out much longer than was standard. At one point, they simultaneously opened their eyes while their tongues were down each other's throats and they broke into a grin, which, really, was *so not* West Hollywood. A chemistry was building, and they remained dangerously clothed far longer than was usually permitted.

Three hours and two showers later, having broken every sacred rule of afternoon-trick etiquette, they walked into the kitchen to obtain some bottled water. Kim was due back at Rob's place and Leon had a million things to take care of, but already they were forming a bond. As veterans of strenuous, hard gay lives, they knew something rare had happened.

When they finally pried themselves away from each other, Leon, shocking himself, asked Kim for his phone number.

"By the way," said Kim. "I'm helping a friend with a party and I'd like you to come. It's on Saturday, the fifteenth, in Beverly Hills. It's going to be a huge deal, trust me. Tents, food, legitimate porn stars, the works! It's being given in Brad Sherwood's honor."

"Is that so? Well, guess what? I've already been invited. My ex-roommate is Brad Sherwood's boyfriend."

"You're kidding. And I thought Sydney was a small town. Look, I'm helping out with the arrangements. Why don't you come a little early, before all the madness."

"I'd love to. But I hope I can see you again before that."

Kim put his hands underneath Leon's shirt. "I was hoping you would say that. You're like a fantasy to me. A real American. I'll come back tonight."

"Hurry."

"I will."

"Wait! Oh, shit, I forgot. I ran a yellow light last month and I have to go to gay traffic school from six to ten. I can't miss it."

"No worries, mate." Kim planted a soft wet one on Leon's cheek. "I'll just come after."

CHAPTER 24

When word of Brad's successful takeover of Magnet Entertainment was announced, telephone service in the 213 and 310 area codes of Los Angeles registered a 1 percent uptick above normal. In the papers, all the nattering pundits felt compelled to say that it was the eighties all over again, when, of course, it was just the nineties all over again, minus the compassion.

Brad's deal was so smooth, so sexy, yet so . . . not flashy. Everyone knew Brad was a crafty player, but this wily maneuver had taken everyone by surprise. It was said they had all underestimated his scope of vision, and now, in hindsight, there was a worldwide orgy of teeth gnashing, envy, and bitterness.

The Magnet board came off looking like fools. Most of them immediately announced the need to attend important monetary-policy seminars in places like Biarritz and Sardinia.

Brad issued a press release that explained everything about the daring new synergistic marketing opportunities he had planned, which included globalization, diversity, multitasking, freestanding cyber-workstations, and jumping into the coming digital revolution—although that, of course, was already here. Then, by ceaselessly chanting "Content" like a mantra, he reached critical mass on the spin; soon it was clear to all that his coup would enrich the lives of each and every American citizen personally!

And they all bought it.

The phone in the Wilshire apartment had been ringing nonstop since four that morning, and Brad took every call. At six, he got Corrine out of

bed and asked her to get to the office to handle everything. He pro-
grammed the call forwarding, turned off the ringer, and then crawled back
under the sheets.

Kevin, having slept poorly, did not appreciate Brad's roving hands.

"Let me sleep," he implored.

"Come on, Kevin, I made history today. Get up, there's everything to do.
Don't you get it? Don't you realize that you are now in bed with the fourth-
richest man in Hollywood? This is the greatest day of my life. One week
ago I was the nineteenth-richest man in Hollywood."

"You mean I've been sleeping with the nineteenth-richest man in Hollywood for all these months? How humiliating."

Brad jumped up and down on the king-size bed and Kevin had to laugh.
Brad had increased his wealth to almost a billion dollars, but really, was that
any reason to act like a little kid?

He threw himself down and smashed his lips against Kevin's face. "Ugh.
Were you smoking cigarettes last night?"

"I had a few," said Kevin.

"When did you start smoking?"

"I have a few now and then. On the set. With the models."

"Well, you better quit before you get addicted."

Of course, Kevin had been already addicted for quite some time. He just
never smoked around Brad. Usually, he snuck out of the apartment and
smoked up by the rooftop pool. Or if it was really chilly, he'd steal a few
puffs in the fire stairwell.

"Whatever," said Kevin.

"Oh, God, there's so much to do today and nothing at all to do," Brad
said. "What do you feel like doing? Shall we go buy a new airplane? A new
house? A few senators? Oh, God, this is going to be fun. Maybe I'll buy my
parents a yacht. Nah. They hate the water. How about a little loving before
breakfast?"

"I'm not in the mood."

Brad was not pleased with the tone in Kevin's voice. Surely he deserved
fellatio on such a great day.

"You could have bought all those things before," said Kevin. "What's
the big difference?"

"Well, yes, I suppose I could have. But there *is* a big difference. Trust me."

Brad had all the toys he needed, that much was true, although he would get another plane. But now he would also write a check for five million dollars to Aids Project Los Angeles. Then another to Project Angel Food. And after that he would pump up Rob's coffers with a few million as a thank-you present for keeping quiet and for all the years of loyal friendship. Then he'd funnel some money into South Central, or maybe even visit. Then he would set up a foundation in his father's name for struggling musicians. Finally, he'd adopt some kids, get the legislation for gay marriage passed, and generally break balls everywhere. But this time around, he could do it gently. With class.

"I have to get to my office and say a few words. No one knew about any of this."

"Not even me," said Kevin.

"I know," Brad replied. "But if you read up on this deal in *Fortune* magazine next month, where I most certainly will be sitting on the cover, I think you'll understand why I had to keep everything top secret."

"Oh, bull, Brad. You didn't trust me."

"I didn't trust anyone, Kevin. It's not as though I singled you out."

"I'm not just anyone."

Brad kissed Kevin on the forehead. "No, you're not. I'll make it up to you. Do you want to come to the office with me? I'll only be there for an hour. I need to reassure some people, maybe fire some others, and then write another statement. Afterwards we could go to lunch at the Ivy."

Kevin imagined the block-long stream of glad-handing executives focused on Brad and ignoring him. "No. I have to go to the gym."

Jeremy buzzed the penthouse at seven A.M., and as Brad rode down the elevator, he decided he wouldn't fire Jeremy right away. He'd need him around for the next few days. Maybe he'd find him a job doing something else.

Now that his company was loaded with debt, of the wealth-preserving tax-deductible kind, Brad needed to make some cosmetic changes in the business so it would appear that the restructuring was wise and sage. On the spot, right there in the elevator, he decided to cancel the fresh-flower order everyone had in their offices.

"Jeremy," called Brad from the back of the limo, "I think we need to have a short talk. I want to put you in another position, one that's not so hard on your back. I'm going to be using a team of bodyguards who will double as my drivers now, so I want you to think about the trajectory of your career path. If there is something else you would like to do in the company, let Corrine know. I'm also thinking of a severance package if you'd like. That way, you could take a year off and go to school for retraining."

Jeremy was floored. This is not what he imagined at all. Going back to school, at his age! Well, that's what they were telling all the oldsters these days. It didn't matter that he knew every shortcut on every surface street in LA. He was screwed.

At the office, Brad found Corrine in the main lobby with a disorderly posse of senior executives and Matt, the new kid in talent coordination. When Brad came in, Corrine started the applause and the other executives, anxious about their futures, felt compelled to join in. Brad felt a little speech was called for, so he reminded himself to smile.

"Thank you all," he began. "I feel a lot of love in the room, and that's what this business is really all about. I think this news is probably a big surprise to most of you and I want you to understand why I did it this way. So let me fill you in."

The Armani-swathed assemblage hung on every word.

"Magnet is now uniquely positioned to be at the forefront of all the new entertainment technologies. As you know, over the years we've trailblazed many artistic frontiers, but believe me, that was only the beginning. Now we are at a new starting point, which is why I no longer can contain the good news. In keeping with the dynamic nature of our new streamlined operation, I will soon be announcing a new name for our company. But since you all are family, I will share it with you now. I am pleased to announce that starting today, Magnet Entertainment will henceforth be known as . . . Digisynth."

The group of stunned executives recognized that it was an appropriate moment to once again applaud their leader. But their hands came together slowly. Corrine scanned the room with a steely eye and the volume picked up.

"Digisynth will usher in a bold new era of leisure-time exploitation. Already we are the leaders in animatronics. But what is our real goal? Well, I'll tell you! No less than complete domination of the marketplace, total *saturation!* We'll be deploying all of the new groundbreaking entertainment technologies. Now, some of you may be nervous, wondering how you'll fit in, but let me assure you there will be no restructuring for the time being. There will be changes soon, true, but rest assured that . . ."

Brad's eyes fell on Matt, who was licking his lips and smoldering in a hungry, lewd way. Why shouldn't I let this kid blow me in my office, thought Brad. Why wasn't Kevin here beside him—or at least waiting out in the car? What the hell did Kevin have to do that was so goddamn important?

". . . that, well, all will be bigger and better and tremendously exciting here at Digisynth. These are revolutionary times and we will be the innovators. Guess we'll all finally have to learn how to program our VCRs!"

Everyone laughed on cue.

"If you have any questions, get in touch with personnel. Oh, and by the way, the personnel department will be getting a new name, too. From now on, personnel will be known as 'the people department.' Because that's what you are. You're not just numbers. You . . . are . . . *people!* Hold on to your hats!"

The group, in shock, applauded again automatically. Out of the whole speech, they had only heard four words: "There will be changes." Any minute now, there would be a stampede to the unmonitored pay phones across the street.

The job search, the endless merry-go-round of interviewing, would begin again for many of them. Groveling skills would need sharpening. Job security? What a decadent notion. But of course, it's always the children that suffer the most; many of them would be asked to attend public schools.

One lactose-intolerant accountant near the back, with his breakfast lodged in his throat, rushed into the bathroom. Pale, and finally knowing what a genuine panic attack felt like, he bent his head over a toilet bowl and heaved. His eyes bulged and a long string of sputum threatened the lapel of his suit. He reached above the bowl and grabbed a seat cover to wipe off his chin. As his eyes refocused, he took a moment out his life to read the fine print on the cardboard seat-cover box: SANI-SEATS: PROVIDED BY THE MANAGEMENT FOR *YOUR* PROTECTION!

When the applause died down, Brad strode toward the elevator bank and crooked a finger at Corrine, signaling for her to follow. As he passed Matt, he gave the kid a wink. Just for fun. Matt, who was unconscionably cute and who only looked about sixteen but was definitely twenty-one, winked back.

"Now, Corrine," said Brad, closing the office door behind him, "this is what I need. I need you to . . . come over here and give me a big hug."

Corrine was only too happy to do this. As part of senior management, her stake in the company grew tremendously valuable overnight. Few in the company would benefit so substantially.

"Just to put a little icing on the cake," said Corrine, "Tell That Girl Hi will be debuting at number one. Roger over at *Billboard* just called."

"Oh, that is just too perfect. Synchronicity!" Brad gloated. "Let's buy each of the girls a BMW roadster. Find out their favorite colors."

"You give cars out like tips," Corrine mockingly scolded.

"Is that so wrong?"

Corrine and Brad laughed, grinned stupidly at each other, and then hugged again. For possibly the first time in his life, Brad felt truly relaxed. He had reaped all the rewards of years of frenetic work, and the monkeys were finally off his back. With the fate of his company now resting on the shoulders of the people who owned junk bonds as part of their retirement portfolios, Brad could let the whole company go down the tubes . . . or build another empire—either way, he would not lose a cent.

"All the press has been favorable, too," Corrine continued. "And every studio head is sick with envy, so they all sent gifts. Mick Jagger called from London to invite you to his country house. And the head of the Federal Reserve put a call in, too, to offer his congratulations. He said you were a model for entrepreneurial excellence. Oh, and here's one from Deepak Chopra."

"Good. Now, about tomorrow night, is everything all set with my parents? I spoke to Rob and L'Orangerie is all set up with security. You are aware that I'll be introducing Kevin to my parents, aren't you? Oh boy, this is going to be trickier than I thought."

"Relax. I told Rob that Richard and I would pick your parents up in our car and then take them home after. I just thought that would be easier for them. So they would have some company on the way."

"Oh, thanks. That gets them out of my hair."

"We're all terribly excited about meeting Kevin. It's really wonderful. Everyone's been waiting so long to meet this mystery man."

Brad smiled. God, this was the scariest thought of all. Everyone important in his life would be meeting Kevin tomorrow night. He was sure it would all be fine. All he would have to do is get through the dinner.

There was a knock at the door and Corrine answered it. A secretary poked her head in. "I'm really sorry to be interrupting, but it's the White House."

"Thank you," said Brad. "Put them on hold."

Across town in West Hollywood, a more subdued celebration was taking place. Shane and Greg were standing in front of the full-length mirror that Shane had bought at Home Depot when he started his bodybuilding regime.

Shane was completely nude and Greg had his face about four inches from Shane's newly enlarged penis.

"The doctor said the scars will fade soon," Shane was telling him, "and then I can go in for more electrolysis around the base of the shaft. He told me he could have made it thicker, but there wasn't enough fat in my thighs to suck out. He said to lay off the gym for three weeks, eat a lot of ice cream and junk food, and then he would try again."

"He wasn't serious, I hope. Well, anyway, it looks pretty good," Greg commented. "Does it still work?"

"I haven't tried it out yet. It should. But the important thing is, now I have a really good bulge for when I pose down."

"Yeah. A big bulge is all that counts, basically."

Shane hitched up his shorts and Greg went into his gym bag for the steroids. The walls of Shane's apartment, like Greg's, were now lined with pictures of bodybuilders. Shane used to have neatly framed snapshots of his airline friends on display, but he had taken them down. Now, pictures of Lee Haney, the Mr. Olympia eight-time champion, dominated the terrain.

"I'll just do you today," said Shane. "I get drug-tested at work now, and I have a flight to Pittsburgh tomorrow night."

"Oh, please," scoffed Greg. "They don't test for steroids. They test for cocaine, shit like that. I mean, like the shit that's bad for you. Imagine putting cocaine up your nose. Talk about low self-esteem."

"Okay," Shane agreed. He needed little convincing. He loved the jamming in of the needle now as much as Greg did. When he didn't have a poke, he felt small and weak.

•　•　•

"So are you coming to this party or what?" asked Kevin. He and Leon were at the Starbucks on Santa Monica, sitting outside in the traffic fumes, drinking black coffees. Kevin was chain-smoking.

"When are you going to give those up?" said Leon. "They constrict the blood vessels around your eyes and make you look puffy."

"They do not," snapped Kevin. Still, he threw the butt on the ground.

"And do you have to litter?" Leon chided. "This is still my neighborhood, you know."

"The world is my ashtray," said Kevin. "Haven't you heard the news? Brad is now worth about a billion dollars."

"Yes, of course I heard. I'm very happy for you. And yes, I'm coming to the party. Oh, Kevin, I have to tell you the most unbelievable thing! I met this guy at the gym the other day, this incredibly cute Australian, and guess what? He invited me to the party, too! He lives in Rob Erikson's guest house."

"You're kidding."

"No, angel face, I am not kidding. Not kidding at all. Furthermore, he came back to the apartment and we had the greatest sex. I mean, the chemistry was just amazing. We even did it in the bed."

"Shame on you. Have you forgotten everything I ever taught you?" Kevin said. "Ugh, sex in a bed. That ain't natural."

"Well, you had it all wrong, Kevin. It was fantastic. And I really like him. We have another date tonight."

Kevin lit up again. "Well, does he have a pot to piss in?"

"God, Kevin, you are so gross. I don't know. I don't really care. He's cute and really nice and, well, I think it could develop into something."

"Oh, God, what an unnatural thought." Kevin put on his new Oliver Peoples sunglasses. "Well, then I guess I'll see you tomorrow night at the party. But what are you doing now? I have to go see Jerry at the salon and get some revitalizing texturizer, but then I thought I might stroll around the Century City mall. Want to come?"

"Can't," said Leon. "Have to work."

"Oh, come on. I'll buy you a new outfit for the party and then we can go have a cocktail at the Beverly Wilshire Hotel. We'll charge it all to Magnet. Excuse me, I mean Digisynth. It'll be fun."

"Nah."

"Well, then, how about we go to the Museum of Television and watch an old *Facts of Life* episode? Brad and I went to a gala there and they gave me a permanent pass."

"Kevin. I'm supposed to be lugging some Mexican paver tiles up to Holmby Hills right now."

Kevin frowned.

"And then I have to get ready for my date."

Kevin's frown deepened, bordering on the sincere. Leon realized with a start that his old roommate looked actually sad, as though he had no one to turn to.

"Oh, sugar cookies," said Leon, relenting. "Well, I suppose I can put off the tiles until tomorrow morning."

"Really? Can you make the time?"

"What the hell. I've been dying to go there anyway, and if I go early I'll miss out on a lot of traffic."

"This is great," said Kevin with, for him, an embarrassing degree of enthusiasm. "You can leave your car here, and we'll take my car, and then I'll drive you back."

"Sounds like a plan."

But halfway down the block, Kevin's new Motorola Star-Tac cell phone, the one Brad gave him, rang. Leon watched as Kevin stood in the middle of the sidewalk going through a series of "uh-huhs," "sures," "mmms," and, finally, "*no problem, Brad.*"

"What?" Leon asked as Kevin rang off.

"Brad wants me to drive out to Malibu with him tonight and help him find an old contract in the storage unit in the garage."

"Oh."

"And then we have a seven-thirty reservation at Geoffrey's."

"That sounds nice," said Leon.

"He needs me to come get him in half an hour."

"Oh."

"Shit," said Kevin.

"Well, hey, no big deal," Leon told him. "We'll make it another time. I really shouldn't be goofing off like this, anyway."

"Yeah," Kevin said. "See you around, Leon."

CHAPTER 25

On the day of the party, all of *tout* gay Hollywood was in a tizzy. There was absolutely no doubt anymore in anyone's mind that Brad Sherwood was the undisputed king of the town, at least for this week, and attendance was mandatory. Those unlucky few that had not been invited scheduled back to back therapy appointments to cope with their shame.

"Darling," said Mike Brazier, on the phone to his wife, "I won't be coming to your mother's tonight. Why don't you and the kids go on without me."

"Oh, so you're going to that big gay thing at Rob Erikson's."

"It's a party for Brad Sherwood," Mike corrected her. "It's business."

"Yeah, right. Can I just say two words to you, Mike? *Community property!*"

Mike took off his headset and looked over at Dan Evans, who was lounging on the couch in his conversation area. "Okay, Dan, so we can go to this together if you want. How badly do you want to come?"

"I need to go to that party."

Mike got up, walked around his massive glass desk, and shut the office door. "Well, that party is the biggest deal in town. And Brad Sherwood is the biggest player in this town. Now, if you were a client I could get you in no problem."

"I understand," said Dan.

"But it's rare these days that I take on a new client," Mike added.

"I know that," Dan answered, downcast and humble. "Everyone knows that."

"Still, I'm only human, Dan. I have certain needs. I'm thinking you might just be the one to take care of them."

Dan went for the top button on his jeans. "On the coffee table like last time?"

"No, Dan, nothing like that. Whatever we had before is now completely in the past. I'm not looking for someone who just wants to, as the old joke says, sleep their way to the middle. No, what I'm looking for now is someone who's willing to go all the way."

"That's me," Dan told him.

"Well, we'll see." Mike launched into a series of rapid-fire questions.

"Do any drugs?"

"No, sir," said Dan.

"Hang out in gay bars?"

"No."

"Willing to sign a contract promising you won't?"

"Sure."

"Willing to take a gay film role?"

Dan hesitated. "No?"

"Why not? You need to play a gay part now and then. It makes people think you're really straight."

"Oh."

"Have any opinions about Scientology?"

"No."

"*Good.* That's the correct answer in this town. Now, let me ask you something else. Do you respect your craft?"

"Yes?"

Mike leaned in close. "To work as an actor in this town is the greatest privilege in the world. There's a hundred thousand members of SAG and Equity, but how many of them actually make a living at it? Why should I give you a shot?"

"Because you know I'm going to be a star," Dan said.

"Stars I have. I want artists. And I don't just mean someone who can win an Oscar. I want someone who thirty years down the road is gonna bag the Jean-fucking-Hersholt Humanitarian Award. At this point in my life, I only want to sign someone who will devote their whole life to building the perfect career. A Gregory Peck. A Clint Eastwood. A Tony Danza."

Dan gulped. Never before in his wildest dreams did he ever imagine he could go that far.

"If we go on this journey, Dan, I'm going to take you very seriously. The question is, are you going to take yourself seriously?"

"Yes," promised Dan.

"I hope you mean that," Mike asserted. "And I hope you realize I'll be in charge the whole way. Pretend you're on death row and I'm the only lawyer in town who has the governor's ear."

Dan nodded his head excitedly. Movie clichés he *understood*.

"Okay, get up," said Mike. "I'm going to follow you in my car back to your house. I have to see what you have to wear to this party tonight."

The hijinks at Rob's parties were legendary, but this event, because of all the prestige, would undoubtedly top them all.

Old-time friends from New York had booked last-minute reservations at the Beverly Hills Hotel, or the Mondrian, or the Chateau Marmont, and were now in their rooms, taking their all-important disco naps.

Three top go-go boys had been flown in from Miami. At the moment they were ensconced in the Holloway Motel, loading up on carbs.

Mylar fig leaf costumes for the waiters had been designed and fitted.

A stage was built on one corner of the property for the star stripper.

Extra permits had been obtained from the City of Beverly Hills for parking. Lavish gift baskets from Neiman's, with hand-signed notes from Rob apologizing in advance for the commotion, had been sent to all the surrounding neighbors.

Light-and-sound directors, their walkie-talkies crackling importantly all afternoon, had finally positioned all the generators, laid all the miles of cable.

But all that stuff was par for the course. Normal. To his everlasting relief, the only issue that would have prevented Rob from sleeping soundly through *his* disco nap was finally resolved: twenty of LA's most decorative boy escorts had been taken out of hiding, and then sternly advised of the most important party directive of all: "*Make sure nobody is ignored.*"

"Corrine is picking my parents up, so we can relax a bit," said Brad.

"Well then let's have some champagne before we go," Kevin suggested. "Are you as nervous as I am?"

"Don't worry. My parents will love you."

"Well, open a bottle anyway while I'm in the shower."

"Okay."

Kevin went padding off to the marble master bath. Brad, already dressed, uncorked a bottle of Taittinger and went into the living room.

He felt totally spiffy in his black Armani suit. He knew that photographers might ambush him at any point, so he wore dark shades that would look menacing in nighttime photos. To jazz it up, he put on a new Hermès tie that Bill from Neiman's had sent over after hearing the news of his coup. His hair, now that he was on his three hundred thirty-fifth plug treatment, seemed almost luxurious.

With nothing to do, he put on "Potion," his favorite cut from the *Tell That Girl Hi* CD. The sexy tune, richer and more melodic than their earlier efforts, wafted out over the terrace. To perfect the moment, and better enjoy the limitless vista of the city twinkling below him, he dimmed the lights.

When Kevin emerged from his shower, Brad met him in the vast master bath with a glass of champagne.

"I'd give you a kiss," Kevin said shyly, "but I don't want to ruin your suit."

"It's tempting, but I respect your sage take on the issue." He handed Kevin a plush white towel.

Kevin, dawdling, drenched himself in Neutrogena body oil while Brad watched.

"Maybe we should hurry a little," Brad said. "Jeremy's been downstairs waiting for over an hour."

"I thought you fired him. You know I can't stand him."

"Well, this is the last time you'll have to see him. I'm arranging for tighter security now."

"Jesus, Brad, tonight of all nights. It's so ghoulish, the way he's always hanging around."

"I know. But just put up with him for tonight, okay?"

"Okay, Brad, anything you want. It's your night." Kevin knotted the towel around his waist and then began the process of untangling his hair with a wide-toothed comb. "Jeremy doesn't really bother me, you know. He's fine. He's got his life, we've got our perfect life. It just bothers me that I've never really been able to win him over."

"Don't worry about it."

Kevin, dry now, turned and let the towel slip from his hips.

"Oh, no," Brad groaned. "Don't start. Finish getting dressed."

"You're right," said Kevin. "Get out of here. Shoo. I don't want your parents to blame me if we're late."

Brad took his glass and went into his office. A final guest list (the third that day) had just been faxed over. By some of the names, Rob had scribbled little remarks. *"Cary and Kerry Sanders: Remember them? Those identical twins off the farm? I got them jobs at Disneyland and they live in Anaheim now. They said they'd drive up."*

Brad continued perusing the list. He knew the names of all the movie executives, and there were others from New York whom he hadn't seen for years. Then there was a hand-picked contingent of retired ice dancers, and a few extraordinary old queens who had lived in Hollywood forever and rarely crawled down out of the hills for anyone. God, it was going to be old-home week.

Brad skimmed further down the list and saw Mike Brazier's name. He liked Mike, had even met his wife and kids. That would be interesting, seeing Mike at an all-male affair like this. He might just make that final leap to the other side. The name just below Mike's was Dan Evans.

Dan Evans. That name again. The name that had created so much unnecessary tension in an otherwise perfect deal.

Brad speed-dialed Rob.

"Darling," said Rob, "Eleanor's dealer is here and I'm not dressed. And the caterers are absolutely gorgeous, but shy, so Kim's racing around trying to find some spare Xanax and Halcyon so they'll feel more comfortable in their fig-leaf costumes . . . and the video guy from Falcon is making such a fuss about the lighting! How could you call me at such a moment?"

"I just have a quick question. I'm looking at the guest list. Who is Dan Evans?"

"Good God, how on earth should I know? I don't know half of all these bad new children."

"Can you get your list? Or find out?"

"Oh, you are such a pain. Hang on." Rob dropped the phone, but came back a few moments later. "Okay, Dan Evans, Dan Evans, uh, here he is. Hmm, well, it looks like he's a last-minute invite, coming with Mike Brazier. He could be an actor or something. Oh darn, there's the door."

"Can't you tell me anything else? His name keeps cropping up at the strangest times."

"Please, Brad. Stop trying to control everything. It's all going to be fine."

"It's just really bugging me."

"He could be anyone! You would not believe who's been trying to get on my guest list. Straights! Straights trying to *pass!* Come on up, darling! Brad,

Elinor is here. Her dealer came through with some coke. She's a gem, that woman. Oh, God, let me go!"

Brad hung up. The *Tell That Girl Hi* album ended and the CD player switched itself off.

"Kevin, what's taking you so long?"

Down the marble hallway, Kevin yelled back. "I'm almost ready!"

Feeling antsy, even vaguely irritable, Brad got up and flipped the switch on the electric fireplace. The flames silently sprang to life.

He wondered if there was anyone else he could call. No, he could think of no one. It was ridiculous, anyway; the party tonight was his coronation, and tomorrow he would be beginning a whole new life. That was the point of the buyout, wasn't it? To make time to see the world, to experience intimacy, to shed his old habits. To discover what else life had to offer besides relentless success and achievement.

Kevin came in quietly. He, of course, looked fabulous.

Not wearing his usual gloomy black tonight, Kevin was dressed in an electric-blue Claude Montana suit with a white shirt and white tie. It was a look suitable only for a Paris runway . . . or a once-in-a-lifetime party. To heighten the drama of his miraculous cheekbones, he had slicked back his hair.

"I hope this is okay. Maybe it's a little too high-fashion for your parents."

"You look amazing."

Kevin went behind the desk and gave Brad one of his well-rehearsed lovey-dovey kisses. But this time there was no hesitation. They were working as a team tonight, and both knew they would need each other.

"I just spoke to Rob, and the party sounds like it's going to be out of this world," said Brad. "I want you to stay by my side."

"I plan to. Every vicious queen in Hollywood will be trying to steal you away from me tonight. Except, of course, for my old roommate, Leon. Seems he has a thing for your friend Rob's little houseboy."

"Really. Say, do you know anyone else who's going?" Brad handed the guest list to Kevin.

Kevin skimmed down the list and when he came to certain celebrities, he admitted to himself that, okay, he was excited about meeting them. But, of course, he did not let on.

"A couple names seem familiar. But Leon is the only good friend. You'll like him."

Brad felt benevolent. "Well, let's have him over next week."

"You might want to use him for a job. He does these really original trompe l'oeil things with second-hand furniture and—"

"Kevin," chuckled Brad, "try to have a little perspective. You must understand that if I use him for anything, he will instantly become the most important decorator in LA."

"I just thought—"

"Forget it," said Brad, a little too harshly. "Let me explain something to you. I'm sure he's talented, but not everyone is ready to step up to the plate. He's involved with a houseboy, for God's sake."

"I see."

"And, besides, I'm no longer in the business of doing favors."

"Gotcha."

"I'm trying to subtract people from my life, not add!"

"Oh, man. Such a tough guy. Give me a kiss. Face it, Brad. You'll always be doing favors. They should make you the pope."

Brad cracked a smile.

"Come on. Let's polish off this champagne and then leave. I hate to see it go to waste."

"Don't worry," said Brad. "There's more in the car."

"*And there always will be,*" thought Kevin, as he pulled Brad into another embrace.

Kevin felt wonderful and complete as he held Brad. The spell, however, was broken when he happened to glance, once more time, down at the guest list.

"Dan Evans? Who invited him?"

"What?"

"This guy . . . Dan Evans."

"Do you know him?"

"Fuck yes! I took some head shots of him once and he never paid me. What a jerk. Let's tell security to keep him out of the party."

"Okay," said Brad, the two syllables carefully measured. "I'll just call Rob."

"Oh, wait a minute. Forget it. We can't let some big queen like Dan Evans spoil this night. I'm sorry for overreacting like that." Kevin looked at the Tiffany clock on Brad's desk. "Shoot. Now we're really gonna be late."

"You're right." Brad went over and switched off the fireplace. "Let me just make a quick trip to the john."

"Yeah," Kevin said. "I'll go, too."

They headed off in different directions.

Brad went into the powder room off the foyer.

What a nice little room, he thought. He could not recall ever seeing it be-fore. It could use a new wall treatment, though. And those tassled brown guest towels were strictly from hunger.

"Big Queen, Big Queen."

After washing his hands, Brad wadded up the towels and tossed them on the basin so that Minerva or Innocencia would find them. He'd have to let them know they could take them home.

Gold Kohler faucets? Those would have to be changed, too. What had the decorator been thinking? Trump Tower. But at least the drain was run-ning well; Kevin must have had the super up. That was thoughtful of him.

"Big Queen, Big Queen."

One night, on the phone with Rob, both of them watching TV, Brad caught a documentary starring Queen Elizabeth. She was on a tour of Harlem. At the small, spotless home of a large black woman, the Queen said, "Just the one room, is it? How nice. It must be nice to live in only one room."

At the time, Brad had no idea what the Queen was talking about.

"Big Queen, Big Queen."

But he did now.

"Are you still in there?" called Kevin.

Brad reluctantly reached for the handle of the door. Never in his life had he felt so sad. He never wanted to leave this small, wonderful powder room.

"Kevin," said Brad quietly, "we need to talk."

"What? We can talk in the car."

"No. This is important."

"What's the matter, Brad? Don't want to go to your own party?" Kevin reached forward to adjust Brad's tie. "Come on. You know we'll have a good time."

Brad grabbed Kevin's fingers and held them.

"Kevin. Did you ever send a fax to a man named Fenny Atkinson?"

Kevin's face drained of color and he fluttered his magnificent eyelashes a few times.

"A fax that said 'Dan Evans is a big queen who has no right to be on television' or some other such nonsense?"

"I can explain," whispered Kevin, his green eyes glittering.

"Oh, God, I hope so." Brad let go of Kevin's fingers.

"This guy," began Kevin, "Dan Evans. He's the kind of guy who always seemed to be in my life until you came along. He owed me some money and he never paid me. Then he thought he could get me to sleep with him. So I just thought I would fuck him with a little poison-pen letter."

"Do what?"

"You know, drop word that he was a big queen. Ruin his chances. *Out* him."

"Kevin," Brad asked, "what are you talking about? We don't out people."

"I know. I know that now. But I was really broke at the time, and he humiliated me. And now he's got this big career. It's not fair."

"Kevin," said Brad, "maybe you think that because an actor is gay he doesn't deserve to be on television, but those of us who have spent our lives in this town think otherwise. It's not that we're saints. It's just harder to get gay actors insurance."

"Look, I know it sounds crazy, but you weren't there. This was an old beef between me and Dan."

"Then why did you drag me into it? Someone I do business with traced your call to a place in Hollywood called Mailbox Center. I know the day and time you placed that call."

"Oh, Brad. I'm so sorry. It was a dumb joke," Kevin pleaded. "But your deal still went through. So everybody's happy."

"Um, not really." Brad paced back and forth. "This is . . . really weird, Kevin. I don't know what to make of this. Where did you get the number?"

Kevin sensed a reprieve. "I had the number already. You'll enjoy this story and then you'll understand everything. Remember the day we met, Christmas Day? You left your address book in my car. So I copied down some numbers. This is Hollywood, right? Anyone would have."

"Maybe anyone would have, yes, but not someone I trust. Not the person I had hoped to spend the rest of my life with."

"Oh, Brad, I'm so sorry. I did this before all the good stuff happened between us. It was stupid, and I'll do anything I can to make it up to you, I promise. There's so much more I want to talk to you about, and you've been so busy. You always are. Can you try to understand?"

"I don't know if we can just forget this, Kevin. Not because you copied the numbers down—I can understand that. But to use them the way you did, well, it's just kind of unbelievable."

"Brad, I swear. It wasn't supposed to affect you."

"Yeah? Well, guess what? It did."

"Look, Brad, haven't there been times in your life when you got pissed off and cut a few corners? Taken advantage of an opportunity?"

"Yes, of course," said Brad. "But not like this. My God, what were you thinking? Do you have any idea how delicate this whole deal was?"

"I didn't know about your deal! You never even told me!"

While that may have been true, Brad could not let Kevin off the hook so easily. His whole carefully crafted world would go to rack and ruin if he allowed people to go about acting upon all their tiny-brained impulses. Still, he tried to give Kevin the benefit of the doubt.

"Let me get this straight. You were, what, trying to get some kind of revenge?"

"Brad, I'm totally ashamed of myself, totally disgusted. But I was really crazy when I did it."

Brad paced up and down the foyer a few more times, considering Kevin's apology.

"Okay," he concluded, finally. "We'll talk about this tomorrow. Thank God you didn't send it to anyone else."

Kevin's mouth dropped.

"Oh, don't tell me," said Brad. "Who else did you send it to?"

"Nobody," mumbled Kevin. "Just a few people around town."

"Who?"

"I don't know! I can't remember. Some agents, some press."

"The *press?*" gasped Brad.

"Brad. I'm sorry. I didn't know you then! If I had, I wouldn't have done anything."

"Where are the numbers?"

"Brad . . ."

"Just do the me the courtesy of answering the question, Kevin."

"I threw them out."

"Jesus. Couldn't you have at least put them in a shredder? The tabloids go through my garbage!"

"But I tore them up," said Kevin.

"Oh, my God. The press?"

"Brad, it was dumb, I know, but this guy really fucked me over!"

Brad stormed away out of the foyer. How many people knew about this little stunt? Had they been laughing at him behind his back for months? He could hear them now, whispering at their tables in restaurants, joking about it before meetings. *"Brad Sherwood's gone off the deep end. He took that sleazy little number out of West Hollywood . . . and actually installed him in his own home."*

Brad returned to the foyer and exploded with rage.

"God damn you! You know, I could forgive you for copying the numbers. And I could forgive you for not coming to me about it. But sending this fax . . . to the press? Kevin. You behaved like a stalker! People go to prison for less than this!"

"Brad, you're blowing this way out of proportion—"

"Never in my life have I been so embarrassed. How could you do something so . . . tacky? So low-rent?"

"Brad, please. Can't we just drop this until tomorrow? I'm meeting your parents in ten minutes."

"Meet my parents? I would never dream of introducing you to my parents now. I could never look them straight in the face again."

"Brad, what's happening? Why won't you let me explain?"

Brad, after so many months of almost unbearable tension, didn't want Kevin to explain. He knew he might regret what he was about to say, but he wasn't about to stop. He was flying too high, fueled now by his own anger.

"Because I'm afraid this little prank says everything about you, Kevin. It says it all. Let me explain something to you. You were nothing when you met me. I took you in off the street. I gave you a home and a career. And this is how you repay me? By faxing this bullshit all around town just so you can get some sort of childish revenge? Do you even realize what you did? You fucked with the money flow! The money that allows you to live like a decent human being for the first time in your shabby life. Thank God I found this out now. For a moment there, Kevin, you almost had me thinking you were different. But I was wrong. You're a hustler. And not even a very smart one at that."

Brad reached up, grabbed Kevin by the lapels and pushed him against the wall. "You idiot! Don't you even realize there is always someone younger and more beautiful ready to replace you?"

There it was. The words had been spoken. It was out. The central truth

about their arrangement, about the town. About the system they all em-
braced. The score.

"It wasn't like that between us," replied Kevin evenly, "and you know it."

"Get out of my house," Brad said coldly. "Back to the street. Go! What
do I have to do, call security?"

"Call *security*?" Kevin began to find his own anger. "Oh, that's great,
Brad. Just beautiful. That is really just so LA. No, don't bother calling security. I'll go. I never belonged here, anyway. But just remember, you took
what you wanted out of this deal, too. You think I had it so easy? Parading
me around, showing me off like I was your new little fuck-toy. Well, go
ahead. Trade me in. Go pick up someone else."

And with that, Kevin flung open the front door and ran down the stairwell.

"You little hustler!" Brad yelled after him. "Get back here. I'm not finished with you! Everything I did I did for you!"

Under the canopy of the building, Jeremy was waiting with the engine
running. When he saw Kevin careening through the lobby, dressed up in
his electric-blue suit, he folded his newspaper and lumbered out of the
limo.

"I won't be needing a ride, Jeremy," barked Kevin as he pushed through
the door. "You can get back in the car and sit on your hemorrhoids a little
longer." He started to move away, then looked back. "He's going to fire
you, you know," Kevin said, then turned and ran.

Adrenaline pumping, Kevin tripped down the ramp and started jogging
down Wilshire. A methanol-powered bus sped by within inches of flatten-
ing him, the close call sobering him into slowing down and moving in
closer to the gutter. A dangling piece of snot was blocking his ability to
breathe, so he wiped it on his jacket. Then he searched his pockets for a cigarette. *Damn*. And to think that a fresh pack was hidden back in the penthouse, in his sock drawer.

Kevin wiped his eyes and squinted into the distance. A bank of at least
seventy cars were revving their engines at a light. Any minute now, they'd all
be bearing down on him. Reflexively, he put his thumb out.

The phalanx of cars roared past, spattering him with a rich mixture of
pebbles and dust. No one, of course, even slowed down, so Kevin waited
for another traffic cycle. After a few minutes, seventy more cars, contain-

ing seventy people, headlights blazing, thundered by. No one even looked at him.

This was ridiculous. A ride was not going to happen.

He staggered along the edge of the dark road, tasting fumes, concentrating on survival. He regretted not grabbing the keys to the Mercedes that Brad had just bought for him, but it was too late to go back now. Knowing Brad, the building guards had probably already been ordered to block his reentry.

His options, in the course of a few minutes, had plummeted from unlimited to nil. And his worst fear had come true: when word about this got out, there would be nowhere he would be welcome in LA. Gossip like this was hard currency, and hookers got respect only in the movies. But where could he go? Not back to New York. Hot Tip Capozi still monitored his every move.

Kevin came upon a panhandler who seemed to be trying to reach the safety of a traffic island. The man held a bent paper cup and a dirty cardboard sign: WILL ACT FOR FOOD. Kevin, so distracted by his current dilemma, actually forgot to worry about airborne tuberculosis as he brushed past him.

As it always does at nightfall in the desert, the temperature plunged, so Kevin was chilled to the bone when he finally crossed over Doheny, the border between Beverly Hills and West Hollywood. Passing Rage, a local bar, he saw a crowd dancing. A clip from *Victor/Victoria* was playing on a video screen in the background. Oh, for crying out loud! Was no one exempt from punishment tonight?

These guys in the bar were not your power-gays—the kind that would be attending Rob Erikson's party. No, these were your working gays, your hapless tourists, your scar-faced regulars. Kevin never had much to do with them. (Acid-washed jeans? *Still?*) He scurried passed the joint with his head down, struck for the first time by the appropriateness of the bar's name.

When he at last made it back to his old Westmount apartment, he was grimy and parched. Never in his life had his hair been this filthy. But did it not look incredible, as though a stylist had mussed it for a shoot? No, it looked frightening. And it took only an hour on the streets to get it that way. Already he was beginning to look and smell like a vagrant.

He desperately hoped Leon hadn't yet left for the party. No lights could be seen through the side window, but he jammed his finger into the buzzer anyway.

The adjacent door cracked open.

"Shane!" Kevin wanted to hug him. "Thank God you're home."

"What happened to you?" asked Shane. "You look terrible. And why aren't you at the party? I thought it was for you and that guy Brad Sherman?"

"Huh? Oh, yeah, him. Well, I'm afraid Brad and I are no longer. Um, can I come in for a minute? I just walked all the way here from Beverly Hills."

"It's not really a good time. I have a flight tonight. I have to iron a uniform shirt."

"Look, Shane, I'm in a bit of a jam. Could I just use your phone or something?"

"Okay. But I have to leave in about forty-five minutes."

"Thanks. You can't imagine the day I've been having."

Kevin slipped into Shane's apartment and gasped. The living room was dimly lit with red bulbs and the walls were plastered with pictures of bodybuilders. They covered every inch of space.

"I see you've really taken this gym thing to heart, Shane."

"I didn't ask you in just so you could make fun of me, Kevin. Why didn't you invite me to your party? I thought we were friends."

"We are. But it was just another industry thing. I didn't think you would have enjoyed it. Anyway, well, you and I are here now, right?"

"Bullshit."

"Mmm. Yeah. You got that right. Look, um, Shane, I feel really bad."

"Don't apologize. I don't want to hear it. I'm sorry, but I just don't, okay?" Shane went over to an end table. "Here's the phone. I picked up a Pittsburgh red-eye tonight for extra money and I can't be late. I'm in enough trouble with the airline already. So make your call and then leave."

"Listen, Shane, I'm in kind of a bind. I think I've worn out my welcome in this town. Can you get me a free flight or something? It would really help. You'd be helping out an old friend."

"Hah! Kevin, there's no such thing as a free flight. The only people who can fly free are spouses."

"But what about all the gay guys? Gays don't have spouses."

"Well, they're shit out of luck, pardon my French. You have to be married or you get nothing."

"That's a pretty unfair system," Kevin commented. And then he remembered Brad talking once about fighting for gay marriage. Brad offered partner benefits at Magnet—all the studios did—but it was pretty thin gruel when you got down to it.

Shane went into the kitchen and set up an old ironing board. Kevin wanted to sob at the horror of it all. Imagine, having to go out to work in the middle of the night. Imagine having to put on a uniform. Imagine having to wear a *name tag*.

He then noticed the backs of Shane's huge arms. They were covered in fiery acne scars. "Shane. Are you on steroids?"

"Maybe I am and maybe I'm not."

"You *are*. God, those are poison. What do you think you're doing?"

"Listen, Kevin. It's none of your business. Some of us weren't born gorgeous, you know. For some of us, it takes a little extra. And in this city, if you're not beautiful, you're in big trouble. Now that I have a body, people like me. I get dates, I get cruised, and if all it takes is a little jab of a needle now and then, it's worth it."

"Gee, Shane, I'm sorry. I didn't mean anything by it. I just don't think it's very healthy."

Shane laughed. "Well, you smoke."

"Mmm," Kevin grunted in acknowledgment. "You may have a point."

"We all need something, I guess," said Shane.

"I don't suppose you have a cigarette lying around?"

"No."

"Didn't think so."

"So, Kevin. You need a ticket." Shane chuckled. "Sounds like you're desperate. Where do you need to go?"

"I don't know. I just have to get out of this town. It doesn't really matter where. As usual, I haven't thought it out."

"Well, there is a way I could get you on my flight tonight. That is, if you want to go to Pittsburgh."

"Pittsburgh?"

"Yeah, Pittsburgh. It's a place in Philadelphia."

Kevin considered the idea of Pittsburgh. Was that the place in the *Rocky* movie? Or was it *Flashdance*? What did people do in Pittsburgh? Oh, as if any of that mattered. It was an option. His only option. He would never get back on the gay A-list, or any list now. That life was officially over.

"Yeah, okay," Kevin decided. "I'll go to Pittsburgh. But how do we do it? I don't have any money."

Shane dragged a wheeled suitcase into the room. "Oh, I can sneak you on the plane. It's easy. Just go to the gate and I'll be there taking tickets. Walk up like you know what you're doing, and then once you get on board, wait for me in the aft lavatory. I'll find you a seat and then you can just sleep the whole flight."

"What about security?"

"Security?" said Shane mockingly. "At an airport?"

"Well, what if the flight is full?"

"It won't be. I just checked on my computer. As of right now there are twelve open seats."

"Will you get in trouble?"

"Do you think I'd do it if I was going to get in trouble? I'm not stupid, you know."

It sounded like a plan Kevin could live with. Sneak out of town—just his style. He could fly to Pittsburgh, hitch his way to Florida somehow, and then crash at his parents' condo. He would work something out. The hell with LA. Enough with these phony, plastic Hollywood types. It would be good to be back on the East Coast with real people.

"Okay. I'll do it."

"Well, wait a minute, not so fast," said Shane. "Why should I do this for you? When have you ever done me a favor?"

"Oh, come on, Shane, give me a break. Brad Sherwood just kicked me out and I'm not in the best mood."

"You've always been really snotty with me, Kevin," Shane stated as he expertly ironed his shirt cuffs. "Don't deny it. But there is one thing you could do for me. In fact, I'd be really grateful."

"Name it."

"It's just a simple blow job. I mean, I've fantasized about you since I moved in here. It would really make me happy."

"You're kidding."

"No, I'm not. It's all I ask. And if you want to get on my flight, that's what you have to do. We midwesterners keep our word."

Kevin was, in the end, not surprised by the request. Isn't that what they all wanted? Wasn't that all Brad had wanted? It was all Anthony wanted, too. Who was he to deny them?

"Okay," Kevin sighed. "What the fuck."

"Great," Shane replied. "Let me just go hang up this shirt. Meanwhile, get out of those clothes."

Kevin, feeling truly whorish, removed his fourteen-hundred-dollar jacket. The shirt and pants came off next. He hadn't, of course, worn underwear. He had wanted to feel especially sexy at the party.

Shane came out of his bedroom. "God, are you gorgeous, even with a little dirt on your face. I wish I had a camera. Mine got stolen out of my luggage."

"Pity."

"Oh, relax. This will be fun for you, I promise. And when we get to Pittsburgh, I'll treat you to a Philly cheese steak. They're world famous and they sell them right at the airport."

A Philly cheese steak? Kevin could only imagine the grease, the grams of fat, the cholesterol.

"Oh, and one more thing," said Shane, as he stepped out of his pants. "I just had a penis enlargement. The stitches just came out, so be gentle."

"What? Now you really have to be kidding."

"Don't laugh at me!" snapped Shane.

"I'm not! No, Shane, I'm not. Really, I'm not."

And then Kevin astonished himself by grabbing Shane and pulling him into a tight hug.

"Thanks for being here," whispered Kevin. "You've been a real friend."

CHAPTER 26

Shane had it all wrong. You couldn't get a Philly cheese steak at the Pittsburgh airport, and certainly not at six in the morning. Instead, Shane bought Kevin a microwaved bagel that came with a small container of cream cheese. Against all his better instincts, Kevin scarfed it down, and it tasted good. But anything would taste good after that long flight with no food.

Sneaking on the plane proved to be one of the easiest stunts Kevin had ever pulled off. Shane simply guided him to a seat near an exit row, slipped him a free headset, and then covered him with a blanket. Before takeoff, the cabin lights were dimmed. Less than half a second into the "Channel Four Celebration of Kenny G," Kevin passed out. He did not wake up until they landed.

"Are you going to be all right?" Shane asked him as the drowsy passengers started dragging their belongings out of the overhead bins.

"Sure," said Kevin. "You've been a real pal, Shane. Thanks for helping me out."

"Thanks for helping me out, too, Kevin. Are you sure it doesn't droop too much?"

"No, it's great. You could hang a Donna Karan car coat on that thing, no problem."

Shane beamed. "Come on. I'll walk you out into the terminal."

Shane proved to be a real mensch. Just before getting back on his return flight, he impulsively withdrew two twenties from a cash machine and handed them over to Kevin.

"Oh, Shane. That's really not necessary. You've done enough."

"Nah, just take them. I have to leave you on your own now. The cleaners are getting off the plane."

"Thanks. Hey, Shane. When you get back to LA, do me a favor. Don't tell Leon about me leaving town. I want to make a clean break."

"Sure. I understand. I guess you fell in with the wrong crowd."

"You could say that."

They hugged.

After Shane left, Kevin purchased a phone card that featured a picture of the Pittsburgh airport.

Boy, people around here look weird, thought Kevin as he stood at a phone kiosk calling Florida information. But then he probably looked weird, too. Not a lot of Pittsburgh types were sporting electric-blue Claude Montana this season.

"Yes, Malloy," said Kevin to the operator. "First name, Patrick."

"Hold for the number."

A mechanical voice slowly read out a series of digits and then a second computer-driven voice made the following announcement: "Global Tele-digicom will connect your call directly after this message, for an extra seventy-five cents. If you agree, press one. If you decline, press two. To repeat this information, press six."

Of course, that message succeeded in instantly erasing the number from Kevin's short-term memory bank, so he pressed one and the call was connected.

Oh boy, thought Kevin, *this is going to be too weird.* He hadn't spoken to his parents in ages. He just prayed his father wouldn't answer. *Hi, Dad. Hi, Dad, how's it going? How ya doin', Dad? How's life in . . . ?*

"Hello?"

"Dad? It's Kevin."

"Hang on, I'll put your mother on."

"Is that you, Kevin?" said Gina, an instant later.

"Yeah. Hi, Ma. Hey, what's with Dad? He didn't even say hello."

"He's got a Promise Keepers meeting this morning and he doesn't want to be late. It's his new hobby. Not that I mind. It gets him out of the house. But, gosh, how are you?"

"Oh, you know, all right. Busy. Mom, I—"

"Well, things sure are busy around here! We've got Diane and Jennifer living with us in the condo now. Luckily, we just got Jennifer enrolled in preschool so we'll have a little peace during the day."

"That's great, Mom. Listen, I—"

"She can be cranky sometimes, that Jennifer, but then all you kids were. I'm not worried—she'll grow out of it. I have to admit it's sort of nice to have a full house again. And I'm getting used to it down here. It's not so bad! The condo association asked me to serve as secretary and we've decided to put in group cable—just basic, for the reception. Oh, but enough about me. How's California?"

"Um, fine, Ma . . . Sort of crazy. Listen, I'm sorry I'm calling so early but—"

"No, no, it's good to hear from you."

"Mom? Do you think—"

"I'm real proud of you, Kevin. You won't have to stay away forever. I know it. But at least I know you're safe out there."

"I was thinking of coming down for a visit."

"Oh," said Gina, taken aback. "Do you really think that would be smart?"

"I don't know, Mom. What could be the harm?"

"Frankly, Kevin, now would not be the best time. Connie and Ralph came down last week and they wore your father out. We made a reservation for them at the Holiday Inn, but after they saw the room they decided to go to the Doral in Miami. Your father was so mad when we drove down for brunch! That was before they left for their cruise. Oh, gosh, so much has been going on, but at least Connie and Diane are speaking again."

"That's good."

"I think everything's going to be okay. But now I need to devote some time to your father. He's going to these meetings now, and he and I have both agreed that I have to start pulling my weight too."

According to a tiny digital display, the pricey phone-card minutes were adding up at an alarming clip.

"That's great, Mom."

"Give it some time, Kevin. And call me if you need anything. Maybe one of these days I'll get your father out to California!"

"Sure."

"Stay in touch."

"I will," said Kevin. "I love you, Mom."

But she had already hung up.

•   •   •

Well, that was not a major box-office triumph. But in any case, the thought of going home to his parents' condo had never held a great deal of appeal anyway.

Kevin considered trying to get through to his sister Diane. It'd been more than five years since he'd seen her, even longer than that since he'd seen his older sister Connie. Why hadn't they been closer? Why did all the kids in his family have so little to say to each other?

I wish I had made more friends, thought Kevin. I wish I hadn't been so cavalier. *I wish I had delivered meals.*

Only one option remained, and just the thought of it left him terrified. But what else could he do? It was time to call Anthony. It was a risk, it was a bad idea, but at this point he had nothing left to lose.

Besides, what harm could there be in a friendly phone call? Anthony probably didn't even live in that apartment on the West Side anymore. What the hell. Two-one-two, here I come, thought Kevin as he reentered the phone codes.

"Yo."

Kevin remembered that voice immediately. It sounded exactly the same as it always had, like when they used to work at Macy's.

"Yo? Hello?"

"Anthony?"

"Yeah, who's this?"

"It's Kevin."

"Holy shit. Hang on, let me switch phones." A few more minutes were eaten up.

"Jesus, Kevin. Where are you?"

"I'm not in New York, that's for sure."

"Well, hell, where you been? How ya doin', you little shit!"

"I'm okay. How are you?"

"I'm doing all right."

"Good, good."

"So when are you gonna come to New York and visit?" Anthony asked after an uneasy silence. "Pop and I sure would like to see you."

"*What?*"

"Yeah, stop on by."

"Won't that piss him off?"

"Oh, no. He's forgot all that shit. He knows I'm gay and he doesn't give a damn anymore. Actually, it would be good if you came around. We could all use a little cheering up."

"What are you talking about?"

"To tell you the truth, things ain't been going too well for us. As a matter of fact we're kind of in deep shit. A few deals in Atlantic City went a little sour and then the legit money wanted in, so we were screwed. A whole bunch of phony racketeering charges came down—you know, RICO bullshit—and then all these low-level politicians wanted to make a name for themselves. And they got lucky, the pricks. Personally, I blame the mayor. Nosy fucking busybody, Italian, too, can you believe it? Anyway, now we're about five months late on the building maintenance. We're about to get kicked out."

"Who's we?"

"Me and Pop. Janice too. We're all squeezed in. And Hot Tip's got emphysema. We're pretty worried about him."

Emphysema? Finally, a bit of good news. As far as Kevin was concerned, the old hard-on should kick tomorrow.

"Sorry to hear that. But can't you do something? Aren't you a rich lawyer by now?"

"Nope. Had to drop out. When you took off was right about the time the money began to dry up. Gosh, it sure would be good to see you, Kevin."

Was that a sniffle on the other end of the line?

"Yeah, you too," said Kevin, uncomprehendingly. "Hey, listen, to tell you the truth, Anthony, things aren't so hot for me either. Actually, I was hoping you could help me out a little bit. I'm in Pittsburgh."

"Sure, Kev. Whatever you need."

Kevin heaved a sigh of gratitude. "Great. I was thinking you could wire me a little money. For, like, plane fare to New York. It really would be great to see you."

"Wire you some money? Hah! I wish I could. I guess I haven't really explained the big picture. We're in *deep* shit here. I'm in trouble, too. In fact, when you called, it was like the answer to a prayer. I was kind of hoping you could help *us* out."

"Huh?"

"We can't put two quarters together," Anthony went on. "Can't even buy milk. We're practically living on pasta handouts. I'm on parole, delivering pizzas, 'cause I can't get a real job—I got a sheet. That's a whole other story, but you know how it is: They came in, made a sweep, and a lot of stuff was in my name. On top of that, a couple of guys we were counting on didn't come through. Fucking degenerate hard-ons. To tell you the truth, the stress has been so bad I've gained a shitload of weight. You wouldn't recognize me."

"Oh," Kevin whispered.

"It sure would be good to see you," Anthony said again. "I should have stuck by you, Kevin."

"Sounds like things didn't go too well for either of us. Listen, Anthony, I have to go now and take care of business. I'll try and make my way up to New York. Don't let the bastards get you down."

CHAPTER 27

Brad, accompanied by an old Harry Connick Jr. CD, swam fifty laps in his pool. Then he slipped into the Jacuzzi. It was five in the afternoon, and the western skies viewed from his Malibu house were, as always, a dramatic yet soothing backdrop. So spiritual, really, out here, and so quiet. You could barely hear the waves today.

Through the kitchen window, Brad could see Rob, wearing a white robe, stuffing carrots into a juicer.

The two of them had been hiding out for a few days now. All the phones had been turned off and had yet to be turned back on. Only Corrine knew where Brad was—she FedEx'ed his messages over. Most of them concerned the arrangements for his upcoming visit to the White House. After that little obligation was taken care of, he and Rob were going to Europe on the new long-range 757 he had just leased. For a long vacation, just the two of them.

Brad hoped he'd be able to pull himself together for the White House visit. The events of the past few months, topped off by the party, had taken so much out of him. He could not overcome a feeling of exhaustion and dread.

He dunked his head under the hot water for a few seconds and then leaned his head back against a blow-up *Flubber* pillow. Once again, he tried to remember what actually went on at the party. He had gone in and out of a few blackouts that night, so the details were sketchy.

The celebration had raged on for almost twenty-four hours. And everyone said it was fabulous.

It was amazing how they all came crawling out of the woodwork—faces they hadn't seen in years. If this were a pitch meeting, it would have sold as a cross between *Night of the Living Dead* and *Interview with the Vampire*. Or maybe it was more like *Weekend at Bernie's II*. Whatever it was, the press reported nothing. Certain stories were simply not offered up for public consumption. But then, the real soul-nourishing Hollywood gossip never got out; it wasn't good for the town.

God, it was decadent. Kind of like South Beach. And as is usually the case, it started out supremely civilized.

Corrine had picked up Midge and Sy on schedule, and then they all had a six-course meal at L'Orangerie, sauce on the side. Brad had never let on to his parents that he was bringing a "friend"; that was going to be a surprise. They believed the big night out was all about the privatization deal, so they didn't pick up on anything. Besides, there was no shortage of good news.

Brad, in no mood for champagne, ordered a Montrachet and proposed a toast.

"To my good friend Rob," said Brad, cool and smooth as ever. "He's stuck by me for all these years and so I'd like to do him a little favor in return." Brad raised his glass. "Rob, I'm going to make a movie about your ice show. I was a fool not to have gotten in at the beginning! But now I'm prepared to offer you a huge sum for the rights. Will you sell them to me?"

Rob blushed. "Of course. If you think you can afford me."

"Oh, I think I can. In fact, I think I'm prepared to drag you up into the ranks of the middle class."

"Excellent. It's about time."

"I've already hired a team of writers."

"Very naughty, but I guess you knew I would agree."

"I want to do a totally realistic animatronic version," Brad said. "No actors . . . only computer generated images and voices. A company in Utah has just about found a way to do it. They can create a full range of voices, hair being whipped around by the wind, anything at all. Totally state of the art. We'll break new ground. In fact, the technology is so advanced we can create new stars based on what we want, not on who's available. We don't even need human models, which means, of course, we won't have to pay them. I have to say, I'm really excited about the business again."

"Movies were always his first love," Midge whispered to Corrine.

Brad ditched his parents by ten, and then he and Rob took the yellow Rolls back to Rexford Drive.

"This is one of the guys I found at the gym," said Kim at the door. "I hope you don't mind, but I've decided to keep him for myself. His name is Leon."

"Oh, hello. Welcome to my house," said Rob. "I'd love to chat, but Brad and I need to go upstairs and change."

Kim winked. "Go right on up. Everything's ready."

Leon offered his hand. "Hi, Mr. Sherwood. You may not remember me, but we've met before."

"I meet a lot of people," said Brad dismissively.

"Enough dawdling," Rob broke in. "Now, Kim, is everything all set? Is there any last-minute crisis I need to know about?"

"No. Everything's fine. The flowers are beautiful, the waiters are getting into their fig leaves, the food, the bar—it's all come together. Security is setting up the metal detectors now. Oh, and the coke that Elinor brought over is in your bedroom. You left it lying out on the table in the breakfast nook."

"Where's Kevin?" Leon inquired.

Brad turned and left the room.

"Very, very sore subject, young man," whispered Rob.

"*Got it,*" Leon replied.

Rob followed Brad upstairs and into the palatial bedroom suite.

"Maybe I should have prepared a few words," said Brad. "I mean, for all the people who flew in. Otherwise, I'll just be repeating myself over and over to everyone."

"Don't worry about that now," Rob responded. "Try to relax. We have a few minutes, Brad. Are you sure you don't want to fill me in on what happened with Kevin?"

"Rob. I'm warning you."

"It's just that you seem so upset."

"Will you fuck off already, you silly old queen! I told you to drop it!"

"I see," Rob said. "Fine."

"Look, I'm sorry. I didn't mean that."

"Of course. No offense taken. We're both tense. Why don't I go down and get us some drinks. I think we both have the pre-party jitters."

"That would be good."

Rob went downstairs in a hurry so they each could cool off.

Brad removed his suit jacket and collapsed on Rob's bed. This party was the last thing he wanted to deal with right now. All through dinner he had been wondering where Kevin was. He could not understand why Kevin had just stormed out like that.

Brad had only given him the standard Hollywood dressing-down. Kevin wasn't actually supposed to *leave*. He had a role to fulfill. He was supposed to be crushed, true, but then beg to be taken back. The whole drill was routine, normal. It was how you trained your assistants, it was how you kept your executives in line, it was *standard procedure*. Why didn't Kevin understand that?

Rob came upstairs with a bucket of ice, two cans of club soda, and a bottle of Bacardi Limón. He fixed them both cocktails and then brought one over to Brad.

"Oh, by the way, I have a little surprise for you," Rob intimated. "I asked old Bill at Neiman's to send over a special outfit for you to wear tonight. It's in the guest suite."

"Really? That's great, Rob. Thank you."

"Don't mention it. It's the least I could do. You're my best friend, you know. And now you're going to do *Fantasy on Ice, the Movie!* Who's better than us?"

"No one!" Brad heartily proclaimed.

They raised their glasses in a toast, all unpleasantness neatly paved over.

"All right," said Rob. "Now, come over here to my dressing table. I think it is absolutely crucial that we both take a tiny toot of the good coke that has been so altruistically provided by Elinor. For God's sake, we're throwing a Hollywood party tonight! Let's slap on the war paint!"

Brad rolled off the bed and trundled over to Rob's stash, where they each took a snort off a hand mirror. Almost instantly, they both felt dynamic and competent. But it was really getting down to the wire. Excited voices could be heard outside on the normally silent street. Rob split up the coke and then hustled Brad off to the guest suite.

Two enormous bodybuilders, each with flowing, dyed-blond hair, lounged naked on the bed. When Brad came in they fell to the floor on their knees.

"Good evening sir," said one.

"We're not guests, sir," the other continued. "Mr. Erikson hired us to bathe and dress you."

"Why am I not surprised?" asked Brad.

"We're total submissive bottoms, sir. We exist only for your pleasure."

"You and everyone else. Okay, whatever. Let's see what you have."

One of the bodybuilders went over to a closet and brought out a black Neiman's garment bag. Handling it carefully, he unzipped it and removed a flowing gold caftan. The other bodybuilder opened a hat box. It contained a colossal jeweled turban.

"I don't think so, boys. You'll never see me in a caftan. I'll stick with what I have on." Brad snorted another line. "But I think I will go for the bath part."

It seemed for a while that Rob had erred: four valet parkers would simply not be enough to handle the onslaught. But then the limo crowd descended, and the only real problem was gridlock. One old driver, ensuring a hefty tip, told his giddy passenger that the party was bigger than the Academy Awards, bigger even than the Streisand concert.

The anticipation was palpable as the crowd was frisked and ID's were checked against the guest list. A black tent sealing the walkway to the front door foiled the stalkerazzi.

Rob, on the phone in his bathroom, rang the line in the guest suite's bathroom. One of the slaves, the one not washing Brad's feet, picked up the phone and held it against Brad's ear.

"Are you enjoying your surprise? Lovely, aren't they? The heat has died down and all the good escort services have their computers up and running again. So I thought, what the heck! I put a pair in every guest room. Anyway, Kim tells me about a hundred guests have already arrived, so I think we better go down soon."

"I'm not wearing that caftan, Rob."

"Oh, what a shame. Old Bill bought it years ago at the MGM auction at Butterfield and Butterfield. He said Valentino had worn it once. Sweet, but so dotty that one . . . so out of touch with the times. Okay, then. Call me back when you're ready. Have the slaves bring you to my room and we'll have one more toot."

The waiters, most of them straight part-time models, were apprehensive about their fig-leaf costumes, but then Kim and Leon passed around a Lalique candy dish full of Xanax and everyone chilled. Kim watched with admiration as his new boyfriend calmly pitched in to help organize them.

The more reserved boys were stationed at the bars set up in the media room, the library, and the living room. The friskier ones were positioned out by the poolhouse. Rob and Brad were hiding out upstairs, so Kim and Leon found themselves manning the entrance foyer when the guests began to arrive.

They poured in. To get an invitation, one had to have one of two prerequisites: looks or wealth. Most had both. Bottlenecks formed. Soon, movie people were pressed up against TV people, who in turn found themselves pressed up against music people—who were angling to get pressed up against all the new computer people. Roving packs of lawyers scavenged everywhere. Studio accountants, agents, designers, models, directors, mutual-fund managers, computer hackers—they all came. Even that notoriously reclusive bed stylist from the Pottery Barn came.

The event coordinator had sequestered the entertainment in the poolhouse, and after everyone got a drink, or a pill, or a snort, or perhaps just a handful of M&M's, the party really began to gel. The DJ gauged the mood of the crowd and put an old Sylvester tune on. Then he layered a jarring, atonal beat underneath and cranked everything up to a deafening level. The famous stripper from Miami, the one that had a talent for maintaining a huge erection for hours while dancing, was fluffed and ready, having injected his shaft with Caverject, an anti-impotence drug he imported from Mexico by the case (which he sold on the side, so he could send money home to his mother).

Backup go-go boys were already outside, strategically placed, costumed, and anxious to start shaking it. Could anyone blame them for their excitement? This could be their big break, and besides, a lot of stars had shown up!

Brad and his slaves enjoyed a leisurely bubble bath. But as the voices outside picked up in volume, Brad became apprehensive. Soon he would have to go down and meet his subjects. He ordered one of the slaves to rustle up a joint. He told the other to massage his wrists. They were sore from shaking hands all day.

Meanwhile, Rob welcomed the Sanders twins into his bedroom, and paged Kim, who brought up a plate of Swedish meatballs. They all did a few lines, after which there was much hair brushing and trying on of earrings, but then Rob hustled them all out and scurried off to find Brad.

Brad, almost dressed, held a fat joint and a bottle of vintage Krug. His eyes were glassy. Both slaves were valiantly attempting to put on his shoes.

"Uh, Brad, darling," said Rob, "it's time to go down. Get a grip on yourself."

"Ooh, weee. There's a good slave!" Brad kicked a Gucci loafer across the room. The slave scampered after it.

"Brad," Rob asked, "how about some coffee?"

"Relax. I'm fine. Just enjoying my slaves."

"Are you sure?"

"Yes, Robbie Rob."

Brad finally rallied, and at the top of the stairs, he and Rob surveyed the developing scene.

"Oh, look," said Rob. "It's . . . him! From last year!"

"Who?"

"Ugh. Nobody. Let's go down."

They descended the staircase and hands reached out. Brad greeted them, touched them with grace, and moved on. Rob took hold of Brad's elbow and together they pushed through the packed rooms.

"Brad! Congratulations," yelled Mike Brazier. "Come meet one of my new discoveries. His name is Dan Evans."

Brad stopped, took a good long look at Dan, and immediately resolved to give the kid a career. It wasn't that he was so impressed by Dan. He just felt an overwhelming desire to spite Kevin. So before pressing on, he uttered the life-giving, magic words: "Call my office. Ask for Corrine."

Outside, hundreds more had gathered.

The little stage that had been set up for the star stripper seemed like a good spot for Brad to get up and say hi to everybody and make a welcoming speech. He headed for it, but at the same moment, the star stripper emerged from his changing room—to find Brad climbing the platform.

"Excuse me, abuelo," he said. "It's time for my show."

"I'm just going to say hello to all my guests," Brad protested.

"I don't think so, honey."

"Excuse me, but . . . I'm Brad Sherwood."

"Who cares? If I don't get up there and wiggle my big Cubano chorizo I don't get my five hundred bucks. So get lost. I got three kids to feed." He pushed Brad aside and climbed up on the platform.

"Why that little tramp," hissed Rob when Brad told him what happened. "Where's the event coordinator? I'll take care of him."

Brad sobered. "Forget it, Rob. I don't know what I was thinking. Nobody is in the mood for a speech. My God, who are all these people?"

But Rob was not ready to let it go. "Imagine! Acting like that in my home."

Then, without warning, the stripper peeled off his towel.

The crowd went nuts.

"Holy cow!" screamed Rob over the din. "Look at that third-world dick! *Now that's the future!*"

It was the biggest fiasco. By three A.M. there were about fifty drunks bare-assed in the pool. Twosomes, threesomes, and foursomes were copulating in every room of the house. Early on, someone got it into their head to snatch the fig leaves off all the waiters—and from there, it only got more festive.

A tray of quail's eggs ended up in the Jacuzzi.

All of the dining-room chairs were broken.

A set of curtains in the library caught fire.

The last thing Brad saw, before he went into a blackout, was the head of business affairs at a major studio leave the house with a television set. *Totally naked!*

Brad woke up in a guest room the next afternoon with Matt from the office lying nude on the Kilim area rug at the foot of his bed. Brad put a blanket over him and looked out the window. The music was still playing. A few people were still out there dancing, if you could call it that. They were really just hanging on to each other, swaying.

Brad reached for an intercom and called out for Rob, but all he got was static.

Matt mumbled something about loving him. Brad told Matt he loved him, too.

CHAPTER 28

That was all Brad could remember.

Getting out of the Jacuzzi seemed impossible. *I'll just lie here a few more minutes,* he thought. He found himself drifting off, but then remembered reading something about hot-tub suicides, and how laughably passé they had become. So he dragged himself out, put on a robe, and went into the kitchen.

"Do you want a tuna sandwich?" asked Rob.

Brad sat down. "Huh?"

"I made them with those gourmet sandwich-size English muffins," said Rob, "and I put a little mustard and celery seed in with the mayo. It's my secret recipe."

"Yeah, okay."

"How about I make you some fresh coffee, too. We need to finish all the packing tonight."

Later, they hung out in Brad's room watching *The Nanny* while Brad threw some clothes into a few suitcases. In a few hours they'd be leaving for Washington. At the crack.

"The navy Armani or the gray?" Brad asked.

"Oh, the navy. To show your patriotic side. In fact, you might as well go all the way and pair it with a white shirt and a red tie. Make it all very Lions Club."

After their quick pit stop in Washington, they were meeting up with the *Fantasies on Ice* cast in Ibiza. It was the end of the tour, and Rob was giving them all a week off at the beach before they went back to whatever the hell it was they did when they weren't chasing each other around a sheet of ice.

"Any word from the foreman about your house?" Brad inquired.

"Picked clean. It will be unlivable for a few weeks, but the insurance will cover everything. Actually, I feel rather grateful to that vicious queen who torched the curtains in the library with her cigarette. Cabbage-rose chintz. What was I *on*?"

"Is he out of the hospital?"

"Oh, no, darling. Not for months. Was that a party or what?"

"Yes," said Brad. "Fabulous."

"I have to go. I'm flying to Washington," Brad told a fellow mogul on the phone the next morning. "I have a dinner with the president. In the family quarters. We're going to discuss the lack of Western television in countries like Bosnia and Ireland, and how that deprivation causes religious wars."

Rob was already in the car. As Brad left the house, a guard intercepted him, spoke a few words into a walkie-talkie, and then guided him to the waiting limousine. Behind the wheel of the car was Jeremy.

This was to be his last trip driving Brad, and it was only for old-times' sake. Jeremy was to be "outsourced" under the new management procedures at Digisynth. The people department "regretted the decision."

Jeremy got a little indignant when he handed over his keys and ID, so Corrine called a guard. But then Brad's new security unit held an emergency meeting and decided that Jeremy should be allowed to drive one more time, "*for closure*."

"*Disgruntled employees kill*" was their motto.

Next to Jeremy sat another armed bodyguard.

The tape of Kevin undressing in the pool cabana on Christmas Day was in the bag beside Brad. He felt he was finally ready to see it, to see what all the fuss had been about. Watching it was going to be a little something extra to christen his new plane with on its inaugural flight. Following a few cocktails served by a nude steward, he'd pop it in the wide-screen TV somewhere over Iowa.

At the freeway entrance, Jeremy went over a pothole and everybody in the car bounced and hit the ceiling. The guards, startled, went for their guns. They were already nervous. Their new boss had not yet said a word to them and he looked like hell. This nut was going to see the president? Maybe they should call for backup.

Boarding his freshly refurbished plane did not seem to cheer Brad up, even though it was lovely, really, to have all that space. And the steward, Lionel, was not only *drop-dead,* but he made gorgeous Long Island iced teas. Brad and Rob were already on seconds as the big jet taxied out onto the runway.

About an hour after takeoff, Brad went over to the CD player and turned off "Take It Like a Woman," the latest single from Tell That Girl Hi. Then he roamed to the back of the plane, scouting out Rob.

Rob was in the rear galley, where Lionel was leaning nude against a counter, showing him snapshots of his new puppy. "I got him at the Beverly Center!" Lionel was saying.

"Hey, Rob," Brad interrupted, "come on up front to the forward lounge. I want to show you something."

"Excuse me, Lionel," said Rob. "My producer wants to speak to me. Why don't you get started on lunch?"

"Certainly, Mr. Erikson." Lionel slipped on a skimpy, custom-made Digisynth apron so he wouldn't burn himself on the stainless-steel doors of the convection ovens.

When Brad and Rob returned to the lounge in the forward compartment, Brad held up the video cassette.

"I lied to you, Rob, a long time ago. I *did* make a tape of Kevin. And I'm going to show it to you now, just so you can finally see what that little trick looked like."

"Oh, Brad, is this really the time? Come back and talk to Lionel. He's adorable, and he has such extraordinary manners. Where did you ever find him?"

"Fuck him, Rob. Or maybe *I* will. Come on, take a look at this. He might be too old for you, but I think you'll enjoy this."

But Rob knew he wouldn't. Brad had changed so much over the past few days. He was so restless and bitter. Rob suddenly wished he were going to Europe alone. Dragging Brad around could only be a trial. Rob supposed he owed him, though. The check for the *Fantasies on Ice* rights had already cleared.

Too bad Kim had decided not to come along—he might have lightened things up a bit. But Kim was always with Leon now and, of course, that was a good thing. You absolutely had to have that one truly passionate affair in your youth, or life later on would become just too unbearable. Rob had his, back as a teen, and the memory always warmed his heart. Oh, those blissful days, back in Gary! Dwayne was the son of a farming-equipment distributor and it lasted all of a summer. The two of them, the picture of burnished youth in their Lee jeans, wouldn't have anything to do with anyone. They shared *everything*: secret looks, milkshakes, a pup tent. It was *all* about hayrides.

But then they lost touch.

Rob understood now that Kevin had been Brad's big affair. But it happened too late, and then it was all over in an instant. And they didn't know what they had.

Brad popped the tape in.

And suddenly there was Kevin, on that first day. He was undressing in the cabana; he looked like he was cold and a little frightened as he rifled through the metal gym lockers. The sweatpants dropped to the floor. The Raymond Dragon bathing suit was sniffed. The camera picked up the hint of stubble on Kevin's chin.

Rob looked over and saw that Brad was pale and stone-faced.

"Brad," he said gently. "Don't you think it's time you told me what happened?"

Brad looked up and spoke in a flat tone. "I told you, Rob. I threw him out."

The scene ended with Kevin striding out of the cabana with the beach towel. Brad rewound it.

"Did you try looking for him?"

"Of course not."

"Well, I know you don't want to hear this, but I think you should. Yeah, all right, I can see he's gorgeous. So are hundreds of other guys. But he made you happy, happier than I've ever seen you. Happier than the first time I took you to Studio 54! Give him another chance."

"I can't," Brad stated. "He did something stupid."

"Oh," said Rob. "I see. That settles it then."

Brad, fuming, downed the rest of his drink.

"Well, if that's all you have to say about it, I'll just go back and finish up my conversation with Lionel," Rob told Brad. "He's much better company."

Brad turned his head and stared out the window. Thirty thousand feet below was some sort of . . . settlement, it seemed.

Rob turned to go. "I'm not going to bother trying to cheer you up anymore. You're turning mean."

"No, wait," Brad spoke up. "Stay."

Rob sighed and lowered himself into a reproduction of an English club chair. On the armrest was a tiny silver plaque that said, "TO BE A SUCCESS IN BUSINESS, BE DARING, BE FIRST, BE DIFFERENT—MARCHANT." There was also a button. Rob touched it, and a miniature humidor, containing a lone Cuban cigar, popped up. A cute touch, but then there seemed to be no end to cute touches on this plane.

"All right, Brad. Out with it."

"I miss him. The day after the party I started to miss him."

"God, was that so hard to admit? Of course you did. Look at him!"

"No, no. You don't get it. I liked having him around, Rob. He helped me through a difficult period. When I met him I was in a really bad space. And I liked living with him. He wasn't really a nice guy when you got down to it—selfish, totally self-absorbed—but he was fun to have around, you know?"

"Of course," said Rob quietly.

"Well, there, I've said it. Anyway, it doesn't matter. I don't know what happened to him and that's that." Brad pushed a button on the intercom. "Hey, steward! Make us two more drinks."

"Right away, Mr. Sherwood."

"Oh, so we're going to get bombed," Rob remarked. "Well, that's always fine with me. At least you're behaving like a human being again."

"Did I tell you I bought him a Mercedes?" said Brad. "And even though he was a jerk, I wanted him to keep it. I made him trade in his other car."

"Wow," breathed Rob. *The kid didn't take the car?* Even Rob was impressed by that. How many cars had the two of them given away over the years . . . ten? Twenty?

"Oh, yeah . . . he was good," continued Brad. "I'll give him that. But he wasn't right for the job. Maybe I should have taken him by the hand a bit more, but hey, life's too . . . well, you know. Anyway, I've been thinking a lot about it the last few days, and I think it's time I took on someone else."

"Excuse me?"

"I like this boyfriend thing. There's this guy Matt, for instance. He works for me at Magnet . . . uh, I mean Digisynth. Now, *he's* respectable. He works hard, even went to Harvard."

"Brad, slow down. Give yourself a little time."

"No, no, Rob, this could work. My parents would like him, and unlike Kevin, he's a team player. Plus, he's younger. But this time I'll do the right thing. I'll sign the car over right away."

. "*Oh, my God,*" Rob whispered. "This Kevin character really hurt you. Someone actually got *in.*"

"No, he didn't. He was nothing but a hustler. If I'm mad at anyone, it's myself. Leaving my address book in a trick's car. I was an idiot right from the start."

"You know, Brad, suddenly I'm not so sure it's such a good idea we go to Europe together."

"What do you mean? It's all arranged," said Brad. "Look, I know I've been a drag lately, but I'm pulling out of it."

"I can't believe how coldly you dumped Kevin. Just put him out like a milk bottle, no severance, no nothing." Brad started to object, but Rob held his hand up. "No, Brad. It's my turn. So he did something stupid. So what? Part of it is your fault, too. You knew he was an outsider when you met him. What did you expect?"

"There's another thing I never told you," Brad confided. "He made me laugh."

Rob flew out of his seat and sat down next to Brad.

"*What?*"

"Yeah," said Brad. "He cracked me up sometimes."

"Wow."

"What should I do?"

"Oh, God. He really made you laugh? That changes everything. I'll tell you what I'd do. I'd hunt him down and drag him back kicking and screaming."

"How?" Brad asked.

"Oh, please—hire a detective, I don't know. God knows you have the resources. Really, Brad. Think about it. Even I could find him if I wanted to . . . and as you know, I'm good for *nothing.*"

PART THREE

PITTSBURGH

Dumped by Brad Sherwood, given the bum's rush by his parents—and Anthony Capozi, not only broke, but *overweight?* And to have to confront all this in *Pittsburgh?* Suddenly, it all seemed a bit too much to bear.

Kevin broke into a sprint, his electric-blue Claude Montana jacket fluttering and flapping voluminously behind him. The deranged look of panic on his face only enhanced his mostly burdensome, often unforgivable sexiness.

The automatic doors leading out to the street whooshed open, and Kevin was hit with a blast of moist, none-too-fresh early-morning air. *Humidity,* he thought, as he stopped dead in his tracks. *I remember this.*

His hair, bone-straight back in LA, immediately adopted a decidedly unstylish curl.

Mixed in with the dense Pittsburgh air particles were clouds of cigarette smoke. A throng of professional road warriors, huddled like hobos around an overflowing ashtray, were getting in a few preflight puffs. Kevin considered bumming a cig, but he doubted any of them would part with one. Clutching their Starbucks grandes, guarding their garment bags with practiced eyes—how much sympathy could they be expected to muster? Who really cared about the tiny human needs of an oddly dressed, down-and-out former kept boy?

Of course, the jacket *did* seem to make an unnecessarily bold statement. Kevin slung it over his shoulder and pressed on.

Halfway down the sidewalk, an eruption of diesel fumes from an airport parking-lot bus engulfed him. When the soot cleared, Kevin found himself in front of a cab stand.

"You know how to get downtown?"

"I take you!" offered the turbaned cabbie, Hanif according to a badge on his shirt. "Veddy much I would like to take you downtown!"

"How much is it?"

"Get in. I take you. And each bag you gip me only one dollar. You gip me your bags and I take you."

"I don't have any bags. Just tell me how much for the ride."

"I gip you the ride for thirty bucks. You come in."

"*Thirty bucks?*" For the first time in what seemed like years, thirty bucks sounded like an enormous sum of money, although Kevin had, on more than one occasion, paid that much for a half a Valium at Prod.

"Forget it."

"Twenty-five," countered Hanif.

"Are you kidding? What a rip-off."

"*What you say? Rip-off? You say I cheat you? Fuck you, motherfucker! I kill you! I fucking kill you, motherfuck!*"

Hanif, livid with anger, was halfway out of the cab before Kevin was back on the run, vaulting over luggage carts. Finally reaching safety behind a bank of arrival/departure monitors, he came upon another group of smokers.

"One dollar for one cigarette."

"Deal," said a grandmother on her way to Vegas.

The gift of clear thinking, made possible by an old moll packing nicotine, was Kevin's. *I'm in Pittsburgh,* he thought as he puffed away. *I've been here over an hour. And I still haven't left the airport. It's time I made some forward progress.*

Newly energized, Kevin tossed the butt away and darted back inside the terminal. After a lengthy series of false starts, multiple baby steps, and a great deal of backtracking, he stumbled upon an information booth. A volunteer from the chamber of commerce promptly directed him toward the municipal bus stop. Which was right outside.

A downtown bus arrived. Kevin snagged a sideways-facing seat and then shakily counted out what was left of the forty dollars that Shane had given him. There wasn't much.

The bus made a dizzying series of wide turns and then barreled through a tunnel, making Kevin pale with nausea. Never in his life had he been in such a tight spot. Never had he felt so abandoned.

Could it really be true that just a scant twelve hours earlier, he had been about to go meet Brad's parents? Could it really be true that he had actually blown his chance to live the life that others could only dream about? Hey, was that a Bed Bath and Beyond outlet store that they just passed?

No. It wasn't. He was obviously hallucinating.

Twenty minutes into the ride, the bus sped by a boutique advertising wigs made of "100% human hair." Kevin's shoulder-length tresses, clumping mussily at the nape his neck, made no sense in this late-spring heat. Hey, why not see if he could sell some hair? Kevin leapt up and reached for the pull cord. But halfway down the aisle, he encountered some elderly black women wearing elaborate hats. They were obviously on their way to church. *Oh, yeah,* thought Kevin. *Sunday.* What self-respecting all-human-hair wig boutique would be open on Sunday?

Dejected, he plunked back down, in a handicap seat near the front. Selling his hair wasn't the worst idea, but, as usual, his timing was off.

I have to get organized here, he thought, as he scratched his sweaty neck. Pulling his hand away, he was horrified to discover dirt under his fingernails.

He desperately needed a place to wash up. And food, too. And then a place to sleep. Oh, yes. That little detail. Maybe he could find a nice rooming house downtown. Full of alcoholics and drifters. Fugitives. Spree killers. *His* sort of people.

Distressed by all the strange stares he was attracting, Kevin jumped off the bus as soon as they reached the city's outer limits.

He landed on the corner opposite a twenty-four-hour free clinic. Remembering his old days in New York peddling sperm, he ran over and immediately sold a pint of blood. This sale netted him enough cash to purchase a few burgers from a dingy walk-up hamburger stand. But he found he just couldn't eat. His endemic Irish mood swings, triggered by the loss of blood, dumped him unceremoniously into a shame spiral.

A revolving kaleidoscope of depressing memories flooded his brainpan. Manhattan, Macy's, Anthony's face. Coffee grounds, his mother, that time he broke a lamp. Newsprint, plastic slipcovers, hundreds of nameless tricks. Gripped by an overwhelming sense of guilt, he ran up the street and ducked into a dollar movie theater.

Some sort of second-run weepie had already started. It seemed to be about a child being dragged across state lines, but so cynically was it written, so obvious were its aspirations, that the plot failed to thicken. Still,

Kevin felt calmer, mostly because of the fleeting presence of Sally Field in a cameo. Despite its flaws, the movie began to work its magic. When the third act capped off with a denunciation of sleazy victories, of cheap values, Kevin found himself wiping away tears. Whether those tears were meant for Sally or himself he could not be sure.

When he emerged from the theater at four o'clock, he felt a little better. Stronger. Ready to straighten out the situation. Where to? Left? Right?

Kevin went left, charging along for a few blocks until he came upon a small storefront church. Inside, spirited voices could be heard singing the praises of the Lord. For a split second, Kevin felt inspired. Refreshed, even. Then, with his ear pressed against the door, Kevin wondered how he could have been so stupid! How could he ever have forgotten the true meaning of the Lord's tenderest day?

Beer bust!

But not in this outfit.

Clipping along as though guided by a divine hand, Kevin found a Salvation Army store, where he quickly negotiated the trade of his fourteen-hundred-dollar Claude Montana ensemble for a pair of jeans and a flannel button-down. The kindly Christian woman behind the counter loaned him a pair of scissors so he could cut the sleeves off the shirt.

Redemption was close at hand, he could feel it, but his work was not yet finished. Now all he needed to do was find the local bar.

"Nine-one-one. Is this a genuine emergency?"

"Darling. I'm at the end of my rope."

"What is the emergency, sir?"

"I need the number for the Gay Suicide Prevention Hotline, please."

"Are you a danger to yourself or others?"

"I should say so."

"This is not the kind of thing we do here, sir. If this is a genuine emergency, I will dispatch an EMT vehicle to the vicinity. Do you have insurance?"

"No, sweetie, I don't. Can't you just give me the number?"

"I cannot do that, sir. What is your location?"

"I haven't a clue."

"If you give me an address, I can dispatch a team of medical technicians in, let's say within the next two hours."

"Can I speak to your supervisor? I think I'd prefer to have my problems addressed by a *trained professional*."

"A frivolous call to nine-one-one is a felony, sir."

"I just want a number!"

"Then I suggest you call information."

"Oh," said Kevin. "Of course. Why didn't I think of that? I'm so sorry. I'm really not myself today."

What luck. The number to the gay hotline was a free call. He would not even have to pull out his newly minted Pittsburgh International Airport phone card.

"Gay hotline," a voice chirped brightly.

"Look, I don't mean to waste your time, but I'm from out of town, and I really would appreciate it if you could give me the address of a gay bar."

"No problem. That's what almost all of these calls are about."

"Somewhere where they're having a Sunday-afternoon thing. A shirtless tea dance would be ideal."

"Can you make a cosmopolitan?"

"Blindfolded."

Kevin took off his top and settled in. He had shown up a bit early, but the action in the joint soon picked up. The music, the same music played everywhere, was spun, although, at one point, the DJ broke out "Who Stole the Kishka," a lively mazurka that seemed to be some sort of home-town fave.

The usual jostling and shoving increased. The "smoke eaters" in the ceiling failed to perform. Folks got sloppy.

It was all deeply comforting.

Kevin's presence created a maelstrom of preening, a buzz, but he was too tired to get up and mingle—not that he ever did mingle. There had never been a need. His feet hurt, so he remained on the sidelines while men sent him drinks. Notes were passed on napkins: "WE'RE HAVING A THREEWAY . . ."

Choices! That was the name of the joint. And after three cosmos, Kevin thought it was *fabulous*.

"Not a lot of new faces blow in here too often," yelled Tom, the guy behind the bar. "What's your rap?"

His rap? Kevin pushed his empty glass across the bar and then slurred, in his famously maddening fashion, "I'm kind of going door to door."

Tom made him the world's weakest cosmopolitan and handed it over, no charge.

By the end of the night, Tom was Kevin's new best friend.

"I was with this guy," Kevin confided boozily, "back in Los *Anga-leez*. We were having a good time, but I never . . . appreciated what I had. I was always carrying a torch for this other guy. But then I screwed up and the guy threw me out."

"Which guy?" Tom asked.

"The guy in LA. Brad Sherwood."

"Yeah? Who's that, pussycat?"

"Only the CEO of Digisynth Entertainment," explained an extremely tall black drag queen who'd been listening in.

"Never heard of him," said Tom.

Tom was the kind of guy they called a "bear." A little beefy, a little hairy, but quick enough with a smile. After watering down a few more drinks, he decided to keep Kevin for himself.

But it was nothing like *that*. Tom just figured that this kid, this Irisher, had nowhere to go. So instead of letting one of the patiently circling vultures at the bar pick him off, Tom thought he'd step in. Since the kid was clearly in *no condition*.

Tom thought he'd fix Kevin something to eat and then set up the cot in the rec room in his basement. But the minute they stepped inside Tom's house, Kevin passed out on the living room couch and slept there for twelve hours.

After a day or two, Kevin told Tom the whole story of Anthony, of Brad, and of his life in West Hollywood. He told him about the beach house, the penthouse, and how he smuggled himself on to Shane's flight. He told Tom everything, and since Tom was a perfect stranger, he did not vary from the truth. He did not leave out a single detail. He was hard on everyone—especially himself. But at the end of the story, Tom just laughed.

Crap like that only happened in the movies.

Tom's take on the whole thing was that Kevin had been one of those runaway types who went out to Hollywood and got used up hustling. Well, hell, that kind of thing went on right here in Pittsburgh, except they didn't make a bunch of fancy TV movies about it.

After a few days of letting Kevin mope around, he decided to fix Kevin up with a job. His sister-in-law's nephew, one of an altogether new and ever-morphing breed of savvy gay entrepreneurs, had bought into a Glamour Shots franchise. Tom figured that if Kevin thought he knew how to push the button on a camera, he could make an honest living.

Folks around here were big on honest living.

The nephew agreed and started paying Kevin under the table. It was a nice little arrangement—the guy was thrilled to find a photographer with Kevin's expertise, and that and Kevin's looks helped bring in the crowds.

Kevin, limping along, finding ignominy not all that bad, came to like his new job. The hours were so . . . regular. And life in the sticks was surprisingly agreeable. Like the time when Kevin got a haircut down at that barbershop Tom went to. Everyone was really friendly, it only cost ten bucks, and it looked okay. And getting around was simple. The buses went everywhere, and the drivers would slow down if they saw you were running a little behind. Oh, sure, the schedule went to hell, but no one seemed to give a good gosh darn.

Plus there was weather. Actual, visible weather. It seemed like every day someone was talking to Kevin about the weather. "Looks like rain," old folks would say at the bus stop and Kevin would find himself jumping right in. "Yeah," he'd say, "I think you're right. *I should have brought an umbrella.*"

It was all so easy, so uncomplicated. *There were no wrong answers.*

Not like back in LA. Once, while developing some photos at Glamour Shots, Kevin vaguely recalled one of his last conversations with Brad, cell phone to cell phone.

Kevin had been in his new Mercedes. "Hi, Brad. I'm on Los Feliz Boulevard just passing the Griffith Observatory and the outside temperature gauge says it's sixty-eight degrees. Can that be right? It seems warmer."

Brad was in his Range Rover. "Hi, Kevin. I'm on Sepulveda trying to avoid the 405 on my way back toward Bel Air and my outside temperature gauge says sixty-eight degrees, too. But there must be something wrong. That part of town is always much warmer this time of year."

Kevin: "Well, I'm sure it's nothing. I was just fiddling with it. Anyway, what are we doing for dinner?"

Brad: "*No!* Kevin! Don't fiddle with the controls! I'm hanging up now. I'm going to schedule an appointment for you with a service manager at the Mercedes dealership. *Don't touch anything until I call you back!*"

Whew! Brad sure was tense during those weeks before his buyout went through. Poor guy. He took on so much.

Or whatever. That was so long ago. Now, Brad Sherwood was just back to being someone he read about, someone they profiled on *60 Minutes*. Someone who slept in the Lincoln bedroom on occasion.

And Kevin was back to being . . . Well, that, Kevin still did not know.

Was he ruing the day he met Brad Sherwood? Did he regret moving into the penthouse with him? Was he sorry he had gotten—as his new friend Tom put it—"too big for his britches"? Not really.

Because a funny thing was happening in Pittsburgh. The ladies *loved* Kevin's portraits. They were lining up around the block. They all seemed to like their hair big—but when you sat down and stopped lying to yourself about it, not nearly as big as the hair back in LA.

"It's a good thing you're out of there, Kev," Tom declared one evening. "People in California ain't right. Hey, why don't you go into the kitchen and get us a couple of beers. Bring that can of Pringles. Thanks, Kev."

Tom wouldn't accept any rent, and soon Kevin had enough money to get himself to New York. The move was finally his to make, but he couldn't find the will. Besides, what reason did he have to go there? To cheer up Anthony and his fat fuck of an invalid father? No, that did not seem like a plan.

Oh, he'd probably pay Anthony a visit eventually, but not now. Because, of course, nothing could ever be the same. It had only taken a few hours in Pittsburgh for Kevin to realize that. The East Coast of his childhood, of his youth—of Anthony—no longer existed. His glorious and tragic past was all just yesterday's news, a sepia-toned dream fragment that would only grow fainter with each passing day. Kevin knew now that if he went to New York, the city, *his* city, would be different, too. Full of *film students*. No, he no longer belonged there. He'd already had his turn.

For now, he was grateful just to rest.

To stay out of trouble.

To steer clear of *love*.

So he stayed put, hung out at Choices!, and helped Tom with the wash. He grew attached to Champ, Tom's German shepherd. After Kevin quit smoking, the dog couldn't stay away from him. Tom was getting a little sick of the arrangement, maybe, but Kevin thought he could get a place of his own somewhere pretty soon.

He'd save some money.

He'd take a class.

Switch to Pert Plus.

Become *normal*.

Pittsburgh. Who knew there existed in the world such a worker's paradise? Kevin found a cheap gym and ran on an old treadmill. He punched an old punching bag. In the afternoons, if business was slow, he'd catch a movie. Most of them sucked, but at least no one pulled a gun on you if you didn't sit through the credits.

True, nothing was exciting. But nothing was too scary, either. One night, Tom had a few friends over to watch a game. As Kevin sat there, in jeans and a T-shirt like the rest of them, he felt a delicious sense of relief flood through his bones. *Nobody in this room is talking about their deal.*

So if the price of all this easy living was watching a team of professional athletes known as the Steelers play the game of football on Monday nights, then hand over the remote! It wouldn't kill him to learn a thing or two about sports. Well, it might . . . but just keeping Tom company felt kind of good.

The dream held and the weeks passed . . . until the day Kevin decided it was time to get some wheels. He went down to the Chrysler dealership and applied for some easy credit on a used K car. After all, the ad on the radio had declared, *"You owe it to yourself not to miss this savings event. No one denied!"*

Kevin gave the friendly sales team Tom's address.

He informed them that he was a full-time employee at Glamour Shots.

And he gave them his social-security number. Why not? He had nothing to fear anymore from Hot Tip Capozi.

The manager came back with his application. "It seems you've been denied."

"I had a few setbacks in LA," Kevin admitted.

"I see that a lease has been paid off on a Miata," said the manager, "but there are still a few pending charges at a number of department stores."

Damn. Kevin had thought he had given all his bills to Brad's accountant to be paid off, but obviously there were a few he had carelessly left out. He wished now that he had filled out a change-of-address form at the post office when he moved into the penthouse. Ugh. But that was the least of his worries back then.

Well, a car would just have to wait.

At home, he found Tom down on the floor measuring the living room for some new baseboards. Tom was like that. Always tinkering with the plumbing, finding a new project. Kevin took a Pepsi from the fridge and hung about while Tom worked.

"Didn't get the car," said Kevin.

Tom, a man of few words, responded with a grunt.

"My credit wasn't up to snuff."

"'Bout time you started thinking about those things."

"I guess."

"Hold down that end of the tape measure over in that corner, will you, Kev?"

"Sure."

"You know, it ain't too fucking glamorous, but someday you're gonna want to buy a house of your own."

His own house? Kevin, in all his life, had never entertained such a ridiculous notion. That was for people who . . . took their lives seriously.

Tom got up to sort through a tool box. "Don't panic. It's not that big a deal. You just have to start worming your way back into the system, that's all."

Kevin rolled his eyes.

"There's no other choice, Kevin."

CHAPTER 30

Eighteen hours later there was a loud rap on Tom's front door. Three federal marshals, in blue nylon windbreakers, stood on his stoop.

"Excuse me, sir. I'm Federal Marshal Crepin. This is Agent McGlynn and over here is Agent Young. We have it on good authority that you are harboring an individual by the name of Kevin Malloy."

"Not *harboring*," Young broke in. He rolled his eyes and leaned in to Tom. "Don't worry, sir. He's not in any trouble."

"Yeah, sorry about him," said McGlynn, pointing to Crepin. "He's a trainee."

Crepin scowled.

"So if you'll just let us in for a few moments," continued Agent Young, "we can probably get this matter straightened out without taking up too much of your time."

But Tom was having none of this. He wasn't a genius, but he recognized a good cop/bad cop routine when he saw one.

"Nobody here by that name," said Tom, a stand-up guy through and through.

"You don't understand," Young responded. "This is an urgent matter. It's very important that we contact him. It would probably be in your best interest if you allowed us to look around."

At that moment, Tom, to his horror, spied Kevin getting off the bus at the corner. Kevin was carrying a backpack, eating an apple, and looking like he didn't have a care in the world—*which he didn't*. Tom wanted to signal to him as he saw him approaching, to warn him to back off, to run, but Kevin, that too-skinny, affable dingbat, was coming straight toward the house.

"That's him!" called a voice from the back of the feds' car.

It was Brad Sherwood.

The feds jumped off the stoop, and before Kevin even had a chance to look up, Young and McGlynn went in for the tackle and pinned him spread-eagle on the sidewalk. Crepin, with no clear role to assume, began rifling through Kevin's knapsack.

"Get off him, you idiots!" yelled Brad helplessly as he struggled with the unfamiliar American design of the car-door lock.

Tom, assessing the situation, darted over and tossed the feds aside. After years of working at Choices! it was easy.

The feds—blameless, really; they were only following procedure—reached for their weapons.

Kevin, dazed and confused, picked himself up, looked around at all the guns, and found himself falling again.

But this time it was into Brad's arms.

Later, after Tom served Brad, Kevin, and the three feds some Sarah Lee cheese danish, which defrosted beautifully in the rotating micro, Kevin explained to Brad how he wound up in Pittsburgh. Oh, sure, he left out a few of the more gruesome details, kept it light, but everyone got the idea.

And then he gave Brad a lengthy tour of his simple quarters down in the basement.

"I think we ought to get a move on, gentlemen," Agent McGlynn stated. "I'd say our mission here has been brought to a satisfactory conclusion, wouldn't you? It's time, however, to return to headquarters. We need to start filing our reports."

"Thanks, men," said Brad. "Why don't you wait outside."

Tom got up, too. "I'll let you guys talk. Give a yell if you need anything, Kev."

When Tom left through the back door, Champ came bounding in. "I love this damn dog," mumbled Kevin as Champ jumped all over him.

"Come back with me, Kevin," Brad began. "That's why I'm here. That's why I've come all this way."

"Aaahhh," replied Kevin. "I was wondering what brought you to Pittsburgh. So, Brad . . . fill me in. What have you been up to?"

"Right after that stupid fight we had, I had to go to the White House. And after that, I promised my friend Rob that I would go to Europe with him. But I cut the trip short. I never really wanted to go, anyway. Everything over there is so *old.*"

Kevin, despite himself, smiled.

Brad leaned across the table. "I had to find you, Kevin. I couldn't stop thinking about you. I hired a detective, but he was no good, so finally I called Washington and hooked up with those three clowns out in the car."

"They may be clowns, but they seem to know how to take a man down."

"Come home, Kevin."

"You know, Brad," Kevin said as he stroked Champ's scruffy fur, "Tom's a great guy. He helped me out at a time when I was so close to losing it."

"Look. I don't have my checkbook, but if you'll write down Tom's address—"

Kevin shot Brad a look.

"Scratch that," said Brad. "How 'bout we invite Tom out to LA? I've got plenty of free time now, and a new plane."

"A new plane . . . Yeah, I sort of remember now you were thinking about getting one." Kevin nuzzled Champ's neck and then stuck his hand in Champ's mouth. The dog bared his teeth and growled threateningly, but it was all just play.

"Give me another chance."

"Stop slobbering, Champ!" Kevin pushed the dog away. The dog came right back.

"I think you're forgetting one thing, Brad. It was you who threw me out. You didn't even come after me. Who's to say it won't happen again?"

McGlynn stuck his head in. "Excuse me, Mr. Sherwood, but we're on a tight schedule."

Kevin dared to meet Brad's eyes. "Oh, shoot. I suppose the least I can do is ride out to the airport with you."

"My old friend Rob put me up to this," Brad explained later, in the back of the car. "I know I came on a little heavy handed, busting in like this, but it's been so dull without you."

"I'm listening," said Kevin.

"You and me. We made a good team."

"That's true. There should have been a headline about us in *Variety*: BRAD SHERWOOD TAKES A LOVER."

"Maybe it was all a little hard for me to live up to."

"Hard for both of us."

"But I love you, Kevin. More than that, I need you. There's so much I still want to do, but without you in my life, well, nothing seems very urgent."

The agent sitting beside Brad, McGlynn, could not believe what he was hearing. Still, the orders for this mission had come from a place really high up. A lot of money had been spread around, and they hadn't had a break in weeks. But now that they had found the suspect, the story was getting even weirder. Christ! Perverts seemed to have the run of the planet these days!

"I'm so sorry about what happened that night," continued Brad, "but we'll spend more time together, I promise. All the time we need. We'll travel, we'll see the world. I've been thinking Fiji. There's a place called Plantation Island. Nothing but beach shacks."

The car slowed at the entrance of the Pittsburgh Airport. A security guard waved them out onto the tarmac. From there they drove to the far end of the property, out by the concrete shacks where they blew up suspicious suitcases.

"And remember—whatever happens between us, just know that never again will you have to live in a basement in Pittsburgh. I'll see to that."

"Ah, but I could, Brad," Kevin corrected him, wagging a finger.

They were now parked directly under the stairs to the plane. It was time to get on board.

No one moved.

"Hey, Kevin. Take a look. What do you think? Do you like my new jet? You can stand up in it without hitting your head."

Kevin glanced sideways, saw eight enormous black wheels, and then jerked his head back.

"It's big," he whispered.

Brad grabbed Kevin's hands. "*Look at it, Kevin. Look at what I'm offering you.*"

Kevin searched Brad's imploring eyes for a long moment before he twisted around and gazed up at the plane.

He saw two pilots, a man and a woman, smiling down at him from the cockpit. He saw tiny rectangular windows that stretched on forever. He saw a gleaming-white tail section that soared five stories into the sky.

A security guard came trotting over and tapped on the window. "Gentlemen, this vehicle can't stay here."

McGlynn flashed his badge, mouthed two words: "*Brad Sherwood.*"

The guard retreated.

Brad unbuckled his seat belt. "Come on. I want to introduce you to the crew."

"Listen, Brad—" began Kevin.

"NO!" wailed Brad.

Now it was Kevin's turn to look miserable.

"Gentlemen," said Brad, "step outside."

McGlynn, Young, and Crepin scampered out of the vehicle.

"Kevin . . . think about what we had."

"I have. I've been thinking about it for weeks now. And believe me, there's nothing I would rather do than get on that plane with you. But too much has happened for us to go back to the way we were before."

"We can put all that behind us."

"No, Brad. You spoke the truth when you said there always will be someone younger. In order for anything between us to work, we've got to try something new."

"Kevin, this is crazy."

"Dammit, Brad, listen to me! Can't you see I'm terrified to go back there?"

"But it will be different this time. I'll take better care of you."

"But that's not what I want," said Kevin. "I've never asked for anything from you, Brad. God knows, I *took*. I took a lot. I took it *all*. But I need to ask you to help me now."

"What is it?"

"Be my friend. Don't make me get on that plane."

"Kevin, I would never make you do something you didn't want to do."

"Brad. Come on. This is me you're talking to. Let me stay. Let me figure some stuff out. I don't want to just run out on everyone. I need to earn some money, visit my family."

"Earn some money? Kevin. Don't you understand at all what I'm saying to you? We'll see my lawyer as soon as we get back." Brad knew he was taking the wrong tack, but he was unable to stop himself. "I could set you up in your own business. You could have your own money."

"Brad, if that's what you think is best, I'll get on that plane. Believe me, it would not be hard. I'll get on that plane and I'll be exactly who you want me to be for as long as you want. Is that all you really want?"

Kevin took Brad's clenched fist in his hand and tenderly uncurled each finger.

"I don't want to be a user anymore, Brad, always manipulating, always figuring out every angle. I don't want to be someone who just takes your money. I want to be someone you trust."

Brad gulped. He had not factored such a possibility into the equation. The negotiation now seemed to be veering irrevocably off course.

"I've always respected you, Brad, even during the times when I was convinced I was conning you so well."

"I didn't feel conned," Brad objected.

"Oh, come now. All those years in Hollywood and you can't spot a con? We both knew we were playing each other. Maybe not all the time, but some of the time. It kept the game fun."

"But that's not how I feel now," said Brad.

"I don't feel that way, either," Kevin admitted. "That's why I can't come back yet. You did me a favor by kicking me out, Brad. You did *us* a favor. But you and I, we don't have time to play games anymore."

Brad slumped back in his seat and rubbed his eyes.

"Okay. Just what exactly is it you want me to do?"

"Just let me stay here, for a little longer. I need to keep working. And I can't just run out on Tom. These people took me in, Brad, no questions asked. I can't just run out on them."

"Alright. It kills me to know that you'll be here, but maybe you're doing the right thing."

"I'm trying to do the right thing. *For once.*"

Kevin took Brad in his arms and they held each other until McGlynn finally opened the car door.

"One word," whispered Brad, "and I'll come and get you."

After they got out of the car, Brad looked up at his pilots and made an economical gesture—that of a key being turned in an ignition.

The turbines in the number-two engine began rotating.

"I miss you, Kevin. Already."

"Don't worry, Brad. You and I aren't finished. This is just the first-act plot point."

Brad smiled weakly. "Will you do something for me?"

"Of course."

"Don't leave until my plane takes off."

Brad stepped onto the air stairs. "I know it sounds stupid, but I'll just feel better."

"I was planning to anyway, Brad."

After the door was sealed up, Kevin made his way over to an unsecured area behind a chain link fence. Once there, he joined a band of men who were watching planes take off. They were following the flight paths of commercial airliners with binoculars, and then scribbling down the aircraft tail numbers in little notebooks.

Plane spotters! Kevin had watched a special about them on *20/20*. Their aim was to roam the country, spotting every plane of every airline, writing down the tail numbers. That was the sum total of the hobby, no more, no less. Sometimes they checked the plane number against a number in a thick manual devoted to fans of the sport, to find out if it was a plane that was rarely spotted. But that was just a frill. Hardly a critical aspect of their mission.

Their lives are working, thought Kevin.

By now he was too far away to see Brad's face in any of the windows of the 757. Still, Kevin held up his hand and waved. He kept waving until the jet reached the end of the runway, just in case Brad was watching.

Curiously, Brad's jet seemed even more impressive from a distance. Of course, it would be nice to be drinking a glass of champagne with Brad right now, and then cuddling up with a movie, but that would all come in time. Kevin sensed he had finally gained a glimmer of Brad's respect and that was more important in the long run. For both of them.

Maybe after Brad's plane takes off, I'll go into the terminal and check on fares to Florida, Kevin mused. Or maybe I'll go back to Tom's, straighten out my credit, and *drive* down. Kevin chuckled to himself as he suddenly remembered one of the central questions of his New York childhood. *Does your family drive or fly to Florida?*

Those were the larger questions of life back then. And they still were now. Life was only as complicated as you made it.

Brad's jet screeched down the runway and took off almost vertically, burning fuel like a fighter. None of these lengthy, lumbering, airliner-type ascents for Brad Sherwood. That plane was out of here! Even the plane spotters were impressed.

Kevin felt momentarily desolate as the jet disappeared from view. But then he bucked himself up. He had plenty of fresh options now. He was free. He could do whatever he wanted. His life had started.

For now, he would go back to his job at Glamour Shots. It was always such a tense moment when his customers came in to pick up their pictures! Thank God they were usually thrilled.

Then, after he put away a little money, he would go to New York and check on Anthony. Maybe break his balls a little, to help him get out of his rut.

But first he would call Leon. It was criminal to have withheld all this gossip.

Kevin knew now that he would eventually return to LA. It was paradise, the place he had been the happiest. But this time he would go back on his own terms. Maybe he'd work really hard. Maybe he'd even direct!

The only real issue facing him now was how he would get back into Pittsburgh. Somehow a bus ride just wouldn't cut it.

"N937302," said one of the plane spotters, in a clipped voice.

"We have that one," whined his partner. "Don't you remember? We saw it only last month in Orlando."

Maybe one of those plane spotters was gay? Kevin wondered. Who could tell these days? Ah, and wouldn't it be just so easy to sidle over, ask a few questions. Bat his eyelashes. Toss his hair . . .

Nah. Today he'd spring for a cab.